RETURN TO SENDER

Ashlyn Kane and Morgan James

Published by
Dreamspinner Press
4760 Preston Road
Suite 244-149
Frisco, TX 75034
http://www.dreamspinnerpress.com/

This is a work of fiction. Names, characters, places, and incidents either are the product of the author's imagination or are used fictitiously, and any resemblance to actual persons, living or dead, business establishments, events, or locales is entirely coincidental.

Cover Art by Catt Ford

ISBN: 978-1-61581-814-3

Printed in the United States of America
First Edition
March 2011

eBook edition available
eBook ISBN: 978-1-61581-815-0

To K and L,
who sacrificed a lot of RL time
so we could bring you this monster.

PROLOGUE

ON A postcard of snowy Boston mailed priority post on December 23rd in a festive red envelope:

Dear Emerson,

You know those times when you get the answer to your burning question and find out you were better off not knowing?

Merry Christmas.

Jonah

CHAPTER 1

NOW

MUZZY-HEADED and confused, Emerson lifted his face from his knees. His eyes were itchy, his tears having unsettled his contact lenses. He blinked, trying to get his vision to focus, then turned to his alarm clock and was surprised to see that it read 5:53. He stared in surprise. Taking a moment to do the math, he figured that he had been sitting there for almost two hours.

He hadn't realized that so much time had passed. He had been sitting alone, wallowing in self-pity and wishing Jonah would come home.

Emerson sniffed and rubbed his nose against his knees. It didn't help that he and Jonah hadn't fought since they'd started dating. Their relationship had been relatively smooth. Until today, when Emerson had come home, and all hell had broken loose.

Emerson didn't know how to deal with it. The achy feeling in his chest hadn't left since Jonah had walked out on him. Which was possibly the worst part of the whole experience: Jonah had just walked out mid-argument. And still wasn't back almost two hours later. Jonah must be pretty mad if he was still cooling off.

For a brief disingenuous moment, Emerson wondered if Jonah would come back at all or whether maybe he'd just run away again.

Okay, that was a bitchy thought. Obviously Jonah wouldn't just run away this time. He wouldn't leave town without telling his boyfriend.

Still, Emerson hadn't felt this awful since the last time Jonah had left.

It had only been a few weeks after graduation, and Emerson had been eager to celebrate Jonah's eighteenth birthday. It was a summer of no responsibilities, and Emerson had been looking forward to how

Jonah would best like to take advantage of that fact. Of course, Emerson wouldn't be eighteen for two more months, and there were limits to the trouble they could get in before their twenty-first birthdays, but getting into trouble wasn't the aim. Emerson just wanted to have fun with his best friend without distractions. Without *girls*.

Jonah was a flirt and tended to get carried away with pretty girls. He wouldn't forget that Emerson was there, but he would split his attention, which, though annoying and somewhat hurtful, Emerson had long ago learned to forgive.

So Emerson had been waiting for Jonah to arrive so they could celebrate. He had showered and dressed in his favorite jeans before settling down on the couch to wait for Jonah to arrive. He waited, and waited, and then, an hour later, when Jonah hadn't answered his phone calls, Emerson grabbed his keys and headed out the door.

Jonah didn't answer his door either. Emerson knocked and called out for him, but the lights stayed out, and there was no response. He had stood on Jonah's doorstep for a long time, staring at Jonah's front door and the car in the driveway, contemplating his next move. The car was in, but the lights were off, and Jonah wasn't answering the door or his phone. Emerson bit his lip, indecisive. Where could Jonah be?

Despite knowing Jonah better than anyone else, Emerson hadn't been able to find him at the baseball diamond in the park. He wasn't getting ice cream around the corner. Emerson even checked the movies, though Jonah wasn't likely to go there without a car.

Another hour later, Emerson was back at home, finally admitting defeat. Jonah wasn't going to be found today. Despite the car in the driveway, he obviously wasn't home, and if he was out and not answering his phone—it wouldn't be the first time that Jonah had gotten distracted by a girl and forgotten to tell Emerson.

When Emerson's parents had arrived home that evening, it had been to find their son curled up on the couch watching *The Princess Bride*. His mother had arched her brows and asked, "Where's Jonah?" and Emerson had only shrugged before telling her that Jonah had changed their plans. He hadn't wanted to admit, even to her, that Jonah had ditched him without a word.

The pain of that day had just been the beginning. Jonah hadn't just ditched him without warning—he had left town. When Jonah's parents got back home the following day, they had phoned Emerson up in a panic. Was Jonah with him? Had Jonah said anything to him? Did he know where Jonah was?

Emerson hadn't known a thing. He had known nothing until they had told him about the letter. The single sheet of paper that Jonah had left for his parents, informing them that he was leaving town for a while to get his head on straight, but with no information about where he was going or when he'd be back, just the promise that he would call.

The concern that had filled Emerson the day before while trying to find Jonah returned and multiplied tenfold. Jonah was gone. Sure, Jonah hadn't exactly disappeared—he said he'd left on his own—but there was no way of knowing that Jonah was still safe or that he would stay that way. And why would he leave without saying anything?

That had been the first day of the worst few months of Emerson's life. It had been a week before Jonah called to reassure his parents that he was all right. Then another month before Emerson stopped imagining Jonah dead in ditches or alleyways as everyone waited for him to call. It took even longer for Emerson to forgive Jonah for leaving in the first place.

But that feeling from the first week of the hollow stomach and the heartache, because of Jonah—that felt just like now. Because Jonah had walked out on him again. At least this time, Emerson knew why.

The sound of the front door opening and slamming shut made Emerson jump. Someone was home. The sound of large boots running up the stairs confirmed that it was Jonah. Emerson swallowed hard and held his breath. Jonah was home! So, Jonah would come see him, right? If Jonah was here, then it must mean that he wanted to talk, because Jonah wouldn't come back unless he was ready to talk again. Emerson knew him, knew he'd stay away as long as his anger was still too hot. So if he was home….

Emerson sat still, his heart thumping in his chest, and stared at the door, willing it to open and for Jonah to be standing there.

It didn't open.

Instead, Jonah's footsteps led into his own room, and then—Emerson jerked at the loud thumping noise. It was followed half a minute later by another one. Okay, so maybe Jonah was still a little angry, *but* he had come home, which was still a good sign. So Emerson would just wait for him to finish whatever he was doing in his room, and then he would see him.

Emerson waited. He waited because Jonah was worth waiting for, as Emerson knew all too well. He waited because he really needed Jonah to forgive him and for everything to be better again. Emerson didn't know what he'd do without Jonah.

It didn't take Jonah long to finish what he was doing. Soon Emerson could hear him out in the hall again. His heart gave a few jerky, fast-paced thumps, but the footsteps didn't come his way. Instead, they were going back downstairs. Strange, but surely Jonah wasn't going to leave. There was silence for a long, long moment. Perhaps two minutes went by with Emerson wondering what the hell Jonah was doing down there. When the silence was broken, it was by the sound of the front door opening and slamming shut.

Emerson's whole body twitched at the violent sound. *Oh.*

Slowly he stood up from the bed and made his way out into the hall. He peered through the open door of Jonah's room to see… nothing. All of Jonah's things—his books, his clothes, his computer—were gone. Emerson stared. Then, turning quickly, he hurried downstairs to see where Jonah had gone. Maybe he had decided to stay somewhere else tonight?

Emerson came to a halt at the bottom of the stairs, his knees suddenly turned to jelly. There on the entrance table where Zack would toss his cell phone and wallet sat a single brass key. Emerson took two mechanical steps forward. He picked up the key and stared at it lying in his palm.

It was a small thing, but… it was the key that Emerson had given him when he had told Jonah he could move in for the summer. Jonah had whooped with delight and kissed Emerson senseless before pulling away from a dazed and horny Emerson to attach the key to his key chain. "I don't want to lose *this*," Jonah had said, and then he had tackled Emerson onto the bed.

Now here it was, left behind on purpose by Jonah, because apparently Jonah wouldn't need it anymore. Jonah had just moved out. Just like that. No warning, no conversation. He just packed his bags and left. Did this mean… was he leaving Emerson too? Did this mean he didn't want *Emerson* anymore?

Emerson's knees gave out, and he felt himself fall to the floor. One minute he was standing; the next he was sitting on the floor in the hallway, staring down at the key in his open hand. Jonah had left his key. Even when they had talked about whether or not Jonah should stay here, Emerson had always thought, had even said, that Jonah could keep his key. But Jonah had left it.

The tears didn't surprise him this time. They came on with a harsh sob and just kept coming. Soon, he curled back into his tight ball, this time propped up against the wall, and the tears weren't just a few drops. He was sobbing and gulping and making harsh, guttural noises into the fabric of his jeans. The tears wouldn't stop. Any time he thought they might, he'd feel the jagged teeth of the key digging into the flesh of his palm anew, and the grief would take over once again.

Eventually, exhaustion and dehydration called a stop to the tears, but he didn't find the energy to rise from the spot. He sat in numb silence, unable to move.

§

THEN

EMERSON hung up the phone and stared at it.

Jonah was still in Boston. Jonah was still alive and safe. He was well in Boston—why he was there was still a mystery, but he was safe. And he still didn't want to talk to Emerson.

Every few weeks, Jonah would pick up the phone and call his parents, and after every phone call, his parents would call Emerson to give him an update. And after the update, Emerson would finally ask, "Did you tell him?" and Jonah's mother would go quiet and tell him that yes, she had, but Emerson always knew by the tone of her voice how unlikely she thought it was that Jonah would listen.

Emerson sniffed and blinked back the tears. God, he was tired of crying over Jonah Cherneski. He was tired of waiting for Jonah's parents to call just so Emerson could feel miserable. Sometimes he wished they'd never call so he wouldn't have to feel this crushing misery afterward.

But Emerson would feel worse for not knowing. Even if knowing Jonah had called also meant asking if his parents had told Jonah to call him and inevitably being told that they had, but that Jonah still sounded reluctant.

Emerson wiped a hand over his face. Who was he kidding—he wasn't done crying over Jonah Cherneski yet.

"Hopefully it will work out better here," a voice said through the newly opened door. Emerson looked up to see two men walking into the room.

He sniffed one last time and tossed his phone onto the bed, watching the two men as they entered.

The one talking was pulling a key out of the door's lock and looking at his companion. He had long black hair and was carrying a guitar. His companion was taller than him, with a shock of ginger hair that didn't look natural. The color didn't suit him.

"Relax, Zack. Why don't you wait until you actually meet your roommate before you decide if you have something to rant about?"

Emerson sat and watched until they noticed him.

"Hello," said the ginger.

"Hi," Emerson said.

The one who was apparently called Zack nodded at him. "Hi. I'm your new roommate."

"Ah. I'm Emerson." There was a pause. "I answer to Em or Emery, if it helps."

There was another pause; then the ginger stepped forward, his hand stretched out. "I'm Greg, this loser's friend and lead guitar."

"Lead guitar?"

"Yeah." Zack closed the door. "We have a band."

Zack and Greg took a moment to look around the room. It was fairly bare. Emerson hadn't had time to put much up on the wall—except for his cork board, which his dad had put up. He figured it didn't look that exciting to an outsider.

"So," said Zack after a moment. He took another look at Emerson. "Are you high?"

Emerson blinked several times. "Um?"

Greg hit his friend with the back of his hand. "What kind of greeting is that?"

"An honest one? I found my new roommate sitting alone with red eyes."

"You're overly optimistic," said Greg.

"Maybe," Zack said with a shrug.

"I'm not high," Emerson said. "I'm just not having—never mind. So, a band? What kind of music do you play?" The subject change was obvious, but Zack and Greg let it pass.

"Rock," said Greg.

"Rock?" Emerson arched a brow. "Beatles, AC/DC, or Coldplay?"

"Peter and the Hanged Man," was Zack's less-than-illuminating answer.

"Uh."

"Us," Greg supplied.

"Oh. But… who's Peter?"

"A saint."

"Right. Literally or figuratively?"

"The first," said Zack. He crossed the room to put down his guitar. "Greg is a Religious Studies major. So let this be a lesson to you—never ask a Religious Studies major to name anything."

"Right." Emerson nodded. "I'll keep that in mind. I'm guessing you're not also a Religious Studies major."

"Music."

"Not surprising," Emerson said with a nod at the guitar case.

"He's here for piano and cello," Greg said, sitting down on the other bed.

"Not guitar?"

"Nope. Need more traditional instruments," Zack explained. "What about you?"

"I can't even play 'Mary Had a Little Lamb' on a kid's xylophone."

"Good to know: don't ask Emery to play back up. But I was asking what your major was."

"Ah. Business."

"Business. Right. Which was exactly what I was suspecting what with the pile of sketchbooks trying to hide under all these pencils." Zack nodded at Emerson's desk.

Emerson looked at his lap. "I like to draw."

Zack walked over and pushed at the books. "A lot, I'm guessing."

Emerson shrugged. "Hobby."

Zack pushed the pencils off the books and picked the top one up.

"So, where are you from, Emerson?" asked Greg.

"Um, Hudson Bend," Emerson answered Greg, but he kept his eyes on Zack, who was flicking through the book. "It's a small town about half an hour away."

"Ah, I've been there. Pretty, slow," Greg said with a nod.

"These are pretty good for a hobby," Zack butted in, still turning pages.

"Thanks." Emerson looked down at his lap again.

"This one isn't done," Zack said, flipping the book around and showing off a half-finished sketch of Jonah. Emerson had started it a few days before Jonah's birthday. Jonah was pictured laughing and beautiful, his face complete, though his neck, ears, and hair were only half-formed. Emerson had lost steam with it after Jonah's birthday.

"Friend?" Zack asked.

Emerson blushed. "Yes." He stood and walked toward Zack. He took the book from Zack's hands.

"Blushing!" Zack crowed. "Boyfriend?" He waggled his eyebrows.

"No." Emerson turned away. He used the excuse of putting the sketchpad away to hide his face.

"He is, isn't he?" Zack smirked.

"What Zack is trying to say," Greg cut in, "is that if he is your boyfriend, or if you have or want a boyfriend, we don't care."

Emerson stared at the sketchbook in his hands. *Oh.* His heart was beating a strong tattoo against his rib cage. Emerson had never told anyone; how did they—?

"Emerson?" Greg said.

Emerson's hands were trembling.

"Emery?" Zack this time. "Shit. Okay, not boyfriend. But you want him to be?"

Still, Emerson stared at the book. He hadn't known them for five minutes, and they had known.

"Emerson?"

"I've never told anyone," Emerson managed to get out. "That I'm—gay."

"Oh. Wow," Greg said.

"Shit," said Zack again.

Emerson let out a strangled, hysterical-sounding laugh. That was—easier to say then Emerson had thought. Possibly because Zack and Greg were strangers? "That was—unexpected," he admitted.

"Yeah. Sorry to drag you out of the closet," Zack said.

Emerson nodded and put down the sketchbook, then turned back to him. "No, it's—good. I—you've saved me from the angst of trying to figure out how to tell you."

Zack grinned. "Atta boy. And Greg and I really don't care."

Emerson gave a small smile. "Good to know."

"You know, Greg was gay once," Zack added.

Greg rolled his eyes. "Everyone experiments in college."

Emerson stared. Greg had just admitted to trying sex with another man. "You…?"

Greg shrugged. "Only once. It was alright—would have been better with boobs."

"Uh. Right," Emerson said again. He wondered if he'd be saying that a lot over the next two terms.

"So, enough talk. Come help me unload my car," Zack said as he put his guitar down by the bed.

That made Emerson blink in surprise. "Me?"

"Sure. If you help, it'll go faster. We'll increase our workforce by half!"

"True, but what's in it for me?" Emerson asked even as he stood to help.

"His unending gratitude," Greg supplied.

"My vow never to play the guitar or cello in our room between midnight and six a.m.," Zack said.

Emerson smiled. "Make it eight, and you have yourself a deal."

§

EMERSON was sitting alone on his bed; the room door was propped open, but he ignored the noise as he idly sketched. It was either sketch something dark and angry, or yell at Jonah's letter again.

Jonah's second letter had arrived yesterday, and it had been as maddeningly vague as the first. When the first letter had arrived, Emerson had been so eager his hands had been trembling, but he had been very disappointed to discover that Jonah had offered no explanation for why he had left. Jonah's apology had been weak and did nothing to heal a heart that had been broken for two months.

Emerson's reply had been… emphatic. He had demanded some sort of explanation as to why Jonah had run off without saying goodbye. Emerson had hoped that Jonah's reply would offer something more than similar, vague statements. He had been very disappointed.

Emerson had freaked out, actually. Thankfully Zack had been out when the letter had arrived.

He hadn't yet made any attempts to write back, still too angry to even try and pick up a pen.

So drawing it was. Though—Emerson cocked his head at his work—definitely darker than usual.

"So I'm walking over here on my way from class and this asshole I've never met before bumps into me and starts yelling at me for not looking where I'm going when I'm the one who dropped their bag! Like, I'm sorry you took up the *whole sidewalk* and don't know how to yield the right of way to someone wearing three-inch heels, buddy! Ugh! He was such a frumious bandersnatch!"

Emerson looked up to see Hayley standing in his room and fuming. She was gorgeous as ever, her red hair a wild mane around her face, highlighting her anger and just making her even more radiant.

"What's a bandersnatch? That sounds dirty."

"It's a… thing." Emerson arched a brow. "It's a nonsense word from *The Jabberwocky*. It's Lewis Carroll," she said finally, as if that should explain everything. Emerson supposed it did.

"Right."

Hayley let out a gusty sigh and launched herself down on Emerson's bed. "Whatcha doing?"

"Drawing."

"So I see." Hayley propped herself on an elbow and leaned over to get a look at the book on Emerson's lap. "Wow. Dark."

"Yeah, I guess."

"What's with you?" Hayley arched a brow.

"Another letter from Jonah," Emerson admitted without looking at her face. There wasn't much point in lying about it; Hayley had a way of always getting stuff out of him, even stuff he didn't want to tell. He had known her only a few weeks before she had figured out that he was gay and pining over Jonah, and unlike Zack and Greg, she hadn't had the luxury of seeing his drawings of Jonah.

"Ooh. As bad as the first?" Her smile was sympathetic.

"Worse. This time I had had questions. Questions that I wrote to him. Questions that he ignored!" Emerson was starting to get worked up again.

"Ouch," Hayley murmured.

"He barely even acknowledged it! He just writes that he's sorry and doesn't want to talk about it, and then he starts talking about Boston!"

"Wow. That's cold."

"So is Boston, apparently," Emerson said with a bitter twist to his lips. There was silence for a beat, and then he let out a sigh. "I just don't understand. Why won't he tell me? Why is he doing this?"

"Because he's a boy? And boys are emotionally stunted."

"Gee, thanks." Emerson gave a dry sniff.

"Also, he's clearly an idiot who doesn't know a good thing when he sees it and should be shot for not snatching you up."

"He's straight, Hayley," Emerson pointed out. He thought he only sounded a *little* bitter.

"So? You are beautiful and awesome, and you could convert any guy! So he's stupid if you haven't got him dancing the YMCA and listening to Judy Garland."

"I'm pretty sure it doesn't work that way."

"Sure it does! I mean, I love dick, but I'd totally give it up for Scarlett Johansson. I mean, have you seen *Iron Man 2*?"

Emerson gave her a small smile at that.

"I love my life," a voice said from the doorway. "My roommate is too gay to steal a girlfriend, but he brings home hot chicks who talk about banging Scarlett Johansson."

Emerson rolled his eyes. "Nice. Way to impress a girl."

"I'm always impressive," Zack retorted as he tossed his notebook down on his desk.

"Hayley, meet Zack," Emerson finally said.

They greeted each other, and then Zack sat down on his own bed. "So, why are you talking about going gay for Johansson?"

Emerson snorted. "Why? Trying to figure out how you can relive this conversation with other girls?" His voice was cutting at best.

Zack gave him the finger.

Hayley ignored them both. "Just trying to explain to Em why Jonah is clearly an idiot," Hayley said sweetly.

"Ah," said Zack, the syllable filled with meaning.

"Great," Emerson muttered.

"What?" To give her credit, Hayley looked genuinely puzzled.

"That boy *is* an idiot. I've been telling Emma that for months."

"Zack…."

"Oh hells no, I am not going to shut up when I have found someone that agrees with me."

"She doesn't—"

Zack cut him off. "He still moping over that letter?"

"Yup. He was doing some emo art when I walked in."

"Emo art? Damn. Violent or just depressing?"

"Very depressing."

Zack stood and picked Emerson's sketchbook up from the bed. "Yikes. See, this is why that boy is no good for you. You sit around in the dark making depressing art," Zack said, looking at the drawing.

Emerson flushed with anger and snatched the book back. "Give me that. He's my best friend, and he left without a word to me. I haven't heard from him in two months, despite knowing him to be alive and in possession of a phone. I think I have the right to be upset. And I have the right to sit alone and draw sad pictures if I want to."

Zack was scowling. "He's making you miserable. Next letter you should tell him to fuck off."

"I can't do that. I—I need to know what I did to make him hate me." He lowered his voice. "Even if it's the last thing we ever talk about."

There was silence.

Zack let out a sigh. "Fine. But don't get your hopes up, Emma."

"Zack is right. He's scummy. Leaving like that and not talking to you was a very scummy thing to do."

"He's not, though, which is why I must have done something to make him angry."

Zack made a furious, aborted noise.

Hayley was the one who spoke. "Em, what he did was an asshole move even if he is mad—you've been worried over his well-being, and making you worry should be a crime." She reached up to smooth a hand over his hair. "Now come on, Em, let's go get some lunch. We'll stuff our faces, and you can get all disgusted while your roommate and I discuss Scarlett." Hayley bounced up from the bed.

Emerson tried to give a good-natured groan. "No, please don't!"

"Sounds good to me!" Zack smiled.

"It would," Emerson grumbled, but he didn't protest when Hayley grabbed his hand and dragged him from the room. "There will be no discussion of breasts or other lady parts while I try to eat."

They both laughed at that.

"I'm starting to regret ever letting you two meet each other."

"You know you love us, Emma."

"Speaking of: Emma?" Hayley arched an eyebrow.

Emerson let out another groan. Zack had started calling him by that stupid nickname after Emerson had made the mistake of commenting on the terrifying chartreuse shirt some guy had been wearing. Zack had arched a brow and asked, "Chartreuse? A.K.A., puke green?" When Emerson had tried to defend himself, Zack had only snorted before adding, "I just realized, you're not gay—you're such a girl, Emma." Zack had refused to let the name drop ever since.

Zack just shrugged at her. "He's a girl, what can I say?"

Hayley tilted her head contemplatively. "I see your point. Tell me more."

Oh yeah, Emerson was definitely regretting letting them meet.

§

"EMERSON?"

He knew it was cliché, but he also knew it was true: Emerson could tell something was wrong the moment his mother said his name.

"Honey, we're at the hospital."

Emerson began to shake. His grip tightened around the phone.

"Kierstyn?" he managed to force out.

"No, your sister is okay. Honey, it's Daddy."

Those words sent a shock through him. "Dad? What—?"

"A heart attack. He's still alive, but we don't have any details yet. You should come down to the hospital."

Emerson nodded in response. He was nodding during a phone conversation and looking for his shoes and wondering how he'd make his way down to the hospital.

"Emerson?"

"Yeah. Yeah, I'm coming. Just—which one?"

He managed to find his shoes and get them on his feet, but he was stumped by the laces. He started to tie them, but then he began thinking about how he had learned to tie his shoelaces. His father had sat him on the stairs by the front door and patiently showed him how to make first one loop and then tie the knot. Dad's pride had been the only thing greater than Emerson's own that afternoon. In a sudden rush, he wondered if his dad would still be around to share that memory or to teach him everything else Emerson needed to learn. His dad was supposed to be the one who would help him buy his first car, his first house. Oh God! A heart attack.

Zack walked in a few minutes later to find him staring at his shoes.

"Em?"

Emerson looked up to see his roommate and closest friend standing in the doorway. "My dad had a heart attack," he said bleakly.

"Right. Tie your shoes, and I'll drive you."

Emerson didn't argue.

§

WRITTEN in a Christmas card dated December 31st:

Jonah,

What? Is that your cryptic way of telling me I'm happier not knowing? Because if it is it's really shit. Not knowing where you were is what nearly k

Then, scribbled underneath a week later:

Dad had a heart attack. He's still alive, but he's unwell. ~~The doctors say they don't know~~ They think there might be another problem that made the heart attack worse.

I miss you.

Emerson

CHAPTER 2

NOW

JONAH stared.

Zack was standing on the doorstep, eyes hard, jaw clenched. He had his hands shoved into the pockets of his jeans and the sleeves of his shirt rolled up to his elbows. He looked like he hadn't slept in a week.

Jonah didn't ask him why he was there.

"Can I come in?"

Wordlessly, Jonah stepped aside, letting Zack step past him into the living room, then closed the door behind him.

Zack cleared his throat. "You probably know why I'm here."

Jonah wasn't an idiot. He could make an educated guess. "If you're here to hit me, you should know my sister beat you to it." Never had he so deeply regretted making sure Natalie knew how to take care of herself should the situation call for it. Luckily, Jonah didn't bruise too easily, but the split lip was annoying.

"I'm not gonna hit you," Zack said. He sounded pretty grudging about that, but at this point Jonah was glad to take anything friendlier than outright hostility.

"Great," Jonah said. "You want a beer?"

"Christ, yes." At least there was something they could agree on.

None of the girls were of age, and Jonah was too protective to let his little sister anywhere near his beer—besides, if he kept it in the fridge, they'd drink it all—so Jonah had to go upstairs to his mini fridge to get it. When he came back down Zack was sitting on the sofa with his elbows on his knees. "Thanks."

Jonah shrugged. "Sure."

"So," Zack finally said half a beer later, "Emerson's pretty upset."

Jonah snorted. Emerson could be upset. That was fine. Good. Great. Because it turned out that Emerson was kind of an asshole.

Also because Jonah was, all things considered, a train wreck. He rarely fought with Emerson, and nothing anyone had ever done had made him feel like this, like a phantom hand had reached into his chest and started twisting things around until he didn't even know which way was up.

There was a crunching sound, and Jonah blinked. Zack reached over and plucked the beer can from his fingers, setting it on the coffee table before Jonah could make a mess. "Looks like he isn't the only one."

Jonah could not even begin to enumerate the ways in which he was upset, and that was actually kind of scary, because he was supposed to be a writer, for God's sake. But he'd never written about something like this, this black and furious and wounded thing that was festering inside of him. He clenched and unclenched his fists instead. When that didn't help, he rubbed at his lip. Finally, he asked, "What are you doing here? You don't even like me."

"I like you just fine when you're not making Emma miserable." Zack scowled and set down his own beer. "Only he won't tell me why you're fighting, which means either I have to kill you, or it's his fault you're here stewing instead of over there making the walls shake where you belong." He paused. "And I'm pretty sure I don't have to kill you."

Jonah laughed bitterly. It would have been easier on him—and considerably more pleasant an experience—if Zack had just needed to punch him in the face. Then he could get on with his life. "Man, I wouldn't even know where to start."

"Look, Jonah, I am trying to help you, man, okay? Seeing you like this is bad enough, but Emma? It's fucking killing me. So whatever it is, spit it out."

Whatever you're trying to say, spit it out.

Jonah swallowed. There was really no delicate way to put this. "Emerson ran into one of my high school girlfriends at the store."

"Okay," Zack hedged.

Jonah worked his mouth, trying to come up with the right words. "She had her kid with her," he finally said.

"O-kay," Zack repeated, and then: "Oh. *Oh.*"

"Yeah," Jonah said miserably.

"Oh, fuck."

That about summed it up as far as Jonah was concerned. It all boiled down to the fact that Emerson didn't trust him. He curled his hands into fists again. Emerson's lack of faith made him angry—made him *livid*, if he were honest.

"How pissed are you?"

God, if Jonah had just been angry… anger he could deal with. But Emerson's betrayal had also carved a hole somewhere up behind his heart, a place that had been full of love and laughter, and filled it up with hurt instead. Emerson might as well have accused him of sleeping around. He swallowed and shook his head, feeling pathetic.

Then he looked up, and Zack actually jerked back at the expression on his face. "Jesus fuck." He rubbed a hand across his brow. "What do you want me to do?"

"Do?"

What little hope had been in Zack's expression faded. "You don't want me to do anything."

Jonah said nothing.

"Fuck!" Zack repeated. "At least tell me how you're sleeping at night."

In answer, Jonah looked pointedly at the beer can on the table.

"That's great, Jonah, but some of us have to work in the morning. Fuck knows how I can sleep through the goddamn commotion you make when you're having sex if I can't even close my eyes if I think I hear him—"

Jonah looked away. He didn't want to talk about Emerson anymore.

After a long silence, Zack finally said, "Alright. I don't like it, and I'll fight you about it, but not right now. Call me if you change your mind," and let himself out.

Jonah drank the rest of his beer and went back to bed.

§

THEN

WHEN Jonah got off the bus in Boston he expected to feel liberated, like the demons that had haunted him over the last two days and two thousand miles had been cut loose from his shoulders. Instead he looked up at the skyline and realized how far away from home he really was.

Jonah had been to cities before, had even lived in Houston when he was younger, but that was a lifetime ago. The concrete buildings seemed to stretch out forever, reaching for the sun like cold, lifeless parodies of Emerson's mother's sunflowers. What the hell was he doing, moving across the country on a whim? What kind of stupidity was that? He should get right back on that bus and go home and beg his parents not to kill him. He should go to college in Austin with Emerson and pretend he'd never seen him and Justin kissing in the yard. He should—

A heavy hand fell on his shoulder, startling him from his internal lecture. "You look like you could use some directions," Daniel said, coming up beside him.

"Understatement," Jonah admitted. He had no idea where he would stay or how he would keep himself safe, let alone feed and clothe himself. He knew he could always go home, that his parents would welcome him back and that Emerson would eventually forgive him for ditching their standing date. But if he came home now, they'd be wondering every time they looked at him what had set him off, how long it would be before he disappeared again.

"Come on," Daniel said. "I'm taking you to the Y. We'll get you set up with a room and some food, and then I'll take you to Pastor Ken."

Daniel had been on the bus for the last nine hundred miles or so and had ended up in the seat next to Jonah's. He was easy to talk to—almost too easy—and Jonah had found himself explaining the whole sordid situation almost before he could consider it. Daniel had left home a few years earlier for reasons he hadn't explained, but Jonah figured that since he'd just been visiting his parents, things had worked out okay for him in the end.

"I don't need religion," Jonah protested feebly. "Or charity," he added, since that seemed like it was the other option. Not yet, anyway, he amended mentally, his stomach twisting.

"No, but I'm thinking you'll probably be wanting a job," Daniel said dryly. "I've been where you are, remember? And I'd still be on the street if it weren't for Pastor Ken."

Well, in that case. "Okay, you've convinced me." Jonah located his duffel in the pile beside the bus and waited for Daniel to grab his rolling suitcase. It was much, much nicer than anyone else's luggage. "Why do you take the bus, anyway?" he asked before he could stop himself. "I mean, you could obviously afford to fly."

"I have to fly for work," Daniel said with a shrug, extending the handle on his bag and dragging it along the sidewalk behind him. "I love my job, but I really, really hate flying. There is not a strong enough word."

"Oh." That made sense. "Lucky me, I guess."

Daniel laughed. "Reserve judgment 'til after you're situated at the Y, okay?"

Perhaps unsurprisingly, it wasn't far from the bus station, and Jonah dropped off his bag, grabbed a quick shower and change of clothes, and picked up a key before buying a pass for public transit. Three stops later they were in front of a high-rise building, housing everything from lawyers' offices to a main-floor pastry shop, and Jonah was shifting from foot to foot with anxiety. "We want the basement level," Daniel said as they got in the elevator, and Jonah pushed the button and waited for the doors to close.

"Why is Pastor Ken in an office building basement?" Jonah asked on the ride down.

The doors dinged open before Daniel could answer, and he led the way out into the lobby area of a clean, if somewhat run-down, gym. "Because he likes to eat, I imagine." Daniel smiled at the girl behind the counter. "Hey, Chrissie. Is Ken in? Got a recruit for him."

The girl, Chrissie, looked Jonah up and down, assessing, before smiling. "Sure. He's in his office. You know where it is."

Jonah shot Daniel a sideways look. "Come here often?"

"Like I said, Pastor Ken's an old friend." Daniel smiled. "Plus, this is my gym. I work upstairs. It's convenient."

Right. Wait—so Daniel was, what, a lawyer? He'd gone from street-kid-slash-runaway to lawyer? Did that really happen? Or maybe he worked in the bakery? But that would hardly explain needing to travel for work.

Before Jonah could speculate further, Daniel led them to a door in the far back corner of the building and knocked.

"It's open," came the answer, and Daniel pushed open the door and ushered Jonah inside.

Pastor Ken was… not what Jonah had been expecting. With his long, dark hair pulled back into a neat ponytail, short-sleeved dress shirt revealing bulging muscles, and the tattoo Jonah could see peeking out from under the band of his watch, he looked more like a biker than a member of the clergy. He stood up as they came in and greeted Daniel with an enthusiastic handshake. "Danny! Long time no see. How was Virginia?"

"Good," Daniel said with a small smile. "Good. Much better than the last time I visited."

"Glad to hear they're coming around," Ken said sincerely, patting him on the shoulder as he turned to Jonah. "And who's this?"

"This is Jonah," Daniel introduced, and Jonah automatically stuck out his hand. Ken took it, his grip firm but not crushing. "He's one of us."

One of…? Surely Daniel couldn't mean what Jonah thought he meant? A gay clergy member? But it would have been impolite to ask, so he kept his mouth shut.

Then Ken said, "A runaway, huh?" and Jonah understood.

"I'm not—I left a note," he said with a blush. "It's—I do plan on going back someday. I just… need some time."

Ken gestured to the chair in front of his desk, and Daniel made his way toward the door. "I've got to get going," he said. "But Jonah—I'll catch up with you later. You can check at the front desk at the Y for messages, okay?"

"Um, sure," Jonah said, nervous now that he was about to be left alone with a complete stranger. Not that Daniel was much closer than that, now that he thought about it. "Thanks again."

"No sweat. See you later, Ken," Daniel called as he closed the door behind him.

"Have a seat," Ken said, and Jonah finally lowered himself down to sit across from him. "So, where are you from?"

"Um, Tennessee originally," Jonah said. "But we've been living in Texas since I was eight or so." This was not at all how he'd expected the conversation to begin.

"I've got relatives in Texas," Ken said with a nod. "Whereabouts?"

"Hudson Bend, just outside Austin."

"Nice city. My people are in Houston. So, how old are you? Are you finished school?"

"I graduated at the end of the school year. And, uh, eighteen. My birthday was a few days ago."

"Oh, well, happy belated, then." Pastor Ken leaned back in his chair and put a foot up on the desk. He was wearing sneakers. They didn't really go with the dress pants. "So, you left home. You want to talk about that?"

"Um." Jonah had thought the answer would be no—he'd really only opened up to Daniel after the first five hundred miles or so. But Pastor Ken's friendly, casual conversation had him completely disarmed. "So I found out that my best friend is gay and has a boyfriend and that I'm kind of in love with him. Sort of all at the same time."

Pastor Ken didn't even bat an eyelash. "Bummer." He *did* reach into his desk drawer and pull out a snack-sized Kit Kat bar, which he tossed at Jonah. "Have to smuggle these in past the health Nazis at the front desk, but it's worth it."

"Thanks," Jonah said, finding himself wanting to smile for the first time in days.

Ken waved him off. "Don't mention it. So, while you're in town I'm assuming you're going to want a job. I can help you with that."

"That would be awesome," Jonah said with feeling, looking up from where he was halfway through unwrapping the chocolate bar.

"Don't thank me yet," Ken said wryly. "We still have to figure out what you'd be good at. Why don't you tell me about your school, what your favorite subjects were, if you did any extracurriculars."

Looking longingly at the chocolate bar, Jonah reluctantly set it on the desk, still in its wrapper, and focused on the task at hand. "English and the so-called soft sciences—psychology and sociology—were probably my best subjects. I always thought I'd end up as a writer, but until that pans out for me I'd like to be able to eat."

Ken chuckled. "When I was a kid I wanted to be a race car driver. 'Writer' sounds pretty down-to-earth."

Jonah flushed. "Thanks. Um, I was pretty good at P.E. too. Captain of the boys' volleyball team. And I did track."

"Volleyball, huh? I'd have said basketball for sure."

"Everyone does," Jonah sighed, but he wasn't about to hold *that* against Ken when he was going out of his way to help Jonah out.

"How much can you bench?"

The seeming non sequitur threw him. "Uh." They'd done a unit in the weight room at school back in May, but he wasn't sure he could still lift that much; he hadn't exactly kept up with it during the summer. "One seventy-five, maybe one eighty," he hedged.

Ken nodded. "Not bad. In terms of hours you're available to work…?"

"Days, nights, weekends, holidays, whatever," Jonah said quickly. "I'm not picky. I usually go to bed late, like after three, but I'm eighteen. It's not like I ever have trouble getting to sleep."

"Okay. Any previous job experience?"

Jonah sighed. "Just cutting people's grass. And I did some community service cleaning houses and doing some minor home repairs for people who were recovering from surgery and stuff."

Ken nodded again, dropping his feet from the desk and leaning forward again. "Okay. Here's the deal. Normally I'd ask around my congregation and my clients here and see if anybody had a use for you, but that takes some time to pan out, and I have something else in mind anyway, if you're interested?"

Oh, God, Jonah hoped he wasn't about to agree to do something stupid. "I'm interested. I think."

Seeming to catch on to Jonah's train of thought, Ken laughed a little at himself and covered his eyes with one hand. "Sorry, sorry, I forget sometimes that not everybody knows my reputation in the community. I'm the head of human resources at this gym, you see. And we need a night maintenance guy. Some cleaning the showers, some changing light bulbs, that kind of thing. It's just minimum wage and only about twenty hours a week, though."

"That's good with me," he said quickly, eager to get any work, especially given the economy. Even if that did sound kind of awful. "I mean, it sounds great."

"But there's a position for a personal trainer opening up soon," Ken continued. "One of our guys just graduated college and will be starting a new job as a physiotherapist. You seem like you get along with people pretty well, though we'll have to stick you with the ladies until you bulk up some, and of course you'll need first aid training and the rest. How does that sound?"

"I—" Jonah suddenly couldn't speak around the lump in his throat. He swallowed hard and settled for merely nodding his head, mortified that his eyes seemed to be filling with tears.

Mercifully, Pastor Ken didn't comment, just opened his desk drawer again and shoved a box of Kleenex across the top. Jonah took one and dried his eyes as discreetly as he could. "I'll take that as a yes."

Jonah nodded again, taking a deep breath and finding his voice. "This is… I mean I can't thank you enough. But why are you being so nice to me?"

Ken raised an eyebrow and pointed upward at the small, unobtrusive cross adorning the wall behind his head. "Kind of in the job description, kid."

"But…." Jonah frowned. His parents weren't overly religious, but he'd grown up in Texas—plenty of other people were. "I thought, you know. God hates fags and all that."

"God doesn't hate people," Ken said, his voice suddenly hard. "People hate people. They just like to use God to justify it." Then he paused, seemingly embarrassed. "Sorry—pet peeve of mine."

"Uh, no, it's okay," Jonah said, overwhelmed and a little stunned. "I… appreciate the sentiment. You know. Coming from where I do."

Ken gave him an assessing nod. "Tell you what," he said. "Finish your chocolate bar, and I'll take you on a tour, okay? Then we can get the paperwork filled out and set you up with some training. You got a place to stay?"

"Daniel took me to the Y," Jonah said around a mouthful of chocolate before remembering himself and swallowing. "It's okay, I guess."

"Not permanent, though," Ken reminded him. "I know a couple people who were looking for roommates come September—students and the like. I'll ask around for you."

"Thanks." Jonah tossed the wrapper in the garbage and brushed off any remaining crumbs. "I'm ready when you are, I guess?"

Ken gave him the grand tour, starting with the pool in the very basement and working his way around. "There's a ladies-only area through that door," he said, pointing, "but they always warn the girls when someone has to come in to do maintenance or whatever. Since you'll be on nights, at least at first, you probably won't see too many people anyway. They won't give you any trouble."

Jonah nodded in understanding.

"Janitor's closet," Ken said, nodding with his head. "Keys are at the front desk. That's where you'll find the screwdrivers, mop, ladder, cleaning agents, that kind of thing. Just make sure to put things back where you found them in case the day people need them."

They went past a row of tanning rooms—"Hypocrites," Ken said with a knowing smile. "They won't even have a Coke machine because pop has too much sugar, but giving yourself cancer is apparently totally cool"—before taking an escalator up a level to the main gym.

"Kickboxing, dance, Pilates, yoga, jazzercise—those all take place in one of those two classrooms." He motioned to his left. "You probably won't need to worry about those, at least not for a while. But you should sit in on classes when you can so that you can sub if necessary. The instructors get paid better."

Jonah made a mental note to make friends with all the instructors, even if he couldn't exactly see himself so much as *saying* the word "jazzercise" with a straight face.

He was familiar with most of the machines from the weight-lifting unit at school, though some of the configurations were new. He paid special attention to how to properly adjust the machines for height so people didn't hurt themselves. Ken introduced him to a few of the other staff—mostly personal trainers and one assistant manager—before declaring the tour officially over.

They adjourned to Ken's office so Jonah could fill out some paperwork, chatting intermittently. He dug out his wallet so he could fill in his social security number, but when he placed it on Ken's desk, a photograph fell out. Ken picked it up before he could stop him.

"This is your family?"

Jonah filled in the last digit and looked up, seeing Ken smooth down the edges of the creased picture. "Yeah," he said. "Mom and Dad and Nat."

"Your sister?"

Jonah nodded.

Ken looked at it for a minute before passing it back. "You're sure you want to stay here and not go home?"

"I want to go home," Jonah said before he could stop himself. "Just not yet." It was difficult to explain, but Ken had done a lot for him already and didn't even know him; he owed it to him to try. "I need to get my head on straight, figure out who I am when nobody else has any expectations. Plus, if I go back now, they'll all just be waiting for me to leave again." He traced the edge of his mother's face, preoccupied.

Ken nodded absently, then said, "It's a nice picture—good composition," and Jonah fought the urge to sigh miserably.

"My friend Emerson took it," he explained. "He's a good photographer, painter, cartoonist…."

"Your best friend Emerson?" Ken clarified.

Busted. Jonah nodded.

"Well, he certainly captured your good side," Ken quipped. "All set with that?"

Jonah looked down and found that he had somehow managed to complete all the required forms. "Yeah, actually."

"Good!" Ken clapped his hands. "How about dinner?"

§

Dear Emerson,

If you're reading this then I guess you're not still mad enough to tear up my letters, so that's good. I wouldn't blame you if you did, so. Thanks?

I'm sorry that I left without saying goodbye. There were some things I had to work out by myself, and I guess I figured that the sooner I got started on that, the better. Please don't ask me to explain. I don't think I understand it myself. I know we always planned to go to school together and be roommates and get shitty college student jobs together, but that just isn't me right now.

How is college, anyway? I called home last week, and they mentioned that you had started. You always were the smart one.

This guy I met on the bus up to Boston got me a job at a gym. The hours suck, but there are some opportunities, so I might stick around for a while. We'll see.

Anyway, that's all I wanted to say.

Jonah

§

Jonah,

So you're alive.

YOU ARE AN ASS OF EPIC PROPORTIONS!

How could you just run off without saying goodbye!? For a week we all thought you were dead in a ditch. And that crappy message you left at one in the afternoon when you knew your parents wouldn't be home didn't do much to make anyone feel better!

How could you just disappear? Didn't you think we'd miss you?

Emerson

P.S. College is fine. My roommate, Zack, is pretty awesome. He's a musician, and he introduced me to his friend and band mate, Greg. I've been going to their concerts at the local bars. I've met lots of new people there and in my classes. I've no complaints.

§

WRITTEN on the back of a flyer for half off a psychic reading:

Emerson,

I guess I deserved that. All I can say is that I wasn't thinking right. I didn't mean to hurt anybody.

I'm glad that college is working out for you. Your new friends sound nice. I'm only sorry that I can't be there.

Boston is a pretty cool (but expensive!) city. It's also frigid. I'm freezing my balls off, and it's only October. Think I'm going to move on before the snow settles in. Don't worry. If I don't hear from you before then, I'll send you a letter from wherever I land next.

Your friend,

Jonah

§

WRITTEN on a University of Texas notepad:

Welcome, Freshmen, to U of T!

Jonah,

I don't even know what to say to your asinine response. Didn't mean to hurt anybody? Weren't thinking straight? That sounds like bullshit to me.

It's your fault you're not here. You could be here going to concerts with me, but you left. So I go to see Zack and Greg play by myself or with Hayley. That's on you.

Emerson

P.S. It's warm in Texas 365 days a year.

§

THREE weeks later, on the back of a bus schedule:

Emerson,

I don't know what else to tell you.

November in Boston is even colder than October. I might lose some extremities to frostbite.

Sounds like you and Zack are close.

Jonah

P.S. There's at least one place in Texas that's cold.

§

WRITTEN five days later on a page pulled from a ringed notebook entitled "Intro to Psych, class 10, November 7th":

Jonah,

A real, proper reason for why you ran away and didn't tell me and just threw away all our plans! Don't act like I don't have the right to be angry when I do.

Emerson

P.S. Zack is my roommate and best friend at college, seeing as he is *at college.*

P.P.S. You expected me to be the same as ever when you left like that? How naïve.

§

AND life went on. Jonah sent a letter to his parents outlining his circumstances—he had only been at the Y a week when Ken had found a pair of students in need of a third roommate, so he even had a place to call his own. He didn't send his return address yet; he didn't trust his parents not to follow him to Boston and drag him home kicking and screaming—but he did call them his first week, just to make sure they knew he wasn't dead. That had been hard—his mom had cried, and he could tell Natalie was angry, but he thought that just maybe his dad understood his need to get out and prove something to the world. And the truth was that Jonah really did think some time away would be good for him.

After two weeks of training and three weeks of the night maintenance shift, which was ten until two, Jonah got the personal-trainer job as well, which was good for his bank account balance and hell on his social life, not that he'd had much time to acquire one. Sebastian and Oliver, his roommates, were nice enough but studious and a couple of years older than he was, and given that he was usually asleep when they were at school and they while he was at work, he didn't see much of them. Especially since he tended to stay at the gym between shifts—he trained, depending on the day, for any number of hours between three in the afternoon and eight o'clock at night.

If nothing else, it was good life experience. He was bored and alone and thought about Emerson pretty much whenever his higher brain function wasn't needed elsewhere, and sometimes even when it was. August turned into September, and he finally got the nerve to write a letter to Emerson. It didn't go exactly as planned, but Jonah figured he deserved the little digs Emerson got in at him and tried not to take it personally.

Then Emerson said *don't tell me I don't have the right to be angry* and *Zack is my best friend* and *how naïve*, and it wasn't like he didn't know what Emerson was doing, but knowing didn't make it hurt any less.

Jonah wasn't a moody person by nature, so someone was bound to notice sooner or later. It was just his bad luck that it happened to be sooner. A week after Emerson's letter, Ken found him at the trainer's station concentrating hard on paperwork he should have been able to do in his sleep.

"Jonah."

Jonah blinked twice at the paper before realizing that *it* wasn't talking to him. He hadn't been getting enough sleep lately. "Oh. Hey, Pastor Ken."

"Can I talk to you in my office for a minute?"

Wordlessly, Jonah rose from the desk and filed the form in the "to be completed" pile. "Am I in trouble?" he asked when the door to the office closed behind him.

Ken turned his head to one side and steepled his fingers together. "You tell me."

Jonah's first impulse was to cross his arms and pout, which was admittedly not very mature, but it did make him feel a little better. "Emerson and I had a fight," he finally admitted.

"Emerson, the boy you're in love with," Ken clarified.

Jonah huffed. "Yes."

"Emerson who is two thousand miles from here."

Jonah decided not to dignify that with a response.

Pastor Ken, however, was not to be deterred. "Did you have a fight on the phone?"

Feeling his cheeks heat, Jonah fixed his gaze to the wood grain of Ken's desk. "I don't call him on the phone." He knew it was ridiculous, but he felt like if he heard Emerson's voice he'd either cry or confess everything. Maybe both.

"So you fought over e-mail?"

There was a strict company policy against using gym computers for personal things, and Jonah wasn't brave enough to risk it. Oliver probably would have let him use his laptop—he was less attached at the fingertips to it than Sebastian was to his—but he didn't know if he could deal with the immediacy of e-mail. Writing things out by hand had always helped him think better. He sighed and pulled the letter out of his shorts pocket.

Ken raised his eyebrows. "You're having a fight with him via snail-mail."

Jonah hadn't actually thought he could feel worse, but now that Ken had pointed out how ridiculous that was, he did. Awesome. "I'm giving him the silent treatment."

"Through letter mail," Ken emphasized.

Jonah kind of wanted to die. "I'm—he said some things," he forced himself to admit. "And I—also maybe said some things, and I know he's just hurting me like I hurt him but I—"

Holding up a hand to stem the flow of Jonah's verbal diarrhea, Ken leaned back in his chair and put his sneakers on his desk again. "Jonah, why did you come to Boston?"

Jonah frowned. They'd had this conversation before. "I needed space. Time to think, to figure out who I am."

"Time away from Emerson," Ken continued.

"Well, yeah."

"Then don't you think that's what you should give yourself?"

Swallowing hard, Jonah took a deep breath. “What do you think I should do?” he said. “I can’t just not talk to him again. I… I can’t do that.”

Ken shook his head. “I don’t think you should, and I’m not asking you to. You said you wanted distance, perspective—give yourself time to get it. Wait a few weeks. Think about what you said to set him off, what made him angry. Do you want to apologize or just move on?”

Jonah nodded resignedly. He knew Ken was right, but with his messed-up schedule, he needed something to keep him sane. It was therapeutic to write to Emerson, and it was going to be hard to stop, hard not to think, *Oh, I have to tell Emerson.* “I know you’re right,” he said at length. “It’s just—I don’t know what to do in the meantime.”

“Ah.” Ken kicked his feet off the desk and swiveled in his chair, rummaging around on the bookshelves that lined his back wall. “I actually have a suggestion for that.” When he turned around again he was holding a battered Frommer’s guide. “Catch.”

Jonah brought his hands up just before the book would have smacked into his chest.

“Seriously, get some culture, please,” Ken begged teasingly. “I’m a member of the clergy, and I think your social life is boring. You need help.”

“Thanks,” Jonah said drily. “I think.”

As usual, Ken just waved him off. “Don’t mention it. Now, get back to doing whatever it is you personal trainers do when you don’t have a client. I have a sermon to write.”

§

ON A postcard of snowy Boston mailed priority post on December 23rd in a festive red envelope:

Dear Emerson,

You know those times when you get the answer to your burning question and find out you were better off not knowing?

Merry Christmas.

Jonah

CHAPTER 3

NOW

"EMMA? Emma, what the hell? Come on, talk to me. Emma, you're freaking me out, so could you please talk to me?"

Emerson blinked. Zack's worried face came into focus. Emerson stared at him.

"You're home."

"Yeah, I'm home. I often come home once I've finished my shift."

"But… you were working until eight tonight."

There was a long pause, and then Zack said slowly, "Yeah, I worked 'til eight. Emma, it's almost nine."

Emerson blinked, absorbing that information. "Oh."

"Emma, how long have you been sitting here?" Zack was frowning still.

"Since Jonah left."

"When was that?"

"Six… six something?" Emerson couldn't remember precisely what time it had been when Jonah had gone the second time. Emerson hadn't exactly taken the time to look at a clock. He'd been too distracted by the front door slamming.

"Emma, have you been sitting here for three hours? And have you been crying? Shit. Tell me what the hell's been going on."

Emerson frowned. *What's been going on?* "I…." Emerson shifted and felt the now-familiar sensation of the key digging into his hand. "Jonah… Jonah left."

"Jonah left… to where?" Zack asked, frowning still.

"I—I dunno. He took all his stuff, and he left."

"What the hell?"

"I don't—I—he just left. He didn't even say goodbye," Emerson said, feeling his breath come shorter. If he hadn't rid his body of all his tears hours ago, he was pretty sure he would have started all over again.

"Right. I think it's time that you were in bed; you are obviously exhausted. Let's go." Zack wrapped two hands around his arms, and then he was lifting Emerson onto his feet. Emerson swayed a little as the feeling came back to his limbs, but he didn't protest when Zack guided him up the stairs to his bedroom and told him to get into bed.

It was Zack who pulled off his shoes and stripped off his jeans, muttering about how he should only have to do this when Emerson was drunk and as such he would have had something to drink too. The last thing Emerson remembered before falling asleep was Zack gently urging him to go to sleep as he pulled the covers over his body.

§

THEN

WRITTEN on plain lined sheets with a few suspicious-looking water marks:

Jonah,

Dad isn't well. The attack took a lot out of him. He's at home again, but he stays in bed a lot.

I don't know what to do. Dad might not get better. ~~I am~~ I got a special sort of pass to take only two classes this term so I can help Mom. I've been running Dad's store while she takes care of him and Kierstyn. Fortunately, the classes I'm taking are at night.

~~I'm thinking~~ ~~Mom needs~~ I'll probably move out of my dorm room. It's just wasted money anyway.

Kierstyn keeps crying. I hear Mom cry at night. ~~I don't~~ ~~I can't~~

I wish you were here for me too.

Emerson

§

WRITTEN on the back of a crumpled flyer for guitar lessons:

Em,

I'm writing this letter at the Laundromat, and I had to steal three different flyers because I don't know what to say. There isn't anything to say. Nothing can make this any better.

It's good that you can be there for your mom and Kierstyn. I know they need you right now. But be careful, Em. I know what you're like, and I know you'll work yourself to death trying to be everything to everyone, and you always put yourself last. ~~It's one of the things I~~

Give your mom and sister a hug from me, and get one for yourself too while you're at it.

Jonah

§

THE bulletin board would be next to come down. Emerson had paused in the middle of packing up his room to notice that the corkboard was still hanging on the wall. The overall effect it had by still being there was almost sad. The bed had been stripped, and Emerson had packed away most of the books, knickknacks, and products littered across shelves and flat surfaces. The bulletin board, with its photographs and colorful flyers, looked very out of place.

With a sigh, Emerson reached for the board and lifted it off its hooks. He stood there a moment, staring at everything that cluttered the board, and considered what to do with it. He could, he supposed, leave everything on it, but he wasn't sure that he wanted his parents to see everything that was pinned to it. There were the pictures in which he and his friends had obviously been drinking. There were missives written out in Hayley and Zack's equally legible hands that said things like "hey, asshole" and "darling" and "quest to get you laid." He didn't think his mother would appreciate such notes. Then there was the small rainbow pin pushed into one corner. No, it would be better to take everything off and put it in a box to be sorted through later.

"Emma!" Zack came sauntering into the room and slammed the door behind him. "How goes the packing?" he asked, his voice somewhat gentler now that he had taken in the empty shelves before him.

Emerson gave his friend a wan smile. "All right. It's not like I have that much to put away. I've only been here one term."

Zack arched an eyebrow. "It's amazing how much shit a man can collect in only four months." Emerson found he couldn't argue with that. It was true. He had been very surprised at how much more he had to pack up to bring home than he had first packed up to bring here.

The cork board emptied, Emerson placed all the pages in an old shoebox and then dumped the pins in with them. He'd most likely be putting many of the pictures back on it once he got home anyway.

"So," Zack began, "when's your mom getting here to pick you up?"

Emerson cleared his throat awkwardly. "She's not. I told her not to bother, that I could manage on my own. Besides, I've got you to help me pack up the car, right?"

Zack let out a snort, but he also smiled and slapped Emerson on the shoulder, so Emerson took it as a yes.

It wasn't until Zack was carting boxes down the stairs and loading them into Emerson's car that Emerson found the letters. They were carefully stacked one atop the other and hidden away in the bottom drawer of his night table. Emerson stared at the pile of paper for a long moment. He should throw them out, he thought vaguely. That would be the best idea. After all, what good were a few letters with everything that was going on? When his life was falling apart and Jonah was who knew where?

Emerson pulled the letters from the drawer and flipped through them. He couldn't help the smile at seeing, once again, all the different colors of paper that Jonah had used to write his letters. Jonah, it seemed, was in the terrible habit of composing letters in strange places and on whatever piece of paper he could find first. The second letter, much to Emerson's surprise when he first saw it, had been scrawled on the back of an advertisement for psychic readings. He wondered now, as he had then, where Jonah had picked the flyer up, if he had been tempted to have his aura read or his future told.

Emerson let out a sigh and shook his head. No, he couldn't throw these out. They were, like it or not, the only ties he had to Jonah these days. The only ties he had to the boy who had been, for so long, his closest friend. Emerson tossed the letters into the shoebox with his deconstructed bulletin board.

A few hours later, Emerson was pulling into the driveway. He turned off the engine but didn't get out of the car. It was stupid—he knew it even as he sat there—to avoid entering the house. He knew that sitting in the car for a few minutes longer wasn't going to make a difference, that when he walked in, things would still be the same. His mother would still be crying, his sister would still look pale and fragile, and his dad would still be absent.

With one last sigh, Emerson opened the car door and, picking up a couple of bags, made his way to the front door. It wouldn't do to put this off any longer. He was home, and he was there to stay, and it was time to get used to that.

Reluctantly, he opened the door and entered the house slowly. He set his bags down in the entrance. Then, instead of going back out to the car—he could empty it later—he headed toward the kitchen. There, he found his mother. She was crying.

Emerson wondered if he could back out of the room unseen. Some days it felt like all he did was discover his mother crying. She always appeared to have been mid-chore or -act when suddenly the tears would hit her, and she would be unable to finish making tea or cleaning the windows or cooking supper. Despite these numerous experiences, Emerson was still at a loss for how to deal with it. He always felt so awkward about it. Parents weren't supposed to cry like this. It was their job to deal with crying children, not the other way around.

"Oh, Emerson, I didn't hear you come in," his mother said, wiping the tears off her face. So much for making his escape.

"Just got in," he explained. Still he stood in the kitchen doorway, wondering how best to proceed. Should he just pretend he hadn't found her standing in front of the kitchen sink, glass in one hand and the other pressed to her mouth while tears slid rapidly down her cheeks?

He decided to strive for normal. "So, got all my stuff. All moved out of the dorms." Still striving for normality, he continued on with his original plan and walked to the fridge to get some juice. He poured himself a tall glass of punch and pretended not to hear his mother pull out a tissue.

Emerson finished his glass of juice and stood in the middle of the kitchen, uncertain and not moving.

"How are you, honey?" Emerson could tell by the tone of her voice that she was asking about his decision to move.

"I'm fine," he said, not wanting to elaborate or argue. He knew she wasn't very happy about the need for him to move back home, but with Dad sick and in the hospital for now, there wasn't much choice about it.

"Okay." She gave him a trembling mockery of a smile that didn't last long. The silence that followed was oppressive. Finally Emerson conceded defeat. He and his mother wouldn't be having any sort of conversation tonight, meaningful or otherwise. Emerson turned to leave.

"Oh, Emerson?"

"Yes, Mom?" Emerson turned back to her, hoping for a moment of the mother he missed.

"When you're at the store tomorrow, don't forget it's inventory time. And file the time sheets so we can get the paychecks out on time. There aren't many, and I don't want the kids to suffer for this." Emerson's parents had owned a small grocery store in Hudson Bend for longer than he could remember. They sold snacks and candy to the local kids and fresh produce and organic foods to their parents. He had been working at the store for most of his life.

"I know, Mom." This was all stuff that Emerson knew. He had known it before Christmas, and he certainly knew to take care of it *now*.

"Right, of course. I just didn't want you to forget."

"Okay."

The silence returned.

"Well, I have homework to get done, and then I'm going to go to bed. Night, Mom."

"Okay."

Emerson turned to go, but just as he was passing through the door, she added softly, "Thank you for this, Emerson. You're a good boy. I'm so proud of you." He didn't turn around. Instead he stood, frozen and embarrassed. He wished she hadn't said anything.

Emerson didn't break the awkward silence, only nodded to let her know he had heard and then continued to his room.

§

EMERSON was shocked out of his sleep by the sound of Garth Brooks telling him he had friends in low places. Blindly fumbling to find the source of the noise, he decided that Garth was right. If Zack and Greg weren't low, then Emerson didn't know who was, because they were clearly to blame for his current hung-over state.

Emerson's hand finally landed on his cell phone, and with a pain-filled groan, he brought the screen to his face. Thankfully he had apparently remembered to take his contacts out last night, even if he couldn't remember going to bed, but that meant he was as blind as a bat. The cell phone told him that Zack was calling. Which meant that Hayley had stolen and reprogrammed his cell phone again.

Thumbing the phone on, Emerson groaned into it. "Wha'?"

"Emma! How are you this morning?"

Emerson whimpered.

"Look, did you make it back to Hayley's okay? You kind of wandered off last night."

He let out another groan. "Did I?" His face was still smushed into his pillow. Emerson tried to remember what had happened last night.

"Don't you remember?" The bastard was laughing at him.

He remembered Zack dragging him out to a frat party. Zack had been bugging him for weeks about working too hard and not getting out enough, so when he had started on about this frat party that Peter and the Hanged Man were playing at, Emerson had caved. He had let Hayley pick out his skinniest jeans and his tightest T-shirt, and then he had let them take him to a *frat* party.

Emerson, of course, had felt woefully out of place. He had also lost track of Hayley about fifteen minutes into the party, because Hayley was a bit of a slut who wanted to get laid. Since the only other people that Emerson knew at this party were the entertainment and therefore unavailable, he had grabbed the closest unopened bottle of beer and begun to drink.

Emerson had downed two bottles of beer while wandering around the party, feeling awkward and conspicuous. Standing in the middle of the frat house, he couldn't remember why he had ever thought that this would be a good idea. That was until he stumbled into a new room and into—someone tall, dark, and gorgeous. Emerson hadn't been too drunk at the time to realize that having to tilt his head back to look the guy in the eyes was a major turn on.

"Hello," the stranger had said with a wide, charming smile. And then Emerson realized that he had planted his hand on the man's chest to steady himself and was, at that point in time, petting the firm muscle under his touch.

Emerson let out a piteous groan and heard Zack chuckle in response. "So, starting to remember?"

"Oh God, I ran into… oh God! I can't remember his name!"

Zack laughed.

"Za-ack!" Emerson moaned, feeling quite sorry for himself. Though he couldn't remember the other guy's name, he certainly remembered what they had done.

After several minutes of flirting and staring up into interested brown eyes, Emerson had let himself be led into a closet. Yes, a closet, but it had been private, and the guy had been nibbling on his neck. Emerson had, since starting college, kissed a few other boys at parties, so it wasn't anything shocking. Still, this whole making out thing was pretty new to him, and none of the other guys had ever been this talented, he'd thought dazedly as he tilted his head back so that the guy could nibble bellow his ear.

And then Emerson, drunk on two beers, had let the stranger….

Emerson groaned again. "Zack… I think I lost my virginity last night, and I can't remember the guy's name."

A long pause greeted this. "Are you serious? Jesus, Emma."

"I just… it's not like I meant to!" Emerson wailed and buried his face deeper into the pillow. "We were making out, and then he just… stuck his hands down my pants!"

He had. It hadn't been done with much finesse, either. The guy had just rammed his hand down there with little regard for Emerson's comfort. His hand had been large and rough and had pulled at Emerson with harsh strokes. Emerson had gasped in surprise, and the guy had taken the opportunity to shove his tongue down Emerson's throat. It was about that time that Emerson thought maybe he wasn't having fun anymore. Apparently being a good neck nibbler didn't mean you were good at giving hand jobs.

Zack let out sigh and murmured, "Christ." Then, louder, "Only you could accidently get a hand job, Emma."

"It wasn't a very good one," Emerson mumbled. "I'd almost think he's never given one before."

It had been so bad that Emerson had just stood there while the stranger jacked him off and then used Emerson's hand to get himself off. Afterward, Emerson had said the fastest goodbye he'd ever given and then run away. Quickly.

Once he'd escaped from the closet, he had stumbled around for a while before finding more beer. Emerson had downed several cups of the stuff, trying to get the memory out of his head.

Then Hayley had found him. No, that wasn't right, because Hayley had found him outside, so he had made his way outside first. He had gone outside because he had wanted to find a mailbox because—

"Oh, shit!" Emerson bolted upright in bed. Panic adrenaline filled his veins. Oh God, he hadn't, had he? He vaguely remembered finding the flyer and the pen, and then—"Oh God… Zack, I think I sent Jonah a drunk letter last night."

This was greeted by silence. "Oh?" It was really unfair that Zack could lace one simple syllable with so much disapproval and meaning. "What did this drunken letter say?"

"I think I told him I got drunk and lost my virginity," Emerson whispered, mortified. Maybe he should just smother himself with a pillow.

Zack burst into laughter.

Emerson pulled the pillow over his head.

"Sorry, Emma, didn't mean to laugh, but shit, only you could get drunk enough to drunk dial, but then actually write and mail a letter instead." There was a pause as they both considered this. "Maybe you didn't actually mail it, or maybe you didn't address it right?"

Hope began to fill Emerson's chest, and he sat up, letting the pillow fall to the side. Zack was right. It was ridiculous to think that Emerson had not only written the letter but had addressed and stamped an envelope as well.

Then Emerson remembered how he had made out an envelope just yesterday to write Jonah a letter. He had decided, on a whim, that he would write Jonah this morning and tell him about the party. Knowing that he'd be in Hayley's dorm room, he had gathered up the needed supplies—envelope, paper, stamp—and then decided he might as well get the envelope ready so that he wouldn't lose the stamp.

Emerson whimpered in despair.

"Right, I'll take that as a no, that you actually managed to successfully drunk mail Jonah."

"Zack!"

"Oh no, don't whine to me, you loser. I've been telling you for months that you should just stop writing that boy. He's bad for you."

"Have sympathy," Emerson begged. "I just told the man of my dreams that I gave it up while drunk at a frat party!"

"Remind me to never call you the morning after you've been drinking again. Hangovers turn you into a drama queen."

Emerson suddenly felt like crying. Then Hayley walked into the room and said, "Oh, Em, you're awake!" and he burst into tears.

Or rather, Emerson sniffled in a very manly fashion and tears started falling down his cheeks. He let out a sob.

"Oh, Christ," he heard Zack say at the same time that Hayley cried, "Emerson, darling, what's wrong?"

He hiccupped. "I'm a slut!" he burst out.

Hayley stared at him, obviously flummoxed. "Em, you are the most celibate person I know."

"I gave it up to a frat boy at a frat party! I'm not just a slut, I'm a cliché." Emerson fell back onto Hayley's bed and covered his face with the pillow again to smother a groan. Through the layers of fabric and down, Emerson thought he could hear Hayley muttering "there, there" and Zack laughing through the phone line.

Hayley sat on her bed and patted Emerson's shoulder comfortingly.

"Emerson." Zack's voice was louder than before, and Emerson wondered if Hayley had put Zack on speakerphone. "How drunk did you get last night?"

And then, "Are you still drunk?" He sounded like he was trying really hard not to laugh.

Emerson whimpered.

Three hours later, after Zack had stopped laughing and after Hayley had got the whole story out of him, and after Emerson had sobered up a bit and had a shower (because he had *really* needed one), he pulled out a piece of paper to write Jonah another letter.

Given that Emerson couldn't remember exactly what he had written, writing the apology letter wasn't that simple.

Well, he knew how to start.

Jonah,

Now, where to go from there? After staring at the page for some time, Emerson decided to go with honesty. He could do that. It took some time, but he finally managed to come up with a letter he was satisfied with.

Oh God! Please tell me that writing you a drunken letter about my drunken activities at a party and then MAILING it is all just a drunken hallucination.

Fuck! I'm embarrassed. I can't believe I did that.

I was trying to follow your advice—make sure I didn't get caught up in work—Zack kept bugging me about going to this party that his friends were throwing and that he was performing at, and I caved. Alcohol is a very bad thing, and I'm never having it ever again. Also, I'm not sure about ever having sex again either; it was kind of pretty awful.

Em

Emerson reread the letter and then groaned in despair. He sounded like a whore! And so one last line was added:

P.S. Oh geez, I made myself sound like a drunken slut! I only had two beers before the making out started. The real drinking happened afterward.

Then, before he could lose his nerve, Emerson placed the letter in an envelope and left the house to mail it.

CHAPTER 4

NOW

"ALRIGHT, I've waited long enough." Natalie didn't bother knocking, just barged into his room—still full of boxes from the furniture he'd been putting together all day—and situated herself on the bed. "Spill."

It had been two days since—Jonah didn't know what to call it, so "since" would have to suffice. When he'd stormed out, furious, he'd needed space to think, so he'd gone for a walk, wanting to be alone. So of course he'd run into his sister and her friends, who were still looking for a fourth roommate. This time he hadn't thought twice about accepting the offer.

He'd slept on the floor the first night, and the next day his dad had come by in the pickup with his bed, and then they'd gone to IKEA.

Next time, Jonah was buying furniture that didn't come in eight thousand pieces.

"Don't you knock?" he said without much real heat. Maybe if he were obnoxious enough she'd go away. "I could have been jerking off in here."

"Please, you are way too emo to choke the chicken right now. You probably can't even get it up."

The sad part was that she was at least partially right. "I don't want to talk about it."

"Obviously. That's why you're sitting up here on the floor making so much noise you'd wake Saint Peter." Natalie made herself comfortable, stretching out on his bed. Then she brandished a nail clipper and threatened, "I'm gonna start cutting right here if you don't spill."

Ugh, that was *disgusting*. "God, where do you get these depraved ideas?" Jonah grumbled, but he put down the screwdriver and flopped onto the floor in defeat anyway. With Natalie it was only ever a matter of time. "Where should I start?"

"Oh, I don't know, how about why you're having a giant love-tiff with your boyfriend, whom you totally adore and cannot keep your hands off of?"

Jonah sighed. He might as well get it off his chest. "Do you remember my ex? Dee Carlisle?"

"Yeah, sure. Girls' volleyball captain, right? She was nice. I heard she was in town for a while." Natalie lowered her voice. "She didn't hit on you in front of him or something?"

"I wish," Jonah muttered. "It was worse."

"How much worse?" asked Natalie cautiously.

"She showed up at the store, while he was working, with her son, Gareth. He's three."

Jonah waited for Natalie to do the math. Then she said, "Oh, he *did not*."

"Accuse me of hiding a kid? Oh yeah." Talking about it—hell, even thinking about it—was like pouring salt on an open wound.

"Wow," Natalie said. "I mean, I knew he was a neurotic basket-case, but this is a little insane, even for Emerson. But you set him straight, right?"

Jonah was silent.

"Right? Jonah?"

He said nothing, and Natalie got off the bed to sit next to him on the floor. "You didn't," she said. "You let him think whatever he wanted. You were too pissed off to care about his feelings."

Well—guilty as charged, but Jonah didn't think anyone could really blame him for that. He sat up. "Hell yes, I was pissed! I'm still pissed!"

"Easy, killer," Natalie placated. "What did he say when you moved out? Anything?"

Jonah kept his mouth shut.

"You didn't talk to him," Natalie extrapolated. She really excelled at this game, which was annoying. "You packed up your shit and left without saying a word. Wow, Jonah, very mature. I'm impressed. The silent treatment. What are you, twelve?"

Fuck it, Jonah didn't have to take shit about his relationship from his baby sister. He stood up. "Know a lot of twelve-year-olds whose boyfriends accuse them of being *fathers*?" he snarled.

Stubbornness ran in the Cherneski genes, though, and Natalie got right up after him. "So Emerson's a basket case. That's not exactly a newsflash, Jonah. You knew what you were signing on for!"

"Are you actually *defending* him?"

"I just called him a basket case! But he's *your* basket case!"

"Not anymore!" Jonah yelled.

The sudden blossom of pain across his face had him staggering backward with one hand on his cheek. Incredulous, he looked down at his hand to find a trickle of blood; she'd split his lip open. "What the *fuck*—"

She was shaking with anger when he met her eyes again. "Jonah, you are my brother, and I love you dearly. But you and Emerson have something most people only dream about, and if you throw that away over this, I swear to God I'll kill you myself."

Then she stormed out, slamming the door behind her, leaving Jonah nursing a cheek that didn't hurt nearly as much as his heart. Weakly, Jonah sat down on his bed, staring at the plain white wall. He should put up some pictures or something, he thought. Only that reminded him of the suitcase full of pictures of Emerson's art he had from his apartment in California, and that led to thinking about Emerson, a practice Jonah was determined to stop.

The door opened again, quietly this time, with the briefest and softest of preceding knocks, and Natalie came in and sat next to him and pressed a cloth-wrapped ice pack to his face. "Sorry," she said, and she sounded like she meant it. Natalie had got their father's temperament, which meant her anger was explosive but over with quickly. "I know you're just…."

"Scared," Jonah said. *Terrified* would have been a better word. He'd lashed out at Natalie because he was afraid that Emerson might not be his basket case anymore. That Emerson wouldn't forgive him for the way he'd acted or wouldn't be able to stop being a neurotic mess just waiting for Jonah to fuck up in a huge, unforgivable way.

"Sure," Natalie said. "That works." She slid an arm around his shoulders in a sideways half-hug. "I'd be scared too."

He covered her hand with the one that wasn't holding the ice to his face. "Thanks."

"Thanks for teaching me how to throw a punch," Natalie said sheepishly.

The funny thing was that he'd never actually thrown one himself. He'd learned how in gym class. He shrugged a little. "I kind of needed it?"

Natalie leaned her head against his shoulder. "You did something, right? I mean I know you're mad at Emerson, but you usually don't get like this unless you're mad at yourself too."

Wincing, he leaned back into her. Sometimes she knew him a little too well.

"It's okay," she said. "You don't have to tell me."

He *wanted* to. He just couldn't—not yet.

§

THEN

JONAH was manning the desk in the main gym when it happened. He was filing some paperwork between snatches of the muted *Survivorman* episode that was playing on screen eight. He was just looking up after filing Helen Yarman's latest workout stats when a shadow fell across the desk.

Blinking as his eyes adjusted to the sudden lack of light, Jonah said, "Can I help you?" Then his vision cleared, and he had to remind himself to close his mouth, because the man on the other side of the desk was....

He wasn't exactly tall, though he wasn't short either. He had shaggy, somewhat curly, glossy black hair, obviously still damp from a shower Jonah could practically smell. Dark eyes, a smooth, perfect cinnamon complexion, and a row of even white teeth behind a full set of smiling lips completed the picture.

Hot, Jonah's brain supplied for him. *The word you are looking for is "hot."*

"Yeah, I just—" Something clicked against the desktop, and Jonah stood up to get a better look... at the object, a thin gold chain with a cross on the end, not at the guy holding it—that was just a bonus. "I found this in the shower," he said almost apologetically. "Someone must've forgotten it. There's a lost and found, though, right?"

"Uh, sure, just let me—" Jonah reached into the odds and ends drawer for a sheet. "I have to fill one of these out to help match it to any missing items," he explained, grabbing for a pen and nearly knocking the entire jar over.

Breathe, he reminded himself firmly over the wave of guilt and embarrassment. *So he's hot. That doesn't give you an excuse to act like a total spaz.*

Jonah filled in the date and time, then looked up again and smiled. "You say you found it in the showers?" he said, trying not to get distracted by the mental image. Mystery Man's T-shirt was clinging to him just right. "The ones in the change rooms or the ones by the pool?"

"Change rooms," Mystery Man said, and Jonah dutifully filled in the appropriate space on the sheet.

"All set, then," Jonah said, locating an envelope to contain the necklace until someone claimed it. "Oh—except I need your name." He waved his hand in the air, dropping the envelope as he did so. "Shit. Sorry."

He got the distinct impression Mystery Man was laughing at him. "It's Evan," he said. "Evan van Horne."

"Nice to meet you," Jonah offered, attempting to staple the found sheet and the envelope together and being foiled by a staple jam. It was just not his day. He gave up and put it down, offering his hand across the desk instead. "I'm Jonah."

Evan's eyes sparkled. "Yeah, I know." He gestured. "It's on your nametag."

Jesus, of course it was. "Well, not everyone can read, you know," Jonah said lamely. "Um, not that you look like someone who can't read." Maybe the universe would do him a favor and engulf the whole building in flames. Evan was looking at him blankly. *Oh, God, say something else*. "So, do you come here often?"

Evan smiled widely while Jonah died inside of utter mortification. "Are you always like this?"

Jonah shuddered. "Oh, God, I hope not." Seppuku was looking pretty tempting right now.

Laughing, Evan stuck his hand over the desk. "You're cute. Let's try this again. I'm Evan."

Unable to resist the smile pulling at his lips, Jonah shook it firmly, though he could still feel the color staining his cheeks. "Jonah. Nice to meet you."

"The pleasure is all mine," Evan assured him. "So, you must be new? Or sort of new, anyway."

"New to this shift," Jonah explained. "I was only on afternoons before."

"That's why I haven't seen you, then. I'm here on my lunch break three days a week." He grinned. "Got to keep up appearances."

Yeah, Jonah could see that. He licked his lips unconsciously at the muscle definition he could see through the T-shirt. "Well, we'll probably be seeing a lot more of each other, then," he said reasonably.

Evan laughed again. "I hope so," he said, looking Jonah up and down in a way that could not be misinterpreted. Then he took a step back from the desk and winked. "See you around."

§

WRITTEN on the back of a neon-yellow flyer for a frat party:

Dear Jonah,
I just lost my virginity at a frat party. I'm a college cliché.
Word of advice: bad idea.
Em

§

WRITTEN on the back of an advertisement for *Les Mis*:

Dear Emerson,

Wow. I could have told you that. You didn't have to go and experience it firsthand.

Sorry, I didn't mean that to sound—I'm just surprised. That's so unlike you. Although I guess you probably needed to cut loose a little. Also, where were your new friends to keep you from making bad decisions? The least they could've done was stop you from sending the letter.

Anyway, I would be offended if you didn't tell me about it. Too bad it was awful. Maybe you should join a convent.

Since we're on the subject, I've sort of been seeing someone. Not sure if it's going anywhere yet, but Evan is really nice, so I guess we'll play it by ear.

How's your dad doing? You usually mention something.

Jonah

§

Two weeks later:

Jonah,

Dad's back in hospital. He's not recovering. He went back in two days before the frat party, hence my bad-decision-making skills.

My friends, the finks, were busy with other things, and so they didn't help me one bit. Though given the way Greg and Zack won't stop laughing about the letter (and my morning-after freak out) I'm not sure they'd have been much help at stopping me from sending it.

How nice of you to have found a girlfriend. I'm putting serious thought into your convent idea.

Emerson

§

JONAH was with a client the next time he saw Evan, who gave him a short wave from the treadmill, and the time after that he had to sub in for a weight-lifting class and missed him, so it was a week later before they had a chance to talk.

"Hey, Jonah."

Jonah almost dropped the towel he'd been using to dry himself—he'd just bid farewell to the last of his students after subbing for the Aqua-fit instructor, who had a nasty stomach bug. "Hey," he answered back, trying not to feel self-conscious but draping the towel around his shoulders anyway. It was kind of embarrassing that a lot of the gym's patrons were better built than he was, since he worked there, not that anyone ever mentioned anything.

"Didn't know you taught," Evan commented, pulling his shirt off and tossing it into his locker.

Jesus. Jonah averted his eyes from the sculpted muscle and reached into his own locker for his shower caddy. Looking at Evan made him feel guilty, like he was betraying Emerson even though Emerson had no idea how he felt. But Emerson had Justin, Jonah reminded himself. It wasn't like Emerson was just sitting at home waiting for him.

Maybe Jonah *should* look. It was just looking, right? "Just a substitute," he said with a sideways cut of his eyes. "Marie has that stomach flu that's been going around."

"Well, it doesn't sound like anyone's going to lodge a complaint, so you must be pretty good. Almost makes me want to sign up."

Jonah flushed. Okay—at first he thought he'd been imagining it, a wishful thinking kind of thing—but Evan was flirting with him, right? "Thanks."

Oh, God. Evan shoved his shorts and boxers down and reached into his locker for his towel. Jonah averted his eyes again, feeling his face heat intensely. *Right—back to not looking. Much safer.*

Unfortunately, he'd just come out of the pool, and he needed a shower of his own.

Well, there was nothing for it. Jonah hadn't exactly been known for his modesty before now, and he wasn't about to start acting bashful just because he'd figured out he was attracted to guys. At least he was over that awkward stage he'd gone through in his first year of high school where he got a boner when the wind blew the right way. Steeling himself, he pushed down his swimsuit and wrapped his towel around his waist.

"Listen—"

Jonah couldn't help the automatic reaction to turn around when Evan spoke, but thankfully the other man had followed Jonah's lead with the towel. Knowing that he didn't have anything on under it was bad enough. "Yeah?"

"I'm making you uncomfortable," Evan said regretfully, backing up a step and grabbing a bottle of body wash from his gym bag. "Sorry. I must have misread you."

"I—no," Jonah said as bravely as he could. "You didn't—I mean, I am bi." It was the first time he'd actually said it aloud, and he couldn't help feeling that it should have been a bigger deal. He should have felt freed or maybe exhilarated or something, but he was the same as he always was. The men's locker room at a gym was probably not the best spot to admit that, but he'd been paying attention—there were enough obviously gay men around that no one should have a problem. Besides, aside from himself and Evan, there weren't many others in the locker room. Feeling the need to follow up with an excuse for his spastic behavior, he continued, "I've just never…." He stopped there, deciding Evan could fill in the blank however he liked. There were limits to how candid he was willing to be, and his inexperience with men was suddenly kind of embarrassing.

"Oh." Evan blinked in apparent shock, and Jonah tried not to squirm as his eyes flicked over him quickly. "Seriously?"

Jesus, this literally could not get any more mortifying. "Uh, no. Just, you know, with girls."

"But you are interested," Evan clarified, sounding hopeful.

Was Jonah interested? Evan was hot and nice and apparently not put off by the fact that Jonah was, at best, a novice when it came to dating men. He wasn't Emerson, of course, but Emerson wasn't here. That was sort of the whole point.

And Emerson was… seeing people… anyway. "Yeah," he admitted.

Evan beamed. "Cool. Have dinner with me Friday?"

"I… okay." Now that that was out of the way, he could relax a little.

"Great!" he enthused, then raised a sheepish hand and scratched at the back of his head. Jonah tried hard not to stare at the way it made the muscles in his bare arm bulge, but he was only human. "Well, that was awkward. Remind me not to be naked next time I ask you out, okay?"

Jonah snorted, and the remaining tension disappeared under the weight of his grin. "No promises."

§

Emerson,

I'm sorry to hear that. Is there anything they can do? A transplant or something?

Your new friends are clearly inferior.

Evan is less of a girlfriend and more of a, um, experiment? That sounds awful, but, you know. I've never dated a guy before, so. Uh. Surprise, I guess.

Don't be mad that I didn't tell you. I'm only figuring it out for myself just now.

Jonah

P.S. I definitely still like girls. If you were wondering, I mean.

§

WRITTEN three days later on note paper labeled with the name "Hayley," in pink ink:

Jonah,

What?!

No, seriously, what? You're dating a guy but you still like girls? So you're like bi or something? Since when?

Emerson

P.S. They don't know what's wrong. They think the heart failure is a symptom, not the problem.

As you weren't there when Greg held me up over a toilet while I puked or when Zack got in a fight at a bar on my behalf, I'll let that ill-informed comment about their inferiority pass.

§

Emerson,

I am pretty sure that is the definition of "bi," yes. Since always, I guess. I'm not exactly Mr. Self-Examination, Em. I didn't know until suddenly I did. If it makes you feel better, you're still the only person at home who knows.

Obviously it's me who's the inferior friend.

Keep me updated on your dad.

Jonah

P.S. the pink ink was a nice touch.

§

ON THE back of a quiz for Business Economics with a score of 10/10:

Jonah,

Ugh, I read your letter on the way to lunch with Hayley, and obviously I couldn't just let a bombshell like that go unanswered ASAP. Blame the pink ink on Hayley: it was all she had.

You'd like her, a lot. She's smart and witty and very sassy. She told Eric Gleeson that if he didn't stop trying to touch her boobs she would ram her stylish, pointed toe, designer boots up his ass before removing the possibility of his polluting future gene pools. I've never seen a grown man look so terrified in my life. You'd get on well with her. I know it. You'll also get on well with Greg and Zack. Well, okay, with Greg. Zack is an overprotective douche, so it'll take a while before you convince him to like you too. I'm not worried, though, you always do.

Dad's not looking any better.

Emerson

(Who still likes you even if you are a bastard who runs away and drops Megaton bombshells AND sometimes dates men—though that was never in question of making me like you less.)

§

WRITTEN on a cocktail napkin from a place called the Pink Flamingo, complete with stylized pink bird, labeled "Emerson," standing on one foot in the corner:

Dear Emerson,

Sorry to hear about your dad. That really sucks, man.

As I am not yet 21, and no one in their right mind would ever let me have alcohol, I had Evan pick up this napkin. I thought you and Hayley might like it. Hopefully it will cheer you up a little, at least.

Both Hayley and Zack sound scary. I am not sure I am safe all the way in Boston, to tell you the truth. I went shopping for a codpiece today just in case. You can buy just about anything in the city.

The bi thing seriously doesn't bother you? I expected a micro freak-out, at least. I'm pretty lucky to have a friend I can be straight with. Well, so to speak.

Whoops, got to go—my break's over. Once more into the sweaty breach.

Jonah

P.S. Business economics? What happened to graphic design?

§

Jonah,

Hayley and Zack aren't that scary. Okay, Hayley isn't that scary. Mostly she's just spunky. Zack is 6 feet of compact muscle. But you'll like him. He's a musician—what's not to like?

Also, can you really buy a codpiece in Boston? This is disturbing news.

Why would you being bi bother me? You haven't suddenly stopped being Jonah, the dorky kid I grew up with who is too tall and lives with his foot always and firmly planted in his mouth, have you?

Graphic design is a useless degree that won't get me a steady, stable job. Business will.

Emerson

P.S. I'm a pink flamingo now?

§

ATTACHED to the classified section of the *New York Times*, with several job postings circled in yellow highlighter:

Emerson,

Don't you dare try to pass that BS off as your own opinion. Not to me.

Jonah

§

TWO days later, on the back of a computer printout of a picture of Jonah holding up the codpiece:

You like it.

§

Jonah,

In response to the picture: I'm terrified. Seriously. Scary.

As for that BS… what was I going to do with a degree in graphic design, anyway? Take pictures for a book?

Emerson

§

"HEY," Oliver grunted, dropping into the kitchen chair across from Jonah. "You cooked?"

"It's been known to happen sometimes," Jonah said drily as Oliver helped himself to a bowl of spaghetti. "It's not like pasta is complicated."

Oliver took a big bite and sighed happily. "God, I love carbs." He spent the next few quiet minutes stuffing his face while Jonah skimmed the newspaper, and then he pushed his bowl away and put on what Jonah could peripherally see was his serious face. "Have you thought anymore about what we talked about?"

Jonah hadn't actually thought about anything else all day. He held up the page he was skimming—classified section. "I'm thinking about it," he promised. Which—okay, earlier he'd actually been browsing through the travel section. He wasn't convinced he wanted to stay in Boston yet, and he wasn't sure how that made him feel. He had a good job and a boyfriend who maybe loved him, was certainly good to him, and it felt awfully selfish to think that maybe that wasn't enough. "I know you guys need to make a decision or start looking for another roommate soon. Can I let you know by the end of the week?"

"That's reasonable," Oliver nodded. For a minute everything was quiet and a little awkward, and then he said, "Listen, I know we aren't close, and that's at least partially my fault. But you seem like a pretty cool guy, and I'd be more than happy if you stuck around. I know Sebastian would say the same." He gave a wry smile. "If he was capable of having a conversation about something other than eighteenth-century France right now, anyway."

"I'm surprised he still knows how to speak English," Jonah confided. "And thanks—you guys have been really great, and I'm sorry we haven't hung out more. It's just—I don't know, I think I want to see the world. Or at least the country." He owed Oliver at least that small measure of honesty.

"Can't say I blame you for that," Oliver admitted as they stood and started clearing their dishes away. "Midterms suck, and when they're finally over, it's exam time."

"The two of you do seem to spend a lot of time at the library." Setting the pot in the sink to soak, Jonah turned around. "Is it okay with you if I take care of this later? I'm supposed to be meeting Evan at his place."

Oliver waved him off. "No, go on. I imagine you have things to talk about." Then he grinned. "Mind you be home by midnight."

Jonah laughed his way out the door, though the idea of *talking* about things with Evan made him want to do the opposite.

It was a couple of blocks to Evan's, and he usually just walked it, but today he just happened to be passing by the bus stop at the same time as the bus, so he hopped on. The early March weather was freezing cold, anyway, and it wasn't like he needed the exercise. He did almost miss his stop, however—too busy staring out the windows at the gray concrete and grayer sky and trying too hard not to think about what he was going to do.

When he reached the apartment building, Evan buzzed him in immediately, then met him at the door with a kiss and a mug of hot chocolate. "You're awesome," Jonah said feelingly, pressing another quick kiss to his mouth before hanging his coat on the back of the door and wrapping both hands around the mug. "How was work?"

"Same old," Evan smiled, leading him into the living room. "Mitch got his tie stuck in the photocopier. Got a picture with my phone before the IT guy arrived, see?"

Jonah had only met Mitch once when a few of Evan's work colleagues had gone out for dinner, but from what he remembered and the way Evan usually talked about him, the photocopier attack was just part of the universe's karmic retribution. "Wow. I didn't know people's eyeballs could actually bulge like that."

Snickering, Evan turned his phone off and set it on the table. "I know. I'm thinking of sending out a company-wide e-mail on photocopier safety. Just trying to figure out if I can get away with it without being fired."

Jonah took a quick sip of hot chocolate, then put it down beside him; it was still too hot to drink. "Probably not with a picture attachment," he said with a mock-regretful tone.

"No, probably not," Evan agreed. "Pity. Anyway, how was your day?"

Jonah shrugged. "It was alright. I got a new client, another yuppie housewife," he teased, knowing how Evan felt about the majority of his clientele. It wasn't his fault the yuppie housewives seemed to find him charming and nonthreatening. Besides, he liked them; they were nice and never treated him any differently because he had a boyfriend. "She seems nice."

"That's awesome, Jonah. You'll be making more money than me soon at this rate."

Jonah poked him in the stomach. "Not unless you quit your job to become a street busker or something."

"Well, I do know how to juggle. You never know."

Jonah did know, actually—Evan loved being a chartered accountant and the money and prestige that came along with it. Jonah was just never going to understand the appeal of something so seemingly artless; he loved words and images and color too much to enjoy crunching numbers. "Whatever you say," Jonah said with a roll of his eyes.

He must have zoned out for a minute, because the next thing he knew, he was reaching for a cold mug of hot chocolate, and Evan was saying, "Jonah? Something on your mind?"

Where to begin. Jonah stared down at the mug in his hands and told himself to just spit it out already, that he might want to move, that he might be leaving, but what he said was, "It's Emerson."

Coward.

"Your pen pal?" Evan clarified, his voice holding enough of a frown, Jonah didn't need to check to see if his expression matched. "Is his dad okay?"

"He's still in the hospital," Jonah said shortly, rotating the mug to the left, then right again. "But that's not…." He huffed finally and put the mug on the table before steeling himself and turning to face Evan. "I'm mad at him for throwing his dreams away, and it's distracting."

"Okay…," Evan hedged.

"It's just—he always wanted to go to art school, and somehow his parents conned him into getting a soulless business degree."

"Gee, Jonah, tell me how you really feel," Evan said, a hint of bitterness to his tone.

Jonah blinked, then realized what he'd said. "No, that's not—I get that it's what you love, really. Come on, it would be kind of ridiculous if I thought everyone should be a starving artist, wouldn't it? Besides, it's not like I can talk." Not when he had no real education to speak of. "I'm just frustrated. I want him to be happy, you know? That's all."

"I believe you," Evan said calmly, shifting so he was sitting facing Jonah. "Is there something else bothering you? You're not usually this jumpy."

Fuck. There was nothing for it—he might as well just own up. "Our lease is up for renewal in a couple weeks," he admitted. "Oliver asked if I wanted to sign, but it's a year contract."

"I thought you liked that apartment?" Evan said. "Have you been fighting with your roommates or something?"

Jonah shook his head. "No, nothing like that. They're great guys, even if I do hardly see them." He looked at his lap.

After a moment Evan said, "Oh. I think I know where this is going."

Relieved, Jonah whipped his head around to look at him. Evan didn't look mad. Actually, he looked… what, happy? Indulgent. "You do?"

"Well, yeah. I mean, I was going to wait a little longer to say something, but if your lease is coming up now, there's not much point, is there?"

Wait, was Evan breaking up with him? That… actually that would make his decision at least a little easier, wouldn't it? But then why was he smiling? "I guess not," Jonah said tentatively.

Evan fidgeted a little, but there was a smile fighting its way past the corners of his mouth. Jonah suddenly had a bad feeling that this was not at all going where he thought it was. "I know you're a lot younger than I am, and it used to freak me out a little, but you're so much more mature than I was at your age that it doesn't even matter anymore. I know you don't like to talk about your feelings, but you know that I love you, and I think—I hope—you feel the same?"

Oh, God. The bottom dropped out of Jonah's stomach. This was definitely not where he thought Evan was going with this conversation. This was the opposite. "Evan—"

"No, let me finish. It's early, but I think we get along well, and maybe this is just the universe's way of telling us that it's time, you know? So what do you say?"

Jonah silently prayed that a bolt of lightning would strike the apartment and interrupt the coming question, but to no avail.

"Move in with me?"

"I'm leaving Boston," Jonah blurted.

Evan blinked hard, like he didn't quite understand what Jonah had just said. "Finally going to visit your parents?" he said faintly.

"No." Jonah stood up, suddenly frantic. He didn't want this. How had he ever convinced himself that he did, that this was any kind of acceptable substitute? It wasn't. Jonah was still too in love with Emerson to want anyone else, and now Evan was going to pay the price for it. "Look, I—you've been really good to me. Good *for* me. But I'm just a stupid kid. I don't know what the hell I'm doing, and I have a lot more growing up to do."

Evan flushed, then stood as well, putting his hands on his hips and then just as quickly removing them. "I don't understand—are you breaking up with me?"

"I'm not ready for this kind of commitment," Jonah said frankly, horrified to hear how his voice shook with the words. "I'm not."

"That's—you don't have to," Evan said, taking a hesitant step forward, reaching for Jonah's hands. "I'm sorry. That was too sudden. Let's just—forget it."

Jonah took a step back. "No, you don't understand. I wasn't ready for the level of commitment we already have." He swallowed what felt like a mouthful of cut glass and ran his hands through his hair, tugging. "I never meant for things to get this far. God, what a fucking mess."

"Jonah—"

"I'm leaving," he repeated, too quickly, unsteady. "You, Boston, my job. I've been lying to myself. I need to go."

"*Jonah—*"

He couldn't listen to it, couldn't take the pleading tone. "I'm sorry," he said, trying to make it sound final.

"You're making a mistake," Evan told him, and for all that Jonah knew his heart was breaking it didn't sound like anything but anger now.

"Yeah, well," Jonah said bitterly, "it wouldn't be the first time."

When he got back to his apartment, Oliver was already in bed, and the apartment was dark. Jonah washed the dishes as quickly and quietly as he could, not wanting to wake his roommates, but his hand slipped as he was drying Oliver's stainless steel measuring cup, and somehow he ended up with a wide red crescent blossoming on his right knuckle.

The measuring cup fell to the floor with a deafening rattle, and Jonah swore, grasping his hand around his wrist to try to stem the bleeding before it got everywhere. "Shit." God, it *hurt*, and the fact that he'd got dish soap in the cut wasn't helping any. He gritted his teeth and turned around to head for the bathroom to get a bandage.

"Jonah?" Oliver appeared in his bedroom doorway wearing track pants and a holey T-shirt. "What's the matter?"

"Nothing," Jonah said a little roughly. What a fucking *fantastic* day it had been. Now he was capping it off by ruining his roommate's sleep habits. "I just cut myself on the measuring cup, that's all."

Oliver took a couple of steps forward; he glanced briefly at Jonah's hand, then up at his face. "Are you okay?"

"It's just a cut—"

"You're crying."

Jonah stared at him, then down at his hand. A salty droplet landed in the cut, and he hissed. "I broke up with Evan." He wasn't convinced that was why he was upset, but it was a good enough cover for now.

"I'll get the peroxide," Oliver said after a short silence, and he disappeared into the bathroom.

He made Jonah sit on the couch while he cleaned the cut and bandaged it with some gauze and medical tape. "I guess this means you're not sticking around."

Jonah stared at him. "How did you know?"

Oliver stood. "You're not that hard to read, Jonah."

Except for when it counted; apparently he'd had Evan completely fooled. "I'm sorry."

With a final pat on the shoulder, Oliver headed back to his room. He paused at the doorway and turned around just for a moment. "I hope you find what you're looking for."

Jonah hoped so too.

§

TUCKED inside a summer course catalog for U of T with all four art night classes marked with sticky notes:

Emerson,

Well, it is huge. I can see why you'd be afraid. But I promise I'll be gentle.

Did you not so much as glance at the classifieds I sent you? Advertising, corporate logos, web design, clothes designers, video games, art directors for films, need I go on? If you're going to throw away your dream, at least do yourself the courtesy of admitting the real reason.

I'll be moving again in a couple of weeks, so if I don't hear from you before then, I'll send you another letter from wherever I land.

Jonah

§

Jonah,

As someone who isn't here, you don't get to judge.

Emerson

§

Emerson,

Sorry about the delay. My funds lasted longer than I thought they would—I made it all the way to Jackson Hole, Wyoming. It is probably the coolest place in the world.

I got a job working at the tourist information center, which is pretty sweet. It doubles as a travel agency (Jackson Hole is really tiny) so I also get discounts on bus fares. You should come and visit when exams are done (not by bus though)! I will show you the Grand Tetons, and we'll go hunting for dropped elk-antler souvenirs. Maybe we'll even camp out at Yellowstone.

There's a writer's workshop that meets every Sunday night at one of the local cafes, and I think I'm going to start going. I've really been itching to put pen to paper lately. I haven't had that since I left home. Maybe it's a sign.

Jonah

CHAPTER 5

NOW

IT WAS two o'clock in the morning and Emerson was awake. His face was pressed into his pillow as he attempted to keep himself quiet.

Emerson was used to having to use a pillow to stifle his noises in the middle of the night, but that was because he had no other way of stopping the noise if he used two hands to jerk off.

He wasn't jerking off now.

No, he didn't have the energy or inclination for that.

The next sob that tore its way up Emerson's throat was loud and painful. God. Crying again. Sometimes it felt like all Emerson had done for the past three years was cry.

His body shook, and the tears fell with wracking spasms. Emerson was tired of crying, but tired also of the pity. No, Emerson didn't want Zack to try and calm him this time. So, he was crying in the middle of the night with his face pressed to the pillow. This way no one would know. Emerson just wanted to get some of the pain out.

The pain of missing Jonah, of knowing that he had chased him away. God, Jonah was gone, and this time Emerson had no one to blame but himself.

Another sob and more tears come out. Even he could tell his voice was filled with pain. Emerson's fingers spasmed and gripped his blankets.

Jonah had left two days ago, and Emerson was starting to get worried that he would never come home. That he would never want Emerson again. Emerson knew where he was, but not because Jonah had told him. Jonah hadn't spoken to him since he ran out of the house in anger, and such a long silence from Jonah didn't bode well. The only other time that Jonah had given Emerson the silent treatment had been when he had run all the way to Boston.

Emerson's heart was breaking over Jonah Cherneski once again.

He cried into his pillow still. Sobs still breaking and tears still falling.

He stayed there until exhaustion overtook him, and he finally fell asleep with the slowing of his sobs.

He woke the next day dehydrated with a head that felt like it had been stuffed with cotton, long after the clock had ticked past noon.

§

THEN

"EMERSON." Mrs. Cherneski hadn't looked terribly surprised to see him standing on her doorstep. "We still haven't heard from Jonah yet."

Her eyes were red and rimmed in black bruises. She had come home two days ago to find her son gone. Obviously she had slept no better than Emerson had these past two nights.

"Uh." Emerson stared at his feet. Then looked back up at her. "I don't suppose you'd mind if I…." He trailed off, looking away from her face. "I don't even know why… it won't help, but—can I… go up to his room?" Emerson didn't know what he hoped to accomplish, just knew he needed to see the room for himself. He needed to see the space, to see if it held any answers for him.

Mrs. Cherneski must have read this on his face, or maybe she had felt something like it herself, because she just opened the door and let him in.

It was weird to be alone in Jonah's room. A dozen memories competed for space in his conscious mind as he looked around the room. This place was as familiar to Emerson as his own bedroom. He and Jonah had wasted away hundreds of afternoons in this room over the years. But now Jonah was gone, and Emerson was left alone.

And Emerson really was alone. There was no one else, no other friends to help bear the loss.

Emerson had always been a worrier. Even as a child he had been prone to anxiety. At three he had been terrified of the vacuum cleaner, even when it was dormant. At six he had worried about being separated from his parents while out in public. At fourteen, it had been that others would discover what he had so recently learned himself: he was gay. A homosexual. A fag.

Emerson had heard them say those words. Kids he had grown up with and known for ten years used "fag" as a weapon. They had tossed it around in the cafeteria, in the locker rooms and classrooms and in the halls. Emerson had loathed hearing it. He had had to school himself so he wouldn't flinch every time he did. So Emerson had pulled away from the other boys whom he had spent his childhood with, all the boys who said that word or who had laughed at it. Jonah never had, and so it had been just Jonah for a long time.

Away from school, things had been more peaceful for Emerson, easier. High school had remained difficult.

It hadn't helped that Emerson was increasingly shy as time passed, and he still had the same lithe body and delicate features of his childhood. He didn't look like a girl, despite his wide eyes and long lashes, but others had still accused him of being one on a few occasions when Emerson had caught their attention.

Not that Emerson had been bullied. He had just been the quiet and reserved shadow to Jonah's popular, shining star. Jonah was the type of teen everyone liked, much as Emerson had been as a child, and so few people had bothered to hate Emerson.

Emerson shook off the memories of high school and looked around the room. It was cluttered, bordering on messy, though there was no trash or dirty clothes lying around. There were, however, various treasures and relics from Jonah's past strewn over the dresser and across bookshelves, pinned to the walls, and a few items even hung on the headboard.

He took in the volleyball trophy that propped up the battered copy of *Macbeth.* Next to it was the baseball that Jonah had had signed by various Texas Rangers. The plaster of Paris hand print that Natalie had made in kindergarten was still propped up on the dresser, next to the painting Emerson had had to make for art class last year. They had had to paint a hero, so Emerson had picked Martin Luther King, Jr., knowing that he'd be gifting it to Jonah. On the desk there were stacks of notebooks with scraps of loose paper sticking out of the edges, and pens of various types and brands stuffed into old coffee cups: one was from Disney World, the other from the Dallas Zoo.

A flash of yellow caught Emerson's eye, and he took in the pennant from junior league baseball hanging over the small desk. The scrap of fabric had to be at least five years old by now, Emerson realized, since it was from when he and Jonah had played as kids. Emerson leaned over and realized that it was from the summer between fifth and sixth grade. It had been a pretty good season.

Attached to the pennant was a team photograph. They had been very different people then. Emerson had been the pitcher and captain of the team—he'd had an arm that tossed straighter than the rest and a personality that the other boys couldn't find fault with. Jonah had been the catcher and then second baseman and hadn't been bad at either, but he had also been new to the league and a little rusty. It didn't help that he had also been very short and scrawny then. Before his growth spurt after ninth grade, Jonah had been small—he had never come up past Emerson's nose—and many of the other kids took potshots at him for being so tiny. The other boys on the team that summer had been especially vocal; none of them had wanted to give Jonah a chance. Jonah had been anxious to prove them wrong.

Emerson smiled in memory as he thought of one particular game in which an interfering old biddy had noticed the tension and had told everyone that Jonah was too small to play well. Emerson had been incensed. Jonah was way too nice to deserve that kind of treatment. His sweet temper also meant that he blushed scarlet when Emerson called a team meeting and told the rest of them off for making stupid plays so they could avoid throwing to Jonah. He had sneered at the boys for worrying about Jonah making them look dumb in front of girls, disgusted at the idea of people hurting Jonah for the sake of impressing anyone.

The team had been angry at Emerson, but later, when Jonah helped make the double play, it had been totally worth it. Even then, Emerson had noticed how much Jonah had glowed for the rest of the day.

The memory was bittersweet now. Jonah was no longer that scrawny, timid kid, and Emerson wasn't the baseball star. And years of secrecy on Emerson's part had added a layer of tension to their relationship that Emerson always felt very keenly.

Emerson found a photo of himself and Jonah sitting on his dresser. He lifted one hand up to touch it. Jonah had an arm around Emerson's shoulders; they were smiling at the camera. It had been taken last fall, shortly after they had finished all their applications for college. Which explained Emerson's relaxed look and smile—application time had been a frustrating few months for him.

He and Jonah had decided sometime before the end of eleventh grade that they'd go to college together. Emerson wanted to be an artist, a graphic designer, a master of computer art; Jonah had always wanted to be a writer, though of what genre was often in flux. They had spent a lot of afternoons planning out their future in this room. They had made plans to travel together, Emerson snapping photos while Jonah wrote journal entries that they could turn into a travel book. Or maybe they would make graphic novels with Emerson penciling drawings or doing art David McKean-style. Or perhaps they'd even use Emerson's artistic eye to put one of Jonah's stories on film. The plans had been varied and unending, but they had all started with time at college together, where they'd have adventures while studying and learning their crafts.

Emerson's dad hadn't liked the plan. He wanted Emerson to be sensible. He had been frustrated with Emerson for years, Emerson thought bitterly, ever since the start of his anti-social tendencies. Emerson had once heard his parents arguing about what to do about it. His dad had wanted to intervene, to get Emerson playing baseball on a team again, to force him to be with old friends. Fortunately his mother had felt that Emerson was simply reevaluating himself and who he wanted to be, and that it was also possible that his brain chemistry was changing with age. That these changes in Emerson were his to make, and they should be careful not to make him feel guilty for not being who they wanted him to be.

Despite his mother's insistence on not pressuring him, his father's disapproval was constant. As such, the disagreements over college tended to be… intense. Emerson often ended up running to Jonah after a fight.

The worst had been right before Emerson had made his decision to fill out a School of Business application. He and Jonah had sat in the park on a Saturday afternoon for over an hour while Emerson vented his frustrations.

"He keeps telling me I'll like business once I start. I can't get him to understand."

"That you need art like breathing?" Jonah finished for him, his head tilted to the side as he gave Emerson an assessing look. "Just keep trying, Em. He'll come around."

"I'm not so sure," Emerson had sighed, frustrated, and crossed his arms. "He also told me I'd thank him when I was older and a successful businessman. He just doesn't get that I'd be happier poor and making art than I'd be rich and running a business."

Jonah's eyes had been filled with understanding as he watched Emerson frown miserably. "You tell him that?"

"Tried. He said: being a starving artist sounds romantic now, but when I'm married with children, I'll come to my senses." Emerson had felt a thrill of embarrassment at having repeated the words about having a wife and kids, knowing they'd never be true.

Jonah had laughed. "Then he really is crazy. Everyone knows that with that face you'll be able to find yourself a rich sugar momma to take care of you while you paint." Emerson blushed hotly; Jonah grinned. "So I know that ice cream and blowing shit up is not going to solve anything, but want to buy a cone and then go back to my house and play Just Cause 2?"

Emerson had smiled at Jonah's offer of comfort. "Yeah."

On the way out of the park, two girls from their class had giggled to see them. "Hey, Jonah," they said coyly. "Emerson." They gave him pleased smirks. Figured. On a day Emerson was feeling like crap, but at least he had Jonah all to himself, two girls came along trying to have Jonah for their machinations. But Jonah had just grinned sunnily, saying, "Hi Mandy, Brittany," without breaking his stride. "So, I'm thinking triple scoops," he told Emerson, and tossed his arm over his shoulder. Emerson had just smiled wider in response.

Emerson let his hand fall from the photograph and turned away, not wanting to see Jonah's smiling face anymore. He sat down on Jonah's bed and found Jonah's blanket, an old quilt that folded into a pillow and had been given to him as a baby. Emerson hadn't seen it in years. He picked it up and examined it. He worried the loose threads and fingered the grape juice stain on the corner.

Jonah's room, of course, provided no answers. Its familiarity only filled Emerson with very little comfort and a much greater feeling of loss.

He resettled himself on the bed, arms around the quilt, and didn't try to stop the tears that fell.

Emerson wasn't sure when he fell asleep, but he woke up several hours after he arrived at the house with a blanket tossed over him.

Untangling himself from the blankets, Emerson rose from the bed. He made a silent exit, not wanting to deal with anyone else. He didn't want to confront their grief right now. Nor was he sure he could bear to face them after he had embarrassed himself by falling asleep in Jonah's bed.

§

SENT after exams are over on the back of an exam schedule:

Jonah,

The doctors finally figured out what was wrong: Coronary artery spasm. Basically the arteries into his heart keep spasming and cutting off blood flow. They can't fix it, only treat it.

I'm still taking care of Dad's business for him, and I've taken some summer courses this year to catch up on my courses. I won't have time to leave Dallas.

Jackson Hole looks nice, though.

Send me a short story when you write one,

Emerson

§

ON THE back of a parking permit for Yellowstone National Park:

Emerson,

Turns out Old Faithful isn't so faithful anymore anyway, but here's a postcard showing you what you're missing.

At least now that they know what's wrong with your dad they can do something. Maybe you can come visit when he improves. I'm renting the basement apartment of someone's house, and the couch is all yours whenever you want it. Just thought you should know.

I sat down to write a short story the other day and came up for air 4,000 words later with no end in sight. Maybe I have what it takes to be a writer after all. It's not particularly fictional, but I'll worry about that when I'm closer to finishing. The girls at the writer's workshop seemed to like it, at least.

Jonah

§

Jonah,

They put Dad on some drugs; we're waiting to see if they take.

I've missed reading your stories. I'm glad you're still writing them. The girls at the writer's workshop? When do I get to read it?

Zack and Greg both went touring around the state, doing bar gigs for the summer. Hayley's still around and living in Austin, so I get to see her on the days that I have class. But being stuck in Hudson Bend sucks. All of our friends are gone, so I've only got Kierstyn for company.

I just got a call while writing this. Zack has invited me down to meet up with them in San Antonio next weekend. They're putting on a few shows in the city, and he thought I might like to catch Saturday's. Since I don't have classes on the weekend, I think I can manage it. It'll be good to see them. And to get out of Hudson.

Maybe I'll send you something from San An.

Emerson

§

Emerson,

I'm glad I am too. I was worried for a while there.

"Girls" is kind of a misnomer. Four of them are in their thirties. Then there's Roberta, she writes these steamy romance novels. She's about eighty-five. I think she mostly does it to embarrass her grandkids. At least that is the impression that I get when she tells the stories about reading certain passages aloud to her college-age grandsons.

You can read it when I type it up. Seriously, Em, I don't have a photocopier. It's fifty handwritten pages and still going strong. It wouldn't even fit in your mailbox.

I submitted a couple of other things in the meantime. I'll let you know if I hear anything.

I'm telling Kierstyn you said that.

Jonah

§

ON THE back of a flyer for a Peter and the Hanged Man show at Bond's 007 Rock Bar in San Antonio:

Jonah,

Fuck! I can't wait until you get to hear them. They are awesome, and you're going to love them! They totally rocked San Antonio!

I'm writing this while drunk, again, but I promise no bad sex this time. Not in a BAR in San An. That would be stupid.

Emerson

Oh! I bought you a present!

In the same envelope was a card that read, "*Told you I'd buy you something—Emerson*" with a red pocket Moleskine notebook and a new pen with "San Antonio, Texas" written along the shaft.

§

Jonah,

I'm sorry for once again sending you drunken correspondence. Seriously, it's an issue.

San An. was good, though I could do without the hangover. I'm not entirely sure what I wrote before, but Zack and Greg know how to put on an awesome gig.

I'm seriously disturbed by the image of Roberta and her torturing her grandsons. I am, however, very grateful that she is not MY grandmother.

I have to wait until you type it? But you're a crazy "the work must first be written out by hand, in full, or it's no good" writer. I'll have to wait forever!

Don't tell her I said anything! Or I'll start telling Natalie where you hide your porn!

Emerson

§

EMERSON bought his textbooks the week before courses started.

After realizing he would be stuck close to home all summer, Emerson had decided to make up for lost time. He hadn't been able to take a full course load last term, so he'd take a few courses now.

Emerson had put in the research about what summer courses there were and had picked out a second-year marketing and an accounting course. He had been very surprised to find himself signing up for "Survey of the Renaissance through Modern Art" and "Drawing for Non-Art Majors."

Emerson had walked away from registering, stunned by his actions. Then he had bought his textbooks as soon as he could.

When the classes started, he threw himself into his studies like he never had before.

Business wasn't as captivating as this. Lectures on the great artists and how to capture a moment on paper were the best classes of his college career.

At times, though, like when he realized that his drawing skills were well beyond his peers', he felt a sharp stab of regret. He had been accepted to the Design program. Emerson had spent weeks on his application and had sent it off well in advance of the closing date. But his parents hadn't been very happy about his dreams. Emerson was smart, much too smart to waste himself making pictures. No, Emerson was smart enough to grasp his father's business, even had a talent for keeping the books.

It had been due to their insistence that he had applied to the School of Business. They had been thrilled when he had received his acceptance letter. Emerson had been disappointed—he had hoped that he'd only be accepted into Design, and thus the battle about which to attend would be over.

The debate, if one could call such a one-sided conversation a debate, had been ongoing when Jonah had left. With Jonah gone, all their plans to attend college together, to match Emerson's degree in design with the one that Jonah would get in English to create books and more, were ruined. And when his father had argued once again for Emerson to go to business school, Emerson had folded under the weight of parental pressure and of grief over loss.

He never regretted his decision more than when he was sitting in those art classes.

It was halfway through the summer, and Emerson attended each class religiously, never letting something else get in the way of his twice-weekly dates with artistic heaven.

After Professor Monroe called an end to the day's session, she looked up at Emerson and asked him to stay a moment. Worry filled Emerson's stomach, and he wondered what he might have done to displease her. Emerson had always done his best to please the teacher. It was in his nature, and he wasn't happy to hear that he might have done otherwise.

After the last student had filed out, Emerson slowly shouldered his bag and made his way toward Ms. Monroe.

"Well, Emerson, how are you today?"

Emerson swallowed hard. Her tone was pleasant enough, but he had learned from Mr. Watson in the fourth grade that that didn't mean much. "Fine, ma'am."

She smiled at him. “I wanted to ask you, Emerson, what are you doing in my class?”

Emerson blinked at her, stunned. What? That didn’t make sense. Emerson was good at this! And he had been doing well mark-wise! Why did she suddenly want to kick him out? “Um… I don’t understand. I thought I was doing well.”

“Oh, you are. That’s thc point. Why are you taking a drawing class for non-art students?”

“I’m not an art student.”

“Yes, I know. I looked you up. Your file says Business. My point is: why are you taking business when clearly you have the talent and the soul of an artist?”

“Uh….”

“Emerson, you sketch must faster than your classmates and with end results that far surpass any of them in terms of accuracy and polish. So why on earth are you wasting your talent away in business?” She arched a brow at him then, giving him a rather pointed look.

“I….” Emerson looked away, staring down at the strap of his messenger bag. “Business is practical.”

She snorted. “I see. And who, pray tell, has been dripping that poison in your ear?”

Emerson’s head shot up, and he stared at her in surprise. “It’s not—”

“Emcrson, I don’t know if you are aware of this, but your file also says that you were accepted into the Design program. A man of your talent, with the proper training, could get any number of jobs in the field of creative design. So when you tell me that a business degree is more practical, I can only assume that you are repeating the rhetoric that has been beaten into you by someone else.”

Emerson stared at her, absolutely floored.

“If I thought for one moment that your true passion lay in business and not in the arts, then I would let the matter drop and leave you alone. But I don’t think it does, and I think you know it.”

Emerson had nothing to say to that. To say anything would be to admit she was right. And he wasn’t sure he could, because admitting she was right meant admitting he’d made a huge mistake.

Ms. Monroe began collecting up her papers and pencils. “It’s not too late, you know. You can change your degree. Some of your business courses will count as electives, and I do believe you are also taking an art theory course this summer that would count toward a degree in the arts.”

Emerson just kept staring at her. He didn’t know what to say to this woman who was telling him to just rewrite his life.

“Just think about it,” she told him as she stuffed everything into her bag and turned toward the door. Emerson watched her make her way from the room, his feet unwilling to follow.

“Oh, and Emerson? If you need any help or a reference when it comes time to convince the registrar’s office into letting you change programs? Let me know.” Then she was out the door, calling over her shoulder, “See you next week!”

And Emerson was left alone, mind racing and heart thumping at the very thought of the new direction his life could take.

CHAPTER 6

NOW

JONAH looked up from second edits at a knock on his door and decided he might as well call it a night. It wasn't like he was in any shape to be concentrating anyway. "It's open."

It was Natalie, of course, balancing two big glasses of sweet tea and a plate of veggie sticks. "Brought you a snack," she said hopefully.

Jonah didn't doubt for a second that she had an ulterior motive—whether it was trying to cheer him up or cajoling him into doing her share of the household chores—but he'd been sulking alone long enough for one day.

Besides, he was hungry. "Come on in."

She did, setting the glasses and plate down on the desk and then flopping onto his unmade bed. Then she reached for a carrot stick and bit down, munching loudly.

Jonah gave up pretending to himself that he wasn't just going to give her whatever she wanted and selected a slice of bell pepper. "Am I on suicide watch?"

"Just nutritional-eating watch, for now," she told him seriously. "You'll know by the straightjacket if I reconsider."

Well, he had been drinking too much and not eating a lot of anything. Though he was fairly sure he'd demolished a significant portion of one of the girls' ice-cream stashes from their freezer. He felt kind of guilty about that. "Okay." He bit into the pepper; it was sweet and juicy, with a good crunch. He'd forgotten how satisfying vegetables were. "What do you want, then?"

Natalie rolled her eyes. "Chew and swallow, then talk," she instructed. "Heathen."

Jonah made a point of chewing with his mouth open, but all the reaction it earned him was a disgusted face and Natalie silently threatening to get broccoli crumbs in his bed, so he relented. Swallowing carefully, he said, “Well?”

“Keep eating, I want you feeling as benevolent as possible.”

Rolling his eyes, Jonah did as he was told, washing it down with a few long gulps of sweet tea. “Okay, I’m full up on benevolence. Hit me with it.”

Now that Jonah was right where she wanted him, Natalie wasted no time. “So there’s this boy.”

Obviously. Jonah really should have seen that coming. “Uh huh,” he said. “Go on.”

“He’s super cute, Jonah. Like, he should be on TV or something.”

“And how do you know this boy?”

“He makes my coffee.”

“You don’t drink coffee.”

“I *didn’t* drink coffee,” Natalie corrected him. “I do now.”

“Because of a boy?”

“Yeah, yeah,” Natalie waved him off. “The things we do for love, I know. Anyway, he’s an art student at the college.”

“Why do I already not like where this is going?” Jonah wondered aloud.

Natalie ignored him. “As you may know,” she continued, “some art students from the college are doing an end-of-summer exhibit. I guess they have time to do it now, but they’re too busy to do it during the semester or something.”

It sounded familiar—Emerson had probably mentioned it at some point, though Jonah was sure he wasn’t participating. Most of his efforts this summer had been concentrated on the children’s book Jonah was still trying to perfect. “Okay.”

“I was thinking that you need to get out of the house more,” she told him with a syrupy smile. “And as it just so happens, I need a date—”

Whoa, whoa. That was far enough. “What do you need a date for if you’re going to be trying to pick up this guy, anyway?”

Natalie made an exasperated noise. "Because only a *loser* would go alone, Jonah."

"You could take one of your girlfriends," he pointed out.

"Please, and risk one of them stealing Matt from right under my nose? They wish."

"Aren't you going to look like more of a loser if he finds out you came with your brother?"

"I'll just tell him you're there to stalk your estranged boyfriend. I'm there solely for moral support."

Ouch. Jonah winced. Estranged boyfriend, huh? Unfortunately, that was a little too apt.

Natalie seemed to realize she'd gone too far, because she sat forward on the bed and patted his leg comfortingly before going on. "Sorry. I know you're going to work it out."

If he didn't, Jonah was pretty sure Natalie would resort to castration. He sighed and nodded for her to continue.

"Anyway, none of them would work anyway. I need you, big brother."

He sighed. "Alright, I'll bite: why me?"

"Because he's an *art student*," Natalie said obviously. "He works in a coffee shop. And he's very, you know, *pretty*."

Oh, God, she couldn't be serious. "You want to use me for my gaydar," Jonah said flatly. "I'm ignoring all the stereotypes you just bought into, by the way, and you're welcome for that."

"For God's sake, Jonah, it's not like I don't know the manliest-looking guy around could just as easily be a friend of Dorothy as he could be a *Playboy* subscriber." She waved her hand at him. "Case in point."

Jonah valiantly fought off the headache that was trying to start between his eyes by pinching the bridge of his nose. "Thanks, I think."

"But he's tripping *my* gaydar," Nat said. "Which used to be pretty good. I don't want to make him uncomfortable or make an ass out of myself, okay? Besides, it might be fun to do something as siblings. Please?"

He sighed. "You knew I was always going to say yes, didn't you?"

Natalie grinned knowingly. "Yeah, but it would've been impolite of me not to at least pretend I was asking."

Resigned to his fate, Jonah figured they might as well iron out the details. She'd never let him live it down if he forgot and picked up a shift at the gym. "When is this shindig? Does it have a dress code?"

"Friday night in the art building," Natalie said promptly. "I think it's part fundraiser, so no blue jeans."

"No blue jeans" meant Nat was going to spend an hour and a half before the thing making Jonah change clothes until she found a combination that suited her, but he figured he owed her one. "Okay, but you're buying the tickets."

"Of course!" She smiled winningly, then got up and started to collect their dishes. "I'll just leave you to your work before you can change your mind, shall I?"

When the door had closed behind her, Jonah stared down at his attempted revisions again, discouraged. He hadn't been at this sort of a loss for words since he'd left Boston.

§

THEN

WHEN the plane touched down on the tarmac, Jonah knew right away that he'd made the right decision.

In the airport in Boston he'd determinedly bought a ticket on the first domestic flight out with an available seat, but Salt Lake City was just not a place he could see himself settling. He'd had enough of city life to last him several months, and though his fingers had been itching for a pen as they flew over the Great Lakes and Colorado, the urge felt stifled the second he got off the plane in Utah. He was just lucky that, after so many months of working and saving as much as he could, he was able to get on the next available flight to the middle of nowhere.

From the runway, Jackson Hole, Wyoming, was the most beautiful place Jonah had ever seen. He pressed his face to the tiny plastic window and tried to breathe it in. The majestic, glacier-capped Grand Tetons towered in the near distance, stretching high into the sky. A blanket of snow still covered the plains and the sloping roofs of every building he could see. The sky was clear and the sun was high, and he could smell the mountain air the second the cabin door opened to let them out onto the tarmac.

Emerson would have loved it. Hell, Jonah was in love with it, and he stayed that way even after he discovered that Jackson Hole was even colder than Boston.

There were a few advantages to small towns, one of them being that Jonah only had to ask three people before someone knew someone with a room to let. Mrs. George was a spritely, no-nonsense widow with a vacant basement apartment, and after Jonah promised he wasn't averse to cleaning eaves troughs or shoveling driveways as the weather necessitated, it was all his.

From there he should have gone straight to finding a job, but there was something he had to do first. In the very bottom of his hiking backpack was a crumpled notebook; Jonah grabbed it and the leaky ballpoint pen from the front pocket and walked down Main Street to the park.

It was fucking cold, but he didn't care. Wrapping his scarf as tight as he dared around his neck, Jonah hunched his shoulders and began to write.

§

JONAH unlocked the side door that led to his basement apartment behind the garage and bent to pick up the pile of envelopes that littered the floor. Gloria, his landlord, usually left them in the kitchen, but she was visiting her son in Denver, and her cleaning lady usually just unlocked Jonah's door long enough to scatter his mail all over the floor. Jonah was still looking for the hidden cameras.

Nothing from Emerson, but that wasn't a surprise; Jonah had just written him two days ago, hardly enough time for his letter even to have reached Emerson, never mind for Emerson to reply. A cell phone bill he'd already paid—he went to the bank at the end of the month to take care of all of his bills simultaneously, otherwise he'd forget. An envelope addressed in his mother's precise handwriting. He'd save that for a day he was feeling maudlin. A couple letters from minor magazines—by now Jonah recognized the typical form letter more or less stating that they weren't considering unsolicited work at the moment, but they would keep his work on file. That was pretty easy, since all of those submissions required a self-addressed, stamped envelope. A few random coupons and assorted junk mail.

At the bottom of the pile was a somewhat larger and thicker envelope not marked with Jonah's own handwriting. A quick glance at the return address made Jonah's pulse speed up, and he hurriedly closed the door behind him, taking the stack of envelopes with him into the small sitting room.

First, he forced himself to open and read the rejection letters, just in case. Setting them aside in a pile on the table, he debated between his mother's letter and the other one, the one from the travel publication put out by AAA.

Well, if the one from AAA was a rejection letter too, he reasoned, he'd always have his mother's letter to cheer him up afterward. With no small amount of trepidation, he slid his thumb under the paper flap and tore the envelope open.

Dear Mr. Cherneski,

Across AmericA is interested in publishing your article in a Midwestern-themed issue to be published at the end of next month. Because of the time element of the publication, please review the attached contract and return it at your earliest possible convenience. Electronic copy should be forwarded to Samantha Burns in our editing department....

Jonah stopped there and went back to the top of the page. *Mr. Cherneski*. Yep, that was his name.

Published at the end of the month. Holy crap. Seriously?

He skimmed through the rest of the letter twice before he managed to force himself to take in the salient details. It was a tiny, insignificant article in a fairly cheap magazine with a very specific target audience, so the compensation wasn't very good, but Jonah wasn't nearly as interested in the money as he was in the fact that he was going to see his name in a byline in a real publication. And if he could sell one article, he could sell another. Hell, maybe even a short story. Maybe someday, he'd be lucky enough to publish the half-finished novel he'd written on scrap pieces of paper and collated into a makeshift notebook. Suddenly his dreams didn't seem so impossible.

Jonah allowed himself a wry smile. Well, *some* of his dreams didn't seem so impossible, anyway. He still couldn't wait to tell Emerson.

§

STAPLED to the cover of a travel magazine, with page 37 sticky-note bookmarked:

Emerson,

As promised, the long-awaited first published work. Sorry that it's nonfiction, but it turns out I am actually pretty good at that.

Don't worry, your drunken letter was much less embarrassing this time, though you did make a point to mention that you didn't let anyone defile you in the men's room. Thanks for the present—I'll have to think of something good to put in it. Can't go putting just anything in a Moleskine notebook.

Roberta would absolutely love you—and you'd love her back. It's impossible not to. I don't know what it is about little old ladies telling dirty jokes, but it's hysterical.

I threw out my porn before I left. Weird, I know.

Jonah

§

Jonah,

That is fucking awesome! I can't believe you got something published! I showed Kierstyn and Mom. They both say congratulations.

I'm glad you liked the notebook. I picked it out in red especially for you.

Only you would think that an old lady telling dirty jokes is hysterical. Sometimes I worry about you.

I just wrote a midterm exam for one of my summer courses. I think it went okay. I mean, no promises, but I think I might have aced it.

You threw it out? Bastard! Now what am I suppose to lord over you in threat!?

Emerson

§

Em,

Thanks. See—dreams do come true. (Ok, a tiny part of a dream. Whatever. I'll take it.)

If Roberta told you a joke, you would pee your pants. I'm not kidding, Emerson, the old lady should have gone into stand-up. Yesterday she had us all in stitches talking about her oldest granddaughter's dog. Apparently he keeps eating the crotch out of her underwear (the granddaughter's, not Roberta's. Even I think that would be too far).

Congrats on the midterm victory, like there was ever any doubt.

One of the guys who does the guided tours of Grand Teton broke his leg rock climbing last week, and since I'm out there all the time hiking, they asked if I could fill in until they find a permanent replacement. Looks like I'll be pretty busy the next little while!

Jonah

§

WRITTEN on the back of a Travis Lake, Texas post card:

Jonah,

You're going to do guided tours to replace a guy who broke his leg?! Please tell me that the broken leg is completely unrelated to the tour giving!

One of the kids that Dad hired to work at the store suddenly quit yesterday. Kierstyn and I are working overtime to cover for him until I can find someone new. Fortunately there's a supply of neighborhood kids who will take the work. Until I hire someone, though, I'll be pretty busy.

I'll have to take your word on Roberta.

Emerson

§

ON THE back of a piece of junk mail advertising life insurance:

Emerson,

I called Natalie, and she said the last time she saw you, you looked like you hadn't slept in a week. Enjoy your new employee and feel free to make her work nights and weekends. She doesn't need a boyfriend at her age anyway.

You're welcome.

Dude, Gavin broke his leg rock climbing while trying to impress a chick. From what I've heard, it was pretty epic. Amazingly, he actually did score a date with her after the fact. My mind is blown. The actual job involves walking around with bear spray and a walkie-talkie and making sure nobody does anything stupid. I am so ridiculously overqualified.

I did see a grizzly the other day though.

Jonah

§

ON A birthday card with a picture of a grizzly bear holding up one paw on the front with the caption "Give me a high five":

Jonah,

"... And a great big BEAR HUG!

Have a BEARY HAPPY BIRTHDAY!"

No, I didn't forget. And no it's not very funny, but it seemed like a good way to segue into: What?! A grizzly bear? A fucking *bear*? Jesus Jonah, quit this job, please!!

Natalie is awesome. Thank you.

Have a very happy birthday, dude.

Emerson

Attached was a parcel wrapped in gaudy, cheap birthday paper: the 2009 Writer's Market Deluxe with access to writersmarket.com.

§

ON A postcard of a rearing grizzly:

Emerson,

Thanks for the book, man. It is definitely going to come in handy!

Yeah, a grizzly bear. It was really cool, Em! Not that I didn't pee my pants a little, but come on—how often do you see a real live grizzly bear in the wild?

No need to quit, though. They finally hired someone last week. Thank God, because working sixty-hour weeks was *killing* me. I missed two writer's workshops in a row because I was sleeping! How pathetic is that? I guess I must officially be old or something.

How are those summer classes coming along, Mr. Workaholic?

Jonah

§

SENT mid- to late August:

Jonah,

I know it's been a while, but I've finally finished my courses. I now have two weeks off before fall classes start. Time enough to write you.

I think I did okay in my classes, but I won't find out for a while.

Dad is finally starting to do much better. They've got him on a drug that seems to agree with him. He's getting some of his energy back, so I'll probably be taking three or four courses this fall.

Natalie and Kierstyn are still my lifesavers. They've pretty much been holding things down here. Of course, Kierstyn's only twelve, so Natalie does more of the fort-holding, but they're a wicked team. Though did your brat sister tell you about what she did the other day? I fell asleep over the accounting books over a week ago, and Natalie took pictures and then plastered them on the corkboard behind the cash desk. It took me *four days* to notice them! Now I've got all the older customers telling me how adorable I am when I sleep.

Emerson

§

SENT four days later:

Em,

Don't worry about it. I know you're a busy guy. I know how it is to work way more than is good for you, and I'm just a lowly peon employee instead of the guy in charge.

You mean those pictures that she made copies of and sent to me? Those ones? You drool in your sleep, you know. Adorable. Did you get new glasses?

If you can believe it, the leaves are already starting to turn up here. I'd complain about that, but it's gorgeous. See attached picture for proof!

There are a couple new faces at the writer's workshop. Non-cougar faces, even. Maybe if I'm lucky one of them will be partial to tall, dorky butternuts. Unlikely, I know, but hey, it's possible they're brain-damaged.

Jonah

§

"SHE'S going to find out," Jonah said. "You know that, right?"

"Sure," Gavin said easily, "but by that point she'll be so into me she won't care."

Jonah stared at him for a moment. He was contorted on his sofa in the living room, watching carefully as he clipped the toenails on his left foot, the one not encased in a walking cast. Every once in a while, an errant clipping would fly off in one direction or another; a few even hit him in the face. He made no discernable effort to pick them up, and Jonah shuddered. "I don't know, dude. Isn't this kind of skeezy?"

Gavin's apartment was full of what might have generously been termed "junk." At the moment he was using the cast on his leg as an excuse for not tidying up, but frankly Jonah couldn't see why he'd kept half of his stuff in the first place. There was a plasma screen TV with a crack the size of the Grand Canyon straight down the middle. It wasn't even plugged in. An old VCR with a video still stuck in it, the tape pulled out and tangled and spilling over onto the floor. Three nonfunctioning video game consoles, two of which had already been replaced by new, working models. And that didn't even count the few luridly colored items Jonah never bothered trying to identify—he had the sneaking suspicion at least one of them was a sex toy. It wasn't like the toenail clippings were the strangest or even most revolting thing Gavin had lying around.

Gavin brushed the last of his disgusting DNA onto the floor and shoved the nail clipper into the couch cushions. "I won't tell her I *wrote* it," he said patiently. "Come on, man, I'll owe you one."

To avoid making eye contact, Jonah continued his mental catalog of Gavin's collection of broken electronics. As ridiculous as it sounded—as frankly psycho stalker as it sounded—Jonah was tempted.

Against incredible odds, Gavin was a good friend, and he wasn't actually as horrible to his girlfriends as he sounded.

Then he saw it. Covered in a thin layer of dust on a shelf over a derelict computer was a complex-looking digital camera. Next to it on the shelf was a detachable zoom lens with a manual focus. Jonah reached out and brushed a finger through the dust on the pop-up flash.

"It's broken," Gavin said, seeing what he was looking at. "It fell off the desk, cracked the lens."

Jonah took the lens cap off and surveyed the damage. It seemed pretty superficial to him, but he wasn't an expert. But there was a camera repair shop in town that specialized in exactly this sort of thing. And Emerson's birthday was coming up… and Emerson loved photography. Emerson would love to have a camera like that, but he would never buy one for himself, could never justify the expense, and it wasn't like Jonah could afford it either, not a new one, but….

"Dude, do this for me, and it's yours if you like it that much."

Jonah finally decided that if the girl was stupid enough to believe Gavin had written her poetry, she deserved what she got. "Alright," he said finally. "What's she like?"

Unfortunately Gavin took this as an invitation to go on, in great length, about Sylvie's great tits and ass. It took some extremely pointed questions from Jonah to glean anything useful at all—that she had dark hair and eyes and was new to Jackson, that they had met on one of Gavin's stupid hikes, that she was staying with her aunt and was studying to be a nutritionist.

"Okay," Jonah said at last, figuring that was about as much useful information as he was going to get out of Gavin without scarring himself for life. "I think I can work with that."

"Seriously?" Gavin seemed surprised. "Cool."

Even though he was praying it would be worth it, Jonah had to wonder what he'd got himself into.

§

Jonah,

I can't believe she sent you those! There was no drool! And I'm not adorable!

But yes, those are new glasses. Zack wouldn't shut up about my needing new ones whenever I was too lazy to put in my contacts, so Hayley helped me pick some out. She says the thinner frames and squarer look suits me better. I don't know anything about fashion, but who am I to argue with a woman of taste? Besides… the old ones were *really* old.

Being the guy in charge sucks. You have to worry about everything. I can't wait until Dad comes back to work. He says he'll start taking care of some things again, like stock and order forms. I can't wait.

Non-cougars? Pretty, young aspiring writers, then? I keep telling you that referencing your Tennessee heritage by calling yourself a butternut is woefully uncool. Seriously, that's probably too dorky for most people.

Emerson

§

ON A computer-enlarged copy of one of the incriminating photos:

Oh, Em. The camera doesn't lie.

You should listen to Hayley more often. Things between you must be pretty serious if you're consulting her for such life-altering decisions.

Turns out the new girl (her name is Xie) actually *likes* dorks, and get this—she's spent her summers with her aunt and uncle in Jackson Hole since she was seven, but she actually grew up in Houston, so we already have something in common. I think you'd really like her, Em, despite the fact that she is vertically challenged. Actually, she's a photography major at the University of Wyoming.

Glad to hear that your dad's feeling better. Hopefully you are taking better care of yourself now that there's someone around to supervise you.

Jonah

§

Jonah,

I can't believe you have these pictures. You should burn the rest of them like I did.

I listen to Hayley in a lot of things, things much more important than new glasses—though was that sarcasm, or have I misled you to believe that Hayley and I are dating? I suspect sarcasm, but just in case....

If you like her, then Xie must be awesome. You've always had great taste.

Dad is feeling good. He's been doing inventory for the past week, which is good because classes have started up again. Zack, Greg, and Hayley are all back in town. Zack and Greg are staying in a townhouse off campus, so I've been by to see them a few times. I stayed at their place last Friday night after we went bar hopping.

They're both already talking about gigs on and off campus this fall. I'm looking forward to another night out with Hayley listening to Peter and the Hanged Man. Think you might be able to join us soon?

Emerson

§

Emerson,

I'm keeping the pictures forever just in case I ever need to blackmail you into doing what's best for you. So there.

No, I didn't really think you and Hayley were dating. I know better than that. Come on, now. You are way too square to go out with someone that cool.

Things with Xie are really great. We went on a couple of dates and really hit it off. She's a little busier now that she's back at school, but it turns out these art majors usually have Fridays off, which leaves us lots of time to get to know one another better.

That's great that your dad is feeling so much better. You deserve a break after working yourself half to death (don't deny it; I have photographic evidence, remember?).

Bar hopping again, huh? Making good use of a fake ID?

Tourist season is starting to wind down before gearing up again in the winter. Maybe I'll see if I can get some time off.

Jonah

§

WRITTEN on the back of a "Welcome Back!" concert flyer put out by the Faculty of Music:

Jonah,

That's it. I'm going to maim your sister. I'd threaten death, but then I'd be down one employee. Which would be really tragic, as it would drag me back into full-time employment at the store.

Dad's doing really well. You wouldn't believe it. He's almost the same man he was before. It looks like next term I'll be taking a full course-load.

It's good to hear you're so happy about the way things are going with Xie. Though you always could charm just about anyone, so it's not a surprise.

Not so much fake ID as it is knowing the right people. Zack and Greg are both known in a lot of the local bars. Some of the guys at the door look the other way, and some of them seem to think I just *look* young. Still, Zack has some "interesting" contacts, so I've got an ID that looks genuine.

Speaking of Zack, this flyer is from the concert he's going to be in at school. His mom was worried about him not having an education and wasting his life on his music, so she sent him to college. He's taking Music Business and Composition, so I'm not sure how much she's reassured. Anyway, the music students put on all these shows. It's pretty funny to see Zack dressed up in his black and white dress suits to play.

No time off at Christmas? What kind of barbaric heathens do you work for?

Emerson

§

JONAH'S phone rang at an absolutely ungodly hour. He normally resisted getting even a cheap local cell, but he had needed this one earlier in the year in case one of the other guides called in sick and he had to go into work at the last minute, and he hadn't gotten around to canceling it yet.

"Gavin, if you are calling me to tell me you got laid, I *will* kill you."

It had to be Gavin. No one else would call at—at—Jonah squinted at the clock, but his eyes couldn't make sense of the numbers, too full of sleep.

There was a pause. "Jonah?"

Shit. "Xie?" Jonah sat up a little in bed. It was the middle of the week, so she still had classes, and she didn't usually call him from her apartment in Laramie. "What's going on? Are you okay?"

"I—no." She paused. "Would Gavin really call you in the middle of the night to gloat about sex?"

"Probably. Now are you going to tell me why you called? You should tell me why you called so that I can make it better, and you can go back to bed."

"So *you* can go back to bed, you mean," she corrected.

"Potato, po-tah-toe."

Silence.

Jonah prodded, "Xie?"

A gusty sigh filtered down the line. "I can hear them," she admitted quietly.

Hear them—? Oh, Jesus. "Xie, man, you should find someone to take over your lease. This isn't good for you." He could have counseled her to man up and tell her roommate off for sleeping with the boy she knew Xie had been in love with since the summer after eighth grade, but it hadn't worked the last forty times he'd suggested it, and it probably wasn't going to work now. "I thought they broke up?"

"They are currently making up very loudly," she hiccupped.

Jonah thought he maybe heard an errant bedspring through the speaker and guessed that she wasn't exaggerating. "I'm sorry, baby."

"Oh, it's not your fault, don't be stupid. I'm sorry I called you in the middle of the night like a lovesick teenager."

"If you can't call me in the middle of the night like a lovesick teenager, what the hell else am I good for?" Jonah retorted. Certainly it had been useless of them to try to date each other. Jonah thanked God Xie had been brave enough to 'fess up, on their fourth or fifth or whatever date it had been, to her abiding unrequited love for her childhood sweetheart. Once he'd owned up to his own set of issues, the friendship between them had been cemented. Tried though they had to make one another forget, they had been unsuccessful, and Jonah couldn't help but think that it was at least partially because they didn't *want* to be in love with anyone else.

He could hear the slight smile in Xie's voice. "Well, I can think of a few things."

"Oh, is that what you wanted me for?" If she was joking about *that*, she would probably be just fine. The arrangement between them was less than ideal, but Xie was hot and kind and got just as much out of the sex as Jonah did; it was a good distraction. "You're coming home next weekend, right?" he asked, a vague plan forming in his brain. It wouldn't fix anything, but it might take her mind off it for a time.

Xie pretended to think. "Hmm, that depends. Are you going to make it worth my while?"

"When have I not made it worth your while?" All right, he'd been somewhat inexperienced with women, if not technically a virgin, before Xie had come along, but she'd never held that against him. Besides, he had other skills.

"Cute." Xie laughed a little, which Jonah counted as a major victory. "Okay, I think they're done. Thanks."

"Don't mention it," Jonah said around a yawn. "I'll see you in a week, okay? And we'll do something fun."

He heard the rustle of blankets and then a soft sigh and imagined Xie settling down into her blankets and the small mountain she had the gall to call pillows. "You know, your mystery man back home is really missing out."

He shook his head. "Goodnight, Xie."

He barely heard her answering murmur before the line went dead.

CHAPTER 7

NOW

EMERSON woke up at five in the morning. He looked at his clock, remembered what had happened the night before, and then turned over and went back to sleep.

The second time he woke up, his clock said 11:23.

When he walked into the kitchen, Zack said, "So he's alive after all."

Emerson grunted in reply. He wasn't in the mood to hear Zack be cute.

He stumbled to his coffee maker and pressed at the buttons until rich coffee started dripping into the pot. He made his way to the cupboard, where he found a bowl, a can of ravioli, and the can opener. By the time his pasta was hot, his coffee was ready to drink.

He sat down at the kitchen table and began to eat.

Zack broke the silence. "So. You going to tell me what happened between you and Jonah yesterday?"

Emerson took a sip of coffee. "We had a fight."

"I figured that." Zack didn't look amused.

Emerson put his fork down, not feeling hungry anymore. He stared down at his ravioli, trying to avoid Zack's gaze.

"You going to tell me anything else?"

"The fight was pretty bad," Emerson admitted. He brought a finger up to push at his coffee mug, spinning it with a press against the handle. "We yelled, Jonah got mad, and then he left."

Zack made a humming noise. "Right. That's all you're going to say, then?"

Emerson shrugged and pushed his glasses up his nose—screw contacts today, they were a pain to put in. He stood then and began cleaning up his breakfast. He tossed out the last of the ravioli and started to clean the bowl.

Zack let out a gusty, put-upon sigh.

In the silence that followed, Emerson became aware of the new song playing on the radio: "Hot Blooded." Mick Jones was inviting Emerson to take his temperature. Emerson jerked at the sound of the familiar tune. The last time he had heard this song, it had been in this kitchen when he had come home to find Jonah cooking and singing along.

Jonah was a terrible singer and an even more terrible dancer, which was why Emerson had burst into laughter when he saw him. Jonah had whipped around, smiling widely. Because Jonah was Jonah, he had refused to be embarrassed about being caught at being a dork. Instead, he just danced badly over to Emerson, still singing along.

"'Come on, baby, do you do more than dance?'" Jonah had asked as he grabbed Emerson around the waist and pulled him close. "'I'm hot-blooded, hot-blooded.'" Jonah was murmuring by the time he reached the end of the line, placing his mouth right over Emerson's in a sweet greeting.

Emerson had reveled in the kiss for a few seconds before his curiosity got the better of him. "You lunatic, what are you doing?"

"Making dinner for my gorgeous boyfriend. He's been working hard all day."

"I meant the terrible singing." Emerson had let out another laugh that continued on as Jonah pulled back to grab his hands so he could drag him into the middle of the kitchen. He was laughing so hard he could barely stand as Jonah tried to dance him around the kitchen.

By the time the song had ended, Emerson had been crying with laughter. With the final strains, Jonah moved in to kiss him again.

Emerson rose from the kitchen table, passed Zack, and brought his hand down violently, shutting the radio off.

"Okay… you suddenly have a hate on for Foreigner?" Zack asked with a cocked eyebrow.

Emerson ignored him and went back to his coffee.

§

EARLIER

EMERSON sat behind the cash register, elbow propped on the counter, leaning his head in his hand. Today had shaped up to be rather boring. It seemed no one needed any organic groceries. Despite it being summertime, the store was often quiet on weekdays.

On this particular day, Emerson had taken to passing the time by thinking of Jonah.

Things hadn't been that great this past week, what with Jonah wanting to move in and Emerson resisting the idea, but last night had been good. The tension had broken, and they'd spent the evening making passionate, desperate love. Emerson could remember the bliss that crossed Jonah's face when he finally pressed inside. Emerson had just felt intense relief to know that, despite their disagreement, they could still do this. That the sex was still as good as ever.

Emerson shifted his hips and couldn't help but smile at the feel of that pleasant ache of the morning after. Emerson really did like that feeling. The reminder the day after of what they had done, of where Jonah had been and of how close they had pushed their bodies together, was something Emerson relished.

Emerson was in the middle of constructing a pleasurable scenario for the evening in which he pushed Jonah down on the bed, straddled Jonah's lap, and went about renewing that achy feeling when the bell over the door rang.

Emerson jumped and looked toward the door to see—nothing. He frowned. The door *had* opened, he was sure, but…. He heard a giggle. Emerson looked down and grinned when he spotted the small boy walking through the aisles.

The boy was adorable. All round cherub face with hazel eyes and thick brown hair. He was giggling, and when he spotted Emerson, he held one chubby hand up to his face and made a loud shushing noise. Emerson grinned before lifting a finger to his own lips and nodding in return. He'd be quiet.

Emerson figured it would be easy to keep an eye on the kid today. The shop was quiet, so he could make sure the boy didn't hurt himself or get into trouble.

Emerson was still smiling and watching the adorable child hiding behind a rack of postcards when the overhead bell rang again. The child let out another string of giggles. It seemed his caregiver had arrived. Too entranced by the adorableness of the kid, Emerson didn't look up at first.

"Hm," said a voice from near the door, and the child giggled once again. "Now I'm sure I saw my Gareth come this way," the voice said again, and the child giggled even louder. Emerson grinned before looking over to see the boy's mother standing in the doorway with her hands on her hips.

Emerson stared at her for a moment, wondering why she looked so familiar. He was derailed by the sound of more laughter from the child.

Emerson watched, grinning, as the mother conducted a game of hide and seek, loudly wondering where her child had gotten to before at last stumbling on the giggling child and scooping him up in her arms. The boy squealed as his mother planted kisses over his face.

When she was done, she propped the boy onto her hip and turned toward Emerson. "Thank you for keeping an eye on him; he snuck away—Emerson?" Her eyes went wide when she spotted him. "Oh my God, Emerson! It's so good to see you!" She was smiling with delight now.

Emerson stared back. She did look familiar, but he couldn't yet place her. She was tall with blond hair and blue eyes. She was quite startlingly pretty and very young.

"It's the hair, isn't it?" she said with a grin. "I've been getting that look a lot these past few days. It's Deanna. Deanna Carlisle."

"Oh." Emerson stared at her. Deanna had gone to high school with him and Jonah. She had been well-liked, often the lead in drama productions, girls' volleyball captain, and valedictorian. She had also, more famously in Emerson's memory, been Jonah's date to the prom.

Emerson realized suddenly that he was just staring at her. "Um, hi! Yeah, the hair did throw me," he said, trying to smile.

Deanna smiled back, wide and brilliant. "So how have you been?"

Emerson shrugged. "Good. Going to U of T at Austin."

"Ooh, wonderful. Are you studying art like you wanted to?"

He nodded. "Design. So, um, is this your…?" Emerson let the question hang, feeling awkward about making assumptions about the kid being hers.

"Oh yeah, he's mine. Gareth is my darling boy, aren't you, sweetie pie?" She leaned in toward her son to rub their noses together. The boy laughed, delighted.

"Wow," Emerson said. There was a pause then, and Emerson was sure she could tell what he was thinking. He covered up the silence with an easy gambit. "So, are you going to be living in Hudson Bend again?"

She smiled. "Nah, we're just up for a visit." She stepped closer to the counter and deposited the boy onto it. Then she smiled at Emerson and said, "It really is good to see you. I was hoping to catch up with old friends." Her smile widened then, and she asked, "So how's Jonah doing these days? You two still best friends?"

Emerson blinked at her. "He's good. He, um, spent a few years traveling. He's living in Austin again."

She smiled at that. "Well, maybe I'll drop him a line, see if he's up for lunch. It would be good to see him again. Wouldn't it, baby?" she asked her son, who was starting to look bored. Once again, she rubbed their noises together. "Wouldn't it be a good idea to see Jonah?" The boy giggled in delight. "I knew my Gareth was a smart boy," she praised, then kissed the top of his head.

Emerson froze. He felt like his veins were filled with ice, and his heart began beating too fast. *Gareth.* Why hadn't he noticed before? She'd given her son Jonah's middle name. Her son who looked so much like a tiny Jonah and who must have been conceived while they were still in high school.

Dread filled Emerson's stomach. He recalled then how excited Jonah had been before prom. How he had rented the tux and the limo. Emerson had used his wisdom teeth being extracted as an excuse for not attending. Jonah had been insistent, and Justin had kept hinting at going, and Emerson had been on the verge of caving and buying a ticket under Jonah's watchful glare, fully intending to get a well-timed twenty-four-hour flu on the night of the event, when he had visited the dentist.

The dentist had offered several options for which day to pull them out, and Emerson hadn't hesitated when he saw the day before prom listed. He told Jonah he hadn't had a choice in the date. Fortunately, Jonah was too good-natured and oblivious to be suspicious.

Unfortunately, he had still left Justin bitter. Justin had kept giving Emerson suspicious looks, as if he had known Emerson didn't want to go just because he didn't want to see Jonah having fun with a female date in a heterosexual wonderland. (Emerson later suspected that this was exactly what had been going on with Justin.) Justin had cattily informed him the next school day that Jonah and Deanna had never shown up to the dance. Emerson's imagination had been able to fill in the blanks.

So, Deanna had a son who was the right age to be—

"Anyway, I just stopped by to pick up some summer squash. This guy loves the stuff so much he ate through mom's home-grown stash." She ruffled her son's hair.

Emerson jerked. "They're, uh, just behind you, one aisle over." He always knew the state of their summer squash inventory, since it was the first thing Jonah went for when he came over.

"Awesome. Could you watch him for a sec?" she asked with a smile, and Emerson automatically reached out with one hand to curl it around the boy's waist.

She came back with the squash, and Emerson tallied up the total. "Anything else?" he asked her on autopilot.

She smiled again. "A promise to go out for a drink with me before I leave Hudson Bend?"

Emerson jerked in surprise. "Um, sorry?"

Her smile dimmed a little, but she repeated herself. "I mean, I don't do too much partying, what with this monster around, but it would be good to go out for drinks with old high school friends."

Emerson tried to give her a smile back. "Yeah, sure. Um, maybe? We'll see how things go." He tried not to say anything that would commit him or sound too rude. After all, he might be seeing a lot of her in the future.

He took her money and bagged the squash. He watched as she scooped up both child and groceries before waving goodbye. "See you later, Emerson. It was so good to see you again!" Then they were gone.

Emerson stood still, staring after the woman who had just walked out carrying a boy who was eerily familiar.

Oh God. Was that…? Had that been Jonah's child? Had Deanna gotten pregnant on prom night—what a cliché!—and moved away while still pregnant? Had her parents sent her away? Did parents still do that?

The boy had looked so much like Jonah and had even displayed Jonah's sense of humor and love of summer squash. Staring at him had been like seeing Jonah as a baby.

Did Jonah know? Had he known that he had a kid for all these years and not said anything? No, that didn't sound like Jonah. Maybe he didn't know he had a kid? But then that didn't sound like Deanna either, to keep something like that hidden. He had never figured her to be the type of girl to keep such a thing quiet, to never tell a man he was a father.

But Jonah wasn't the type of guy not tell anyone that he had a kid. Unless…. Emerson thought about the timing. Thought about how Deanna probably would have done the confessing around the same time that Jonah had run away from home. He wondered if she had told him just before and if that was one of the reasons Jonah had left. Or maybe she had sent an e-mail that Jonah *hadn't* ignored.

If Jonah had learned in those first few months before he had written to Emerson…. It wasn't exactly the kind of thing that Emerson would have welcomed hearing about when Jonah had first started writing to him. And then after that it would have been easy to fall into a pattern of wanting to tell but not knowing when and getting more reluctant to reveal the secret the longer it was kept.

Oh God. Emerson was involved with a father who hadn't told him he had a son!

§

Now

DESPITE Zack's prodding to open up about what had happened, Emerson stayed close-mouthed. He wasn't entirely certain as to why he was so wary about telling Zack about it, though he was pretty certain that Zack would have a few choice words about how Emerson had come home to pick a fight. Also, he wasn't entirely sure that Zack would take his side on the whole Deanna thing. He could be wrong, but he didn't want to take the chance that Zack would tell him off too. This way, at least Emerson knew Zack would take care of him while he wallowed.

Zack was still persistent, though. Two days after the fight, Emerson had returned to his bedroom to find Zack sitting on his bed and examining Emerson's latest drawing.

"This is some strange shit, Emma."

Emerson grunted and ignored him. He settled himself on his bed again, resettling into his cocoon.

"Seriously. Did you draw this yesterday?" Zack held up a half-finished drawing. Emerson had picked up a pencil and paper yesterday only to get halfway through a drawing filled with pain and regret before he'd got sick of the picture, sick of himself, and thrown the sketchpad and pencils onto the floor before burying himself under the blankets once again.

"So?"

"So? It's fucking depressing, that's what. Christ, Emma. Why won't you just tell me what happened?"

Emerson picked at the weave of his blanket.

"Emma…."

"I don't want to talk about it," he mumbled. "Can we just… not?"

"You owe me." Zack's voice was stern. "After all the times I've let you cry on my shoulder, don't you think I deserve to know why you're being a mopey bitch?"

He looked up at Zack, surprised. That was a low blow. Emerson knew that he'd always been kind of a mess and that ever since he'd met Zack, he'd looked to the other man to help him pick up the pieces, but Zack had never sounded like he minded before.

"Shit. Don't cry," Zack muttered, and he shifted over. He settled on the bed next to Emerson and let their shoulders press together. "Alright, fine, so I suck at the tough love thing. I think we both already knew that."

"Only sometimes," Emerson agreed.

"When you're ready to talk, you're going to tell me, though. Don't think you won't."

Emerson nodded and tilted to rest his head on Zack's shoulder. "Yeah. I know."

§

THEN

WRITTEN inside a birthday card filled with dirty jokes written on four different-colored sticky notes, predominantly in old-fashioned, spidery handwriting and signed by all the writers' workshop members, complete with a photograph of the whole gang:

Dear Emerson,

Happy birthday! Hope you enjoy the jokes. When I told her it was your birthday, Roberta insisted. The others might have chipped in a little on the tamer ones.

I debated for ages on what to get you, but eventually an opportunity arose that I couldn't pass up. I don't have your eye, but I attached a couple of samples (had to make sure it worked, of course). Don't worry, it's not as extravagant as you think.

Jonah

Emerson laughed as he read the letter and then turned to the box. As quickly as he could, he peeled away the paper. Inside was a slightly battered SLR camera. Emerson stared. A camera. Jonah had gotten him a camera.

His fingers trembled as he worked to get it free from the box. *A camera.*

Suddenly, Emerson was swamped by his feelings for Jonah. He was filled with love and adoration for a boy several hundreds of miles away, a boy who, despite the distance, knew Emerson better than anyone else. Which was the problem, wasn't it? It had been his problem for years, really. Jonah did know Emerson best and always managed to do just the right thing to keep Emerson ridiculously attached and in love.

A camera.

God, he hadn't felt this giddy in love since that hot August afternoon on the beach when Jonah had reached out one long-fingered hand to smooth sunscreen on Emerson's nose. They had been laughing and talking, and Jonah had pulled out the sunscreen to "reapply—Jesus, Em, don't you ever learn?" He had poured enough into his hand so that he could smear the greasy substance all over Emerson's nose. Emerson had stood there trying to stifle his laughter and watching Jonah's oh-so-earnest expression as he worked to re-cover Emerson in sunscreen. Jonah's brow had been furrowed, his eyes serious, and Emerson had thought that Jonah was kind of awesome and wonderful. It had been then, standing on a beach with Jonah's fingers running over his nose, that he suddenly thought to himself, *I love him.* Emerson's heart started beating too fast, and his stomach filled with a thousand butterflies. *I love him. Like, want to spend the rest of my life with him love. Oh my God! I'm in love with my best friend!*

He had continued to stand there, letting Jonah slather sunscreen on him without arguing. Emerson couldn't move. He was stunned by the revelation. God, he was in love with Jonah!

The panic over being in love with a straight boy—and his best friend!— had come later. At that moment in time, Emerson had simply reveled in the light sensation filling his whole body at the knowledge that he was *in love*.

It felt a lot like that first moment when he held his new camera.

God, a camera. Jonah bought him a camera. Emerson bit his lip as he stared at it. No one knew Emerson better than Jonah. No one.

He wondered…. All those months ago when Jonah had confessed to having a boyfriend, Emerson had wondered about the possibility of them like he never had before. When he had thought Jonah was straight, it was easy to limit those what-ifs to accidental thoughts during jack-off sessions, but after he found out Jonah was interested in men, the what-ifs had become much more difficult to keep at bay. And now—Jonah sent him letters all the time, and Emerson found himself often thinking of Jonah and wondering what Jonah felt for him.

Now, looking at the camera that Jonah had sent him, hope bloomed in his chest. Maybe Emerson wasn't so stupid to still be in love with Jonah after all this time. Three years was a long time to be in love with a boy who didn't love you back, but if he did… three years wasn't that long to wait for somebody.

Emerson allowed his heart to beat double time. He would push things—no, not push, but… things would move forward, he was certain.

Grabbing his camera and his coat, Emerson hurried out the door, eager to try out his new present.

Several hours later, Emerson and Hayley were sitting on Zack's bed while Emerson uploaded all the pictures onto his laptop. There were several hundred of Hudson Bend and Austin and everything in between, and he wanted an empty memory card for his birthday party.

"He gave you a camera?" Hayley was holding it and turning it this way and that. "An expensive gift for a best friend."

Emerson blushed. "He said it wasn't that extravagant, and it looks beat up. He probably got it second-hand."

Hayley arched a brow. "Even second-hand, it would cost." She set the camera down. "So… loverboy send you another letter filled with unresolved sexual tension?" Emerson kept his gaze locked on his computer screen. His usual denials about the letters not being from a lover or filled with sexual tension of any kind didn't form. Not today.

"Ooh! I know that look! Lemme see!" Hayley made grabby hands. Emerson caved and handed over the letter.

Hayley cackled when she found the dirty jokes. Emerson had just unplugged his camera when suddenly his hand was being grabbed, and he was being dragged down the stairs and into the kitchen.

"Jonah sent jokes!" Hayley called to get Greg and Zack's attention. Then she proceeded to read out all the jokes one by one and then post each one on Emerson's Cork Board of Communication. The board had been instituted when messages to Emerson had repeatedly failed to reach him. After he had made a meal for three people only to discover that Zack and Greg had picked up a last-minute gig, it had been a must.

Then Zack was pressing a beer into Emerson's hand and telling him to "start drinking, Emma." Within a few hours, Zack and Greg's house was filled with anyone that Emerson might classify as a friend. There were classmates and fellow Peter fans, and he was pretty sure he saw the girl who sold him coffee once a week.

Emerson was weaving a few hours later as he walked away from the beer pong table, though he didn't sway as badly as his opponent.

"Emery!" Eve popped up in front of him. Her dark curls were a mess around her face.

Emerson had met Eve when she had followed Hayley to Zack's dorm room last spring. The girls had met in Hayley's Intro to Art History course second semester, and Eve just started showing up to gatherings as if she had always been there.

Eve was… Eve scared him a little. She was unlike anyone else Emerson had ever met. Her long hair always looked like it was ready for a shampoo commercial. Her brown eyes were framed by cat's-eye horn rims, and a silver tongue stud peeked out between her teeth. Emerson wasn't as afraid of her beauty or fashion sense, though, as he was about her brazen honesty regarding three things: one, sex; two, being into chicks; three, sex with said chicks. Eve was an unapologetic lesbian.

Her out-and-proud attitude threw Emerson. He wasn't used to people who made the announcement so unselfconsciously—or during the first five minutes of meeting them. He also wasn't sure what to make of her art. She was taking the Design program, and any of her work that Emerson had seen tended to have lots of breasts and vaginas.

Still, Emerson had a soft spot for the girl who could make Hayley seem prudish.

"I'm victorious," he told her.

"So I saw, darling—beer pong champion." She smacked a kiss to his cheek. "Have you been having a good birthday?"

Emerson nodded. "Yes. Jonah sent me a camera."

"Ooh. The elusive Jonah!" Eve gave a grin. "So, let's see it, darling."

Emerson spun on his heels and looked around. "I left it… kitchen!"

He led Eve toward the kitchen, giggling with her as they went. Emerson went to the cabinet where he had stored the camera before playing beer pong and pulled it out.

"Ooh. Expensive," Eve said, properly impressed.

"Yep!" Emerson nodded.

Eve looked from the camera to his face. "Oh my—Emery, did you know that you're glowing?"

He blinked at her. "Am not?" He wasn't feeling too confident about that denial.

"Are too."

Emerson couldn't tell if he was blushing, his face was already so flushed with alcohol. "Am not."

"Too. Does he know?"

"He who?"

"Mysterious Pen Pal! Does he know?"

"Know what?"

"That you're glowing!"

"Well, he's not here, so I'm pretty sure he doesn't know what I look like right now…."

"I meant, does he know you're completely in love with him?"

"I—" Emerson stared. "No?"

Eve laughed. "Why so unsure?"

Emerson looked down at his camera and didn't say anything.

"Oh Emery, honey! You're blushing! Don't be embarrassed! You know I'd never hold loving cock against you! Loving cock is wonderful if that's what you're into."

Staring at her really was the only possible course of action. He really should have been used to Eve by now.

Fortunately, Emerson was saved from having to find a response to that by Hayley's arrival.

Unfortunately, Hayley had arrived to pull him into a conversation with some of her hot friends from her history class. Meeting the cute boys wasn't a hardship, but Emerson began to feel very uncomfortable when Eve and the newly met Devon started up a game of "Never Have I Ever."

"Never have I ever had sex in an empty classroom," said Devon to start.

Hayley took her shot without shame. As did Brian, Emerson noticed.

"My turn!" Hayley said with a grin. "Never have I ever slept with a frat boy!" She shot Emerson a coy smile.

He took his shot. Eve stared at him.

"You didn't! Ooh. You did!"

"I—"

"Emery, you slept with a frat boy?"

"I… think he was?"

"You think? Did you have a one-off lay at a frat party?"

"Okay! Next question!" Emerson said desperately.

"My turn!" Eve gave a wicked grin, and Emerson suspected he was about to pay for shutting her down. "I've never had a crush on my pen pal!"

Emerson glared at Eve.

"Drink up, Emery!" Eve cried.

Hayley cackled.

Emerson drank.

"I've never been caught with my pants down by my mother," said Brian when they finally resumed the game. Devon drank.

"Your turn, Em!"

"Never have I ever had to pee so badly before!" Emerson said before jumping to his feet.

"Boo!" Eve cried out drunkenly.

"That's cheating!" cried Hayley.

"But I have to pee!"

"You better come back!" Hayley called.

He waved a hand at her. "Sure, sure," he called, then weaved his way through party-goers, trying to find a bathroom.

It wasn't until he had stumbled into the bathroom that Emerson realized he was still clutching his camera. Setting it down carefully, he proceeded to drunkenly attack his button and zipper.

When Emerson stumbled out, once again holding his camera, he looked hard for a distraction worthy of missing the rest of "Never Have I Ever."

Fortunately, Zack was very obliging.

"Emma! Birthday boy! How's the party going?"

Emerson grinned. Oh yeah, no one better than Zack to offer up a distraction.

Hayley found them in the kitchen thirty minutes later, laughing over the dirty lyrics Zack was penning.

"Emerson! You didn't come back! You lied to me!" Crap. Hayley was pouting.

Emerson shook his head in denial. "No—I ran into Zack!" he said, pointing.

"So Zack is more important than me?"

"No!" Emerson shook his head vehemently. "But Zack was distracting. And I'm drunk," he added for good measure.

"Right. Well, I demand that you come spend time with me! You left during me time and didn't come back!"

"Okay, okay," Emerson said, happy to give in. Though mostly happy that Hayley wasn't going to continue pouting.

"Good!" Hayley grabbed his hand and pulled. "Greg was just showing off the checker board! We're playing!"

"Checkers?" Okay, Emerson might be drunk, but that really didn't sound right.

"Yes, checkers."

What kind of drunken game was that? Emerson wondered. Then he saw the board, and everything made sense.

§

Jonah,

Thank you! The camera is awesome and filled with pictures.

Last night Zack threw me a birthday party. He insisted. It was at his townhouse, and there was a lot of alcohol. Also, pretty much everyone I ever met while on campus. Seriously, I think I saw the girl who sells me coffee on Tuesday mornings.

Anyway, the night was pretty awesome. I won at beer pong and lost at checkers (no, really, Greg has this awesome checkers board that has shot glasses for playing pieces. Every time you lose a piece you have to drink the contents. Unfortunately for me, Hayley is a total shark!).

Fortunately, your present arrived in good time, so I got a LOT of pictures—far too many to print out or e-mail. I'll see about getting them put onto a CD for you.

Tell everyone at the workshop I say thanks for their good wishes. I'm not sure about the dirty jokes, but Hayley thought they were a riot. Especially when I told her about Roberta. She pulled each sticky note out of the card and pinned them to the corkboard of messages I keep at Zack's (I'm there a lot—they use me for my cooking skills, and Zack and Greg always forget to tell me shit when I'm around).

I'm not sure how a camera isn't as extravagant as I think, but I guess I'll have to take your word for it. I'm seriously hoping, though, that you didn't shoplift it or take out a loan—I like it too much to give it back.

Having had a very awesome birthday,

Emerson

§

EMERSON readjusted his grip around the pillow under his head. His fingers had been gripping the down for so long that they creaked as he let go and then gripped the fabric again.

The body behind him shifted, and two large hands palmed his naked ass. He shivered when the thumbs slipped between the cheeks.

It hit him then that Karl was pulling them apart to see his hole, to eye the entrance into Emerson's body. He shivered again and wondered for a moment how it was that he got here in the first place.

It started at the party, he thought. Well, this part had started at the party, when Karl had approached him. Emerson had already had a few drinks by then, and so when Karl started flirting, Emerson had flirted back. He had let Karl lean in close, speak in his ear and run his hand up Emerson's arm. He even leaned in toward Karl and glanced at the other man from below his lashes.

When Karl had moved on to kisses, Emerson had opened his mouth and welcomed them. He had even reached up to twine both arms around Karl's neck. He didn't object when Karl curled large hands around his hips before running them up his torso, rubbing up and down.

They had curled around his waist and palmed the small of his back and between his shoulder blades. Emerson moaned and pressed closer and let his tongue reach out to Karl's.

When Karl had hotly suggested that they go back to his place, Emerson had readily agreed.

Emerson was startled out of his reverie by the feel of a lube-coated finger pushing past the ring of muscle guarding his body. The finger pushed in slowly, and—Jesus! Karl must have some experience with this, because he went straight for Emerson's prostate. He moaned loudly at the shivery feeling running through his body. God, but he loved his prostate! He had long ago tried slipping his own fingers into his body when he jerked off; the feeling of a finger inside him was familiar at least. The slow, unerring massage turned Emerson into a moaning, shivery mess. He pressed his face into the pillow and tried to stifle some of the moans. Seeing as how Emerson was drunk, stopping the moans before they escaped him was impossible.

Karl was good at this, Emerson thought dazedly as another finger pushed in with the first. He pushed his face deeper into the pillow and wondered if he could get more control if he distracted himself from the pleasure.

He tried to think of something else, ran his day through his mind. He had woken up, made himself breakfast, and then said goodbye to his parents and Kierstyn when they left for the day. Emerson's dad had an appointment in Austin, so he and his wife were spending the day out and dropping Kierstyn off at a friend's there. Emerson had had the house to himself, which turned out to be a bad thing when he opened and read Jonah's latest letter.

The most recent letter had been written on stationery from someplace called the Rustic Inn Creekside Resort and Spa. Something about the name had made Emerson's stomach curl with dread.

The sour feeling in his stomach only got worse when he read Jonah's story about where his camera had come from. He couldn't help but be disappointed at knowing that his camera was not just second-hand, but that Jonah hadn't even paid for it. It had been the broken, discarded toy of a friend.

The feeling only got worse when he read about *why* Jonah was at the Rustic Inn.

I am looking forward to having some privacy from Gavin was a deceptive start to the paragraph. Emerson's stomach plummeted as he continued to read: *It seems another one of his shortcomings is that he doesn't like to knock. That or he just wants to see Xie naked.*

He had kind of suspected that Jonah and Xie probably weren't just kissing each other goodnight, but he didn't appreciate having it spelled out for him. Unbidden, the image of Jonah having sex with a cute girl came to him. He could imagine Jonah kissing her, undressing her, petting her and fu—

Emerson had stopped himself. He wasn't going to picture Jonah with his girlfriend having a romantic "stay-cation" at an inn and spa that gave them their own Jacuzzi. He wasn't going to do that to himself.

He had reread the paragraph. Emerson had *really* wanted to find some evidence to tell him he was wrong. He didn't find any.

God, he had been such a fool. After Jonah had confessed his bisexuality, Emerson had allowed thoughts he had suppressed for so long to have some legroom. Had imagined what life might be like if he and Jonah were the couple he had so long wanted them to be. And then Jonah had sent him a camera, a gift that was not only thoughtful, but also expensive. Emerson had started to think, to hope, that he wasn't being foolish in his dreams. That Jonah really did feel something for him, too, wanted him too.

But this latest letter just proved how much of an idiot he had been. Jonah wasn't pining after him in return, wasn't wishing that Emerson could be something more. He wasn't like Emerson, who was waiting at home for someone who would never love him. He wasn't turning down dates and keeping his romantic experiences limited to make-out sessions at college parties. He wasn't being a pathetic loser wasting his life away while he waited for the object of his hopeless crush to love him back.

The rest of the afternoon passed away in a strange blur after that. The first thing he'd done was to find the Rustic Inn's website, which had filled Emerson with longing as he imagined what a weekend there would be like. It also prompted him to decide that Jonah had been lying about his bisexuality. That he was, instead, bi-curious, and now that he had found Xie, he would marry her, and they'd have the perfect life together. They would, Emerson suspected, have loads of beautiful babies, to whom Emerson would be godfather, while he stayed a lonely bachelor living with his bazillion cats and perving on Jonah from afar for the rest of his life until he died.

That was when Emerson went hunting for liquor. He found the Smirnoff Lime Twist in his parents' cupboards and took two shots to calm his hysteria.

A little tipsy, Emerson had reread the letter again. Jonah didn't just have a girlfriend—he had a lover. Emerson then spent half an hour obsessing over what Xie looked like and how long she had waited before she let Jonah fuck her. He wondered how many times they had fucked since the first.

When the image of Jonah fucking some girl good enough to make her scream in delight started to torture him, Emerson took another shot of vodka.

Half an hour later, Emerson was stumbling out of the house to escape the letter and his own thoughts and running into a neighbor, a fellow student on his way to a party. Two hours after that, he was at a campus party drinking bad keg beer and getting chatted up by Karl.

"I can't wait to fuck you," Karl growled, shocking Emerson back to the present. He was still on his knees, and Karl still had fingers up his ass. "Bet you're tight. Can't wait to get in your tight little ass."

Karl followed thought with action. He pulled out his fingers, leaving Emerson feeling open and obscene. Then Emerson heard a condom wrapper tear and then the sounds of Karl stroking himself. Then Karl was guiding his cock to Emerson's ass and pushing in.

It hurt. Karl was hot, hard, and unforgiving as he pushed steadily into his body. Emerson gasped into the pillow, tears stinging his eyes. He felt like he was being split in two. When a tear escaped, he rubbed his face into the fabric, wiping it away.

Karl was groaning and moaning behind him. He gripped Emerson's hips tight and started to move in even strokes.

After a minute it felt all right. It wasn't unpleasant. But the pain had sobered him up, and Emerson suddenly felt lonely, even as Karl puffed away behind him. He bit his lip, trying to will it better, trying to get more pleasure out of this.

He thought of Jonah and the Rustic Inn and wondered if Jonah was fucking Xie right now. He thought of the pictures of the Inn and suddenly felt a deep longing to be with Jonah instead. He closed his eyes tight. The thoughts went away, but a new one came instead. He saw himself at the Rustic Inn, kneeling on that big bed with Jonah behind him. He pretended for a moment that it was Jonah thrusting into him with increasing force.

The sex didn't get better. It didn't get worse. Or, at least, the physical act didn't get worse. The sick feeling in Emerson's stomach yawned and widened when he suddenly remembered the promises he had made himself once. The promise to be careful about who he had sex with after the drunk hand jobs at the frat party. And the wistful promise he had made years ago to let Jonah be the first.

After Karl finally came, he flipped Emerson over and sucked him off. The relief Emerson felt when he came was mostly about being thankful that the whole experience was finally over.

Luckily, Karl passed out. Alcohol and sex had proved to be too much for him.

Emerson just crawled out of the bed and back into his clothes. He was definitely too drunk now to find his way back to the Bend, but fortunately Zack and Greg's was within walking distance. It took him almost twenty minutes to get there with his slow, swaying gait.

When he discovered that no one was home, he was glad that Zack had long ago given him a key to the place.

Emerson headed straight to the kitchen and fished out Zack's bottle of Jack. Then he stumbled his way to Zack's bedroom—he didn't much feel like seeing Greg right now—and started drinking.

§

ZACK found him in his room, a few hours after the fact, pissed drunk and sprawled out on the floor. Emerson's shoulders were propped up against the edge of his bed. He had tried sitting but found that lying down was much preferable and, after a lengthy consideration of Zack's bed, he had opted for the floor instead.

"Em! What the hell are you doing here?" Zack asked, surprised. Then, after a long pause, he said, "Are you *drunk*?"

He sounded very incredulous, which Emerson thought was unfair, since he had seen Emerson drunk before.

"Yes," said Emerson, trying not to sound petulant at all.

"Emerson…." There was another pause, and then Zack was sitting down on the floor next to him. "Emma, why are you getting drunk alone in my room at two in the morning?"

Emerson tilted his head back, trying to get a proper view of the alarm clock. Was it only two? That meant that it had only been ninety minutes since he had left Karl's, and not yet three hours since he had told Karl he could…. Emerson let his thoughts drift away from that line of thinking.

"Emerson!" Zack poked his shoulder, hard.

"What?" Emerson hadn't meant to sound that whiny.

"What's going on, Emma?"

He took another swig from his bottle of Jack. "You'd be so proud of me," he told Zack. "I went and found myself a boy whose name wasn't Jonah Cherneski and who wanted to fuck me."

Zack sighed, his warm breath tickling the side of Emerson's face. "Em, what did you do?"

"What you keep saying I should do. I found another boy to fuck me."

This was met with silence. Emerson took another drink.

"Emerson." Zack's voice sounded so disappointed that Emerson raised his bottle again, only the mouth never reached his lips as Zack snatched the bottle from his hand.

"You've had enough," Zack told him, sounding like Emerson's dad.

A hollow feeling filled his stomach. "No, I haven't!"

"Yes, you have." His voice was firm. Then Zack put the bottle an arm's length away from him, on his other side. Emerson eyed the bottle, peering across Zack's chest, but decided, ultimately, that it was just too far away.

"Emerson, tell me you didn't."

"Didn't what?" Even through the drunken haze, Emerson knew he sounded like a child.

"Tell me you didn't let some stranger—"

"Pop my cherry?" The words tore out of Emerson with a vengeance, as sharp and quick as any weapon. "He was tall and pretty and nice, so yes, when he asked if he could, I let him. I told him to- to put his cock up my ass." Suddenly Emerson's eyes felt itchy. "I let him… I told him to fuck me because I….” A sob kept him from finishing his sentence.

“Oh Emma,” Zack murmured sympathetically. He snaked an arm around Emerson’s shoulders and pressed his cheek to the top of his head.

“It hurt.” The words spilled out of Emerson on the tail end of another sob, much to his surprise. “It still hurts.”

Zack let out another sigh. “Emma….”

“It was awful, Zack,” Emerson said. The tears wouldn’t stop falling. They just kept coming, and Emerson could hardly talk for the all the sobs.

“Shit, you do get yourself into it, don’t you?” Zack rubbed one hand up and down Emerson’s arm and didn’t complain when Emerson turned his face into Zack’s neck and cried onto his shoulder.

§

WRITTEN on the back of a flyer for an in-faculty music soirée, never mailed:

Jonah,

Went out again last night to another party; drank too much. Have hangover from hell and Zack is being mean and glaring at me.

Ugh, can’t remember anything about yesterday, but did get your letter, you God-damned son of a lying bitch and why do you do this shit to me—

§

ONE week later:

Jonah,

I don’t think I want to know anything more about Gavin. What you’ve told me and hinted at is enough to scar me for life. Despite that, thank him for the camera.

Wow. A weekend away? I didn't realize you and Xie were that serious. Congrats, I guess? (Zack, Greg, and Hayley are all sluts who refuse to give me proper experience on how to deal with my friends dating for longer than five hours. So… sorry I don't know the right thing to say.)

Went to a party last weekend and had too much to drink, as evidenced by embarrassing make-out session mid-dance floor with a classmate I barely talked to before that night. Zack was an evil bastard the next day. He had no sympathy for my hangover. Anyway, I was so busy recovering and then trying to get all my homework done that I didn't have time for you and your letters until this weekend.

I really should go, though—I don't have that much free time today. Natalie's minding the shop, but Dad's not working weekends again yet, so they're still my responsibility, and I've got some homework and reading to get done.

Emerson

CHAPTER 8

Emerson,

It's alright, I know you're busy. Hell, after all the shit I've pulled, I'm probably lucky that you still talk to me at all.

It wasn't a weekend "away" per se. Unless you mean away from Gavin, of course. You *should* stay far away from him. I am pretty sure there aren't any airborne STIs, but you can never be too careful. If the government was going to weaponize that shit, Gavin would be their go-to guy.

I just gave myself goose bumps.

It's not really a "congratulations" thing. It's—what's the opposite of complicated? That's what it is. It started out romantic, but now we're just kind of mutually pathetic and horny. (Is that too much information? It's probably too much information.) Anyway, it turns out we're not actually that compatible, romantically, but Xie is a good friend. I guess that isn't going to help you learn what to say if you ever meet anyone in a functional relationship. Sorry.

You need to be more careful, Emerson. Who knows what could happen at these college parties you're going to? I'd hate for you to get hurt. Then who would I send Roberta's filthy jokes to?

Jonah

§

WRITTEN on the back of an internal map of the campus library:

Jonah,

Uhh, yeah, still a no on the meeting Gavin—ever—front.

You have a friends-with-benefits arrangement with someone? What happened to the dork who ran away? Sometimes I wonder if I'll recognize you when you come home.

I was fine. I know how to take care of myself—yes, Jonah, even at a college party. I didn't have that much to drink, just enough to make me think that dancing would be a good idea.

Dirty jokes? Geez, you're as bad as Hayley. The other day she started a conversation with, "So last night, the guy I picked up was eating me out like he was a fucking vacuum. I mean, like, seriously, sucking on my clit." Then she started giving me advice for oral sex. I'm pretty sure the whole conversation was about making me blush. She says it's amusing. Frankly, I just think she's evil. What else is a guy suppose to do when a woman starts talking about last night's oral sex?

Well, I've got to wrap this letter up. I'm meeting up with a classmate for coffee and studying, and it's time for me to hightail it across campus, but I want to mail this first.

Emerson

§

Hey Em,

Even dorks grow up, I guess. You ever hear that saying, "you can never go home again"? Everything changes, Em. That's the only thing that ever stays the same.

I didn't mean to imply that you don't know how to take care of yourself. I meant to say I don't think you *do* enough of it. There's a difference.

Hey, free sex advice is always good. Most guys would be taking notes, dude, at least if they could divert enough blood from their boner. From what you've told me about Hayley, guys would probably kill just to be a fly on that wall.

I finally got out a short story just for you. Sorry about the bad photocopy; the machine at work needs a tune-up.

Jonah

§

WRITTEN on a lined sheet torn from a notebook:

Jonah,

I really can take care of myself just fine. And I do, too, do enough of it.

Free sex advice from Hayley is, and always will be, sex advice *from Hayley*. There is no way that that will ever stop being wrong and upsetting. It's Hayley. That's like… getting sex advice from Natalie. So, there is no boner when Hayley talks about sex.

Wow. Jonah, your story is amazing. I can't get over it. I've read it about five times already. I had no idea that anyone could give a park bench so much personality, but you did. It's very different from what you used to write; I guess it must come from all those new experiences you've been having. Did you come up with the idea sitting on a park bench, wondering who else was there before you?

Yesterday I was taking a short cut across campus when I had to stop to take this picture for you. Your work was good inspiration.

Emerson

P.S. I've never believed that stupid saying about how you can never go home again. It was coined by someone who couldn't have been loved very much.

§

On the back of page two of Jonah's resume:

Emerson,

If you say so.

I'll have you know you have killed any and all boners, present and future, forever by mentioning Natalie and sex in the same sentence. Thanks a lot, asshole. Ugh.

I wrote the whole thing sitting on a park bench, actually. My ass was completely numb when I got up, but it was worth it. The picture is perfect—it looks so lonely, you can just imagine it absorbing bits and pieces of the people it shelters over the years to keep itself company. I was in kind of a maudlin mood when I wrote it. Yes, it even happens to me sometimes. It just seems that no matter where you go, what you do, someone was always there before you. Someone beat you to it, someone faster, better.

Xie has finally finagled a date with the boy she's been in love with since eighth grade, and who might actually love her back. I hope he does. She deserves it.

Jonah

§

EMERSON found Hang Out on U of T's website for clubs and societies. It was the only informal LGBT group without another agenda. Unlike the ones that wanted to promote social or political change, this group was all about meeting others who understood what you were going through. He read on their website that they met for coffee once a week, so Emerson made note of the time and place, and the following week he got ready to go.

And now here he was, standing outside of a coffee shop, arms crossed and staring at the door. All he had to do was go through those doors, and he'd be meeting others just like him.

Now: to step through the door.

Emerson was bound and determined to walk through that door, because he had made a promise to himself. After waking up to discover that he had fallen into bed with someone while drunk yet again, this time as the direct fallout of Jonah's latest letter, Emerson had made his decision. He was tired of being lovesick and hung up on Jonah. He was tired of feeling depressed and angry. He was tired of pining after Jonah, of getting his hopes up one letter and having them dashed the next. Emerson couldn't take the yo-yoing emotions anymore.

So Emerson had made himself a promise: he was going to get out of the house, he was going to meet new people, and he was going to get the fuck over his stupid unrequited love.

Someone walked up behind Emerson, and they clipped shoulders as he passed. He gave an apology but kept walking to the door.

See, it was easy, Emerson thought. That guy had gone in, and so could he.

He pulled open the door and walked to the counter. After ordering his coffee and dumping in an appropriate amount of sugar, Emerson hesitated, looking around the shop. The place was fairly lively, but Emerson was pretty sure that the group he was looking for was located in the far right corner. There was a large group of laughing and talking students, not terribly unusual for a coffee shop so close to the college, but this group looked a little different. There were a larger number of girls with short hair and piercings and boys wearing bright colors and effeminate clothes. There were also several very nondescript, average-looking students.

"Hi."

Emerson jumped and turned to see the guy who had bumped into him standing at his side.

"Thinking about joining us?"

"What?" Emerson stared at him, trying to look like a man who didn't have homosexual thoughts and who wasn't thinking about joining an LGBT club.

"Was wondering if you were just going to stand here all day or if you were thinking about actually sitting down and joining us."

"Us?"

"Yeah. Hang Out." Emerson jerked to hear the name, and the guy just grinned in response. "We don't bite—we're actually real friendly." He gave Emerson a wink, and it was then that Emerson noticed that this man was really quite attractive. He was tall, with dark features, warm brown eyes, and curly black hair. Emerson swallowed.

"I've never…."

"Been to any sort of LGBT meeting? That's okay; we're all a little shy the first time. I'm Alex." He held out his hand for Emerson to shake.

"Emerson."

"I know." Emerson blinked in surprise. "You showed up at my photography club meeting last week. I… noticed you."

"Oh." Emerson blushed at the knowledge of being noticed and at not being able to remember the other man.

"So… you going to come and join us?"

"Um, yeah. I'd like that," Emerson managed to force out of his dry throat, and he followed Alex over to the group in the corner.

Emerson had never felt so comfortable or happy with a group of strangers before in his life. They had been warm and welcoming and had had this knowing air about them that had been nice instead of awkward. It had also been a bit of a revelation when he found himself hearing so many jokes and casual comments about being gay. Emerson had never met so many people who were so comfortable about it.

By the time Alex walked him back to his car, Emerson was high on adrenaline. He felt the hot rush of success and the pleased buzz of having met potential new friends.

And then, of course, there was Alex. Alex, who had flirted with Emerson over coffee and who had lingered with him before offering to walk Emerson back to his car. He had accepted, enjoying the feeling of interest and mild arousal curling in his belly. It had been too long since Emerson had felt that while sober and with someone who wasn't Jonah Cherneski.

"So, Emerson… I was kind of hoping that you and I could maybe go out again, grab another cup of coffee or maybe go to dinner?" Alex gave him a shy smile.

Emerson found himself smiling back. "Yeah. Yes."

"Okay, then." Alex's grin was wide. "So, Friday at six? Do you like Thai food?"

"Thai sounds good."

"Great. Meet me at Titaya's? They have a great banana roll with coconut ice cream for dessert. I'll even share a bite or two," he added with what might have been a suggestive smile.

Emerson blushed. "Maybe I want my own banana roll," he said, not quite believing his own nerve.

Alex laughed, obviously delighted. "Suit yourself. I'll see you Friday, Emerson."

Emerson watched him leave, a pleased smile spreading inexorably across his face.

§

WRITTEN on the back of a flyer for the Texas Photography Club:

Jonah,

Writing fiction while sitting in the park? Wow, how very… romantic poet of you. Next you'll be telling me how you wrote poems about your walks in the woods.

I'm sorry to hear about Xie. Someone will come along for you too.

So as you can see, they have a photography club at U of T, so a couple of weeks ago I decided to check it out. I figured, what with all the free time I have these days not minding the shop, I could totally join a club. You'd be proud. I went on my own and everything.

The meetings so far have been good. We took a walk around Austin last week looking for subjects. It was good to share the experience with people just as obsessed as I am. I don't think I've ever spent so much time talking about camera lenses and light angles before. Several of us went for coffee afterward, and we didn't break up until late. We almost spent more time at the coffee shop than we did on the outing. Paid off for me though: I ended up with a date. Three, actually. I saw Alex twice in the last week, and we're going to meet up again tonight.

Actually, I should go—I need to shower and change now if I want to mail this before my date.

Emerson

§

WRITTEN on a blank sheet of computer paper stapled to a quarterly arts magazine and a check for $500:

Emerson,

I forged your signature for the rights to the photo. The contest called for a short story with accompanying photograph. Attached is your cut of second place. Congrats! (Please don't be mad.)

I'm not sorry about Xie. She deserves to be happy as much as anyone. I know there's someone out there for me. I'm not worried yet; we're still young.

The photography club sounds pretty cool. Alex must be pretty cool, too, if he's already got to the third date. I'm happy for you, Em.

Jonah

§

WRITTEN the same day he read Jonah's last letter:

Jonah,

You just sent me $500. Any anger I might have had about forging my signature totally went away at that. I don't know what to do with all this extra money!

I'm guessing the "he" wasn't a typo. So, you know? Zack keeps telling me I'm too much of a queer for people not to guess—I guess he's right. I wanted to tell you, but I was kind of terrified—it's not like there's a successful and popular PFLAG chapter in Hudson Bend. I haven't told anyone else yet except for Hayley, Zack, and Greg.

Emerson

§

Em,

Save it. Someday you're going to need a better camera.

I don't make typos when I'm hand-writing, Emerson. I figured it out in twelfth grade when you started spending more time with Justin. I'm out here, but you're the only one back home who knows. Well, I think Natalie suspects, but she's sneaky like that. Watch out for that one. Anyway, I don't want to tell my parents on the phone or, worse, in a letter. They deserve to hear it in person. I just don't know when that will be.

I actually got another part-time job at one of the local hotels here for the ski season, but it's not posh or anything. I'm just the maintenance guy. Anyway, if it takes me longer to reply than usual, you'll know why.

Jonah

§

Jonah,

I'll definitely need a better camera if I plan on taking more pictures for your stories.

Oh, Justin… Justin wasn't—I mean, okay, yes, he sort of was, because there was one incident, but mostly he wasn't.

Natalie is totally wily. I don't trust her for a second (i.e. pictures of me sleeping!). She always seems to know everything—especially now that she's working at the store. Seriously, if you need to know anything about anyone in Hudson Bend, ask Natalie.

Ugh—I'm so exhausted. I just got home from forced servitude. While I was writing this letter, Hayley showed up and insisted that we go shopping. She dragged me to all these clothing shops and made me buy a few things. She says that if I want to go on more dates, I need nicer clothes. I thought the clothes I wore to class or to church with Mom were nice enough, but Hayley just gave me this look like I was from Mars when I said as much. Seriously, what's wrong with jeans, tees, and sweaters? Hayley says everything, but whatever. I now have more button-down shirts in my closet, and I'm completely wiped after following Hayley around clothing and shoes and "accessory" stores.

I'm going to bed.

Emerson

Jonah put down the letter with shaking hands and found himself gnawing on his thumbnail a moment later. What—how—

I mean, okay, yes, he was, because there was one incident, but mostly he wasn't.

Oh. Oh, God, Jonah was such a tool. He'd left—he'd *left the state*, left home, run away from whatever this thing was that he felt for Emerson, and it had all been for nothing. He could have stayed, could maybe even have had Emerson himself if he had waited, if he'd been patient, only now he was in Wyoming of all bloody places, and Emerson was back home in Texas where he belonged and from where, if Jonah was honest with himself, he would probably never leave.

He was such an idiot.

He knew Xie's phone number by heart—she was almost as good for talking sense into him as Emerson was, and he couldn't go to Emerson with this for obvious reasons—so an hour and a half before he had to leave for work, he found himself sitting cross-legged on his bed, the only place in the apartment he got a signal, and dialing the ten digits he needed to get hold of Xie.

She picked up on the third ring, sounding sleepy and happy. "M'hello?"

"God, I woke you," Jonah said abruptly, remembering the time change—Xie was visiting with Bryce's grandparents in New York—and the fact that not everyone worked nights.

"No, no, it's fine," she assured him, already sounding much more awake. There were a few rustling sounds—he imagined her rolling out of Bryce's bed, closing the door quietly behind her so she wouldn't wake him—"You never call unless it's important; I'll make time. What's going on?"

"I think it's possible that I might have been a giant tool."

Xie let that one sink in for a few minutes, probably for his own benefit as much as hers, Jonah thought darkly. Then she said, "Uh huh, Jonah, we know this. After all, you let me go, didn't you?"

Jonah appreciated the attempted at levity, but he was freaking out and had to work in an hour and a half, and now was so not the time. "Xie—"

"Relax, Jonah, I was kidding. You don't owe me anything. Now, what did you do to Emerson that required you to call me and interrupt my nap?"

"The day I left," Jonah said.

"Yes? You're going to have to be more specific, honey."

"I thought—I told you how I walked in on Emerson and his boyfriend kissing?"

"Whereupon you realized your tragic big gay love for your best friend? Can we get to the point, please?"

"It wasn't," Jonah said bleakly. "I mean—Justin wasn't his boyfriend. It was just. And I left, Xie; *how can I ever tell him*—"

Thankfully Xie interrupted him before he could become any more hysterical. "One, stop running your hands through your hair, it makes you look like a hobo."

Jonah frowned guiltily and pulled his free hand away from his head, wondering how she'd known.

"Two, take some deep breaths and think this through. Let's go over your list of reasons for leaving, other than your wretched unrequited love, of course."

"Why are you so mean to me?" he asked, bewildered, plucking at his bed covers. "And why does it make me feel better?"

"Because I'm not giving you time to feel sorry for yourself. So, reasons for leaving. Go."

Only the set of reasons pertaining to Emerson were the slightest bit valid, so Jonah jumped right to those. "Sexual epiphany, in love with best friend, major freak-out?" he recited dutifully.

"And what exactly were you freaking out about?"

Jonah took a deep breath and once again marveled at the force of nature that was Xie. His hands were no longer shaking, and he was starting to feel like he might make it all the way through getting to work and even the end of his shift without having a breakdown. "That apparently I was bi. That I was in love with my best friend, who obviously didn't see me that way. That Emerson would find out how I felt. That even if the thing with Justin ended and we did get together, it might not work out, and it would ruin our friendship."

"So you decided it was better to go away because?"

"I needed time," Jonah said aloud, hearing the truth in his own words. "There was too much at stake at home. I've never been in love before. I don't know what it's like, and what if I—"

"What if you fucked up your relationship with Emerson for good because you were wrong?"

"Yes!" Jonah paused, feeling a shiver go through him at the idea. "Oh."

"Yes," Xie said, "oh. Most of your reasons for leaving are still valid, Jonah. I'm not saying running away was the smart choice or the brave choice or even the choice I'd have made, but it was *a choice*."

"I guess."

Xie's voice gentled. "Jonah, how long have you been away from home now?"

"Uh." He glanced toward the calendar he'd hung on the wall in the kitchen, but it was too far away to see. "A year and a half, I guess."

"And how do you feel about Emerson now?"

Jonah closed his eyes and kept his mouth shut, because if anything, he was more in love with Emerson than ever.

"Maybe it's time to think about going home, Jonah, don't you think? Or are you going to pine after him forever? Nothing's ever going to happen as long as you're apart."

Jonah thought about the manuscript he'd written painstakingly in three or four different notebooks and on bits of scrap paper, pieced together at the library in brief Word documents and so recently submitted to a handful of publishing houses. If any one of them picked up the book for distribution, his secret would be out anyway. He could wait that long. "Not forever," he said at length. "Thanks, Xie. I have to go now."

§

Emerson,

I promise I'll tell you next time I need a photographer so I don't have to resort to forgery.

I don't think I'll ask what you mean by "incident." Maybe I got the wrong idea.

Sorry about your indentured labor with Hayley. Xie made me go shopping with her once, but it was mostly to hold the bags, I think. She didn't even attempt to get me to try anything on, and she gave up asking my opinion on what looked good about two outfits in. Anyway, who cares what you wear on dates? Especially if it's not the first one? You wouldn't date someone that shallow! Besides, you look fine in a T-shirt and jeans.

We have like seventeen feet of snow. Remember that drought we had in sixth grade? When it finally broke, we were in the middle of the last baseball game of the season, but nobody wanted to come in from the rain because the summer had been so unbearably hot and dry? Well, the snow here is like the sun that summer. Any more, and I'll need to invest in snowshoes. Or a dogsled.

Jonah

§

Jonah,

Good idea on the photography front. I'd hate for you to have to go to jail for identity fraud.

"Wrong idea?" About Justin? I don't know what to say to that. We did a project together and kissed once; I'm not sure how you could get any ideas.

It wasn't so much indentured labor with Hayley as it was cruel and unusual punishment. Apparently, for a gay man, I show appalling fashion sense. Also, it would be the first date? Alex turned out to be not that cool in the end, but I met someone else through a club, so Hayley decided I needed help.

If you're going to keep whining about the snow, I want a picture of you up to your ass in fresh powder. Just saying.

I hate this time of year at college. It's after midterms, but professors are gearing up for end of term, so I've got all these essays and projects that are coming due at the same time in about five weeks. Not fun. I've been spending most of my free time in Austin in the library on campus. Fortunately, Hayley, Zack, and Greg are all awesome, so I have people to eat with and somewhere to crash, even though they keep giving me food orders and making me cook for them. (Lesson learned: if you're working on an essay until midnight and have class the following morning, don't drive home when there is a couch with your name on it just five minutes away.)

Well, my study break is over now (actually it probably really ended about five minutes ago, but who's counting?), so I should sign this.

Emerson

P.S. Winters aren't very snowy in Texas, you know.

§

Emerson,

Do you think there are people bigger than me in prison?

I thought people weren't supposed to judge you for what you wore in university. How high school of them. That sucks about Alex, but I guess it's good that you met someone new.

Sadly, there is no camera to borrow for me to take pictures to send to you. I've seen you at work on Photoshop, though, if you want to see it that badly, I'm sure you can make it happen.

You mean college is trying to teach you time-management skills? How utterly appalling. Seriously, Emerson, trust me when I say this, college is so much better than the working world. It has to be. Because the working world is drudgery. At least, the hospitality industry is. And the shift I'm on is pretty dead—I haven't really met any new people other than the mohawked kid who works the late shift at my local Java Bean. (He is pretty cute, though.)

There are a lot of great things about Texas, Emerson, but that doesn't mean there's nothing else out there.

Jonah

CHAPTER 9

THEN

IT WAS a Wednesday when Emerson came home from campus feeling crappy and listless.

He had suspected by the third date and known by the fourth that he and Alex weren't going anywhere. Despite a really hot hand job at the end of the third date that had been the first sober and good sex of Emerson's experience, he knew he and Alex weren't meant to be. Alex had been hot and sweet and a great catch, but their chemistry hadn't jibed.

It probably hadn't helped, either, that the day before their fourth date, Emerson had spent a good hour freaking out over Jonah's recent letter. Knowing that Jonah knew he was gay, and he hadn't told him, had rocked Emerson to the core. Poor Greg had spent an hour trying to calm him down. Emerson had kept telling himself that Greg was right: obviously Jonah did not have a problem with it. If he did, he would have said so before now. Besides, he wasn't a hypocrite. Unfortunately for Greg, it wasn't until Zack got home and said, "Emma, it's really not that difficult to figure you out," that Emerson really stopped hyperventilating. Instead he had clung to Jonah's parting line about how Jonah was happy for him. He had been pretty distracted the next time he saw Alex.

Still, Emerson wasn't exactly happy about having agreed with Alex not to go on more dates.

Having poured a glass of water, Emerson headed up to his room. Listless, he began to do his readings, but he soon found he was unable to concentrate. Emerson had really liked Alex. He hoped that things didn't get awkward at Hang Out or the photography club.

Tapping his pen on his textbook, Emerson stared blankly at the words. Despite the lack of success at long-term happily-ever-after, he had liked dating. He had liked going out, not knowing if he'd get a kiss at the end of the night. He liked the dance of getting to know someone and wondering how things would turn out. No, Emerson would do this again. The next time he met another nice, good-looking guy who was interested, Emerson was going to say yes to him too.

Maybe if he was feeling really brave, he would even do the asking himself.

By the time Emerson was called to dinner, he was feeling much better, though still a little melancholy. He wasn't feeling the bone-deep sadness of when Jonah had left, but he still wasn't feeling all that happy. He definitely wasn't feeling up to hearing his mother's news.

"Oh, Harper called today."

Emerson looked over to see that his mom was smiling.

"He was able to get time off this Thanksgiving," she announced, "so he's coming up to visit us next month."

Emerson held back a groan. His dad looked pleased and started grilling his wife about when their son would arrive. He looked eager at the prospect of seeing Harper again soon.

Emerson didn't share their sentiments. Harper had left home almost ten years ago. He had moved to New York City for college and never came home except, of course, for holidays. Harper had studied law with a diligence that was rewarded with high marks and a high-paying job out of college. He kept himself busy with work, going from one case to another. He was careful to regularly call home and talk to their mom and dad, but he showed little interest in making regular visits or talking to Emerson and Kierstyn.

Harper and Emerson had never been close. An eight-year age gap in combination with a distance of several thousand miles meant they had never developed a relationship that could be described as intimate. Visits from Harper were always awkward and stilted as far as Emerson was concerned. Neither of them knew how to speak to the other. To make matters worse, in the past few years, Harper had taken to using women as the topic of choice to create common ground.

The year before last, Harper had cornered Emerson in the den for the most awkward conversation of Emerson's life. Harper had begun by apologizing for his absence and explaining how he felt there was something he should do as Emerson's older brother: pass on the wisdom of experience. Then he had proceeded to give Emerson a long talk about women and sex, giving him advice on how to pick them up, date them, and fuck them. The last topic had ended with a strong warning about safe sex. He had threatened to do Emerson bodily harm if he got a girl pregnant because he didn't wear a condom. Then, to cap it all off, he slapped a large box of condoms in Emerson's lap. If Emerson never had to hear his brother say sentences like "if you let her be on top, it's easier to hit the G-spot" ever again, he'd be eternally happy.

Emerson wasn't at all hesitant to admit that his reluctance to live through another such conversation—or any conversation about women at all—was the strongest reason he wasn't looking forward to Harper's visit.

Unsurprisingly, Emerson found that he couldn't muster up the energy to fake excitement over Harper's impending arrival.

§

Jonah,

Despite what you may mistakenly believe about your gargantuan size, there are actually people who are bigger than you are. In fact, there are a lot of people who are wider than you are, beanpole.

Thanksgiving is coming up soon. Mom's talking about having Natalie and your parents over for dinner next week. She wants to thank them for the help they've been. Your mom's brought more than one casserole over ever since Dad got sick, and Natalie continues to be awesome (if wily), so maybe on Thursday, maybe Saturday. I guess we'll see what your mom says.

Harper called yesterday and said that he's got business in Austin, so he'll be coming by for a visit Thanksgiving weekend. He'll be flying in Sunday and plans to come here Wednesday instead of going home. Mom, of course, is totally excited about it. Dad's pretty happy about it, too, though he's not saying as much as Mom is.

Anyway, back to the old college grindstone.

Happy Thanksgiving, Jonah.

Emerson

§

Emerson,

Re: my gargantuan size: you noticed! But you forget that I have spent a good portion of the last year and a half doing physically demanding jobs. I have graduated from beanpole to stripper pole, at least.

In related news, some girl came up to me on the street yesterday and said, "I love a guy who wears pink shirts!" I always thought I'd be flattered, but she was *scary*.

Elijah (mohawk) has the soul of a poet, Emerson. Probably in a jar in his room somewhere, actually, and probably Byron's, but still. He's real, genuine, and I've met enough people who aren't that that counts for a lot. We're actually going to spend Thanksgiving together volunteering at the local soup kitchen. Say hi to everyone at home for me and tell them I love them.

Jonah

§

HARPER arrived at the house late on Wednesday afternoon. It was weird to think that Harper would be in town for three days without seeing them, but he had insisted that it would be easier to give his family his full attention if the visit waited until after his business was done.

The reunion took place shortly before dinner. Hugs were had, greetings given, and even presents passed out.

Emerson had been uncertain how to react to the brand new iPod Touch. Kierstyn had, of course, squealed and gibbered and hugged Harper before calling him the best big brother ever. Emerson had just been relieved that it wasn't full of porn to further his education.

After the pleasantries, they had all found themselves in the kitchen. Mom had needed to fix supper, and Harper had complained about a dry throat. So Emerson found himself leaning against the counter and listening to an update of Harper's life.

"Tell us about New York. How's the job?" Mom asked.

Harper shrugged in response, digging a cola from the fridge. "Same as always. Not much is new." Harper gave a small smile and patiently answered all of his mother's questions: the job was good; yes, it was very busy; no, he didn't have a girl; and no, he didn't have bad jetlag. After some time, when their mom had begun to slow down, the time between her questions lengthening, Harper gave a smile and said, "Enough about me! Tell me what's new around here!"

"Oh, you know how little things change around here. Emerson and Kierstyn go to school, Dad runs the shop. Hudson Bend isn't as exciting as New York." Their mother smiled, and Harper shrugged. "Besides, you hear about it when we talk on the phone," she added without irony. Emerson guessed she felt she was much more thorough in her reporting.

Harper snorted. "Not everything. You never told me about Em being gay now."

There was silence.

Emerson felt his fingers go numb. He stood there staring at his brother, dumbfounded. How had Harper known? Why had he said anything?

His father broke the silence first with a surprised demand of, "What?" It was followed closely by his mother wanting to know, "What on earth does that mean?"

Harper frowned. "I saw Emerson in Austin with his boyfriend? Well, I thought he was… they were kissing."

"You must have been mistaken," said Mom. "It's been two years since you last saw him; obviously you were mistaken."

"Mom, I know my own brother when I see him," said Harper, sounding exasperated.

"Obviously you don't! Not if you think you saw him kissing a man!"

Emerson's stomach lurched violently at his mother's words.

"Ask him!" Harper waved a hand in Emerson's direction in a wide, sweeping arc. Four sets of eyes turned to regard him. Emerson's throat was suddenly so dry he couldn't swallow. He didn't think he could speak. *Oh God. They know. They all know!* He felt like he might swallow his tongue. Throwing up was also a likely response. He stared back at them, silent.

His lack of protest was damning. His mother went pale and murmured a soft, "Oh," before turning back to cooking the pumpkin for tomorrow's pie.

"Emerson?"

Emerson moved his wide-eyed gaze to his father. He wondered desperately what his father would say. Would he ask Emerson directly if he had been kissing another man in public? He wondered what he would say to that in response. *If* he could talk—Emerson was starting to think he'd misplaced his tongue.

"Wait," said Harper, sounding bewildered. "You really didn't know?"

"Of course we didn't know," Dad snapped. "There's nothing to know. Obviously you were mistaken. Emerson is not gay."

Emerson flinched at that and pressed his body closer to the kitchen counter behind him.

Harper snorted. "Dad, he looks like a deer in the headlights. I think it's safe to say I was right."

His father turned to look at him again. Emerson stared back. "Emerson, don't you have anything to say? Or are you just going to ignore this?"

Emerson opened his mouth, but no words came out. His father turned away from him, seemingly unbothered by his silence. "This is ridiculous. I don't even know why we're having this conversation. Emerson isn't gay! He would have told us! And I know my boy. He wouldn't go around kissing men—anyone—in public. Or get in a relationship without saying anything."

There was a loud squelching noise, and everyone turned to look. Emerson's mom was violently attacking the pumpkin with a potato masher. She seemed unfazed by the noise and apparently didn't notice the attention.

Emerson didn't know what to do about that either.

"Linda?" Emerson saw his father frown at his mother. Then his expression shifted, and he started to talk again. "Calm down, Linda, there's no reason to attack tomorrow's dinner."

Her movements began to slow until they finally stopped, but she didn't loosen her grip on the handle of the masher. She just stood there, silent and still, doing nothing.

Oh God, Emerson thought numbly. *I've broken my mother.*

For a long time there was silence, though it was far from still. Emerson's dad had taken to shifting and gesturing agitatedly. The silence was broken by a sob. Emerson's eyes widened when he saw his mother's shoulders shake. She was crying! Emerson had made his mother cry.

The last time he had seen his mother cry had been during that weepy phase after his dad's heart attack. *Your homosexuality is as awful as a heart attack. It's like near-death, like watching someone almost die,* a bitter voice whispered in his mind. Emerson tried to stamp it down.

"Oh Jesus," murmured Harper. Emerson realized then that he wasn't very successful at shutting the voice up when he got the sudden urge to yell at Harper for spoiling everything. What had given Harper the right to say anything?

Their father shot Harper a dirty look before walking up to his wife. "Linda?"

"I'm sorry!" she gasped. She turned away from the pumpkin, and Emerson could see her in profile then, though her back was now to her eldest and her husband. She lifted her hands to cover her face.

"Linda? Why are you crying?" She took her hands away from her face and moved to wipe the tears from her cheeks. "Emerson's not—" he began again. This time he was cut off.

"Oh, John, don't be a fool. Of course he is—just look at his face." Then, suddenly, everyone turned to look at Emerson once more.

Emerson stared back, uncertain as to what to say or do. What could he possibly say to that?

"Emerson, are you—?" His father didn't so much finish the question as he did start waving his hands around in the air in some incomprehensible way that was, apparently, meant to mean "gay."

"Uh," Emerson managed to get out. They kept staring at him. Apparently this would require an actual answer. "Yes?" he whispered.

Harper snorted. "Are you not sure?"

"Harper!" snapped their mother, and Harper cringed.

"What?" It seemed that Emerson's father had regained his voice after a brief moment of shocked silence. "But—you never said.... Since when?" His eyes were baffled as he stared at his son.

Emerson shifted under the scrutiny. "Uh," he said again. He cleared his throat. His fingers clenched, and he realized he was still holding his water glass. "Since ninth grade." His voice was rough, and his sentence rose slightly at the end, making him sound uncertain once again.

"Ninth?" His father asked. "Since you were fourteen?"

"That was five years ago," his mother whispered. "You didn't tell us for five years?" She turned away from him.

"Uh," said Emerson, not sure what to say to that.

"And is Harper right? Do you have a boyfriend?" His father's voice rose as he asked the question, visibly disconcerted by the prospect.

"No," Emerson blurted. "It was just a date."

"A date," muttered his father. "With another man." He ran his hands over his head before shaking it. "I don't know what to say—what to do about this."

"Do?" Emerson asked, voice small. He remembered then all the stories he had heard of gay teens being tossed out of their house. True, Emerson was nineteen now, an adult, but he needed his parents' money to live and go to school. Without them, his life as he knew it would be completely changed.

His father grunted.

Emerson wanted to ask him if "do" might include tossing his second-born out onto the streets, but he didn't have the courage.

"I don't understand," said Kierstyn suddenly. Emerson jumped; he had forgotten she was there. Judging by the way others reacted, he wasn't the only one.

"Emerson's gay, honey," his mother started to say, but she was interrupted when Kierstyn rolled her eyes and continued.

"I got that—I know what it means, but—" She hesitated, looking uncertain now. "Why are you crying?" She looked genuinely puzzled. "You always said that there was nothing wrong with being homosexual, even if other people said there was. What's the big deal?"

Their mom started to cry harder.

Emerson just stood there, frozen. He wanted to move, but he didn't know where to go. He felt like crying but knew no tears would come.

He wanted to repeat Kierstyn's question. They weren't homophobic, so why were they acting this way? But then, part of him had always guessed they wouldn't react well, or he would have told them years ago.

Emerson felt guilt fill his stomach, causing it to curl. He wished suddenly that he wasn't here, that he was wherever Jonah was.

Emerson looked down and stared at his water glass. He wasn't feeling very thirsty anymore. In fact, he was pretty sure that he wouldn't be able to swallow anything. Turning, he placed the glass on the counter. He didn't fail to notice the way his fingers were trembling. God, he wasn't ready for this. He really wasn't ready to tell them, and he certainly wasn't ready to deal with the fallout.

"This is…." Emerson's dad was talking again. "This is crazy—how can you be—Emerson, how can—" He went on like this for some time, rambling about Emerson and the shock of his being gay, especially lingering on how Emerson had never given them a sign of this before. When he said, "I just don't understand how you could never tell us. You never even gave us a sign," Emerson's mother let out a gasp. Her shoulders were twitching with the force of her tears.

"Christ," Harper murmured, turning away.

Kierstyn, Emerson noted, was also looking distressed. She was biting her lip, and her eyes were shining with tears, but she didn't hesitate when she moved to walk over to him. She stood next to him, and after a moment, she reached out to grip one of his trembling hands in her own. Emerson licked his lips and tried to find his voice to thank her but was able only to mouth the words.

It was then, as he stood clutching his sister's hand while his father kept pacing and gesturing, while his mother cried, and his brother turned his back on them, that the doorbell rang. It was then that Emerson remembered that the Cherneskis were due for dinner.

§

EMERSON wrapped his arms around his legs and buried his face in his knees. He had placed himself on the floor, leaning back against the other side of the bed, using it as a buffer between himself and his bedroom door. As an extra precaution, the door was locked.

He had retreated to his room not long after the Cherneskis arrived. The chaos they had prompted had made the whole situation unbearable for him.

Mr. and Mrs. Cherneski had shown proper concern when they had arrived to find his mother weeping and his father incoherent. It was Kierstyn who had oh-so-helpfully told them the cause. Emerson wasn't upset with her about it, though—despite the wisdom she had shown at holding his hand when he needed the support, she was still only twelve.

Mr. and Mrs. Cherneski had both looked shocked at Kierstyn's blurted announcement and had stuttered in their first attempts at responding. Obviously neither knew how to react to such news.

Emerson sniffed and rubbed his face against the fabric of his jeans. Now that he was alone, the tears were finally coming. He blinked against them, trying to stop them from falling.

He'd been relatively successful at bearing the looks from Mr. and Mrs. Cherneski and at dealing with his parents' distress until Natalie had broken an awkward silence by asking, "Wait, are you all really surprised? You mean you didn't know? I thought we were all just waiting for him to tell us." Emerson had been stunned—*Natalie* knew?

Her remark had been met with similar shock from the others—except for Emerson's mother, who had made a strangled noise before letting out a loud sob and crying in earnest. It was then that Emerson had decided that he could no longer deal with the situation. He had untangled his fingers from Kierstyn's before making his retreat.

Now he was hiding in his bedroom, his door was locked to keep anyone else out, and he really, *really* wanted Jonah.

Jonah, who wasn't here and was unreachable by phone.

Emerson picked up his cell. He hesitated over the contacts. Part of him wanted to phone Zack—the man he always ran to with his problems these days—but he knew Zack would be volatile and indignant, and Emerson didn't want that right now.

He considered Hayley, but she too was likely to get angry at Harper and his parents. What Emerson really wanted was a calming influence. Greg it was, then.

Greg answered with his usual sleepy-sounding, "'Lo?"

"Greg, my life just turned to shit," was Emerson's opener.

There was a pause, then Greg said, "Okay. Tell me what happened."

He did. Emerson recounted the whole evening, ending with, "Mom just started crying harder, and I couldn't take it anymore." Greg had listened in almost-silence, making short comments or noises of sympathy.

"Where are you now?"

"My room. Door's locked."

Greg made a slight snorting sound. "So you're hiding."

"Maybe." Emerson rubbed a hand over his face. "My parents hate me."

"They don't hate you, Em. They're just reeling. Give 'em some time to adjust."

Emerson sniffed.

"Look, Em, I know it seems bad right now, but give them a few days to get used to the idea before you decide that they hate you."

Emerson bit his lip and shifted. "Okay."

"Adjusting to the fact that their baby boy likes to suck cock will take some time," he said. Emerson could hear the smirk. He groaned. He had forgotten that there was a good reason Greg hung out with Zack.

"Feeling calmer now?" Greg asked.

Emerson nodded and then, remembering the phone, grunted an affirmative.

"Good. Now, you pulled me away from apple pie. I like pie. So go and get some sleep. Things will look better in the morning."

Emerson wasn't so sure about that, but he didn't have the energy to argue with Greg. Instead, he said goodnight and hung up.

He stared at his phone for a long minute and wished that he could call Jonah. Thoughts of the other man only made him miss him more. He missed Jonah like crazy—he always did, but right now, he really wished that Jonah were here to hold him and tell him that everything would be okay again.

When the tears threatened to come this time, Emerson couldn't stop them. He gasped and pressed his leaking eyes into his knees, once again wrapping his arms around his legs. Sobs wracked his body and made him shake and tremble.

Some minutes later, when he was able to calm himself, he lifted his face from his knees and uncoiled his arms from his legs so that he could wipe the tears from his cheeks.

It was then that he decided that if he couldn't call Jonah, if the only means of communication he possessed was letters, then he would write Jonah a letter right now.

He leaned over to grab a notebook and pen from his desk and started to write. He'd mail it tomorrow. It wasn't Jonah's voice or arms, but it was all he had, so Emerson would take it.

§

Jonah,

I'm writing this while hiding in my room. The door is locked, and I'm contemplating just staying here until Monday. I can leave for Austin on Monday and just stay there all week. Zack and Greg love me enough to let me live on their couch.

Right, okay, so I should explain instead of rambling so much.

Last Monday night, I had a date. It wasn't serious or anything, but it wasn't the first with this guy, so I let him hold my hand and kiss me a few times. Which turned out to be the biggest mistake ever. I didn't notice him at all, but Harper SAW US. He saw ME on a DATE with another MAN!

Today he showed up, and we're all standing around talking when he suddenly comes out with, "When did Emerson become a fag?" God, everyone went silent, and then Mom and Dad started demanding to know what he meant, and I was just staring at Harper, and then he tells them about seeing me KISSING A MAN!

Mom started crying, and Dad kept rambling, and I couldn't tell what Harper thought. Kierstyn's been awesome, as she's the only one not freaking out.

Things got so much worse, though, because your parents and Natalie showed up for dinner, and we hadn't even set the table yet, and Mom was still crying, and so Kierstyn told them too. I wasn't sure if I should start laughing or crying when Natalie said, "Well, yeah. You didn't know? I thought we were just waiting for him to tell us?" Which made Mom cry even harder.

I ran away after that. Hid in my room. I've been hiding here since. I don't have plans to leave my room anytime soon (midnight snack and bathroom runs don't count as leaving). I don't think I could handle seeing Mom cry again.

I really wish Zack, Greg, and Hayley were in town, but they all went home for the holiday. Fortunately for me (and unfortunately for Greg), I have their phone numbers.

On the upside, your family seemed totally cool about the being into dick thing?

Emerson

CHAPTER 10

Emerson,

I guess it's too late for the "don't panic" and is time for the "oh, shit" already. In other words: dude, that sucks. Are you sure it's as bad as you think? Your parents aren't just surprised? Maybe they just need some time. Give both sisters a hug from me. As for Harper, I don't know what his problem is—he couldn't have talked to you first? What the hell?! I always thought he was a dick. Wish I was wrong, though. Sorry.

If things don't get better at home and Zack and Greg and Hayley get sick of you, which I doubt, and/or you decide you'd be safer out of state, which I also doubt, you know there is always a place for you here. I wish I could come home for you, but I really can't give up the holiday hours, and it's too late now anyway. This sort of thing makes me wish I had a computer. Maybe next time I get something published I'll look into getting a used one.

Anyway—what's happening now? Is everything okay? Did someone punch Harper in the face? Because if not, I volunteer for the honor. What about your parents? They wouldn't throw you out or anything, right?

Write me back ASAP.

Jonah

§

Jonah,

Oh God, it's awful here. Mom and Dad aren't threatening to kick me out, and they say they still love me, but it's like someone died! Mom's still crying—not all the time, but the other day she literally cried over spilled milk. She says she's not angry at me, that she's just feeling emotional, but… she keeps crying like I broke her heart.

Dad's not much better. He keeps starting weird and awkward conversations. One time it was about whether or not I was sure (yes, I am, very, in case you're wondering too) and another was about safe sex. He practically out and out asked me if I've had another guy's cock up my ass. He was all euphemistic about it, but I could tell he was worried that I was out getting shot up with HIV-infected sperm.

Kierstyn, on the other hand, has been awesome. She keeps coming into my room when I'm studying and sitting down with her homework beside me. The other day while I was writing an essay sitting on my bed, she did her math homework curled up next to me. I love her lots right now.

Sorry to disappoint, but Zack called first dibs on beating Harper up. Fortunately for Zack (I really don't want him in jail), he got to the house a day after Harper had left. Still, he practically forced his way into the house and up the stairs to my room. So now Mom seems to think he's my boyfriend. Anytime someone says the name "Zack," she tears up.

Harper seemed to be a little bit sorry about it but pretty much told me that it was my fault for kissing a boy in public and not having told my family yet. He's gone home now, though, so whatever.

Trust me, I gave Natalie a great big hug the next time I saw her. She is my new favorite person.

Still alive and with shelter,

Emerson

§

ON A card attached to a large plastic container of gummy bears:

Em,

I wanted to get you something with the last letter, but it was important that I send it quickly, and I didn't have time. Anyway, happy belated coming out. Or not so happy, I guess, but anyway, have some candy.

I know it sucks right now, but I'm sure it'll get easier. Just hang in there. Your parents love you. They are just really awkward about stuff. It would probably be the same if your brother had walked in on you having sex with a girl or something, only then they'd be worried about babies too. (Just trying to look on the bright side.)

I wasn't wondering, Emerson, but thank you for the not-at-all reassuring mental images. I'd cry if I thought Zack was your boyfriend, too, so cut your mom some slack.

Jonah

P.S. Remind me the next time I move to go to California, please. The weather here is freeze-your-tits-off cold. The snow actually froze Elijah's mohawk the other day.

§

Jonah,

Ugh, don't make jokes about sex with girls or getting them pregnant. One of the beautiful things about being out is that people aren't supposed to keep putting mental images in my brain of girls and sex and me.

Thank you lots for the candy, though. I've been eating it whenever I'm forced to hide in my room.

Hey! Zack is a great person, and I'm offended on his behalf. I could do worse than him for a boyfriend. At least then I'd know that my honor was always safe, what with Zack around to protect it.

Jonah: next time you move, move to California.

Christmas is going to be here soon. I can't believe it's come 'round again. You getting time off this Christmas?

Emerson

P.S. Wow, I am even less sold on the idea of a mohawked boyfriend now. I didn't think that was possible.

§

Emerson,

Sorry, sorry, didn't realize it was such a touchy subject.

I never said Zack wasn't a good guy, just—look at it from your mom's point of view. Zack is a guitar-playing gym bunny for all she knows (from all you've told me, even). Next you'll be telling me he has long hair and an earring. It's no wonder your mom freaked out.

As a side note, I imagine the part where he'd be simultaneously attempting to protect and violate your honor would be frustrating and likely sitcom-level ridiculous.

I do actually have time off for Christmas—well, I've got a three-day weekend, which is almost the same thing and frankly a small miracle considering where I work—but not nearly enough to come home, of course. I'll be spending the holiday with Elijah and his (apparently completely normal) family in Cheyenne, though, so don't worry about me too much, I won't be alone. Besides, I'm still talking to you this year, so it's automatically better than last.

Jonah

§

Jonah,

Not that touchy. But, I'm tired of being told about girls having sex as if I should be participating in it and enjoying it. Can I have a break yet?

Um, Zack does have long hair and an earring? And he's not a gym bunny—he's an athlete. He does kickboxing and teaches self-defense classes once a week. I'm truly regretful if I actually managed to give you the opinion that he's a guitar-playing gym bunny.

Sigh, yes, if you want to interpret honor as a sexual thing then fine, yes, that would be amusing. Though I was thinking more along the lines of wanting to duel anyone that insulted me (i.e. punching Harper). Though given the incident at a bar a few weeks ago during which some random guy started fondling my ass, Zack protects *that* honor too.

Wow, three whole days for Christmas. How will you ever cope with that much time off?

Zack and Hayley are talking about a road trip, and I think I might be able to swing it. Mostly because they're talking about heading to Hayley's, so a bed's not going to cost that much. Hayley is from New Orleans, so I have to say, I'm pretty tempted. They're talking about New Year's, so I'm thinking we might actually do it. Though, nine hours on the road with Zack, Hayley, and Greg? I'll let you know if I survive it.

Emerson

§

Emerson,

You do an extremely thorough job defending your non-boyfriend. Just saying. Don't ask me how I knew about the hair and the earring.

Wow, a road trip? And here I thought you were chained to the house or something. Soon you'll be telling me you're going to Daytona Beach on spring break.

Since I want to move on to California as soon as possible, the three days at Christmas is not a setback by any means. It gives me just enough time to catch my breath before diving back into the drudgery. The good thing is that keeping so busy helps me to use my spare time wisely, and I am getting a ton of writing done. Sorry, I know it drives you nuts when I tease about it, but I'm a little superstitious; I'm afraid I'll jinx it.

Make sure to send me Hayley's address so I can wish you a happy new year.

Jonah

§

WRITTEN in a cheap Christmas card that read "Merry Christ-moose" over a bad drawing of a moose in a scarf and Rudolph's nose:

Jonah,

Why do you make defending Zack sound so suspicious? Like it's an inadvertent declaration of love? As for the hair and earring, if I thought you had a computer, I'd accuse you of Facebook stalking. As it is I guess I'll just have to assume that you're a freak with lucky guesses.

We're just going to New Orleans for New Year's. We'll drive down on the 30th and home on the 2nd. Dad's feeling well enough now to mind things at the store for a few days without my help. Also, did you miss the part where I said we'd be staying at Hayley's parents'? The only expense will be gas and New Year's—Hayley says her mother loves to feed people, so we won't even have to worry about food.

I can't wait to read what you're writing. I'll get to read it the moment it's done, right?

Emerson

§

ATTACHED to a large, heavy package and shipped via UPS on a card depicting a shiny green Christmas tree with raised ornaments:

Dear Emerson,

Merry Christmas (and Happy New Year, in case the card I plan on sending to you at Hayley's doesn't make it there in time).

Vis-a-vis writing and the computer thing—actually, now that you mention it... is the suspense killing you yet? Long story short—or actually not short, actually, it's just over 100,000 words—er. It turns out I'm a novelist after all. I was just checking my mail—literally, I opened your letter and the acceptance letter was behind it with a big fat advance (ok, not that big or fat, but it's money I wasn't expecting). Anyway, I needed a computer to do the required editing, so I went out and bought one of those netbook things with free wireless access for six months. I'll e-mail you from my new address ASAP.

The book should come out sometime this summer. My contract says I'm not allowed to transmit the file electronically to anyone other than the editors, but I'll see if I can get you an advanced reader's copy.

As for your Christmas present—well. It actually is as extravagant as it looks, this time, and I expect you to use it.

Jonah

§

SENT in a large, bubble-lined envelope with a small rectangular box and a folder inside along with another Christmas card.

Jonah,

Oh, wow. Where to begin?

You got a book deal?! I can't believe this! I can't believe you wrote a novel! I can't believe you wrote a novel and didn't tell me, and I can't believe you wrote a novel that's going to be published! That's so exciting. I'm giving you mental hugs and high fives of congratulations.

Though, you are a bitch for not sending me a copy *before* you signed a contract. I will forgive you, but you're a bigger bitch if you don't get me an advanced reading copy. Seriously.

You bought me a *graphics tablet*? This is just awesome. So awesome that I couldn't wait to use it. The gift in the small box was something I bought you a few weeks ago, but I couldn't leave it at that, not when you bought me a tablet, so I made you some stuff. Nothing special, but I just thought you might like to see your present in action.

I suppose now would also be a good time to mention how much use this gift will get in the new year. After way too many hours spent down in the academic advisory and registrar offices, I am now an art student. I am the newest member of the design program. I took a few courses last summer and last term that they're willing to count toward the degree and to advance me to second-term freshman status.

Merry Christmas, Jonah!

And Happy New Year! I'll send you a card from New Orleans.

Emerson

§

Emerson,

The pen is seriously awesome. In ten years when I am a famous and highly paid author I will tell everyone it's because I wrote everything in the fountain pen you gave me, and all the other famous highly paid authors will be jealous and try to steal the fountain pen mojo, but I will have hidden it away somewhere safe because of course it is too important to go in a desk drawer or something equally asinine.

It's entirely possible I've had too much eggnog.

Congrats on the art program thing! Knew you could do it. Obviously you've been practicing if the stuff you sent me is any indication.

I am actually e-mailing you from Cheyenne! We are heading back early tomorrow (the 26th) and everyone else is in bed, but I couldn't sleep. (The room is spinning. Again with the eggnog. Thank God for spell check.)

Anyway, since my choices seem to be sign off or hurl on my keyboard, I'm going to end this letter and pray it doesn't say something really embarrassing.

Jonah

§

Jonah,

Fountain pen mojo? If this is you on eggnog, we need to feed it to you more often.

Thank you. I'm looking forward to taking lessons in art history over economic history.

It's nice that you have a computer now so that we can communicate in real time (I'm still sending you a post card from New Orleans, FYI), and you are right, it would be best not to damage your new toy by puking all over it. Just saying.

I think it's time to go to bed. Yes, I know it's only nine, but I'm exhausted. Because I am an awesome brother, I took Kierstyn and Natalie out for a day of post-Christmas sale fun. I am vastly underappreciated, as I've received little sympathy for how much my feet suffer. Parents weren't nearly grateful enough considering I saved them from Boxing Day hell.

Tired and sore,

Emerson

§

Emerson,

Oh God, what did I say to you? I told you, you should never let me near alcohol.

It looks like I'll be heading to California the third week in January, much sooner than I anticipated. Elijah isn't going to be thrilled, but I don't think he'll be very surprised either.

You courageous soul, braving the insanity of the mall on Boxing Day. What were you thinking? That way lies madness.

Anyway, happy new year.

Jonah

§

Jonah,

Only that you were going to rule the world of popular fiction with the power of your pen mojo.

California is sunny—I think you'll find it much preferable to Wyoming.

Unfortunately I was only thinking that I was an awesome big brother, and I wasn't thinking about the reality of what I had signed up for.

In other news, Mom came home from the mall yesterday with a copy of *Family Secrets: Gay Sons, a Mother's Story* and *Straight Parents, Gay Children: Keeping Families Together*. She was last seen clutching at *Family Secrets* and crying. At least she's now crying because of other people's gay children?

We're leaving for New Orleans tomorrow, so the next you hear from me may be via snail mail from Louisiana.

Emerson

§

SENT via snail-mail to Emerson at Hayley's New Orleans address:

one paper party hat with pink cellophane pom-pom

one lurid purple noisemaker

one marzipan pig

one blue plastic toy dragon

one singing New Year's card ("Auld Lang Syne")

one roll of Mentos

Dear Emerson,

Happy New Year! Hopefully nine hours in a car with three normal people won't have damaged your fragile nonsensibilities too much. (I am an author now, and I get to make up words if I want to. So there.)

Included are all the necessary items for an excellent New Year's celebration (minus some champagne because apparently you can't be trusted around alcohol either). I was going to include a condom, but given your last drunken sexual encounter, that seemed like a bad idea.

Anyway, enjoy.

Jonah

§

WRITTEN on the back of a postcard with the picture of a donkey on it:

Jonah,

Oh look, I found your picture on a postcard in New Orleans.

Went partying on New Year's. Got drunk.

Lost most of the package; Hayley ate the Mentos.

Happy fucking New Year.

Emerson

§

IN EMERSON'S e-mail three days later, with no subject line: a picture of a donkey with a badly drawn-on frown.

§

THE day after that:

So, I deserved that. I'm sorry, Emerson. I didn't mean to imply—whatever the hell it is I implied. I just shouldn't send you letters immediately after messy breakups, apparently.

I know it's a crap excuse. Believe me, I would take it back if I could.

J.

§

Jonah,

I shouldn't read letters while hung over, I guess. Your joke wouldn't have been very funny while sober, but it packed more of a punch while ill. How about we agree to never mention such things again?

Now stop pouting and no more puppy dog eyes.

Emerson

§

Emerson,

Capital idea. This thing where we get mad at each other is frankly balls.

So, other than, you know—how was the trip?

J

§

Jonah,

I don't like it much either.

The trip was good. Hayley's mom gave us way too much food to eat. So… we had too much to drink and too much to eat. We went partying on the town—and whatever you do, spend New Year's in New Orleans at least once. I took loads of pictures; I attached a few to the e-mail. Just don't tell Hayley you've seen that third one; she threatened bodily harm if I showed it to anyone else.

Classes start in a few days; I get to do my first term in Design.

Emerson

§

Emerson,

So, sounds (and looks!) like you had a good New Year's at least. Word to the wise, don't break up with your boyfriend three days before New Year's Eve; it makes for a shitty celebration.

You must be excited for your new term. I've been using my shiny new Internet access to find myself a place in California that isn't a dump. A job would be a good bonus. It's a bit challenging since I don't know exactly where I want to go yet. Maybe San Francisco. After all, why not?

So, are you finally going to come visit me when I make it somewhere warm?

Jonah

§

Jonah,

I could have told you that—breaking up always makes days shitty.

San Francisco, eh? Good idea—after all, where else should you go?

Your homes not being warm enough has never been the problem, but rather how far away you are. When am I supposed to make the journey out to San Fran? How am I supposed to pay for it?

So Dad just came to talk to me. Asked me if I had a boyfriend. Then he said he was tired of guessing what was going on in my life now, so if we could go back to talking to each other like normal again, he'd be happy. Then he cried. Which wasn't so great, because I'm tired of crying parents, but the first part was good.

So it looks like I've got a dad again. Not sure about Mom, but she's still reading those books.

Emerson

§

Emerson,

Are you implying something? Technically speaking I suppose you're just stating it outright. That's okay, though, I think I'll like San Francisco. I have a couple of part-time jobs lined up—one doing children's programs at a library and one as a barista—don't laugh—and I officially have an apartment. Between the jobs and the writing/editing, I'll be a very busy boy, which suits me just fine. I have decided to retire from romance (Elijah mailed me a dead fish. A DEAD FISH, Emerson. It would turn anyone off of love, I promise you).

I will sell my kidney on the black market if that's what it takes to get you here, Emerson. Of course, I'll probably die of sepsis while I wait. You let me know when you can come, and we'll work something out.

I knew your parents would come around. Although of course this opens the door for all sorts of awkward new conversations.

Jonah

§

Jonah,

Wow, children's programs and barista? You're going to be tired all the time, I think. Is there anything more demanding than children or coffee drinkers waiting for their coffee?

A dead fish? What did you do to the poor man? A dead fish is pretty spiteful.

I'd rather you didn't sell your kidney or die of sepsis. I don't know, Jonah. I still have school to consider as well. We'll see.

None of the conversations yet to come can be as bad as the "are you a gay slut getting infected with STIs?" conversation with Dad from before.

Classes started this week. I have a studio space. A place where I can do art. I'm going to bankrupt myself over the next few months buying art supplies, but I don't care. I have a studio. True, it's in the middle of a large room surrounded by many other students who are doing art and making a lot of noise, but I don't care.

Emerson

§

Emerson,

Barista = free coffee. I'll be fine.

I don't know—it's not like Elijah didn't know I was going to move somewhere else and break up with him. I was honest with him from the start. I didn't mean to break anyone's heart! (If I even did. He might just be bitter.)

You don't have to let me know right away. I'm planning on staying in California for a while. You have all summer to visit me. Maybe we can learn to surf!

No conversation can ever be as bad as the STI conversation. Well, unless you actually did have one. That would probably be worse. Actually, now that I think of it, there are a whole bunch of worse conversations. Let's change the subject.

Sounds like you're really enjoying the design program. I won't say I told you so, but we both know it's implied. I'm thinking if I like California as much as I think I'm going to I might apply to a creative writing program for the fall. It's never too late, right? (You can say you told me so, too, if you want. It's only fair.)

Jonah

P.S. Check out the link to my fancy new future apartment!

§

Jonah,

Well, if you get free coffee….

Re: Elijah: This is what you get for dating a guy with a mohawk.

So you'll be in California for a while then. I see you're still impractical—all summer? I can't leave for an entire summer.

Ugh. Now you've put unhappy thoughts in my head. Thankfully there were no STIs, and let's leave it at that. Mom, though, made her own attempt at awkward conversations today. Asked me if I had a boyfriend. When I said no, she then proceeded to make inquiries about Zack and Greg and did I maybe want either of them to be my boyfriend. It took a while to convince her that I had no romantic interests.

Design is awesome. Much better than business. And yes, I promise not to say I told you so if you won't.

Emerson

P.S. Nice place. It looks so sunny.

§

Emerson,

Lesson learned, my friend. Lesson learned.

Why couldn't you leave for the whole summer? You could crash here, get a job, a real, crappy, college-student job with no responsibility. Anyway I wasn't inviting you for the whole summer. I was inviting you for any time during the summer. Not that I'd object if you wanted to live with me for a couple of months, but sleeping on my couch might eventually get old.

Your mom has good instincts. High five her for me. I'd lament your lack of prospects, but it's kind of nice to have someone to commiserate with about the whole celibacy thing.

Downloaded the application package for USF's English writing program last night. It's not ideal, but hey, the credits will probably transfer, and it's the experience I want anyway, not the letters.

Jonah

§

Jonah,

Because Dad couldn't do without me for the whole summer. I'm not sure I could excuse being away for a week.

Good instincts? For suspecting me of liking Zack or Greg? Or perhaps for being against my dating either of them?

Commiserate about celibacy? I feel no need to complain about that. I'd rather complain about the lack of men who want to date in Austin. Somehow I doubt you'll be having greater dating issues in *San Francisco* than I will in Texas.

USF, huh? Should be good. At least you'll get to meet other aspiring writers.

I've got to go. Hayley's here and complaining that I'm not ready to go. She says I spend too much time in the studio, so she's come to take me for lunch.

Emerson

Jonah! I stole the computer. Don't believe a word this boy says about me! When do I get to meet the sexy best friend, then? - Hayley :)

§

Emerson,

Sorry, I'm a bit scattered. My flight leaves in a couple of hours, and I'm still packing, but I wanted to catch you before I left.

I understand about your parents needing you at the store. I still wish you could come visit, though. Plenty of men to date in San Fran... or so I've heard, anyway. Not that I'll be partaking in the many charms I am sure they have to offer. I'll probably be too busy between working and writing anyway.

The trouble will come when I meet aspiring writers and have to try very hard not to lord my published-ness over their heads. Depending on what sort of reviews the book gets, I suppose. Hrm, maybe I should have used a pseudonym. Oh well.

Tell Hayley I said hello and flexed my bicep just for her—I've got to shove this into the bag and get to the airport, or I'm screwed!

Jonah

§

Jonah,

So have you made it to San Fran yet?

I don't think I want to go to San Fran for a date. Especially since I'd only be getting a few days with you as it is. We'll see about my going.

So you're serious about this not dating thing then? Never going to fall in love again? (I now have Costello stuck in my head… darn, Mom's music.)

Speaking of your published-ness, when do I get to read this book? How long do I have to wait? Two months? Six? Twelve?

Ugh! I can't believe Hayley. She totally distracted me, then sat on my lap and kept me too far away from my laptop to stop her from editorializing and sending that e-mail. I will not tell her you flexed a bicep just for her—it will go to her head, and she will be insufferable (well, more so than she already is).

Did my first photography assignment. We had to experiment with movement. Here's my final print.

Emerson

§

Hey Em,

All settled in. It may be premature of me to say so, but I am never leaving.

Working at the library is pretty cool. I have really young kids three days during the week for an hour and a half at a time, so I usually read them a story, and then we do some kind of craft. Then whcn thcy'rc gonc, I put away any books that have been returned or whatever else needs doing, then at three we have a teen book club. We are never reading *Twilight.* Ever. Anyway, I've only worked two shifts so far, but it's pretty great. I'm already planning on trying to con them into paying me to do a writer's workshop.

As for love—I don't know about never again. Just not right now. When the right person comes around, I'll let you know.

I haven't even got the first edit yet, so I don't know when I'll have an advance reader's copy to send you. June, maybe? You will know as soon as I know.

Your final print has just become my first wall decoration in California. You should be proud.

Jonah

P.S. Attached is a crappy picture of my flexing bicep. You can keep it for yourself or give it to Hayley, whatever.

§

Jonah,

Well, it's good to hear that you like it there. Oh man, they told you to do story time? It's a wonder you ever leave the library! No *Twilight*? What, you don't want to have to engage in epic Jacob vs. Edward battles? What's wrong with you?

You know… that's generally what happens with love. You wait around until the right person comes along.

Glad to hear someone liked my print. Don't know what the professor thinks of it yet.

Re: picture. I'm not giving it to Hayley. And what happened to the beanpole? No way were your biceps that huge when you left here.

I'm in the studio again at the moment, taking a break from my latest assignment. They gave me clay, Jonah. Clay! And told me to make something with it. What am I supposed to make with clay?

Emerson

§

Emerson,

I'm thinking now I might as well write a kids' book. Up to some illustration work? I know it's not exactly the animated movie we used to dream of doing, but it could be fun.

Any teenager who shows up with an Edward or Jacob T-shirt is automatically required to read the first six chapters of *Wuthering Heights*. That usually puts them back in their place pretty quickly.

I'm sure you'll do fine on your assignment. You'll have to send me the next one, too, because my walls are still pretty bare. Or a picture of it, I guess, if you're making it out of clay. Can you make it look like Stretch Armstrong? (That is really the only G-rated suggestion I have for you, man, you know me better than to ask for advice on that! Unless you want to make a model of my bicep.)

Spent all of today learning how to make girly coffee drinks. Just what I needed—caffeine AND sugar. If I spontaneously combust tell my mom I love her.

Jonah

§

Jonah,

Send me a copy of a manuscript for a children's book, and I'll see what I can do. Though I make no promises, considering I don't even know what the book is about.

Haha! *Wuthering Heights*? Forcing classic lit down their throats? Ah, nosy Kierstyn has just informed me about the book's significance. One question: how do *you* know what Bella's favorite book is?

Um, there will be no Stretch Armstrong or bicep sculptures. Nor will there be R-rated sculptures. I don't care what Eve is doing, I'm not making a cock.

Oh God! Who thought it would be a good idea to give *you* coffee and sugar? I lament that anyone liked this idea. I also wonder at the mental health of whoever allowed this to happen.

Anyway, I've got to go. Zack is dragging us out to a bar tonight to watch him and Greg sing, so I've got to get this reading done. Art theory, here I come.

Emerson

§

Emerson,

Sorry for the tardy reply. Worked a double Thursday, then again yesterday. Saturday I didn't have to work at the shop, but I gave myself a tour after the library to acquaint myself with the area. Seriously, you should visit. You'd love it here.

Let me brainstorm for a bit on the book, and I'll get back to you. I have a couple of ideas, but I want to flesh them out a bit first.

The story with *Wuthering Heights* is this: actually a teenage girl asked me for it when I was working the help desk, explained its significance, and then came back an hour later with a very unhappy expression. It was so hard not to laugh in her face.

Well if you're not making a muscleman or a dick, what else is left? The Alamo? Seriously, Emerson. ;)

Re: coffee and sugar. This is why I did a phone interview. They couldn't see me twitching. And it's too late to fire me now, I already have all the regulars' orders memorized. Besides, Katie, the manager, is even more of a spaz than I am. So there.

Enjoy your studying! I am going to go up onto the rooftop to watch the sun sink into the bay. Wish you were here.

Jonah

§

Jonah,

Take as long as you want on the brainstorming. I'm not sure I'll be able to do any illustrating until the summer. I'm so busy with assignments that I barely have free time, and when I do, I'm not very eager to do *more* art.

And here I thought you were sneaking glances at *Twilight* in your free time. Or, perhaps, like Zack, you had made the mistake of dating a girl who's into it. (She lasted all of one weekend, and Zack ranted for about two weeks at how the book was rotting people's brains. He says she told him he could never hope to be as wonderful as Edward Cullen. This is apparently enough to wilt even Zack's… ardor.)

I am not sculpting the Alamo. We had to pick an emotion: desire, fear or jealousy. I sculpted this (the attached picture) instead. I stayed up late last night finishing it so that it could be ready to hand in in a few days.

It's time for me to go. The timer is about to go on the oven, and I have hungry people to feed. Seriously, when Hayley, Zack, and Greg are waiting for food, things can get ugly.

Emerson

§

Emerson,

I can definitely have something ready to illustrate by the summer, and I totally commiserate about the lack of free time. I wouldn't have time for a date right now even if I wanted one.

Thank you again for the unnecessary visual re Zack's ardor. Though I totally sympathize with him over the *Twilight* freaks. Two of the girls in the book club have asked me out, and one of the others is flirting pretty shamelessly. It's... "off-putting" isn't a strong enough word, but "disgusting" seems too far. Creepy, maybe? Yeah. As in they make me feel like an old man. Debating simply telling them I am gay, but with these girls, who knows, that might just encourage them. After all, unattainable is what they are looking for.

Anyway, speaking of creepy, printed the picture of your sculpture—very cool by the way—and hung it over my bed. Mind you, my apartment is so tiny that pretty much anywhere I put it would've been over the bed, unless I hung it in the bathroom, but still. I am not sure I see fear or jealousy OR desire—I mean the last one, yeah, a little bit, but not *primarily* that. It's something else. Yearning, maybe, the way they're reaching for each other. (Apparently I shouldn't have had that wine with dinner. Sorry. I'll shut up now.)

Jonah

§

Jonah,

I've escaped the studio and have about five minutes to write you before I have to go to bed and then again to the studio. I've been so busy recently that I haven't even brought the computer to the studio; it's too distracting.

Well, I'm eager to see what kind of children's book you would write. And to have enough time to draw for it.

Hey, if I have to suffer through such stories about Zack, then you should join me!

Book club girls? Aren't they all teenagers? Jonah, are you attracting sixteen-year-old girls? You dog, robbing the cradle! I suspect you're right about them wanting someone unattainable—at least judging from the way Kierstyn crushes on one celebrity after another. These days she seems set on marrying a Jonas brother—though which one seems to change every other day.

My sculpture's also on the wall? Maybe I should stop sending you pictures, or soon your whole apartment will be filled with nothing but. I hadn't intended to include any fear or jealousy in the sculpture, though I suppose both could also be inferred (as my art prof loves to say). She seems to agree with you, by the way. Congratulated me on creating a piece that incorporated all three emotions.

I think it's bedtime now. Must sleep.

Emerson

CHAPTER 11

NOW

BY THE following Wednesday, Emerson was a prime example of human misery and piteousness. Other than a Friday shift at the store and dinner with his mother, he hadn't left the house. Actually, Emerson had rarely left his room. It was noon already, and he wasn't yet showered. Shifting on his bed, Emerson curled his blankets tighter around himself. He resettled and kept watching *The Princess Bride*.

Emerson had watched it and *The Jungle Book* several times over the past few days. Both films were favorites from his childhood and both were among the first things he pulled out when feeling low. The only things that came close to making him feel better when he was this sad were the film he had worn out on VHS when he was five or the dread pirate in black, who was his first crush at ten.

Westley and Inigo Montoya were fencing with foils and words on his laptop screen when there was a knock on his door.

"Em-er-son!" Hayley's shout came through his bedroom door. She knocked three times before opening his door and bouncing in. She didn't hesitate as she crossed the room and settled herself on the bed. "I've missed you, darling." She kissed his cheek. Hayley had been out of town for several weeks visiting her parents. Emerson was glad she was back, especially now, as she was curled up against him, a warm, comforting weight.

"Are you watching *The Princess Bride* again? Honey, what's wrong?" She looked around the room. She took in the clothes on the floor, the dishes on the desk, and then finally Emerson, unshowered and in his glasses, flannel pants and last night's T-shirt. "Darling, where's Jonah? Why are you moping?"

"I think Jonah and I… broke up."

"What?!" Hayley jerked up so she could lean back and get a look at Emerson's face. "Excuse me? You *think* you and Jonah broke up? I'm sorry, did you just tell me that the wonder couple *broke* up?" Emerson pouted and didn't respond. "And what do you mean by 'I think'?"

"We had a really bad fight."

"'Really bad fight'? What does that mean?"

"I—it was bad. Jonah moved out without saying anything. He's living with Natalie—she texted me."

"Jonah moved out without telling you, and his little sister had to tell you where he is." She stared at him. "Jonah is giving you the silent treatment? *Jonah?* Your boyfriend Jonah? The boy who is so madly in love with you he thinks you're the greatest thing to ever walk the earth, who wrote a book for you? That Jonah?"

"Yes?" Emerson shifted again and watched Westley engage in a battle of wits with Vizzini.

"Emerson?"

"What?"

"Tell me what happened."

"I—I ran into his old girlfriend, and I…."

"*Emerson*, what did you do?"

"I ran into his old girlfriend and her son. He looked just like Jonah, and I may have freaked out and asked Jonah if it was his."

There was a long pause, and then Hayley said in a voice that was very calm, "So let me get this straight: you see his ex-girlfriend and her kid, then you go home and accuse your boyfriend of lying to you for four years about getting his girlfriend pregnant and having a child?"

"Maybe?"

"That's a pretty big lie to accuse him of. That's not an 'oops, I forgot to mention I have a stamp collection' kind of lie. 'I forgot to tell you about my kid' is a big one!"

"I know! I just… I guess I figured if he found out when we weren't talking…."

"Oh, like that makes it okay? Shit, Emerson, you told him that you don't trust him! That you think he can lie like this to you, that he doesn't love you enough to tell you he has a kid! Kids don't go away, they stick around, and not telling your significant other you have one when you're together for a year would be a shitty thing to do. And you said he did that?"

Emerson bit his lip. "I didn't think…."

"Obviously not, since that was a pretty stupid thing to do! God. I didn't know you could *be* that dumb."

Emerson shifted, curled tighter, and hugged himself. "Don't yell, Hayley. I know picking a fight was stupid."

"I'll yell if I God damn well want to! Someone *should* yell at you! Picking a fight wasn't the stupidest part—thinking Jonah could lie in the first place was!" She ignored his pout. "God, it's like I don't even know you! I know you're a head case, Emerson, but this is whole new levels of fucked up. Seriously! What is your damage?"

Emerson turned to her with wide hurt eyes. Okay, that wasn't fair.

Hayley just made an exasperated noise. "Don't even, Emerson!" Then she was tossing her hands in the air and standing up. "I can't even…." Hayley made another noise before she stormed out of the room to the sound of Buttercup shouting, "Do you promise not to hurt him?!"

Emerson stared after her. Now Hayley was mad at him too. Great.

In the silence that followed, Emerson was left staring blankly at the screen. Hayley was right; he was an idiot who had picked the fight that chased away his "one true love." Emerson stared at Buttercup and Westley for a moment and then closed his laptop. He couldn't stand it anymore.

Emerson had been one of those people who actually found true love. He had found that one person made for him, and he had ruined it. He'd been so stupid to think Jonah would lie about having a kid. Jonah would never keep a secret like that from him, despite everything else in their lives. God, how could he have been so dumb to forget that?

Oh God! Emerson was a complete moron! And now he'd spend the rest of his life lonely because Jonah had run away from him! Again! Emerson had already got him to come home once—he wasn't sure if Jonah would do it again.

By the time Zack found him, Emerson was crying again, silent tears slowly sliding down his cheeks.

"Shit. You need to stop the waterworks."

"Zack, I'm an idiot!"

Zack sighed. "Not that I'm arguing with you, but why?"

Emerson wiped at his face. "Hayley's right! I'm neurotic. I chased away Jonah—the love of my life—with my neuroses!"

"Okay, Emma. Take a breath, you drama queen." Zack settled himself on the bed next to Emerson and wrapped an arm around his shoulder. "I won't argue the point. What you did was all kinds of stupid, but this isn't unfixable. Jonah will forgive you if you apologize. That boy thinks you hung the moon. He adores you, Emma, which is why I didn't hurt him for hurting you, and which is also why he'll take you back if you give him good cause."

"What if he doesn't?"

"He will." Zack's voice was firm and confident.

"But what if he doesn't?"

"Then he'll die in a pit of despair and self-loathing much like this one, I imagine. Your co-dependency will kill you both in the end."

"Great pep talk." Emerson gave a weak chuckle.

"Thanks. I try."

§

THEN

Emerson,

Don't forget to give yourself a break just because you're now studying in a program you actually like.

I'm starting to flesh out the children's story—how are you with drawing cartoonish dogs? I seem to remember some pretty good doodles from back in the day, but everyone gets rusty, I suppose.

Oh that Kevin Jonas, he's so dreamy. </sarcasm> Seriously, what is wrong with girls today? Bethany, one of my book club kids, tried to slip me her MySpace page address inside the cover of a novel she was returning. Maybe I'll stop taking showers for a while. That should help, right? (I burned the address, in case you were wondering.)

Don't you dare stop sending me pictures. I still have white wall space! And I can't afford to paint yet. Maybe after my first royalty payment. The point being, keep the pictures coming. I'm thinking of creating a shrine. Should have known you'd still be a teacher's pet.

Jonah

§

Jonah,

I give myself breaks. Just, usually they are breaks at Zack and Greg's. There is food there. Also, frequently guitars in the evening.

How do I feel about cartoon dogs?

[Here, Emerson inserted a doodle of a long-legged shaggy dog with floppy ears and enormous brown eyes.]

Pish, rusty.

Meh, it could be worse than Kevin Jonas. Though seriously—her MySpace page? How very bold of her. Also, I'm a bit creeped out. Do you suppose she'd give it to a teacher she had a crush on too? (Oh I was wondering, though I figured that you had kept it, enshrined it, and then joined her friends list....)

Fine, I will help you fill up the wall space. Though this time around, you will have to make do with the dog.

I better run before Zack tries to steal my laptop. He's very touchy about my using it while I'm at his place.

Emerson

§

Emerson,

That dog looks suspiciously familiar. Nonetheless, he has taken up residence on the refrigerator door. I brought a copy to the shop to show Katie, but then I accidentally left it as a bookmark in the book we're reading in teen book club. Big mistake. I thought it couldn't get worse after the MySpace thing. I am debating asking Katie to make an appearance as my fake girlfriend, but I am secretly terrified of what she might ask me to do in return. She's kinda diabolical.

Re: Jonas brothers. Girls are so fickle. Natalie wanted to marry you when she was about eleven. Don't tell her I said that, though, she'll be so embarrassed. But you were so nice to her when none of my other friends would give her the time of day, and she was an awkward kid. Of course she had a crush on you.

First edit has arrived! I will have a few weeks to work on it, and then I'll send it back. That means I should have a proof a couple of months later. Publication date is creeping up on me!

Jonah

P.S. I am ignoring your jailbaity comments.

When Emerson opened the e-mail and read the line about Natalie, he turned bright red. The next time he saw Natalie, the blush was just as fierce. He never told Jonah about either time.

§

Jonah,

I have no idea what you could possibly mean—that dog is a work of my imagination and shouldn't resemble any other dog out there.

Why not just tell the girls you're gay and taken? At least then they will stop asking you out, even if the staring and eyelash fluttering won't end.

God, you liar. Natalie did not have a crush on me! Don't say such things, as I'd like to be able to face her again someday.

I can't believe you're having a book published. You do realize that when it is, I'll be telling everyone I know that my best friend wrote a novel, right??

New picture for you. I somehow found the time to go on the last photo club outing. We went to a park nearby, and I snapped this photo. Lucky it was such a rainy day to make the picture turn out so well.

Right, dinner time, got to run. Everyone (i.e. me) is home tonight, so family dinner.

Emerson

P. S. Now why would you ignore my jail bait comments?

§

Emerson, the dog has dimples; I don't know who you think you're kidding.

Your wish is my command. I told them I'm in a long-distance relationship with another man, which is totally true. It happens to be friendship only, but they don't need to know that little detail. Of course, just as I predicted, this has only made me more interesting, and now they want to know if we send each other naughty e-mails.

This is all your fault.

Natalie used to doodle "Mrs. Emerson Blackburn" on her school notebooks. Swear to God. Don't worry, she's over it now.

This picture went over the desk in the office area. I like it. It's whimsical. Maybe I'll write a fantasy next.

Jonah

§

Jonah,

I fail to see what's so special about dimples. Lots of people—er, dogs—have dimples.

Oh dear. I suppose the term "long-distance" didn't help much, as the relationship with me seems just as whimsical as the one they've imagined themselves in with you. Cough. Seriously? Naughty e-mails? I think maybe you need to bring in an e-mail from this boyfriend in which he writes about, in great detail, the current weather patterns of Austin.

It is not my fault you can't convince a bunch of sixteen-year-old girls not to be in love with you.

I am totally ignoring this comment about Natalie, who never had a crush on me.

No photo today. Too tired of looking at my own shots. Just spent the last few days working with my pictures, trying to find the best ones to work with, and then giving them digital facelifts. Over 48 hours on PhotoShop is a bitch. Results are awesome, though. It might have been worth it. Ask me tomorrow.

Emerson

§

Emerson,

You're a shitty liar, even by e-mail. It's disgraceful, really.

Well—what's the weather like in Austin, then? I expect a thorough report. Don't skip on the adjectives.

Hey, remember that one summer when Natalie "tripped" and spilled her lemonade all over your shirt so that my mom would wash it? Yeah. I am not the only one who makes inappropriate people fall in love with them. (By unanimous vote, we are now reading *Someday This Pain Will Be Useful To You* in teen book club. Since my big gay declaration, I have a new problem. We have one boy in the TBC. I bet you can guess.)

Still plenty of wall space that needs to be filled up here. Meanwhile, I am debating taking surfing lessons. They have three-day classes in the summer, but space is booking up. What do you say, want to learn something new?

Jonah

Emerson could remember that day. Natalie had had the worst timing ever, as it had happened only shortly after Emerson realized, one, that he was very gay and that was just the way he was, no denying or escaping or changing it, and two, he was kind of totally desperately in love with Jonah Cherneski. Being forced, by Jonah, to strip had been mortifying.

On the other hand, Emerson still had the T-shirt he'd "borrowed."

§

Jonah,

I haven't the faintest idea what you're talking about.

I am ignoring your attempts to get me to remember that painfully embarrassing afternoon at your house. Instead: so you're now reading LGBT teen lit? Those wily kids of yours. Though after looking the book up on Amazon, I can't help but notice that you picked a book in which the teen gets in great trouble for setting his sights on an older man. Kudos, I guess. So, did the gay love confession draw the boy to the group? Has he joined in hopes of meeting a hot young gay man?

Another picture, just for you. Recognize the skyline?

Surfing lessons? Okay. When?

Emerson

P.S. Because I am awesome I'm sending along a second e-mail just for your book club to enjoy. Though please avoid sharing my e-mail address.

§

EXCERPTS from the excruciatingly boring "love" e-mail:

My darling, dearest love,

As it has been so long since you've last been to Austin, I felt the need to remind you of how wonderful it is….

Last night it rained for a very long time. At around five o'clock local time, it started to drizzle. It picked up speed soon enough, however, and by six o'clock we had a full thunderstorm. There was lighting and thunder that lasted for a full forty-four minutes. The rain itself lasted well into the night. Though it didn't pour for longer than two and a half hours, it did rain well past eleven. I can't tell you exactly when it stopped, as I went to bed....

As you know, it's often very sunny and warm here. Just last week we had unseasonably warm weather, the high often reaching up to eighty degrees when usually it doesn't much travel past seventy this early in the year....

Anyway, that's what my week has been like. How's the weather down in San Francisco?

Sincerely,

Your Love.

Emerson

§

REALLY? YOUR'E COMING?

Jonah

§

LATER:

Emerson,

Ok, so now that I have more than thirty seconds on my break at the library:

REALLY? YOU'RE COMING? AWESOME.

Obviously you're thinking sometime after April. School, and thus TBC, goes until the middle of June, and then I have a week off at the library before we start the more hours-intensive summer programs. If you can wait 'til, say, the 21st, I'll be all yours for ten days or so. Let me know, and I'll book our class for that week.

I read your letter at TBC, and I think it might actually have worked. They now think I am the most boring (and celibate) person in the world. Success! Of course, the part that sucks is that they're half-right, but I'm not complaining.

The boy has been part of TBC from the beginning. Originally I thought he was very clever and was using it as a way to get girls. Obviously my gaydar is completely useless when I'm not dating.

Your latest work of art is awesome, Em, and the quality was high enough that I was able to get a decently sized print out of it. Framed it and everything. You'll have to sign it when you visit.

Jonah

§

Jonah,

Yeah, I'm coming. I talked to Mom about it, and she says it's no problem. It shouldn't be too difficult to get a flight from Austin to San Francisco. I'm looking into it now.

I can't believe you actually read that God-awful e-mail to them. Seriously, if they believed that, then I despair of them. If they think that you could ever be involved with someone so boring, they don't know you at all.

Wow. Your gaydar is useless. Possibly completely broken. I feel very bad for you now. How did you ever manage two boyfriends?

Sign a photograph? You are very strange. I'm not sure that that is standard protocol with photography.

Emerson

§

Emerson,

Sweet! Send me your flight details so I can make sure to meet you at the airport. Is there anything special you want to see or do while you're here, or should I plan the itinerary myself?

Teenagers are very gullible. I shudder to think of the stupid things I probably believed about being a grown-up back in the day. Besides, it serves me very well if they think I'm boring. Even Morgan (the TBC boy) is starting to look elsewhere—I caught him making out with one of the library pages the other day, so that's one less heart I'm breaking.

I managed two boyfriends by being completely charming until they asked me out, therefore the useless gaydar did not adversely affect my chances. Eventually they just couldn't help themselves and had to throw themselves at me. They had no chance, really.

What do you do with photographs if not sign them? Watermark? Too late for that, already printed.

Anyway, I have to go—TBC in ten minutes!

Jonah

§

Jonah,

Ticket bought! Follow linkage to flight details.

Are they really that gullible? I suppose they are if Morgan is making out with library pages. Then again, it could all be part of a plot to make you ridiculously jealous. (Are you? Did you fly into a jealous rage and break up the make-out session?)

I'm not sure I believe that you can so completely charm men into falling over themselves to ask you out.

It just seems silly to sign a photograph like it was a painting, is all.

More illustrations to inspire your kids' book writing—two dogs this time.

Emerson

§

Emerson,

Awesome. I just booked our spot in the surf school. Don't forget to pack your sunscreen. You know how you get.

I am not sure if Morgan is gullible or just horny. He is a teenager, after all. I did no such thing as fly into a jealous rage to break up the make-out session. Actually, I may have attempted to steer people away. It's nice to see Morgan coming out of his shell a bit. Er. Pretend that didn't sound absolutely filthy, will you?

You will have to wait 'til you are here, and then you will see me in action. I am unstoppable. No one can resist. No one!

Ahem.

Emerson, you make an adorable dog. The glasses are a nice touch. I'm still ironing out the details of the manuscript, but we can talk about that in more detail when you come visit.

Jonah

§

Jonah,

Yes, Mom, I promise to pack sunscreen. I may be pale, but I do live in Texas. It's not like I've forgotten how I burn.

Um, yes, gladly will forget. Though well done on supporting gay, horny teenagers as they attempt to get laid.

The prospect of seeing you in action has me feeling somewhat alarmed.

I am not a dog :P Though I'm glad you like the drawing. Figured that would please you.

Emerson

§

Emerson,

It's just that if you die of skin cancer, then I'll have no one to mother. Well, Natalie, but she's so grown up and hardly needs it.

You are so the dog, as you will realize when I finally gct around to sending you a manuscript. In the meantime, one of the librarians is on maternity leave, so I'm picking up some extra hours at the library and am actually writing this while hiding in the broom cupboard that serves as our break room. I have to go back out and brave the wilderness that is the Thursday night book club in a few minutes—mostly bored housewives who, from what I gathered before Kelly went off on maternity, are all sleeping with each other's husbands—and I am not subjecting myself to that for a moment longer than I have to. I am wearing my ugliest shirt, just in case.

Jonah

§

Jonah,

"Die of skin cancer"? Gee, aren't you cheerful.

Hrm. I look forward to reading this story.

Umm. I think it's very important that you tell these bored housewives as soon as possible about your gorgeous boyfriend whom you love dearly. I'm thinking bored housewives are much more likely to be persistent in their pursuit than teenage girls are, and seriously, the prospect sounds ten times more frightening.

In other news, I'm now being asked to make a sculpture out of found objects. That is, anything I want so long as it's never been in an art store. My prof is totally pushing junkyards and secondhand shops for this one.

Emerson

§

Emerson,

Ray of sunshine, that's me!

So far only one of the housewives has attempted to cop a feel. I am trying to decide if it's because she was drunk—she always shows up at meetings with a Coke can, and it's always already open, and I could swear it smells like Jim Beam, but I could be wrong. If I was a bored housewife, I'd be an alcoholic, too, so I don't know if I can actually blame her, but my ass is my own. I really don't want to have to file a sexual harassment report at work.

I put a copy of the dog picture on the bulletin board behind my desk at the library and drew a big heart around it in red crayon. So far it seems to be working. Fingers crossed.

The found objects assignment sounds awesome. I'm totally buying whatever you make, so bring it with you in June.

Jonah

§

Jonah,

You always were too cheerful.

She tried to cop a feel? Shudder. Seriously, they cannot pay you enough to deal with that! They certainly couldn't me, and not just because they're women.

Jonah, you haven't even seen what I'm going to create. You can't promise to buy it! That's just ridiculous. You're so—I don't know how to describe you.

Emerson

§

Emerson,

Finally had to talk to my manager at the library about the harpies. It was either that or start wearing the codpiece, and frankly it doesn't fit like it used to. She actually had to make a public announcement at the beginning of each book club about sexual harassment of library employees, since obviously I couldn't do it myself as no one would *listen*. Bethany kept *looking* at me when she delivered the news to the teen group, and poor Morgan just turned this god-awful shade of red; he probably thought he'd been caught snogging the page or something.

I never thought I'd say this, but why can't I have ten groups of four-year-olds?

Too late—I can and did promise to buy it. I hope you make a giant penis. As for your difficulty in describing me, I can think of several words that would work—handsome, clever, insightful, dashing, heroic, modest, etc. I could go on.

Jonah

§

"WHATCHA doing?" Emerson had been sitting at his drafting table minding his own business when suddenly Eve had plastered herself against his back with both arms wrapped around his neck.

"Reading my e-mails."

"Ooh, is that one from Jonah?" She gasped in his ear. "Is he talking about codpieces? Emerson, honey, why is your mystery man discussing his junk with you?"

Emerson blushed. "He's not discussing his… junk," Emerson tried to protest.

"'It was either that or start wearing the codpiece, and frankly it doesn't fit like it used to,'" Eve read over his shoulder. "Oh, he's a dirty boy! I like him," she said with satisfaction before she continued on the main point. "That certainly sounds to me like he is talking about the size of his junk. I repeat, why?"

"He wasn't—he was just referencing an old joke about the codpiece," Emerson argued feebly.

Eve let out a laugh. "Honey, he just told you about how his junk no longer fits inside his codpiece!"

"Jonah has no sense of personal boundaries," Emerson mumbled, mortified. He was very thankful that it was a quiet time of day in the studio and no one else was within hearing range. "Jonah likes to overshare."

"You know you like it!" Eve argued good-naturedly. "You want to know all about his junk. Don't deny it! I know you, Emery!"

Emerson felt himself flush brighter. Okay, so what if he did want to know about Jonah's… junk? He *didn't* really want to have this discussion with Eve.

Flipping his laptop closed, Emerson turned to look at the face still perched on his shoulder. "How about we go get some lunch?"

"Are you trying to bribe me into forgetting what I just read?" She let out a gasp but then tilted her head, considering. "Buy me a mangoberry juice, and I'll forget everything."

"Deal." Emerson slid his laptop into his bag and moved his art supplies into his lockbox. Then they were ready to go.

When Emerson wrote back to Jonah later that week, he refused to address the codpiece remark further. He refused to even mention it in order to drop the topic, not wanting to let Jonah know he was ignoring it on purpose.

§

A FEW weeks later, Emerson opened an e-mail from Jonah and nearly swallowed his tongue. There was a picture of a naked man on his computer. Well, a naked torso—there was no head or anything below the hips, but it was still naked man. A very hot naked man. A young, well-muscled, tanned, and gorgeous naked man.

Emerson sat for a moment, his mind boggling. Why was Jonah sending him pictures of hot naked men? Curiosity finally spurred him into taking his eyes off the picture and reading the text. The e-mail started off the same as usual: Jonah responding to Emerson's last e-mail, with nothing to explain the soft-core porn.

Until: *I keep telling you that I'm not a skinny little kid anymore, but it seems that you need proof. Forgive this crappy photograph; I had to take it with my computer's built-in webcam, so it's kind of grainy. And taking a picture of yourself is kind of awkward.*

Oh. Right. Last week, in response to Jonah contemplating eating junk food to ruin his good looks and thus not have to suffer unwanted attentions, Emerson had written that it would take massive amounts of junk food for that to work. He had been pretty sure that Jonah would be unable to eat enough junk food to counteract his hummingbird-like metabolism. Jonah had always had a sweet tooth and had always been a beanpole.

Emerson stared. Stared at the text and then at the photo. His eyes kept flicking back and forth between the two. His heart started thumping faster. Jonah hadn't been ugly when he left—Emerson had years of crushing on Jonah to attest to that—but he had been a kid the last time Emerson had seen him and had looked the part. This wasn't a kid; this was a man—a well-built man.

Oh God. Just what Emerson needed: more to fuel his fantasies and to keep his crush alive.

Unbidden, the image of Jonah's head attached to a gorgeous torso entered his mind's eye. Emerson could picture it: Jonah with the body of this fit, sexy man. Oh, Emerson could picture it all too well. There was a reason that the men Emerson gravitated toward were often tall and lean and into sports.

Emerson looked at the picture again and swallowed hard. Then he realized that he was hard. As a rock. He glanced down at the prominent bulge in his jeans and bit his lip, considering. He glanced back up at the photo and thought about it. A part of him thought he would feel a little skeevy about it afterward, if he did this. On the other hand, Jonah wasn't here, and he wouldn't ever know if Emerson….

He frowned and hesitated for another moment before reaching down and unbuttoning his fly.

His bottom lip kept clenched between his teeth, he slowly eased his pants down his hips and his cock out of his underwear. Right now, Emerson was feeling very relieved that he had received this e-mail late at night, after everyone had gone to bed.

Emerson looked back to the photo and then noticed the text of the e-mail and suddenly felt dirty again. Desperately, he opened the picture in a new window. Then he grabbed his lotion and reached once again for his cock.

Eyes locked on the picture, Emerson let his imagination run wild as he slowly started to stroke himself. He imagined that gorgeous body attached to the familiar face. He thought about how much stronger than him Jonah would be. He could picture Jonah pulling him close, pushing him down or hovering over him on a bed. Emerson began to pant harshly as his hand picked up speed.

He was still biting his lip, now trying to stifle the moans that wanted to come out. He really didn't want to be overheard, but he had forgotten how hard it was to be totally quiet doing this.

Emerson's eyes fluttered shut, and he let his head tilt backward. His strokes were fast now, and he was so close. Panting hard, he desperately brought his left hand up to cover his mouth. He'd learned long ago he could never stop all the moans from forming. When he came, he was whimpering urgently into his palm.

As he sat there panting harshly, he once again caught a glimpse of the picture. And felt himself blush hotly as embarrassment filled his belly. God, he had just jerked off to a picture of his best friend.

Mortified and sleepy from both the hour and the orgasm, Emerson decided to delay his response.

The following morning, Emerson discovered that being well-rested made little difference: it was very difficult to write a message to your best friend concerning the photograph of him that you had jerked off to.

Emerson stared at the blinking cursor on his screen. He had replied to most everything else in Jonah's last e-mail, but now he was faced with having to acknowledge the picture. He couldn't ignore it; that would be too conspicuous. So, he had to address the picture, that was certain, but what should he say?

He couldn't very well tell Jonah that the man in the picture was hot, so hot in fact that Emerson hadn't been able to keep his pants on. Telling Jonah that he had jerked off to fantasies about him was not an option. Which meant that acknowledging the picture as being Jonah was a fine and difficult line to walk. If he said it was Jonah and agreed that he was more muscular than he had been, then how could he not make a comment about Jonah's insistence that he was now irresistible?

Emerson decided to take the easy way out. He was, for a long moment, thankful that there was no face in the picture. So he called

Jonah a "lying liar" and insisted that he had not been fooled by Jonah's ploy. There was no head and thus no proof that it was Jonah.

Rereading what he wrote, he felt satisfied with it. There was no hint that Emerson appreciated the picture whatsoever.

§

"YOU sure you packed everything?" Zack's voice was amused as he watched Emerson look over the contents of his suitcase one last time. Emerson ignored him. While he might be willing to admit to himself—in the privacy of his own head—that he was maybe being a little obsessive and anal about his packing, he wouldn't give Zack the satisfaction of admitting as much.

In a few short hours, Emerson would be in San Francisco seeing Jonah for the first time in two years. Emerson was feeling pretty nervous about that. He wasn't quite sure what it would be like to see him again after so long. He wondered if Jonah would be as dorky and sweet as he remembered. He also wondered if Jonah would really look like the picture he had sent.

"You sure you don't need a ride?" Zack asked as he walked into the room and settled down on the bed.

"Yeah. Dad says he wants to; he wants to take me to breakfast first." Emerson shrugged.

"Fine, fine," Zack said. "When's he getting here?" The doorbell rang before Emerson could respond. He grinned at his dad's perfect timing.

"Now." Emerson slammed his case closed and zipped it shut.

"See you in a week?" Zack asked as he rose from the bed to follow Emerson.

Emerson nodded. "Have fun at your parents'."

Zack pulled a face. "I'll pick you up from the airport," he reminded him, then wrapped both arms around Emerson's shoulders. "Be good, Emma. Have fun." Then he let go of Emerson so that they could walk down the stairs unhindered.

"Hey, Dad."

"Hey, Mr. Blackburn," Zack greeted behind him; he nodded at them both in return.

"You ready to go?" His dad was smiling at him and reached out to grab Emerson's suitcase as Emerson moved to put on his shoes.

"Yup."

"I thought we could grab some pancakes at Guy's," his dad said, and Emerson grinned. Guy's Diner had the best pancakes.

"Sounds good to me."

Emerson said goodbye to Zack, and then he and his dad were out the door and making their way to the car.

Then things went as they normally did with his dad. He asked about Emerson's life, wondered how his summer was going, how his friends were. He even offered delicately phrased questions about Emerson's prospective boyfriends. By the time they reached the diner and started eating, Emerson was relaxed and no longer actively fretting over his vacation. Sure, he was still feeling nervous about it, but his dad's presence went a long way to keeping him calm.

"So, you better go check out the Golden Gate Bridge while you're there. It's a landmark—you can't go to San Francisco and not take a look at the bridge," his father told him. "Then, once on the other side, you really… you really should go to the park…." He trailed off, then cleared his throat. He lifted a hand up to rub at his shoulder. His face took on a pale hue.

Emerson's throat constricted. "Dad?" he croaked. "Dad? Are you okay?"

"Yeah, I'm fine," he said, but he began to rub at his chest.

"Dad…?" Emerson could feel the chills and tremors in his limbs. "Dad!" His voice rose in pitch. He was starting to feel panicked now.

"Emerson, I'm fi- fine." He went paler still and clutched at chest.

"Da-dad…? Something's wrong. Dad, I—I need… help!" Emerson looked around desperately. Something was definitely wrong. This was—oh God, his dad was having another heart attack.

"Stacey, call 911," a voice called to the woman behind the counter. And then there was a woman standing by their table saying, "Hi, I'm Becky, I'm a nurse." Then she was taking over, asking his dad if he carried any aspirin or other medication with him, working to make sure he was still alive when the paramedics arrived.

Emerson sat there frozen, terrified and uncertain and unable to move. When the paramedics came and bundled his father onto the stretcher, it was all he could do to get to his feet and stumble after them. It was Becky who told them that Emerson was to go too.

At the hospital, they sat Emerson down in a waiting room, and then an administration secretary was in front of him asking him questions. Was that his father? What was his name? Was his mother in town? What was the phone number to call her at?

Numbly, Emerson gave all the information they needed. He didn't hesitate, just told her everything she wanted to know.

He stayed that way, numb and listless, until his mother ran into the room, frantic, and wrapped both arms around Emerson to hold him tight.

It was then that Emerson started to cry.

CHAPTER 12

NOW

WHEN the door opened, Jonah looked down. Then down some more.

Then he remembered to take off his sunglasses so he didn't look so intimidating and crouched down a little too. "Hey, buddy," he said softly, his heart beating double-time in his chest. It was no wonder Emerson had assumed… the kid really did look just like him. Same hair, same eyes. But there was no way, and it was still no excuse. His stomach twisted. "Is your mom home?"

The kid nodded his head with a shy smile and disappeared back into the house, leaving the door open behind him.

"Who's at the door, baby?" Jonah heard from inside the house. "Let's go see, come on."

Once you got past the hair color, Deanna Carlisle hadn't changed much since high school. She was still tall and beautiful, with a friendly, open face and sparkling blue eyes. "Jonah!" she exclaimed. There was never any doubt that her surprise and delight were genuine. She put the little boy down and stepped forward to hug him.

Jonah let her; he hadn't had nearly enough hugs in the past week, and it was good to see an old friend again. "God, you did grow up just right, didn't you?" she teased, running her hands over his back before releasing him. "Have you got time to come in?"

"If you don't mind," he said a little hesitantly, flicking his eyes toward the kid.

"Don't be silly." Stepping back from the door, she motioned him into the house. When she knelt, the little boy ran into her arms. "Gareth, come say hi to Jonah."

"Hi," Gareth said shyly, sticking out his little baby hand.

"Hey." Jonah smiled. Gareth's hand almost fit around his index finger. "Nice to meet you."

"Gareth, baby, why don't you see if you can find your blocks? Mommy and Jonah have some catching up to do."

She put him down, and the kid scampered off in the direction of the living room.

"You want a drink? I think my dad has beer," Deanna said enticingly.

Jonah shook his head slowly. "Trying to quit."

"You're cute. Coffee, then." She flicked on the coffee pot, then motioned to the kitchen table. "I have to admit, I was expecting to hear from you a little earlier. Emerson promised me we'd go out for drinks."

Jonah scratched at the back of his neck. "Yeah, Emerson and I are kind of not speaking to each other right now."

Deanna raised her eyebrows in disbelief. "Seriously? Come on, you guys were thick as thieves. What happened?"

"Oh, you know, nothing serious. Except that he thinks I have a secret family." He looked pointedly toward the door where Gareth had disappeared.

"Oh my God—I never even thought." Deanna put her hand over her mouth. "He must be pretty mad at you, huh?"

"Other way around, actually. Under other circumstances, I wouldn't have blamed him, but…," he trailed off.

Smiling slightly, Deanna shrugged. "Well, I can't say I blame him either. I have a type, you know? I can see why it might have caused a little rift, but why didn't you just tell him the truth?"

This was the part that hurt to talk about. "I already *told* him the truth months ago."

Leaning back in her chair, she hit him with a speculative look. She wasn't angry—she was too laid-back for that—but she was definitely curious. "You never struck me as the kiss and tell type, Jonah."

He took a deep, shaky breath. "Yeah, well, it's kind of an important conversation when you start a relationship with someone."

Deanna's mouth dropped open. "You and—oh my God. Emerson's gay?" She paused. "Actually, that explains why he never seemed to like me that much. So, not so much a rift as a lover's tiff, then, I guess."

"I moved out without saying goodbye," Jonah admitted after a minute. "'Tiff' might not be a strong enough word."

"This is why you're skipping the beer?" Deanna said perceptively.

"I think I had enough this week."

With a reassuring smile, she put her hand over his on the table and gave a quick squeeze before getting up to pour the coffee. "How serious is it?"

"The fight or my drinking problem?" Jonah asked drily.

"The relationship, smartass." She set a mug in front of him. "Though I'm curious about the rest as well."

He wrapped both hands around the warm mug, staring into its depths. "The drinking was situational. And my sister threw out my last six-pack to help me along with kicking that habit."

"Hmm, I knew I liked her." Deanna finished adding sugar to her mug—she didn't use quite as much as Emerson, but it was a close thing—and licked the spoon. "Keep going, you're not off the hook yet."

Jonah took a slow sip, buying himself some time to think. "Everything else is pretty serious. You must have heard Emerson's dad died last June?"

"Yeah, a heart attack," she said sympathetically. "I'm sorry. He was a great guy."

"He was," Jonah reflected. "Emerson was kind of a mess. I was in San Francisco at the time—he was supposed to come visit, but obviously that didn't happen. So I came home instead."

"Go on."

"I stayed as long as I could—I'd booked some time off for his trip—but I had a job and other responsibilities back in San Fran, and I was supposed to start school in August, so I had to go back. Emerson's mom figured it wouldn't be a bad idea for him to tag along, get out of the house for a week or so. She wouldn't take no for an answer."

"Well, if anyone could make him feel better, it'd be you."

That brought a lump to his throat, and it was another few sips before he could continue. Even then, he wasn't really sure what he wanted to say or even how much he wanted to share. "I was—kind of a big chicken about it. I left it 'til the last minute in case things didn't work out, but when he left we were…."

"It's alright," Deanna supplied when he didn't continue. "I mean, I am dying for details, but I get that it's private, and you're not really in the mood to talk about specifics."

"Thanks. Anyway, when I said Emerson was a mess—I don't know exactly what happened while I was gone, but I know he did some things he regrets." Even saying that much felt like a betrayal of Emerson's confidence, but honestly, Jonah needed someone to talk to, and turnabout was fair play. "And I think it maybe made him a little, uh, neurotic."

"He always was kind of highly-strung."

Jonah huffed. "That's one way of putting it. Anyway, after he saw you at the store, he came home looking for a fight. It took him a while to get to the point—he kept just hinting sideways that I was a father and hadn't told him about it, even though he should have known I'd never slept with you. Basically he insinuated that I was a liar.

"I thought he'd finally put his insecurities behind him, you know? I was never anything but patient. Everything was going well. I mean, okay, we were fighting about whether I should move in—I was subletting one of the rooms from one of Emerson's housemates for the summer—but other than that it was perfect. I can't believe he thought I would do something like that."

Deanna squeezed his hand again. "I'm sorry, Jonah. In his defense, Gareth does look just like you."

"And he has my middle name." He was curious about that.

She ducked her head and pushed a strand of hair behind her ear. "When he was born—well, let's just say his real dad didn't exactly step up. I *wished* you were his father. And I liked the name. I never thought it'd cause you any trouble."

Suddenly he found himself blinking hard, fighting off unexpected tears. "Hey—no. Dee. I'm kind of insanely flattered. This isn't your fault."

Deanna laughed a little wetly and wiped at her eyes. "Sorry. The first year was kind of hard. I wouldn't trade him for the world, but it's definitely not the life I thought I wanted." She shook her head. "But we were talking about you."

"Yeah—I've been sort of monopolizing the conversation, haven't I?" he asked, chagrined.

"I don't mind. It's obviously weighing on you pretty heavily."

"This is the first time I've left the house all week."

She gave him one of those incredibly perceptive looks. "You're searching for a reason to forgive him."

If Emerson had apologized at any time, Jonah knew he would have forgiven him on the spot. He wasn't capable of holding a grudge. But he wasn't sure Emerson *would* apologize. He wasn't even sure Emerson knew why Jonah was so upset. "I've never been this miserable in my life." Oh, hell, while he was at it, he might as well tell her the rest. "I… it's not like I'm completely blameless either."

"Nobody's perfect," Deanna said gently.

"No, Dee. I think I scared him." Jonah looked at his hands. They were big, just like the rest of him. Jonah had never hit anyone in his life—he'd avoided fights before he hit puberty because he was small for his age and didn't want to get beat up, and afterward, when he was taller than everyone else, no one ever bothered him. He had a slow fuse; it just wasn't in his nature to get angry.

When he'd stared down Emerson that day in his bedroom demanding that Emerson move, though, he'd been very aware of his size. He could have moved Emerson out of the way easily—and he knew Emerson knew it too.

Jonah hated that he'd done that, but he'd been desperate. At first the realization that Emerson was accusing him of hiding a child had been ridiculous, but when his incredulity faded, it was like being punched in the gut. It hadn't taken much for the deep hurt to turn to anger. He didn't want Emerson to see him like that—to see how upset he was. He'd needed to get away, to clear his head, and when Emerson hadn't let him leave, he'd purposely intimidated him. It wasn't something he could ever take back. It killed him to think that now he'd given Emerson a reason not to trust him.

"Jonah, you wouldn't hurt a fly. Anyone who knows you knows that."

"But I could. It'd be so easy."

"But you *wouldn't*," Deanna emphasized. "I may not have known all the facts about you in high school, but even then I knew you'd throw yourself under a bus for Emerson. That if it ever came down to a choice between the two of us, you wouldn't hesitate."

"You were a good friend too," Jonah said hoarsely.

"I'm still a pretty good friend," she said with a small smile. "Now, pie or cookies?"

"Cookies!" said Gareth from the doorway.

Jonah started and looked up as Gareth flung himself across the kitchen and into Deanna's lap.

"I… pie or cookies?" he asked.

"Super-secret mom remedy for broken hearts," she told him, swinging Gareth up and giving him a noisy kiss where his T-shirt rode up. "Though it'll work better if you actually talk to him."

Talk to Emerson. Jonah didn't know if he was ready to do that.

"Mommy's cookies are the best," Gareth said from his place of honor.

"Well, I guess I won't argue with the expert," he said finally. *Either one of them.* "Cookies it is."

§

THEN

LATER, Jonah would say that he knew something was wrong long before Emerson failed to get off the plane. He was nervous—of course he was nervous; he hadn't seen his best friend in two *years*—and the coffee wasn't helping. He finally threw it away when he was halfway done and sat there in the arrivals area with his netbook balanced on his knee, jiggling in time with the tapping of his foot. He refreshed the flight status page about seven times a minute despite the fact that it was flashing on the airport television screen not twenty feet away.

An hour passed.

Maybe he missed his flight, Jonah thought hopefully, checking the next incoming flight from Austin. It would land in another twenty minutes. *Maybe he got bumped for someone with a family emergency.*

That would be just like Emerson, to give up his seat to someone who needed it more. *Maybe—*

In the corner of the screen, Google Talk blinked with an incoming message from Natalie.

Jonah's stomach sank. Emerson wasn't coming.

He clicked on the message to answer it. "Natalie?" He frowned at her image on the computer screen, sickly pale with serious, sad eyes. *Oh, God, Emerson.* "Natalie, what's going on?"

Natalie rubbed the corner of her eye like she always did when she was pretending not to cry. "You'd better come home."

Jonah was on a plane less than an hour later.

With the netbook still on his knee as they sat on the runway waiting for clearance, he fired off a few e-mails—his landlord, Katie, his supervisor at the library—letting them know he might be out of touch for longer than he anticipated and that he would be out of state. His fingers hesitated for a few moments over the phrase "death in the family," but he'd known John and the Blackburn family since he was ten—if that didn't make them family, neither would blood. Then they were taxiing, and he folded the little computer up and shoved it into its case, the only piece of luggage he had.

At least he wouldn't get held up at the baggage claim.

§

"EM? HAVE you had anything to eat today, hun?" Emerson looked up to see his mother's sister standing in the door to his bedroom. Her eyes were red-rimmed but dry and filled with compassion.

Emerson, who was not feeling particularly talkative, simply shrugged in response to her question.

"Honey, you really should think about eating something."

Emerson simply stared at his knees.

After his aunt had brought them home from the hospital, Emerson had suddenly been overcome by the scent of disinfectant and death on his clothes. He had jumped into the shower and begun to clean himself with single-minded intent. He wasn't sure how long he had stayed in the shower, but he had been there for some time, scrubbing himself down, attempting to remove all trace of the smell.

Once clean enough to satisfy himself, he had returned to his bedroom to stare at his closet for a long moment, contemplating clothes. In the end, it was a no-brainer to pull out his favorite worn jeans and the T-shirt of Jonah's he had kept so long ago. After pulling it on, he had stood there a moment, rubbing the soft green fabric beneath his hand. Then, he pulled on one of his zip-up sweaters and sat down on his bed.

He had curled himself into a tight ball and had been unable to move since. He had neither the energy nor the inclination to uncurl himself from his protective huddle.

His aunt sighed.

"Alright. I won't push it right now, but you're eating something tomorrow, just so you know." Then she ran a tender hand over his head before she left him alone again.

A great, empty ache had filled his chest and hollowed him out. He didn't know what to do now, to do next. He felt crippled by grief. He felt all at once that his whole body would cave in on the yawning ache inside him, and yet that all the pieces of him would float away and bring him to nothingness if he were not careful. He wished Jonah were here. Jonah, who could hold him and comfort him, who would fill the empty spaces and keep the pieces together.

Jonah.

Jonah, who was in San Francisco… where Emerson was supposed to be right now.

Oh. Oh, he had forgotten about his trip, hadn't even sent Jonah a message. Jonah must be so worried by now that Emerson hadn't shown up.

Slowly, his limbs filled with lethargy, though his mind was quick enough, he scooped up his laptop and opened it to contact Jonah. He wasn't on Skype, so Emerson opened a new e-mail. He stared at it for a long time, watching the cursor blink on the blank white page. He didn't know what to write, how to explain. There were certain things he just couldn't bring himself to write, not yet.

Finally, his fingers shakily tapped out, "Still at home. I need you," before they failed him. He could write no more, it seemed. He hit "send."

His laptop stayed open on the bed, waiting to tell him should Jonah respond. The computer stayed silent, and Emerson waited. His eyes still hurt, swollen and itchy from the tears, yet he didn't cry again. He had no more energy to cry. He had energy for nothing. He simply sat and waited. He waited to stop hurting. He waited to have energy. He waited for Jonah to contact him.

He could hear a knock at the front door. Someone, probably his aunt, answered. There was talking, and Emerson could see her, in his mind's eye, talking to a neighbor or maybe a salesperson, trying to explain that the family was in no condition to talk to anyone, friend or stranger. A fresh wave of grief interrupted his musings, and he lost track of the noises downstairs.

There was a knock on his bedroom door, and then it was opening, and then Jonah was there. Jonah was standing in his bedroom, looking serious and wan, but still like Jonah. His Jonah.

Emerson stared, frozen with shock. Then Jonah took one hesitant step toward him, and Emerson was unfrozen. He was unfolding his limbs and stretching out and reaching—

Jonah wrapped both arms around him and held him tight. One large palm curved around Emerson's waist, while the other was around his shoulder. Emerson felt safe for the first time since his father had first turned pale.

"Jonah," Emerson gasped, only to be answered by a soft, soothing shush and Jonah murmuring his name. Emerson broke. Huge, gulping sobs climbed their way up his throat and forced themselves out of his mouth. He gasped and shuddered in Jonah's arms as the tears came unrestrained. He could not stop them now, not now that Jonah was here to keep him safe.

§

NATALIE met him at the airport, still ashen pale and too quiet, and she was the same girl Jonah had taught how to swing a bat and climb a tree, only taller and more grown up, as if he needed something *else* to be sad about. He caught her up in a fierce hug as soon as he saw her, not saying anything, and it was a long time before he was able to let go.

Then she pulled away and put her hand on his arm and gave him one of those brave smiles their mom was so good at, and Jonah knew it was time to go.

"Do you want to drive?" she asked.

"Do you want to live?" Jonah asked back, and could have punched himself for it. "No, you—I haven't driven in years, Nat."

"'Kay."

Mom and Dad must have got a new car while he was gone—he vaguely remembered Mom mentioning something about it during some phone conversation or other, but he hadn't really been paying attention—because he nearly walked past it in the parking lot. He got a quick flash of that brave smile again as Natalie unlocked the doors with the key fob, and then he was sliding in, smacking his head on the side of the roof and nearly breaking his knees on the dash before he found the lever to move the seat back.

By the time they made it into Hudson Bend, Jonah's nerves were completely frayed. Natalie signaled to turn down into Emerson's neighborhood, but Jonah put his hand over hers on the gearshift. "Don't," he said. "I'll walk from here. I could use the air."

Natalie didn't argue, just threw the car into park long enough for him to get out.

It was only a ten-minute walk, but despite the four-hour flight and the hour-long drive, Jonah knew he wasn't ready yet to face the situation inside the house. Not that he would ever be ready. He could hardly think of facing Mrs. Blackburn and Kierstyn, never mind Emerson, but he wasn't going to back out now.

It was no time at all before he found himself ringing the doorbell, and he almost fell over in relief when Emerson's Aunt Brenda answered the door. She apparently hadn't heard much about his flight from Austin and surrounding area, because she didn't look surprised. Instead, all she said was, "He's in his room," and it wasn't like Jonah was ever going to forget where that was. He toed off his shoes and left them on the rack and made his way up the too-quiet stairway in the too-quiet house until he was standing in front of Emerson's door.

Then there was nothing left to do but go in.

He knocked once on the door—but that was stupid; he'd never knocked on Emerson's door in his life. Taking a deep breath, he pushed it open and stood there in the doorway with his heart caught in his throat.

For a half a second he couldn't move, and then, somehow, he was on the bed on the other side of the room with Emerson crushed desperately against his chest.

Jonah didn't know how long it was before Emerson finally, finally cried himself out and fell asleep, or how long he'd been staring at him since, but at some point afterward the bedroom door creaked open. Slowly, Jonah looked up, raising the first finger of his left hand to his lips as Kierstyn appeared in the doorway, looking even worse than Emerson, hair a wreck, eyes swollen and red, skin deathly pale. From the expression on her face, she hadn't quite forgiven Jonah yet for leaving either.

Well, it wasn't like Jonah was going to hold that against her now, of all times. He squeezed over closer to Emerson and nodded his head at the empty space beside him.

Kierstyn only hesitated for a second. Then she let the door latch softly closed behind her and crawled up on the bed beside him. "You made Emerson cry, a lot. Just so you know, I'm still mad at you," she whispered without looking at him.

"That's alright," Jonah said quietly, distracted again by Emerson's steady, even breathing. "I deserve it."

"'S'long as we're agreed," Kierstyn mumbled into his ribcage. Then she, too, went quiet.

§

SOME time later Jonah tiptoed his way out of Emerson's bedroom, having successfully extricated himself from both sleeping Blackburns without waking anyone. He closed the door gently behind him and stood outside in the quiet hallway for a long moment, catching his breath.

Aunt Brenda was nowhere to be found—probably in the master bedroom with her sister, Jonah thought—so for the time being, it seemed that he had the run of the house. Finding himself in the kitchen and at a loss for something to do, he ran some hot water in the sink and washed the dishes, careful to keep them from clanking against the side of the sink. Putting them away was easy—he knew the cupboards here better than his own in San Francisco, and nothing had moved. Then he washed the counter tops and swept the floor and got out the Windex to peel the dead bugs from the window above the sink.

He tidied the living room next—the vacuum would have to wait; he didn't want to risk waking anyone. Then the main floor bathroom, which was far enough away from the bedrooms upstairs that no one would be disturbed by the sound of the running water as he rinsed out the tub. Finally there was nothing left to do, so he went back into the kitchen and cleaned out the refrigerator until a jar of pickled eggs, John's favorite, brought him up short, and he had to take a minute to stop and clench his jaw.

Jonah put the jar back in the fridge, all the way on the bottom where no one would find it unless they were looking.

After that he reorganized the pantry, which was a suitable distraction until he found a bag of soup noodles and a packet of yeast. Two hours later he was taking a loaf of fresh bread out of the oven and sealing up the seventh or so Tupperware container of chicken noodle soup, everything but the loaf pan and the Dutch oven already washed and put away as if he'd never been there.

Then the phone rang, and Jonah dropped the ladle onto the tile floor with a loud clatter. "Shit." He didn't know why Brenda hadn't just turned the ringer off—

He managed to pick up on the second ring. "Hello?"

There was a pause. "Jonah?"

He sighed, bending to pick up the ladle and put it in the sink. "Hi, Mom."

Another pause, and Jonah was sure she was going to ask him when he was coming home, but when she finally spoke again, what she said was, "How's Emerson, sweetheart?"

Jonah made sure the burner was off before retreating to the living room, farther away from the stairs. "Sleeping, for now. He took it pretty hard."

"Of course," his mom answered. Then, hesitantly, "Honey, do you need anything?"

What Jonah needed was for Emerson to be okay, but he wasn't likely to get that, at least not anytime soon. But tangential to that thought—"I need to talk to you and Dad and Natalie, but that can wait. This is more important for now." After all he'd put his family through, he was not going to come out to them on the phone, even if Natalie probably already knew anyway.

"Call me when you need a ride, baby," his mom said. "We miss you."

Jonah swallowed. "I miss you too. I'll call you later."

They hung up just in time for the door to crack open. Jonah felt his shoulders go tense as Emerson's brother Harper pushed open the front door and stood in the entryway just like everyone else seemed to be doing that day. Of course, it was almost ten o'clock at night, and he'd probably been traveling for hours.

"Hey," Jonah said, well aware of how painfully awkward the situation was and that it wasn't likely to be improving anytime soon. "I heard about your dad. Obviously. I'm sorry."

Harper just gave a short nod and ran his hand through his hair before finally making a move to take his shoes off. "Where is everyone?" He looked a lot less intimidating than Jonah remembered, although of course he'd hardly seen Harper in years and years.

"Emerson and Kierstyn are asleep in his room. I think your aunt Brenda is with your mom, though I don't know if they're awake."

Harper continued to stand there stupidly, nodding, until Jonah finally broke down and said, "You want a drink?"

"Yes, please," Harper answered, and followed him into the kitchen.

Just because Jonah wasn't old enough to drink didn't mean he didn't know where the liquor cabinet was, and this was certainly no time for beer. He poured two generous measures of scotch over ice cubes and set them on the kitchen table, where Harper parked himself without actually using his eyes.

"We all thought he was doing better," Harper said at length, curling both hands around the glass and staring down into the amber liquid.

Jonah didn't know what to say to that, so he kept his mouth shut.

"We all thought—" and here Harper interrupted himself by raising his nose into the air and sniffing deeply several times. Then his stomach growled loudly, and he said, "God, did you *bake*?"

"I really suck at this," Jonah admitted in a rush. "I didn't know what else to do."

"Jesus." Harper got up from the table and located the bread apparently using the power of his nose, then cut himself a generous slice. He ate it standing at the counter, not bothering with niceties like butter or cheese. "Emerson should keep you."

Again, Jonah could think of no appropriate response. Instead he said, "There's soup in the fridge? If you're hungry."

Which was how Emerson found them, twenty minutes later, slurping their soup in what was otherwise a companionable silence.

"There's a bowl for you in the microwave," Jonah said in a voice that was less *if you're hungry* and more *and if you don't eat it on your own I'll spoon-feed it to you; I know what you're like*.

Emerson blinked at him owlishly—he must have forgotten to put his contacts in, or pick up his glasses—and hit the power button to reheat it. "When did you get in?" he asked Harper, taking the seat between the two of them at the table.

"Couple minutes ago." Harper passed him the basket of bread. Maybe Harper wasn't such a dickwad after all. "Jonah fed me."

Emerson paused with a thick slice of bread halfway to his mouth. "I didn't hear the fire alarm."

Jonah gave him a crooked, slightly broken smile. "Smartass."

"You're making too much noise," Kierstyn complained from the doorway, and Jonah kicked out the chair on his other side so she could sit down. She took two slices of bread from the basket and slathered them in margarine, then made them into a sandwich like she'd done when she was a child and convinced that she liked neither sandwich meat nor cheese.

Jonah said, "Sorry," and then Mrs. Blackburn and Aunt Brenda came downstairs, too, and he heated up the rest of the soup and got an extra chair from the dining room so they could all sit together.

"Thanks," Emerson said quietly twenty minutes later, slipping out to join him on the front steps.

"Don't be an idiot," Jonah replied, knocking their shoulders together. "Do you want me to come back tomorrow?"

"If you're free. I know you haven't seen your family in years."

Seriously? Jonah turned his head just enough to spit Emerson with a penetrating look. "And they can do without me for a couple more days."

Emerson opened his mouth again, and Jonah said, casually, before anything really stupid could come out of it, "If you thank me again, I will not be responsible for my actions."

It didn't quite get a smile, but considering the circumstances, Jonah would take what he could get.

A minute or so later Natalie pulled up in the driveway, and Jonah pulled Emerson up and into a hug before he could talk himself out of it. "Go back to bed," he advised. "I'll be back in the morning."

Natalie gave him a sideways look when he got in thc car, but Jonah just closed the door and buckled up and let out a long breath. "Can we talk about it when we get home?" he said at length.

"Whatever, Jonah, you are the least subtle person on the planet," Natalie told him, throwing the car into reverse. "You can tell me whenever you want."

He tilted his head back against the seat. "Thanks."

§

BALANCING the tray of coffees and the bag of pastries in one hand, Jonah reached for the doorknob with the other.

Behind him, Natalie said, "You're not going to knock?"

"I haven't knocked since I was thirteen," Jonah pointed out, finding the door unlocked. Yesterday didn't count. He kicked his shoes off onto the mat and held the door open long enough for Natalie to follow him inside. "Careful of that board"—there was a small step up to the main part of the room—"you only need to stub your toe on that once, and you'll never forget it."

Natalie didn't comment on that, following him into the living room silently, but when they didn't meet anyone in the kitchen either, she asked, "Are you sure they're even awake?"

"Kierstyn's bedroom light was on," Jonah said absently, taking a plate from a cupboard for the pastries and arranging them neatly before setting them on the table. "And she makes a lot of noise in the morning. Besides, Emerson slept most of yesterday afternoon."

He didn't need to turn around to know exactly which look she was giving him. It was the same look she had given him this morning when he'd come to breakfast in a T-shirt that was two years old and, it had to be said, a little small in some key areas. "Gee, I wonder who you're trying to impress," she'd said, and Jonah had closed his eyes and begged, "God, not today, Natalie."

She'd let it drop after that. It wasn't like Jonah had any choice apparel-wise; he hadn't exactly packed for this trip.

Unfortunately for both of them, Mrs. Blackburn was the next person into the kitchen that morning, though she didn't look particularly surprised to see Jonah, at least. "Oh, good morning," she said, obviously on autopilot since there was nothing remotely good about this morning. Her eyes were horribly damp and red, though she managed a small smile. "And you brought breakfast." At that she swallowed hard and wiped beneath her eyes with her third finger.

If Jonah was feeling awkward, he couldn't even imagine how poor Natalie felt. "It was nothing," he said modestly. "The bakery was on the way." Then, steeling himself, he said, "Natalie's just come for the keys to the store, and then she'll be off."

Mrs. Blackburn faltered. "Oh—but we told everyone—"

"Can't have the produce going bad," Natalie said with forced cheer. "And there's supposed to be a delivery today. I called in some favors. We'll take care of it, Mrs. B."

Mrs. Blackburn let out a big sob before she got control of herself and fell upon Natalie in an excruciatingly awkward hug. Natalie endured it like a trooper, and when Mrs. Blackburn pulled away to find the keys to the store, she was composed again.

Natalie took the keys and hightailed it to the door, but not before Jonah could mouth a heartfelt "thank you."

"Thank you for coming," Mrs. Blackburn managed a few moments later, her back turned to the process of selecting one of the coffees Jonah had brought. "You've been a godsend, and I know Emerson missed you."

"I should never have left," Jonah admitted softly, and almost swallowed his tongue when he heard footsteps on the stairs behind him.

"Well, you're here now, and that's what matters," she said with a brave sniffle, and she planted a kiss on his cheek. "Emerson, Jonah brought breakfast."

Still fighting down the urge to blush—pretending fiercely to himself it was from the motherly kiss and not his stupid, ill-timed confession, which Emerson had no doubt overheard—Jonah added, "And coffee—the big one is yours." Three creams, five sugars, and it was a wonder that Emerson hadn't developed diabetes or at the very least an unattractive paunch. Not that Jonah could talk; he liked his almost as sweet.

Emerson gave him a bleary stare from behind his glasses, his expression inscrutable. Maybe it was too early for him to work out exactly what it was that Jonah had meant. "Thanks," he said, his voice hoarse from sleep.

Jonah suppressed the urge to shudder. "Sure."

Emerson took a seat at the table, his gaze seeming to stare through the wooden top, though he did manage to choke down half of a chocolate croissant. Jonah watched him for a few minutes until he was satisfied that Emerson wasn't going to starve himself, then let his eyes and thoughts drift.

Emerson's dad had redone the kitchen when they had been in tenth grade, and they had been conscripted for the weekend to work pulling out the old cabinets and peeling away the old linoleum so that new tile could be laid. By the time they had finished at the end of the day they'd been too tired and sweaty even to walk as far as the lake for a swim. Instead they'd laid on their backs in the grass until they fell asleep, only to be woken hours later with sunburns and empty stomachs. Emerson's mom had given them cold fried chicken and her special potato salad, and they'd had a watermelon seed-spitting contest until the setting sun made it impossible to determine a winner, and they called it a tie.

"Jonah."

Jonah looked over at him, at where he was sitting, rigid and uncomfortable, at the kitchen table, and wondered when the hell they'd gotten so old. Emerson's mom was gone, and so was the last half of the chocolate croissant. He blinked in recognition.

Emerson sounded a hair away from losing it. "Take me away from here. Please."

Jonah let out a long, shuddering breath. "Yeah, alright," he said. "Let's go for a walk."

They hadn't walked much of anywhere together since before Jonah had got his driver's license in eleventh grade, and Jonah found that the mindless locomotion was soothing, falling into step just ahead of Emerson with an ease that spoke of long years of friendship. He'd thought he had no particular destination in mind, content simply to be with his friend under the hot Texas sun, but then he heard the resounding crack of a baseball hitting wood and realized he'd directed them to the ball diamond they'd played on as kids.

Jonah bought a couple of Sno Cones from the canteen, blue raspberry for him and cherry for Emerson, and then they picked out a spot on the rusting metal bleachers, the sun-borrowed heat burning for a moment even through the fabric of Jonah's jeans.

If they attracted a few stares—and they did; Jonah had been gone for almost two years, and news of Emerson's father had traveled fast—Emerson, at least, seemed not to notice, and the few scattered parents and friends apparently knew enough not to approach him in his grief. The red team, it seemed, was up by several runs, as evidenced by the fact that their coach called them into the dugout before the green team got three outs, some kind of mercy rule like they hadn't had in Jonah's time. Back then the bleachers had been almost brand-new, a vibrant ultramarine, and the concessions stand had smelled of fresh paint as well as popcorn and hotdogs. But the summer sun still held the same relentless Texas heat, and the field had recently been mowed, the smell of the fresh-cut grass bringing back memories.

§

BEFORE

THE batter swung the bat hard and connected with the ball, sending it into deep left center. Jonah cursed under his breath, watching the advancement of the runners helplessly. The ball went well over the fielder's head, landing somewhere behind him and to his left. If he hurried, he might make the throw in time to beat the runner, who had been on second, home. Then Jonah would have a chance to make a play.

But the fielder looked between the ball and Jonah dubiously and threw it in to the second baseman, where the batter was already waiting, and a few seconds later the runner crossed the plate with a triumphant grin to cheers from the stands, just like the three before him. It was near the end of the second game of a double-header, and there was only Emerson to pitch—it was obvious he was getting tired, and Jonah didn't blame him.

Behind Jonah, he heard one of the away team's older fans—probably someone's grandmother—lean over and say, in a voice that may have been intended to be soft but which carried across the flat, dusty diamond as easily as if she'd used a megaphone, "They won't throw him the ball because they know he won't catch it."

Flinching, Jonah ducked his head in shame and kicked at the dirt, feeling sick. It had been two years since he'd played on a team, and it was true that he was rusty, but he always played well in practices. But he was short and scrawny and awkward, and people took it for granted that he wasn't good at sports. It was difficult to have confidence when nobody wanted to give him a chance to prove himself.

The next batter stepped up to the plate, and Jonah raised his head again to meet Emerson's eyes where he was standing on the pitcher's mound. They were narrowed into slits behind his lenses, and he looked like he'd swallowed a mouthful of vinegar. "Time out," he said loudly, and Jonah's heart hammered in his chest as Emerson waved the other players in from the outfield.

The boy who'd fielded the ball, Tim, glared defiantly, and Emerson hadn't even said anything yet. "Tim, do you want to win this game or not?"

Tim scoffed. "We're down four runs in the bottom of the seventh, Emerson. I'd like not to be an embarrassment."

"Glad to hear it," Emerson said acidly. Jonah stared determinedly at the dirt. "Is your arm bothering you?"

"What?" Tim answered. "No."

"So there's no reason you couldn't throw the ball where it would do some good? Home plate, for example, where it would have prevented another run?"

The second baseman spoke up. "He was trying to make the easier out, Emerson."

"Does he need glasses?" Emerson asked rhetorically. "Because he can borrow mine. The batter was already on the base."

Jonah kind of wanted the ground to open and swallow him up, preferably erasing any evidence that he had ever lived, or at least this conversation, from history.

Tim and Eric, the second baseman, gave Jonah guilty sideways looks. "Look, Sarah Waters and Allie Sparks are in the bleachers, okay? We look stupid when he doesn't catch it."

Jonah flinched again, but he couldn't stop himself from looking at Emerson, and he saw that his friend's face had gone hard. "You'll look a lot stupider when I bench you and put Jonah's sister in instead! At least she knows how to play on a team, and she's not going to let some *girl*"—here Emerson's lip curled up—"distract her from the game! Jonah is perfectly capable of catching the ball. I see him do it every time one of the batters misses. Maybe you just need to work on your aim."

Jonah felt his ears heat at the praise, but he took care to make sure the other boys didn't notice his pleasure. The last thing he needed was for Emerson to be accused of favoritism.

"Now," Emerson said, while Tim and Eric were still busy staring furiously at a spot over his shoulder, "can we play some baseball here, people?"

§

THEN

EMERSON looked better, Jonah decided as they walked back to his house. They'd been at the diamond most of the day watching the kids play, eating hotdogs, and just generally existing in the same small pocket of space. Emerson's face had got a bit of color back, and he'd eaten some lunch, and if there was a red slash of sunburn spreading over the tips of his ears and nose, for once, Jonah wasn't going to complain about it. Apparently neither one of them could be trusted to remember sunscreen at a time like this, and that was fine.

They had just come into view of Emerson's house when Emerson pulled up short, presumably at the sight of the black Trans Am hugging the curb at the end of the driveway. Emerson said, "Oh, no."

Jonah looked from him to the car and back again. "Friend of yours?" he asked warily.

"It's Zack," Emerson explained, looking pained. "Hayley must have told him when he got back from seeing his parents."

"Well, it's good that he wanted to check that you were okay?" Jonah hazarded.

"Yes, no, Zack is great, absolutely, it's just." Emerson finally met his gaze. "He kind of hates you."

Oh, well. That wasn't so bad. Jonah was mostly just glad it wasn't an ex-boyfriend—or current one. Wait a second—"Wait, why does he hate me? What did I do?" *Everyone* liked Jonah, and aside from the attempted ass-grabbing, he was mostly okay with that. He was just gregarious. People couldn't help it.

"He's just." Emerson looked a little panicky now. "He's kind of protective. Um. A lot." He scratched the back of his neck, then winced, and Jonah realized that that was burnt too. Damn it, he was going to have to be more careful. Next time they would sit in the shade. Too bad he hadn't brought that 100 SPF. "And when I first met him, you were, you know…."

Gone, Jonah realized, and not speaking to Emerson at the time. Well, he could see how that would color Zack's opinion. But *hating* him for it seemed kind of extreme. Unless…. "Exactly how badly did you take that?"

Emerson flushed under about forty new freckles and looked away, so, pretty badly, then. Jonah didn't know whether to feel guilty about it or pleased that Emerson cared about him so much. He didn't have any time to decide, however, because at that moment the door to the house opened and a guy Jonah decided must be Zack jogged out of it, making a beeline for Emerson.

"Hey, Emma." They—well, hugged wasn't exactly the word; it was a lot manlier than the hugging Emerson usually did. "Hayley told me what happened. I came as soon as I could. I'm sorry, man."

Emerson nodded, pulling back, and wiped at his eyes once, and then Zack took a step back and looked over at Jonah.

This was probably going to be ridiculous, but Jonah stuck out his hand anyway. “Hi, I’m Jonah. You must be Zack.”

Zack gave him a flinty-eyed stare and let his hand hang there in the air for a moment, but eventually he reached out and attempted to crush Jonah’s fingers. He was just lucky his hand was proportional to the rest of him, or he might have had to go to the hospital. “Pleasure,” Zack said, tone indicating clearly that it was anything but.

“Um, while this macho display is good for my ego, I am choking on the testosterone,” Emerson broke in.

Zack let go of Jonah’s hand, looking thoroughly unchastened. Jonah pointedly did not shake his hand out in spite of the throbbing.

A rumble sounded in the distance, and Jonah looked up to see the blue sky rapidly clouding over. “I should get home,” Jonah said regretfully. With Natalie at work, he’d have to walk, and it was definitely going to rain. He didn’t exactly want to leave, but it wasn’t like Emerson was going to be alone. “Call you tomorrow? I should probably spend some time with my parents after the bombshell I dropped on them yesterday.”

Emerson blanched under his sunburn, and Zack gave him a narrow-eyed look that told Jonah his opinion was being rapidly re-evaluated. “You told them…?”

Jonah shrugged, trying to be nonchalant. “No time like the present. See you tomorrow?” he asked, meaning, “Will you be okay if I leave you with this guy?”

“Yeah,” Emerson said finally. He’d been doing so well all day, but all of a sudden it seemed like you could have knocked him over with a feather. “Yeah, sure.”

“Alright then. It was nice to meet you, Zack,” he said as sincerely as possible. He waved goodbye just as the gathering clouds blocked out the sun.

“Zack could drive you,” Emerson offered as he was walking away.

Jonah smirked a little as he turned around. Emerson looked embarrassed, Zack thoroughly unimpressed. “No, he couldn’t,” he said, watching Zack shrug at Emerson unconcernedly. “See you tomorrow.”

§

THEY hadn't even made it to the church yet, and already Emerson wanted to fall apart. Aunt Brenda had volunteered to drive the family out to the church, and so he was sitting in an uncomfortable suit in the back seat of her car. Kierstyn, by reason of being the smallest, had been elected to take the middle seat. She was pressed firmly against his side, and Emerson tried not to think about anything else but the comforting warmth of her body. If he didn't, he might recall what it was that they were doing today.

They rode in a silence that was broken only when Aunt Brenda announced, "Here we are." It was a long moment before Emerson reached for the door handle. By the time he and Kierstyn pulled themselves from the car, his mother and Harper were already standing at its bumper, staring at the church.

They walked in together as a family, and Emerson wished he could take more comfort from that fact. They were not a whole anymore, not without Dad.

Emerson blinked hard and shied away from those thoughts.

He followed his mother and Harper down the aisle to the front pew, and when Kierstyn snaked her hand into his own, he didn't argue. He simply squeezed her hand back.

Back stiff, and heart aching, Emerson kept his mind carefully blank and held Kierstyn's hand tight. He didn't notice the other attendees arriving. In fact he hardly noticed when the pastor began the ceremony.

Emerson didn't take notice of the proceedings until Kierstyn untangled their fingers and went to the altar. There, looking sweet and pretty in her black dress, she carefully and deliberately recited the words to Frost's "Nothing Gold Can Stay." Hearing his little sister recite his father's favorite poem made Emerson want to cry again.

He zoned out again when the pastor started up once more and didn't come back to himself until it was Harper talking.

"I wish I knew all the right words to say to encompass the man that our father was. Unfortunately, I don't, and I probably won't do the man justice, but I'm here to try."

Emerson sat and listened, his chest aching to hear Harper try to give a eulogy for their *father*.

"My father was a man who loved his children more than anything else. My whole life, his love for me was never in question. No matter what we did or what we told him, he never stopped loving us. And we tested that. I tested it when I moved across the country for college and forgot to phone regularly. Kierstyn's not old enough to have given Dad a proper test—I think that takes teenage hormones—but all the little everyday tests didn't pass Dad by. He even forgave her when she quit ballet and cut off her pigtails." There was tittering in the pews at that, and Harper gave a small smile.

"Emerson… Emerson perhaps gave it the biggest test when he came out, but Dad… Dad took that the same way he took everything. In fact, the day he passed he had breakfast with Emerson, and Em says Dad was just as nosy about his love life as always."

There were more titters about that, but not as loud as the ones before. Not everyone at the funeral had been entirely accepting when they had heard that Emerson was gay, and the awkward laughter was proof of that. Emerson suddenly felt a pang of great love for Harper, who didn't flinch away from telling the truth.

"We'll miss you, Dad," were Harper's final words before he folded his paper and stepped away from the altar.

Then his Uncle Ed who lived in Tulsa got up and commemorated his baby brother. Ed's eulogy was for a boy who hadn't existed for forty years and a man who hadn't in twenty. Emerson felt awkward listening to an uncle he barely knew talk about a man that he didn't.

His awkwardness increased when it was Uncle Ed who said, "In order to commemorate his father, John's middle child elected to say good-bye in the way he does best. Emerson created this slide show of his father's memory. The music is, I believe, an original composition by some friends of his, created for today."

They played the slide show. The song had been written by Greg and Zack. Zack had been working the melody out on his piano for weeks, and after John's death had enrolled Greg into helping him create the lyrics. The song was for Emerson, and he found he couldn't both listen to his father's elegy and watch the photos of his life. He looked away.

Then the service was done, and they were moving outside and watching the casket being lowered. His mother was pushing him forward, and Emerson was scooping up earth and tossing it in the grave.

The priest ended with an invitation to the wake at the Blackburn home, and Emerson walked back to his aunt's car. Just as suddenly, they were back in the driveway, and then Emerson was standing in his house, waiting for people to arrive with food and more condolences. He stood by the kitchen counter, staring into a glass of water.

"Hey."

Emerson looked up, and there was Jonah, tall and handsome as ever. He was beautiful in his black suit.

"Hi," Emerson said back. It was apparently all the permission Jonah needed to walk right up and wrap his long arms around Emerson. Emerson was engulfed, but it didn't feel stifling. He just felt precious and cherished, safe. Jonah was good at that. Emerson allowed himself the luxury of placing his head down on Jonah's shoulder and soaking up all the love and attention that he could.

They stayed in the kitchen with Jonah holding him close and Emerson's fingers curled in the fabric of his coat until Brenda came walking in carrying a casserole, with guests carrying more food on her heels.

Jonah released him then, and if Emerson hadn't been so tired, he might have blushed at being caught in such an intimate pose.

"Oh." Brenda didn't look that surprised to have found them alone together. "Boys, why don't you find someplace else to hide—this kitchen is about to get busy." She gave them a soft smile, which they both attempted to return, before she went back to organizing food.

Jonah followed Emerson through the living room and into the den, then to a far corner where they could sit on a love seat that was out of the way and far from popular traffic.

"You need anything, Em?" Jonah asked softly. Emerson shook his head. No. He didn't need anything that Jonah could give him.

Emerson shifted on his seat. He felt stiff and uncomfortable. He didn't even know how to just *sit* anymore, it seemed.

"Hey, settle down," Jonah murmured. He wrapped an arm around Emerson's shoulders and pulled him in close. Emerson didn't argue as he was settled against the back rest, leaning into Jonah's comforting presence.

His mind was still moving, but at least his limbs weren't. "Jonah?"

"Yeah?"

"Thank you."

"Emerson?"

"Yeah?"

"Don't thank me again."

"Oh. I just wanted you to know…."

"Yeah. I know. Just so long as you do too."

"Yeah."

Silence reigned. Emerson let it consume him.

Kierstyn found them first. She crept into the room as though she was sneaking away from or to something. Kierstyn didn't hesitate to climb onto the couch next to Emerson, and Emerson never thought to deny her. She was so somber; he had never seen her like this before.

Unfortunately, she wasn't the last person to find them.

Sedate guests in dark colors kept wandering into the den and spotting Emerson and Kierstyn, insisting on offering condolences. They kept coming and coming, even after Kierstyn had fallen asleep curled against the armrest. Emerson hated them for their pity and their *I'm sorrys*. Mostly he hated them for making Jonah so uncomfortable that, upon arrival of the first guest, he had coughed, embarrassed, before lifting his arm up and away. Emerson's shoulder felt cold without Jonah's warm weight. He kept shifting his back and rolling his shoulders uncomfortably, anxiously, until Jonah grabbed his hand and laced their fingers together.

"Hey, quit twitching."

"I'm sorry. I just…."

"Hey, I know. It's just… you're starting to look like you've got a rash or something."

Emerson turned to look at his best friend and found that Jonah was giving him an attempt at his usual mocking smirk.

"Gee, thanks."

"Well, we wouldn't want all these lovely people to get any ideas." Jonah arched a brow.

The smile was genuine if small. "You're always so thoughtful."

"Yup."

Emerson opened his mouth to respond but was interrupted by a call of "Emerson! There you are. I've been looking for you. I just wanted to say…." He turned to the newcomer, nodding to her in all the appropriate places, acting as if he actually cared what she said.

Jonah stayed all afternoon and into the evening. He didn't move from his spot except to head to the bathroom. He didn't even leave to find food, though that might have been possible only because food was brought to them. Jonah just stayed with him, their hands locked together, all day long. Emerson wasn't sure he had ever loved him more.

§

"IF YOU try to do up my seatbelt for me, I'm changing seats," Emerson threatened as Jonah finished putting his carryon in the overhead compartment.

"Oh." Jonah thought about wheeling Emerson's suitcase through the airport, and bringing him his sugared-up coffee, and keeping track of his boarding pass and ID, and never letting him out of sight for longer than it took to take a leak in privacy, and decided he might've been a bit of a mother hen. "Sorry?"

Emerson sighed and sat back in his seat. "It's fine. I know you're just looking out for me. But I'm not going to break. I am a mostly functional member of society. Promise." Emerson gave a little tremulous smile.

"I know." Truth told, Emerson was doing a much better job of keeping his shit together than Jonah was, and Jonah wasn't the one whose dad had just died. But Jonah was trying to make up for two years of absentee friendship *and* be supportive to someone who was grieving, and he had less of a clue how to do the latter than the former, which was to say he had no fucking idea. Compounding this was the further complication that he happened to be in love with Emerson as well. Basic chivalry had seemed a good start originally, but then, Emerson wasn't a girl.

Jonah was more than just aware of that fact.

He sat down in the aisle seat—no one had claimed the window yet; Jonah was hoping it stayed empty—and tucked a paperback he'd nicked off his dad into the seatback in front of him. "Nervous?" he asked.

Emerson shook his head. "I'm okay. Excited." Emerson chewed his lip. "Worried about leaving my mom alone, but I guess that'll happen when I go back to school anyway." Then Emerson turned to him and asked with an obvious attempt to change the subject, "What about you? You're the one with a book release in less than two months. Aren't *you* nervous?"

Sure he was, but he was a lot more nervous about having Emerson in his apartment for a week and trying to keep his hands to himself. "I—believe it or not, no."

"I can't believe I haven't even read it yet," muttered Emerson.

Jonah tensed.

"Not that—I'm not complaining," Emerson assured him. "Just, I thought I was going to have my hands on it a week ago, and now I'm going to be hanging out with you for a week, so I'm not going to have time until I head back home."

"You know I'd have given it to you if I could," Jonah said gently. Emerson only ever babbled like that if he was nervous, and his leg was bouncing. "Are you sure you don't want some Gravol or something?"

"Yes!" Emerson assured him. "I'm fine. I keep telling you—" and then the plane started pulling away from the boarding area, and his face went white.

"Are you going to do up your seatbelt now?"

He did, his hands trembling slightly in the process. When he pulled them away from the belt it was to curl them around his chest, hugging himself.

The plane turned to orient itself to the runway, and Emerson started jiggling his leg double-time. It was making *Jonah* nervous, and Jonah hadn't been nervous on a flight since his family's vacation to Disney World when he was eight. Before he could think about it, he reached out with his right hand and pressed down on Emerson's knee.

Oh. That had been a mistake, because the denim underneath Jonah's hand was warm from Emerson's skin, and Emerson had gone still like he was *waiting* for something, only he couldn't be, and

Jonah—couldn't take his hand away. It was like it was permanently magnetized to Emerson's leg.

"Sorry," Emerson said, sounding a little off. In the background, Jonah heard the pitch of the engines increase and managed to shake himself enough to pull his hand away.

He cleared his throat. "It's fine."

Somehow, Jonah made it through takeoff with Emerson white-knuckling the armrests beside him and breathing hard like someone was—well, like he was having a lot better time than he really was. For a second Jonah wondered, somewhat wildly, if he could calm Emerson down by blowing him in the restroom, and then he spent the next half an hour deeply regretting that moment's indiscretion, because he *could not stop thinking about it*. The second the fasten seatbelts sign went off, he muttered an excuse about needing a piss to Emerson and made a beeline for the bathroom.

No sooner had he slid the latch closed behind him than he had his jeans down around his knees and one hand curled tightly around his dick.

What would Emerson be like, he wondered as he frantically scrabbled for tissues with his left hand. Would he be shy? Wanton? Some intoxicating mixture of the two? Would his skin pebble into goose bumps under Jonah's touch? Would he shiver? How would he taste?

Jonah gave himself a rough experimental stroke, knowing he wouldn't last long. Emerson would take some coaxing, he decided. Jonah knew he hadn't always had the best luck with sex, however little they talked about it—which was to say only when Emerson had had too much to drink. So he'd be nervous. Jonah would have to convince him that it was good for him, that he wanted—God. Everything that he wanted. Which was a lot.

What kind of noises would he make? Jonah wondered. Little quiet gasps and snuffles of pleasure? Would he hiss in satisfaction when Jonah licked at the head of his cock like he was currently dying to do? Or maybe—Jonah clenched his jaw at another long, hard stroke—maybe he wouldn't contain himself. Maybe he'd be loud. God, that would be hot. Jonah hoped he was a screamer….

Jonah barely managed to catch the mess before it sprayed all over the bathroom and his jeans, shuddering with aftershocks so strong, they made him dizzy. Jesus Christ, if this was what it was like to jerk off thinking about Emerson, actual sex would probably kill him, but what a way to go.

Making sure there was no physical evidence of his activities, Jonah washed his hands thoroughly and flushed before leaving the bathroom. There wasn't even a line-up yet. That was just embarrassing.

Jonah plopped back down in his seat, trying very hard to act like a normal human being and not someone who'd just frantically jerked off in an airplane bathroom while fantasizing about sucking his best friend off. For all the attention Emerson was paying to anything that was not hyperventilating and trying to dent the plastic with his fingernails, Jonah might as well have come out of the bathroom naked with his dick still hard. "Emerson. Come on, man, breathe. It's another four hours to San Francisco."

"Oh, God," Emerson said.

"Come on, the movie's going to start soon," Jonah coaxed. "You can use my headphones. I kept them from my last flight." He fished them out of the seat pocket and plugged them into Emerson's armrest, flipping through the channels until he found something that sounded classical and soothing. "Here." He hooked the speakers over Emerson's ears, more challenging than it sounded when he was limited to one side.

Emerson managed a shaky smile. "Thanks."

"*Relax*," Jonah commanded, and he automatically put his hand on Emerson's knee again, *God damn it*. For a second he could only stare down at the hand like it had betrayed him; then he snapped out of it. "Sleep if you can, 'cause I'm going to keep you very busy all week."

If Jonah hadn't known better, he would have said Emerson flushed at the words.

CHAPTER 13

NOW

JONAH was brushing his teeth when his cell phone started ringing, the sudden sound startling him so much that he jerked his head up and hit it on the open medicine cabinet and swore through a mouthful of toothpaste. He spat quickly and dropped his toothbrush into the cup by the sink before bolting out the door, following the sound of his ringtone.

"Maggie!" he shouted. What if it was Emerson? He didn't want Emerson to think he was screening his calls. Damn it, he knew he should've assigned his boyfriend a ringtone. "Can you help me find—"

"Got it!" his roommate cried from the living room.

Thank God. "Emerson?" Jonah mouthed hopefully at her when he skidded to a stop in the doorway. She shook her head regretfully.

"Some girl," she mouthed back, handing over the phone.

Jonah tried not to be too obvious about his disappointment, but from the way Maggie patted his shoulder as she left the room, he was fairly certain he'd been unsuccessful. "Hello?"

"What, you don't answer your own phone anymore, mister big shot?"

Jonah held the phone away from his ear for a second in disbelief. "Xie?"

"In the flesh!" she chirped. "Well, sort of."

"It's good to hear your voice," Jonah told her honestly. Okay, he'd been hoping for a call from Emerson, but if he couldn't have that, maybe he could at least vent to someone who'd understand.

"Back at you," Xie said. "E-mail just isn't the same. I miss you, you know?"

Jonah felt his throat start to close up. God, how he knew. He could really use a friend like Xie at the moment. Preferably closer than a phone call away. "I do know," he said, managing to speak without tipping Xie off to his mood. "To what do I owe the pleasure? I trust from your chipper demeanor that you're not having problems with Bryce."

"God, no," she laughed. "He's wonderful. I'm calling for your mailing address."

That was odd—she could have just e-mailed him for that. It would have been more convenient. "It's—uh—hold on," he said, rummaging through the pile of junk mail by the door for something with the house number and zip code on it. "I haven't got it memorized yet."

"No hurry. We just got a long-distance phone plan," she teased.

Jonah tried really hard to be happy for her, but he couldn't help but feel the sting. He and Emerson weren't living together, were maybe not even together anymore at all. "Okay, I found it," he said at last. "Ready?"

At Xie's affirmative, Jonah rattled off the address. Xie read it back to him to ensure she had it down right.

"That's it," Jonah confirmed.

"Good! Oh! That reminds me." Jonah could hear her flipping through the pages of some kind of notebook. "I've forgotten Emerson's last name."

Jonah started feeling uneasy. "It's Blackburn. What do you need it for?"

"Well, it would be sort of rude to put 'and guest' on your invitation when the two of you have been together so long."

"Invitation?" Jonah echoed in a whisper.

Apparently she couldn't keep it in any longer. "To the wedding."

Oh, God. "Wedding?" he parroted.

"Bryce proposed!"

So it did mean what he thought it had meant. "Congratulations," he choked out as sincerely as possible. "That's really great, Xie. When's the big day?"

"This May. You're going to come, right? I'll finally get to meet Emerson?"

"Of course I'm coming. I want to meet Bryce, too, you know."

"And Emerson? He's not taking summer courses again, is he?"

Shit. Should he tell her? "Not that he's mentioned," he hedged.

He knew he was busted when Xie's silence went on way too long, and he sighed and folded like a cheap piece of paper. "We had a fight," he admitted.

"What!? You and the boy wonder? You could have led with that," Xie reproached him.

"I didn't want to rain on your parade! I really am happy for you."

"Never mind about my parade. It's not for another nine months. What happened?"

Jonah opened his mouth to answer, but nothing seemed to want to come out. Apparently he was all talked out.

That probably made it action time.

"Jonah!" Natalie bellowed from the top of the stairs. "We're leaving in twenty!"

Crap. The art exhibition thing was tonight. Making up with Emerson would have to wait until Natalie was done torturing him. "It's kind of a long story," he said. "And I've got to go. With any luck, by the next time I talk to you, there won't be anything to tell."

§

THEN

JONAH handed him a beer and took the lawn chair next to him as the sun sank over the bay. "Man, I can't believe it's your last day here." *I can't believe I've been such a pussy for an entire week*, he amended in his head. He couldn't be sure without asking, but he thought—he *thought* Emerson might possibly have the same kind of feelings for him that Jonah had about Emerson. He'd certainly caught him looking a time or two when Jonah had stepped out of the shower. Not that Jonah would hold that against him either way. He spent time at the gym on purpose to cultivate that kind of reaction. But he wanted it to mean something more coming from Emerson.

"Me neither," Emerson admitted. "Although I can certainly see why you don't want to come back home. You have a great view."

The view was pretty great, Jonah thought, but he was looking at Emerson's profile burnished pink and orange by the setting sun and not at the water. He couldn't help but think that he'd go back to Texas in a heartbeat if only Emerson asked him to. "I have no complaints."

They watched the rest of the sunset in near-silence, and then by mutual unspoken agreement they folded up the lawn chairs and went back inside. Jonah stashed the chairs inside the tiny coat closet and kicked his shoes in after, but Emerson paced farther into the apartment, going all the way to the window that looked out over the street. Everything about him screamed "agitated." Especially when he wrapped both arms around his torso.

Jonah frowned. "What are you thinking?"

Jonah saw him worry his lower lip for a moment before he released a long breath. "I'm thinking I should really—I was supposed to ask you why you left," he said in a rush. "I've been putting it off because… but I'm leaving tomorrow. I can't wait anymore."

Swaying like someone had just hit him with a sledgehammer, Jonah swallowed.

"I was starting to think you'd forgotten."

"I was so angry with you when you wouldn't tell me," Emerson went on. "I mean I was pissed you left in the first place, and then you didn't trust me—"

"It was never you I didn't trust," Jonah assured him. God, he'd been waiting for this moment for fucking *years,* and he still wasn't ready. "Maybe you should sit down?"

He could practically feel Emerson's anxiety ratcheting up another ten notches, but he did sit, and Jonah took care to keep as much distance between them on the couch as possible. "You're not dying or something, are you?" Emerson half-whispered.

"Jesus, fuck, no, Emerson, I'm not, I promise." Christ, if that was what Emerson thought, then Jonah had been a bigger asshole than he'd given himself credit for. "I'm fine, okay? Picture of health."

Emerson let out a deep breath and finally met his eyes. "Okay. What then? What could be so bad that you'd…?"

And here it was, the moment of truth. Jonah swallowed hard past the lump in his throat and resolved to finally put his money where his mouth was. "It was my birthday," he interrupted. If he didn't build up some momentum, he'd never get the story out right. "We were going to see a movie, remember? I was going to pick you up."

"I remember."

"Only when I got to your house, you weren't anywhere to be found. Not in the living room, dining room, or kitchen. So I went upstairs to your room, and that's when I saw you through the window." He didn't dare meet Emerson's eyes now, just kept his gaze focused on the twinkling lights of the city out the window. "When I saw you kissing Justin."

There was an impatient, curious noise from the couch beside him. "Jonah, I told you, it was only once, nothing to write home about—"

"But I didn't write home, did I?" Jonah cut him off. "I *left* home. Emerson, God, I know you say it didn't mean anything to you, but it meant a lot to me. All it took was that split-second, and then…." It was getting more and more difficult to continue, but he'd come this far.

Emerson's voice was almost too quiet. "And then?"

Obviously Emerson wasn't going to let him off the hook either, and that was good, Jonah told himself. But it didn't make the next part any easier. "And then I knew." It was an effort of sheer will, but Jonah forced himself to turn his head and meet Emerson's gaze head on. "I was furious, Emerson. It was an innocent kiss, I know that now, but for those few seconds I wanted to tear Justin's throat out. And then I had to stop and ask myself why, why the sight of my best friend kissing another man really bothered me. As I hauled ass somewhere else, by the way, because I couldn't let you know that I'd seen you. At first I thought maybe it was because you hadn't trusted me enough to tell me your secret. Or maybe I was just envious because you had someone and I didn't. But that didn't explain why I was so angry with Justin. When I was finally able to be honest with myself, I had to admit that it was because"—he took a deep breath and plunged ahead—"because I wanted you for myself."

By this time he was so deep in memory that the sharp intake of breath from Emerson barely registered. "And that just led to more questions. Did that mean I was gay? Bi? How strong were these"—he stumbled a little despite his best efforts—"feelings? Was it lust? Love? Was it possible that you felt the same? What if you did? Could we really be together? And if something did happen, what then? What if it didn't work? Would I lose my best friend as well as my…." No, he couldn't say the word. Couldn't say another word, in fact. Between the trepidation and relief building into a solid mass in his throat, he counted himself lucky to keep breathing.

§

BEFORE:

SHOVING his car keys into the pocket of his cargo shorts, Jonah slammed the door and headed up the drive, his flip-flops slapping happily against the interlocking brick.

The day was overcast—probably going to rain, Jonah thought, or maybe even thunderstorm like it had been threatening all week—but it didn't put a damper on his mood. He had a wallet full of birthday money and a car to use for the weekend while his parents went with Kierstyn to a soccer tournament in Houston. So far the plan was to pick up Emerson and hit the movies together. Then, when they inevitably ran into some girls from school—Hudson's Bend was a tiny little town, and it was Friday night after all—maybe go out for ice cream together. If that didn't work out he and Emerson could hit up the Blockbuster down the road from Emerson's parents' store and rent a couple horror movies, buy half a shelf of junk food, and spend all night on Jonah's couch until they were too terrified to move.

On second thought…. Jonah paused at the front door and looked up. The best ice cream in Hudson's Bend had no indoor seating and only a cloth awning to keep off the sun and a light drizzle. Maybe Plan B was a better idea.

Whatever. He'd see what Emerson thought. "Em?" Jonah opened the front door and toed off his flip-flops. "Mrs. B?"

No answer, but that wasn't too surprising; it was early, so they were probably still at work. Emerson usually got home around four, though, so maybe he was in the shower.

Jonah headed up the stairs, listening for the sounds of running water. Nothing. "Em?" he called again. He had to be home—Kierstyn would've come running already, and the door had been open. "You're not jerking off or something, are you?"

There was no response, so he figured it was probably safe to push open Emerson's door, but his room was empty too.

Weird. He was probably outside, then, Jonah decided, going over to the window. Emerson was a total dreamer and occasionally spent an hour or two lying on his back in the yard, watching the sky and getting sunburned. Not that that would be a problem today. Pushing back the curtain, Jonah peered out the window into the yard.

And frowned. Squinted. There *was* a boy in the yard, but it wasn't Emerson, hair a little too long and dark and shoulders a little too slender. But—oh. There was Emerson coming out of the lake, shoulders pink despite the cloud cover. Would he ever learn to put on sunscreen? Jonah wondered.

Emerson smiled when he saw the other boy, and when he picked up a towel to toss at Emerson, Jonah recognized Justin, Emerson's biology lab partner.

Now that he knew where Emerson was, he should go downstairs and demand the attention that was his due—it was his birthday, after all. But something kept him glued to the window, watching the scene unfold below him.

Jonah knew that Emerson had been spending more time with Justin since they had been partnered together in school, but he hadn't realized how much. Though he couldn't hear what was being said, he didn't need to. His normally shy, reserved friend was smiling and laughing, his posture assured and open.

Emerson ran the towel over his face first, then through his hair, causing it to stick up in damp clumps. He patted his chest and shoulders down more gingerly, Jonah noted with a roll of his eyes—probably sore. Jonah noticed the set of Justin's head as Emerson threw the towel on the picnic table and froze, suddenly feeling like he very much needed to be out in the yard with them and simultaneously unable to move. He was too far away to see Justin's eyes, but it seemed like—surely Justin wasn't looking at Emerson like—like *that*?

Justin put his hand on Emerson's arm, and Emerson turned around. Jonah caught just the hint of a blush before his face was turned the wrong way.

Jonah wasn't happy about that. Now he couldn't see what was going on with Emerson—well, he could extrapolate from Emerson's posture, which was still totally relaxed, though he was doing that fidgety thing with his left hand that he did when he was impatient. Did Emerson not think this was weird? Justin hadn't let go of his arm yet. Not even Jonah touched Emerson *that* much.

If seeing Justin's hand on Emerson's arm had Jonah anxious, watching the other hand come up to settle on his waist had him in a full-blown panic. Or it would have, if he had been able to do anything other than stare helplessly as Emerson's own hand came up and rested on Justin's arm. As he ducked his head like he did when he was *embarrassed* and looked up quickly again. Jonah's brain supplied an unhelpfully vivid vision of what he'd look like with those green eyes burning through his lashes. As Justin leaned down and pulled the world out from beneath Jonah's feet without a thought by smoothly tipping Emerson's face up into a kiss as if they'd been doing it for months.

Jonah didn't even stop to put on his sandals on his way out the door, just scooped them up by the thong and got into the car and drove.

He finally brought the car to a stop in the parking lot at the local ball diamond just as the first peal of thunder rumbled in the sky. With shaking hands, he killed the engine, then leaned his elbows on the steering wheel and put his head in his hands.

Okay. First things first.

Jonah was… shocked. Though, of course, now that he thought about it, perhaps he shouldn't have been. He had never known Emerson to display much interest in girls, despite their fascination with him—Jonah had always simply attributed this to Emerson's somewhat antisocial nature. And naturally Emerson had never mentioned his interest in boys, though that "dare" to watch *Brokeback Mountain* on television together when it had first aired a few years ago now made a lot more sense. So he was shocked, and a little hurt—because of course he'd taken the dare, and though they'd never spoken of it again, Jonah knew he hadn't given Emerson any reason to think he was homophobic. Because he wasn't.

Jonah curled his fingers into his hair and pressed his forehead against the steering wheel. Shocked, and hurt—and jealous. There was no avoiding that.

He was jealous of Emerson's time. It was Jonah's birthday, and they always spent it together. Justin had infringed on that, but that didn't account for the rising tide of hot emotion swelling in Jonah's chest.

It wasn't that Justin was a boy. Jonah was fairly sure he wasn't homophobic, but he was smart enough to realize that seeing something on television and experiencing it in person were different. He tested his theory by imagining Emerson kissing a girl—any girl, it didn't matter— and winced at the tug on his hair as his knuckles went white.

And it wasn't that Emerson had someone and Jonah didn't. Until two minutes ago Jonah had been perfectly happy being single.

No, Jonah was jealous because Emerson had kissed someone who wasn't Jonah. And apparently Jonah wanted Emerson all to himself.

"Fuck," he swore, closing his eyes tightly as the first drops of rain spattered against the windshield and lightning lit the cloud-covered sky. Sitting there with the rain pounding down on the roof of the car, he came to three realizations: first and second that he was in love with Emerson and it *sucked*; and lastly that he was apparently bisexual. *Hell of a fucking birthday*, he thought bitterly.

What would happen now that Emerson had a boyfriend? Someone who would share his life in ways Jonah couldn't? Would Jonah be able to watch Emerson fall in love with someone else from the sidelines? Could he put aside his own wants and be happy for his friend? He wasn't sure.

And what about in the fall? He and Emerson had always planned on rooming together in college, but how could he handle that sort of temptation? What if he ever interrupted Emerson and Justin in a private moment? How would he react? What would happen when Emerson found out about Jonah's feelings?

And then what if Justin broke Emerson's heart? Jonah knew how sensitive Emerson was, how easy it was to hurt him. Could he stand to console his friend? Would he be able to offer impartial advice when his own heart hung in the balance? Or what if they broke up and Jonah convinced Emerson to give him a chance? What then? Would anything more than friendship ruin their dynamic? What if—God forbid—it didn't work out? Could they be friends afterward? How would Jonah cope without Emerson once he'd kissed him, touched him, learned his body like he knew his own?

No, Jonah couldn't do that to himself—to them. Making up his mind, he turned the key in the ignition and headed for home.

§

THEN

EMERSON stared at his friend, wide-eyed and silent. His breath was caught in his throat. Oh. Jonah felt the same way. Jonah returned his feelings. Emerson looked down and noticed that his hands were shaking. He curled them into fists.

"I needed to get away, to think," Jonah was saying now. "I just—I needed to take some time to figure some stuff out. To find answers to some of those questions, like gay or bi?"

Emerson looked up again. Jonah was still staring out the window.

"I was kind of overwhelmed by it all, you know? All I could think was that I needed space to think, so I hopped on the first bus out of town to get it."

Oh. Jonah had left because—he had left to—"You needed to get away from me?" Emerson's voice was quiet, but it carried.

"No! That's not—I needed to get away from everyone. My world had turned upside down, and I couldn't turn to you or anyone else about it."

Emerson looked down again to see that his hands were still curled into tight fists. This was it, he was sure. This was the moment when Emerson had to make his own confession. He'd never get another moment as perfect as this.

Rising on shaky feet, he took a few hesitant steps forward before he spoke. "The kiss meant nothing." Jonah's shoulders tensed, and he looked like he might speak again, so Emerson hurried on. "It meant nothing because I didn't feel anything for him. He kissed me, and all I could think was, 'I wish he was Jonah'."

Jonah spun around. "What?" His eyes were wide, but they looked eager. He took a half-step in Emerson's direction. "Em…?"

"I—I pushed him away afterward because I wanted him to be you, and he wasn't," Emerson blurted out. "And I thought that spending the day with you at the movies sounded so much better."

"Emerson." Jonah was starting to smile. He took another step toward Emerson, but he wanted to get this all out, to reciprocate some of the emotional sharing.

"I tried dating other people, but it never works. Because no matter what I do or who I date, I can't ever get over you. I've done some stupid shit trying to make myself forget about you, but it never works. I'm still…." Emerson stumbled to a halt, the words failing him. He wasn't ready yet to say "love," but everything else seemed trite.

Jonah, it seemed, didn't care how Emerson finished that sentence. He had been moving closer and closer until he was standing in Emerson's space and wrapping two large palms around Emerson's face when his verbal outpouring trickled to a stop. Emerson looked up—and wow, did Jonah ever look tall when he stood so close—and saw that Jonah's eyes were dancing and his lips were curling at the corners.

"If it's all right with you, I'm going to kiss you, now."

Yes. Emerson's mouth went dry at that. He tried to nod instead, but Jonah was still framing his face. He must have looked pretty ridiculous, because Jonah huffed a small laugh. Then he was inching closer and bending his head down.

Emerson's eyes fluttered shut as Jonah's lips met his own.

For a long moment, Emerson didn't move. He just stood there stunned as Jonah pressed their lips together in a sweet, lingering kiss.

Jonah is kissing me. He felt giddy and lightheaded.

Jonah moved one hand down, stroking the length of his torso before long fingers curled around his hip. Then Jonah was trying to pull Emerson in closer, even as his lips were parting and asking Emerson's to do the same.

Feeling rushed back into Emerson's limbs. He stumbled forward into Jonah in answer to the pressure on his hip. His fingers, no longer numb, lifted to curl into the fabric of Jonah's shirt, his hands now resting on broad shoulders. And his lips....

His lips parted under Jonah's. Jonah nibbled on his bottom lip in thanks. Then his tongue teased forward, licking at Emerson's mouth with playful intent. Emerson gasped and let his own tongue move out to meet Jonah's.

Jonah was kissing him. Emerson was intoxicated with it. His limbs felt as though they were filled with buzzing electricity. It was getting harder and harder to keep his breath even. He pulled deep, desperate breaths through his nose. He felt dizzy, out of his body, and he was glad that Jonah was holding on to him, because all of his blood was rushing south.

Jonah pulled his mouth away, gasping desperately. He pressed his lips to Emerson's cheek and murmured his name.

Emerson just pressed closer, pulling in deep breaths of his own.

Jonah wound both arms around Emerson's body, and Emerson responded by winding his around Jonah's neck. They were kissing again when Emerson noticed something hard pressing against his belly. Jonah was hard for him. For once, the feel of another man's arousal was exciting and welcome.

Emerson groaned and pressed closer. A thrill of delight made him shiver when he realized that their hard-ons were pressed together.

"Emerson," Jonah murmured as he pressed eager kisses to the corner of Emerson's mouth and his jaw by his chin. A hand rubbed up his back, while the other rested warm and comfortable above his tailbone. A nibble to his lip and a kiss to his nose, Emerson shivered and moaned, drowning in all the delicious sensations.

It was wonderful. It felt amazing to be here with Jonah. Emerson threaded his fingers in Jonah's long hair, like he had wanted to do ever since he first saw the new style. He placed a few haphazard kisses of his own, trying to reciprocate, but it was obvious that Jonah had more practice. Which was okay. Emerson was fine with that and not intimidated in the slightest.

He pulled a ragged breath and closed his eyes when he felt Jonah's touch skate up the skin of his back. Right, Jonah was definitely putting all that practice to good use, and Emerson was seeing the benefits. He let his head fall down onto Jonah's shoulder, then pressed kisses to his neck. With one last fleeting thought of trying to return the favor, Emerson drifted off on a haze of lust, letting Jonah guide the way.

§

THE first taste of Emerson's lips was heady, but Jonah was only human, and he'd had a hard-on for Emerson since he was little more than a kid. Eventually he was going to want more than just Emerson's admittedly luscious mouth moving enthusiastically against his own. Luckily, he hadn't been going to the gym for nothing. It was a simple thing to reach out and put his hands on Emerson's waist and drag him within acceptable heavy-petting distance, and then….

At the first hint of Jonah's palm on the smooth, warm skin of his back, Emerson tensed, and for a second Jonah thought he might pull away. But no—his hands tugged a little harder at Jonah's hair, and he shuddered so slightly that Jonah wouldn't have noticed if he didn't have his *hands* on Emerson's *bare skin*, a fact that was incredibly distracting. Speaking of hands, he let them wander lower, wondering exactly how much Emerson would let him get away with, how much he was comfortable with. He didn't want to push his luck, but God, he'd been waiting *forever*.

He scored his nails almost accidentally up Emerson's back, and Emerson broke away from his mouth with a gasp and buried his face in Jonah's neck instead. When Emerson took the opportunity to apply his tongue to the pulse point pounding away there, Jonah decided that was just fine. "God, Emerson, if you had asked me about this on Monday we could have spent the whole damn week in the apartment." He didn't say *in bed*, though he was thinking it. He knew that was across the line.

Emerson made a tiny noise of agreement that reverberated all the way to Jonah's dick—no surprise there. Everything he did was going to Jonah's dick at this point—and Jonah thought, *Fuck it*. If he didn't push his luck now, he'd be waiting 'til Christmas at the earliest. He nudged Emerson down until he was sitting on the couch again, then followed him and slid his hands over Emerson's front, tracing the contours of the flat stomach and firm chest. "Take your shirt off."

Emerson bit him, momentarily derailing that train of thought as blood roared in Jonah's ears. In response, he smoothed his hand over firm flesh until he found the tight bud of a nipple, brushing first with his thumb and then pinching and massaging lightly until Emerson detached from his neck and let out a gasp that did nothing to ease the raging erection between Jonah's legs. Encouraged, he reached up with his other hand, giving the other nipple the same treatment.

Emerson moaned, and his hands tightened in Jonah's hair. Not ready to take his shirt off yet, then, Jonah thought, and decided to help him along by applying his mouth to the sweet little patch of sunburned skin behind Emerson's ear.

Emerson's breath hitched. "Jonah—"

God, if Emerson sounded that wrecked *now*, when Jonah had barely touched him anywhere, he had a feeling that all his brain cells were going to melt out his ears when Jonah finally got to his dick. Emerson had a voice made for the very best porn, and he was going to be *loud*, Jonah just knew it. He proved himself right when he slid his lips lower, sucking hard on the tendon in Emerson's neck, and the air filled with the sound of Emerson's groan.

Emerson released his death grip on Jonah's hair, and for a minute he thought he'd been convincing enough for Emerson to let him take his damn shirt off so he could get his mouth on his chest already, but Emerson was going for the hem of Jonah's tee instead, hands scrabbling across skin that had never been so sensitive. Reluctantly, Jonah dragged his hands away from Emerson's skin and raised his arms so Emerson could pull it over his head.

Maybe that was a little too real for Emerson just yet, because once Jonah had his shirt off he just sat back a little on the couch, eyes wide and glued to Jonah's chest, and yes, he was pretty built, but it wasn't a damn competition. Emerson needed to remember that. Jonah shifted around on the couch and put his hands on Emerson's waist again, this time depositing him right into his lap. "Stop over-thinking it and just kiss me again, Emerson," he demanded, and he skated his hands right up the back of Emerson's shirt again for extra credit.

That was all the coaxing he needed, apparently, because he pushed forward on Jonah's lap, so close Jonah could feel his excitement through his jeans, and there was no way Jonah's own erection was going to go unnoticed—Emerson had probably already felt it when they'd first kissed—but fuck it, that was sort of the point, wasn't it? Disentangling his hands from Emerson's shirt, he slid them up to the back of his neck instead and dragged him down to lip level.

Jonah licked into Emerson's mouth, chasing the last hint of beer from his lips, teeth, tongue, stroking strong and sure, then fading back into a tease until Emerson whined high in his throat and pushed his whole body into Jonah's, shoving him back into the couch as he fought for control of the kiss. "Fuck," he murmured into Emerson's mouth. He was trying like crazy to keep his hands above the belt, but unless Emerson actually told him to stop, he wasn't going to be able to. The last week had been like one excruciatingly long striptease, and now he only had a few hours left to touch Emerson in all the ways he wanted to, and it was never going to be enough time. "I can't believe you have to leave tomorrow, maybe we can change your flight—"

Emerson put a cautious, exploratory hand on Jonah's abs, almost like he was counting the ridges, and that was just *it*.

"Jesus Christ, Emerson, get your shirt off *now*."

Jonah didn't miss the telling shudder or the poorly disguised moan or the way Emerson thrust hard down into his lap, but those things were for investigating at some other juncture, preferably once they had had six or seven orgasms to take the edge off. For the time being he contented himself with pulling the offending cotton up and away from Emerson's skin so they could press their bare chests together.

It was electric—more than electric; it was fucking *nuclear*. Emerson's gasping sob echoed from the walls, and Jonah felt the surge of energy fill him up, make him act. Somehow he got one hand under Emerson's implausibly incredible ass and the other between his shoulder blades and flipped him onto his back on the couch, following after and pressing his thigh up between Emerson's, feeling the erection that was trapped there.

Emerson made a noise like he was dying in the best possible way, so Jonah did it again, coupling it with the flicker of his tongue over Emerson's nipple. Emerson jerked his hips beneath him, bringing his pelvic bone into delicious contact with Jonah's dick, and one of his hands flew up to his mouth and stifled a perfectly delicious moan of enjoyment. "Fucking wanted this for years," Jonah murmured into Emerson's collarbone, licking first and then biting gently before stopping to suck a round purple bruise in the hollow of Emerson's throat. "Thought about you like this, what I wanted to do to you." A bite at one dusky nipple, a thrust of his hips, and another, louder gasp of encouragement from Emerson. "What I wanted you to do to me."

Shuddering all over, Emerson let his head fall back, his hands, clammy with sweat, making their way to Jonah's back, urging him closer. "What—" he started, cutting himself off with a moan when Jonah sucked another bruise higher on his neck. "What should I—"

Jesus. Jonah groaned. "Anything, God." He pushed himself up on one hand long enough to grab Emerson's arm, followed it down, turned and directed him until Emerson's palm was pressing against the bulge in his jeans. "Just, fuck, touch me, *please*—"

Emerson did, tentatively at first, just a tease of pressure, almost more frustrating than not being touched at all, and Jonah ducked his head down, bit at his earlobe until Emerson's whining pants filled the room. "So fucking hot," he whispered between licks down Emerson's neck, his own breath catching as Emerson got more daring, increasing the pressure on his cock. "Knew you would be, Em, always knew it would be like this."

He mouthed Emerson's Adam's apple, pushed his knee up against Emerson's erection until he sobbed loud into the room. "Fuck," Emerson swore, thrusting his hips up again. "God, Jonah. That's…."

"You like it when I talk dirty to you, Emerson?" he asked huskily, not that he could stop if he wanted to. "Like knowing how hard you get me?"

Emerson gave a choked-off cry as Jonah sucked up another bruise, this one just under his jaw line, and ran his thumbnail over his left nipple just hard enough to scratch. He fumbled frantically with the fly of Jonah's jeans for a few excruciating seconds, and then his hand curled hot and firm around Jonah's dick, and they both groaned.

"Jesus, yes," Jonah hissed, not bothering to resist thrusting into Emerson's palm. "Like that, fuck, harder, Em, I'm not going to break—"

Emerson licked his lips, whimpered, and fuck, Jonah had to kiss him, a truly filthy open-mouthed kiss that was all slick tongue and unadulterated desire. "Fuck, God, Em," he gasped a minute later as Emerson's thumb swept wetly over the head of his cock. "Yes, like that, Emerson, so hot, gonna make me come—"

A strangled gasp fell from Emerson's lips and Jonah licked it away while making good on his promise, fucking hard into his hand and spraying ropes of thick white come everywhere as his vision dimmed, and his heart pounded in his ears. He kissed Emerson sloppily, his mind still comfortably fuzzy, before drawing back enough to survey his handiwork.

Come had spattered all over Emerson's chest and stomach from his shoulder to the waistband of his jeans—and they hadn't been spared either. The sight left Jonah feeling like he'd been kicked in the stomach. His mouth went dry, and his dick gave a valiant twitch indicating its interest. But now was really not the time for that. He'd already given Emerson too much damn time to get his head back on straight, and if he gave him any more, he was going to start panicking. Already was, if he was reading the renewed tension in Emerson's posture right.

Jonah drew an idle finger through the mess on Emerson's chest, tracking the movement as he circled a nipple and swallowing hard. "This is a surprisingly good look for you," he said hoarsely before sinking back down onto his elbows and kissing the apprehension out of Emerson's mouth. It wasn't long before the tension was gone, and Emerson was pushing his body up against Jonah's again, obviously looking for some stimulation, but now that Jonah had him right where he wanted him, he wasn't in any hurry. "You really need to read the fucking book I wrote you, Emerson," he murmured, trailing his lips down Emerson's neck to his chest again, heedless of the salt-bitter taste of his own come.

"Oh, God," Emerson whined when Jonah took one nipple between his teeth. "Jonah, please."

"Please what?" he asked, switching sides and sliding his right hand down to the front of Emerson's jeans. "Please keep touching you? Please have my way with you? Please tease you all night until you wake all the neighbors with your screaming?"

"Oh, God," Emerson repeated. He tried to rub himself up against Jonah's hand, but Jonah pulled away just in time.

Deftly undoing the top button of his fly, Jonah pressed on, letting his fingers linger in the trail of sparse hair that led to Emerson's dick. "Please make you come?"

"Yes!" Emerson sobbed desperately. "Yes, okay? Please, Jonah."

Jonah drew down his zipper slowly before peeling back the fabric and trailing his fingers ever-so-lightly over Emerson's cloth-covered erection. Suddenly he could smell Emerson's arousal, and the scent made him lightheaded, dizzy. "I want to suck you," he said, and Emerson shivered all over, moaning continuously. "I haven't thought about anything else for a week, not since the flight. You were so nervous, I just wanted to shove you into the bathroom, get on my knees and make you forget." Heart pounding, Jonah reached into Emerson's boxers and pulled out his cock, already wet with pre-come. Emerson gave a wordless cry and tried to thrust into his hand, but Jonah kept his grip light. "I jerked off in the airplane bathroom thinking about it, Emerson. Like I was fucking fifteen again." He slid his body lower, pressing open-mouthed kisses and love bites all down Emerson's torso, scraping his teeth across the skin around his navel. "Let me do it, Emerson. It'll be so good." Emerson's stomach was heaving as he practically hyperventilated. "Emerson. Can I? Can I suck you?"

"Yes!" Emerson practically shouted. "Yes, yes, God, whatever you want, just—"

§

EMERSON'S fingers were trembling when he pressed them over his eyes. Oh God. It was too much. Jonah was, at that very moment, pulling down Emerson's pants so that they weren't in the way when Jonah went to suck him. Jonah was going to suck his cock.

Emerson whimpered.

God, if the idea alone was enough to make him want to come….

"Yeah, Emerson." When Jonah spoke, warm puffs of air blew over Emerson's dick, making his thigh and stomach muscles tremble in response. "I can't wait. Been dying to do this. To suck you."

He whimpered again. If Jonah didn't stop talking he was going to spontaneously combust.

Jonah leaned down, and then—

Oh! That was Jonah's tongue. On his dick. Licking all. The way. Up.

His lips pressed together to muffle the moans, but when Jonah reached the head and gave it an extra lick, Emerson couldn't stop the next one.

Nor could Emerson stop his hands from moving away from his face. One flew out to grab the back of the couch. The other landed next to his hip, where it curled in the gap between two cushions. Emerson felt like he might fly off the couch.

He looked down and saw Jonah shoot him a filthy smile before he shifted his body and readjusted his grip. One large hand curved around Emerson's hipbone, the other around his cock. Then Jonah leaned forward and wrapped his lips around the head. Oh so slowly, he started to slide down the length of it.

It was too hot to watch. Emerson's head fell back onto the armrest, and more whimpers flew out in a rush. The hand clutching the couch cushions rose without Emerson's permission and gripped Jonah's hair, which Jonah liked, judging from the way he let out a long moan around Emerson's cock. The vibrations made heat spread through Emerson's belly and out toward his fingers and toes. Emerson could feel the moan building, and fuck, he knew it would be loud.

Desperately, he brought his left hand up, relinquishing his remaining hold on the couch to slap his palm over his mouth. God, he wished he could do better than simply muffle the noise. He wished more than ever that he could just shut himself up, but he had learned long ago that he could never keep himself quiet. The only thing he could do was try and stop some of the sound and keep the embarrassment level to a minimum.

Jonah pulled up slowly until only the head of Emerson's cock was in his mouth. Emerson could feel his tongue working at it, stroking and licking.

Oh God!

The other hand flew up to join the first, both pressing hard against his mouth, trying to keep the mortifying noises inside.

He felt Jonah pull his mouth away and heard the obscene popping noise it made. Oh Jesus, Jonah was trying to kill him.

"Emerson." And now Jonah was stopping to *talk to him*. Emerson kept his eyes shut tight and his head tossed back. Maybe if he ignored him Jonah would go back to what he was doing with the licking and the sucking. "What are you doing?" Jonah asked him. His voice sounded kind of funny, husky and sexy, but also confused. Emerson squeezed his eyes tighter.

"Emerson? Are you trying to silence yourself?" Jonah's hands suddenly slid up his body and then his arms. They wrapped around his wrists and then began to pull on them.

Emerson let Jonah pull his hands away. He could bring them back later.

"Em, look at me." It really wasn't fair of Jonah to ask that, because Emerson couldn't resist him when he used that voice.

Letting his eyes flutter open, he looked down his body to see Jonah between his thighs. Oh, Lord, that just wasn't fair.

"Now, how about we try this again, but this time you don't try and stop all those delightful noises before they leave your lips?" Jonah was grinning.

"What?" Emerson blinked at him, uncomprehending.

Jonah smirked and crawled up Emerson's body, speaking all the while. "I like the noises you make. I want to hear you." Their faces were level now, and Jonah leaned in to place a soft kiss on Emerson's mouth. "So stop covering your mouth and let me."

Then Jonah was sliding back down his body and swallowing Emerson's cock down deep.

Christ!

Emerson couldn't help the way his back arched or the loud moan that pushed its way up his throat. Or his automatic response of slapping his hand over his mouth.

"Hmm, I can see this might be a difficult habit to break," said Jonah. And then he was pulling at Emerson's arms and placing Emerson's hands in his hair. "Next time you get the urge to do something else with those? Don't."

Emerson stared at Jonah wide-eyed, confused, and unbalanced. Jonah wanted him to make a fool of himself?

"Jonah," he managed to get out. "I… I get really *loud*," he muttered, embarrassed to admit it.

Jonah's response was to grin widely. "Oh, I *hope* so." And funnily enough, he really sounded like he did. "Emerson, I like the noises you make. Now, let me suck you off."

Then he was leaning down and taking Emerson's cock into his

mouth once again. It was different this time, more focused. Jonah was sucking hard, bobbing his head up and down. His enthusiastic motions were so good that Emerson started to moan again. He pressed his lips together automatically, and his left hand started to uncurl from Jonah's hair, but Jonah reached up and held Emerson's hand where it was. Then he pulled up, sucking the whole time and running his tongue along the bottom of Emerson's dick.

It was too good. It felt too amazing, and Emerson couldn't hold *this* moan back without his hands. It burst forward loud and obvious, and had Emerson not already been flushed with desire, he would have colored in embarrassment at the sound.

Except… Jonah let out a moan in response and screwed his lips down farther than they had been before, while a hand reached down to stroke Emerson's balls. Okay. Judging by the positive reinforcement Jonah was employing, he hadn't been lying about liking Emerson's noises.

Jonah liked the way Emerson was when he was turned on.

Jonah kept "encouraging" him until Emerson was soon making near-continuous noises of pleasure. Many were still muffled behind his clenched lips, and he kept trying to use his hand to cover up the loudest of them, but he was louder than he had ever let himself be before.

"Jonah, I'm gonna… oh God! Do—more! More! Jonah!" Emerson wasn't sure when exactly he had started babbling, but he thought it might have been around the time he realized he was about to come.

He clenched his fingers and felt the silky strands between them. Jonah moaned encouragingly. One hand was curled around Emerson's hip to keep it in place. The other was around the base of Emerson's cock, jerking frantically.

Emerson's toes curled, and his thighs tensed. He started muttering, "Jonah, JonahJonahJonahJonah," and he was still calling out for Jonah when he came hard down his throat. Emerson's eyes were tightly shut, but the world still went white. His hips tried to push up, stopped only by Jonah holding him in place.

The sound of Jonah's satisfied moan, the feel of his large hands holding him still, and the strong suck Jonah added at the end had glorious aftershocks shaking Emerson's body.

Emerson lost some time. One moment he was coming, the next Jonah was leaning over him and smiling. "Emerson," he said, making it sound like an endearment. Then he was kissing Emerson long and sweet. Emerson wrapped both arms around Jonah's shoulders and didn't fight it when the kiss made his toes curl.

§

"ARE you freaking out?" Jonah asked casually, flat on his back and staring up at the ceiling.

"No," Emerson blatantly lied into Jonah's chest. It was really the only way to comfortably fit the two of them on the couch lying down. Not that Jonah was complaining.

Jonah grinned. "Liar." It was okay. Emerson only freaked out when he *cared.*

"Yes," Emerson admitted, sounding equal levels of annoyed and contrite.

It took all of Jonah's remaining energy to lift his head and look down at the man sprawled across his pecs. "Why?"

There was what Jonah might call a very pointed silence. Then he said, a little more gently than he'd intended, "Do I need to spell it out with Shakespeare, Emerson?" Silence. Jonah's lips quirked into a fond smile. "*Hamlet* or *Romeo and Juliet*?"

"How about something that didn't end in disaster for everyone involved?" Emerson stopped, and Jonah could practically feel him backpedaling. "Not that I—I mean if you *have to*—you don't—"

Jonah pouted theatrically. "That's not fair. All the greatest love quotes are from tragedies." The comedies were useless. "'O, never say that I was false of heart, though absence seemed my flame to qualify.'" He carded his fingers idly through Emerson's hair. "'As easy might I from myself depart as from my soul which in thy breast doth lie.'"

"Jonah. Don't tease me."

"Do I sound like I'm joking?"

A long moment of nothing, and then a gentle, juddering sigh. Jonah went on, "I'm not going to take it back. I love you, and now you are stuck with me. Is that clear enough, or do I have to write you a sonnet?"

Pause.

"Emerson?"

"I'm thinking!" Emerson said, mock-indignant, and Jonah laughed.

"You don't have to decide right now. In fact, please don't decide right now." A sudden thought occurred to him. "Emerson. This is why Zack hates me, isn't it?" He propped himself up on his elbows so he could watch Emerson blush. He was so right. "That's adorable."

"Shut up," Emerson muttered into his trapezius.

"Oh, make me," Jonah challenged lightly, and Emerson surprised him by lifting his head, a calculating expression on his face, and crawling up a few inches to kiss him thoroughly.

"So there."

There was no way to contain the goofy smile, so Jonah didn't bother to try, just stared happily at the ceiling and ran his hands up and down the smooth skin of Emerson's back a few times lazily. "Come to bed, Emerson."

Emerson froze.

"To sleep, idiot," Jonah chided, though he couldn't blame Emerson for thinking that when the evidence of Jonah's renewed interest was, if not exactly staring him in the face, at least poking him in the leg.

"Oh," Emerson said. "Alright."

Of course, when they got there, there was some amount of shifting around and making themselves comfortable, none of which did anything to ameliorate Jonah's problem. Figuring his choices were to wait until it went away—and it could be a long wait, if he was going to be spending it curled up around Emerson—or go looking for trouble, Jonah took his chances and nuzzled his face into the back of Emerson's neck, curling one proprietary hand over his hip.

"You said we were just going to sleep!" Emerson reminded him as Jonah rubbed circles on his flank with his thumb.

Humming in response, Jonah pressed his lips to Emerson's hairline, nibbling lightly, sliding his hand lower. "Did I?"

Emerson huffed, but his breath was definitely coming quicker. "You know you—" He cut himself off as Jonah wrapped his hand loosely around his erection. "You lured me here under false"—his hips stuttered—"false pretenses."

Jonah grinned to himself. "Do you want me to stop?"

Emerson's breathless laugh went right to his cock. "Don't you dare."

§

WHEN Jonah dropped Emerson off at the airport, he wouldn't let Emerson go before acting out a very cheesy goodbye.

Emerson had gasped with surprise when Jonah suddenly wrapped an arm around his shoulders and pressed the opposite hand warm against the small of his back, then tilted Emerson back into a low dip. There, in the middle of the airport, Jonah kissed him thoroughly.

Emerson blushed hotly, embarrassed by such a romantic public display. When Jonah let him straighten back up, he didn't miss the fact that people were watching. Strangers were staring at him.

"You're insane," Emerson muttered as he put his face in Jonah's neck so that he wouldn't have to see them watching him.

"You love it!" Jonah crowed. He was laughing with delight, exhilarated by what he had just done, Emerson could tell.

"You're still a maniac," Emerson said, tilting his head to kiss Jonah's jaw. "Now, are you going to let me go so I can get on my plane?"

Jonah's arms tightened around him. "I don't want you to go. I'm going to miss you. Are you sure you can't just stay here forever?" Jonah asked, flashing puppy dog eyes.

Emerson placed one hand over Jonah's face. "Put those away. They don't work on me."

Jonah grinned. "Sure they do!"

"Well, they don't work well enough to get me to miss my flight back home. Despite how much I want to be with you."

Jonah gave a pleased, sappy grin at that. "Well, alright then. Just so long as I know that you would rather be with me, I'll be satisfied enough to let you go." Jonah contradicted those words with another squeeze.

Emerson laughed. "Seriously, Jonah!"

Jonah just grinned and planted another kiss on his mouth.

Emerson opened his mouth to tell Jonah off again when he heard a boarding call for his plane.

"You have to go," Jonah said, sounding disappointed.

"Yeah, I have to go."

"I'll see you at Christmas," Jonah pointed out. "And we still have e-mail."

"E-mail isn't a very good substitute. I don't get to hear your voice. *You* need to get a phone," Emerson said, tapping a finger on Jonah's chest.

Jonah gave a self-deprecating smirk. "But they're so expensive. Skype is free, though."

Smiling, Emerson said, "That it is. But for now, you have to let me go."

Jonah let out a mighty sigh and kissed him hard one last time, then let him go. "See you at Christmas?"

"Yeah, you'll see me at Christmas," Emerson said before taking a step back. Jonah had clung to his hands for a long moment before finally letting go.

Emerson hadn't been able to help the way that he turned to look back over his shoulder to get one last glimpse of Jonah before he turned the corner and was out of sight.

The flight home felt like it took eons. He was just as nervous flying this time as he was on the first trip, except this time Jonah wasn't with him to make it better.

By the time the flight touched down in Austin, Emerson was a bit of a wreck: he was jittery and sweaty, and he was pretty sure he had tugged and pushed his hair into a mess. He didn't hesitate when it came to getting off the plane.

Emerson was, at that moment, very glad that Jonah had convinced him not to check any luggage. He really didn't feel up to waiting around. Right now, he wanted to get in Zack's car and get home to clean clothes and a shower.

When it had come time to finding a ride home from the airport, Emerson had gone to his friend to act as chauffeur. Fortunately for Emerson, Zack was the kind of guy who would pick you up from the airport so your grieving mother wouldn't have to.

Relief swept through Emerson when he finally caught sight of a waiting Zack.

"Emma! Welcome home!" Zack called out to him.

Emerson smiled back and waved as he approached. "Hey," he greeted once he was within talking distance.

As he was expecting a standard greeting in response, Emerson was rather surprised when Zack replied with raucous laughter. His eyes were dancing, and he even clapped his hands together in delight. "Oh-oh, Emma! Had a good trip I see!"

Emerson frowned at his friend. Considering he probably looked a bit neurotic and tired after that flight, he wasn't sure what it was about his appearance that made Zack reach that conclusion. "What?"

Zack's grin got even wider. "Oh, don't tell me you didn't notice!" When Emerson continued to stare at him, confused, Zack let out another bark of laughter. Then he reached up with one hand to poke a long finger into Emerson's neck. The prodding was surprisingly painful.

"Ouch!" Emerson swatted his hand away. "What are you…?"

"Your boy is the amorous type. Also, I'm thinking very possessive. He marked you up good."

"What?" he asked again, though he could feel the dawning horror.

"You're covered in hickeys. Covered."

Emerson's eyes widened in dismay. "Oh God. Really?"

"How did you not notice?" Zack asked, still grinning as he started to lead the way to the car.

"I didn't shave this morning, so I didn't really look in a mirror." Oh geez, Zack had noticed them straight away, which meant that they were visible enough for other people to have noticed them. He could feel his cheeks flushing with embarrassment. "I'm going to kill Jonah. He never even said anything," Emerson whined.

"'Course he didn't. Probably figured you'd get all embarrassed, and there's nothing you can do about it now. They're there, and you can't wear a scarf in this heat."

Oh man. Just great. Not only was Jonah apparently a vampire, but he was a proprietary and exhibitionistic one. It would seem that he liked to both mark Emerson up and show those marks off. And now Zack was going to laugh at him, and Zack knew—

"Wait a minute, how did you know Jonah…?"

"Left his calling card?" Zack asked, one eyebrow arched as he unlocked the car's doors. "Because no way did you let a stranger mark you up that bad and not notice. Also, any fool could see how bad that boy's got it for you." Then he slid into the car, leaving Emerson to scramble at the door handle and tussle with his bag as he hastily made it into the car.

"What?!"

"Figured it out the first time I saw him. Jonah's crazy in love with you." Zack turned on the engine and started to pull out of the parking space.

Emerson reached for his seat belt and quickly snapped it shut. "You figured out Jonah was in love with me while standing on a street curb with him for… two minutes?"

"Yeah. He's 'bout as difficult to understand as pig Latin." Zack smirked.

Emerson sat in stunned silence, taking that in.

"So, I take it things went well on your vacation then?" Zack asked eventually.

A no doubt silly and stupid grin formed on Emerson's face. "Really well. The week was awesome, but then last night Jonah confessed…." Emerson cleared his throat. "He told me he felt the same."

"I'm glad." Emerson was impressed, as Zack only sounded a little grudging as he said that. "You were due for some good news in your life."

Emerson was surprised at how touched he was by those words. "Thanks."

There was a long pause that was definitely turning awkward. Emerson should have known how badly Zack would do with this kind of conversation.

The sound of Zack clearing his throat very loudly filled the vehicle. “Right, so let’s get you home to your mama.”

Emerson grinned at his crazy friend. It was good to be home. And soon he’d be walking in the front door and seeing his mom and little sister for the first time in a week. Life was feeling pretty damn good, he thought to himself, reaching up to scratch at his neck. He was surprised by another twinge of pain. Right, so life was pretty damned good, despite the array of hickeys. He was going to get back at Jonah for that. First, though, he was going to go home and….

“Shit! I can’t go home after a vacation to San Francisco to see my mama when I’m covered in hickeys!”

Zack’s laughter filled the cabin as they sped down the highway.

CHAPTER 14

NOW

"KILL the redhead, marry Hanna, and fuck Hayley," said Eve with a discreet sip of her wine. Her eyes were sparkling with delight. Emerson shot her an incredulous look. Sure, he had given her the options, but that was not how he thought things would play out. "Have you had Hanna's cookies?" Eve wanted to know.

Emerson blinked at her. "Does Hayley know you have designs on her? Never mind. I suppose I should be grateful you're not going to off one of my best friends," he said dryly.

"And only fag hag!" chirped Eve.

Emerson ignored her. "Also, it's good to know a lifelong commitment from you comes so cheap."

Eve looked affronted. "They have bacon in them, Emerson. Bacon." She sighed. "It's amazing. Miraculous, even. Plus, Hayley is way hotter than Red. Anyway, it's my turn now." Her eyes took on mischievous sparkle. "Fuck, marry, kill: Zack, Greg, Matt."

"Seriously? That's just wrong any way you cut it," Emerson told her. Eve just gave him a look; she wouldn't change her play. He sighed. "Fine. Marry Greg because he knows how to clean a bathroom and put shit away, fuck Matt because yes, he really is that pretty, and kill Zack because he'd hit me if I ever even suggested the other two to him."

Eve gave a delighted laugh. "At least you didn't say marry Matt. And it's not like you can marry Zack in Texas anyway, you know. Alright, go on, hit me with it."

Emerson started peering around the room. "I can't marry Greg either," he muttered distractedly. He stared at all the prospects.

"Neither can I, you know. It's just part of the fantasy," Eve said with a smirk.

Emerson just rolled his eyes. "Um… fuck, marry, kill: Surya, girl in yellow dress in the corner, or…." He took another sweeping glance of the room before settling on—he snorted—"Professor Stacey."

"Kill Surya, fuck yellow dress, marry Professor Stacey."

Emerson couldn't help the gagging noise he made.

"Come on, dude, even you have to admit the woman is pretty hot for forty. And the take-no-prisoners attitude is a total turn-on."

Emerson just stared at her. "That was more than I wanted to know about your kinks."

"Don't lie, darling, you know you like it! Now, FMK: the hottie in the blue shirt, Jerome—he's the one in the corner with the pink tie—or, hmm. Oooh, the guy with the girl in the red dress with the amazing rack. Actually, damn, maybe I want them both to myself." Eve lifted a hand to fan herself.

"Pink tie?" asked Emerson as he started to look around for these three guys. "That's too much even for me. I may have to reject him on principle. Blue shirt has potential, and…," he was saying as he turned to look for the last choice, his eyes finally spotting the bright red dress. The dress was pretty sinful: high hem, low neck, and tight curves. But Emerson was a little disturbed to see that the dress was also on a very familiar body—Natalie—and so the hot guy Natalie was with was—"Oh."

"Emery? Come on, what's the hold-up? Aren't you going to answer? Em?"

Jonah looked—oh, he looked as gorgeous as ever. Emerson's mouth went dry as he stared. Natalie said something to him then that had him tossing his head back to let out one of his boisterous laughs.

"Damn," muttered Eve. "Right, I can see why you're distracted. But come on, Emery, fuck or marry Mr. Gorgeous?"

Marry! Emerson's hindbrain cried. *Marry him!*

"That's—it's Jonah," Emerson managed to choke out.

"What? *That's* Jonah? Oh, damn…." Eve gave him a tentative sidelong look.

Jonah. Jonah was here. Why was Jonah here? This was the last place Emerson had suspected he'd run into Jonah.

"Emerson?" Eve prompted.

"Marry," Emerson croaked out.

"I know. Maybe you should tell him that?"

"I can't—he wouldn't—he was so mad, I don't know if he would…," Emerson stumbled out.

Then Jonah was turning to look at him. Jonah was looking at him first with surprise but then with that same familiar, tender look.

Emerson downed the rest of his wine, then passed the empty glass to Eve. Right. Jonah was what he wanted, and it was time to tell him that.

§

THEN

UNFORTUNATELY for Emerson, there was no way that he could avoid going home. His mother was expecting him and would definitely be disappointed if he didn't show up after being away for a week. So Emerson let Zack take him home.

"Good luck," Zack told him with a smile.

Emerson grumbled and waved the finger at Zack in return.

He stayed outside to watch Zack drive off, but he knew it was just an excuse to delay the inevitable.

When he walked through the front door, it was to a cry of, "You're home!" Then his mother was there, wrapping her arms around him tight and giving him a squeeze.

"Oh, I missed you, baby! Did you have a good time?" she was already asking even before she had fully relinquished her grip. Standing back, she held him at arm's length.

"How was San Francisco? How's Jonah doing?" she asked as she looked him over. Her eyes went kind of funny, but then she was demanding to hear about what he had done on his visit.

Emerson soon found himself being guided to a kitchen chair. His mother placed a drink before him and then added a plate of cookies.

"Are you hungry?" she asked of him, and then she was making him food.

Her prodding was relentless, and soon Emerson was recounting the week he'd had with Jonah. Telling her about all the sights they had visited and the things they had done.

After Emerson had finished telling his mother about visiting the Fraenkel Gallery of Photography and eaten the last of his sandwich, his mother gave him a long look and said, "So, darling, did you do anything else interesting on your trip?"

Emerson took another drink of his juice and considered the question. He'd discussed the Fraenkel Gallery, told her also about seeing the de Young and the Legion of Honor art galleries. He had told her about going to the beach and seeing Alcatraz in the distance, and about the Golden Gate Bridge and Park, Sausalito and the Fisherman's Wharf. He had even told her the story about Jonah and the sea lions.

He couldn't think of anything else that he wanted to tell her, and told her as much.

"Oh. Are you sure?" she asked him. "There's nothing else you wanted to tell me about?" She raised both eyebrows at her son. Emerson felt himself color as he considered what it was that he wasn't telling his mother.

He shook his head.

"Honey, are you sure there is nothing happy you want to tell me about? Maybe something that happened yesterday?"

Her eyes flicked down, and she stared pointedly his neck.

Emerson felt himself color again. "Um." He looked down and stared at the crumbs on his plate. "No?" His voice was hesitant. He reached out with one hand and began pushing some of the crumbs around on his plate.

His mother sighed. "Oh. You know that you can tell me anything, right?"

Emerson looked up to see that his mother was staring at him, her eyes looking kind of sad. He *couldn't* put that look on her face.

"Yes," he whispered to his plate.

"So, you've nothing else to tell me?" she prodded once again.

Emerson sighed. "Um, maybe? Jonah… uh, Jonah asked me to be his boyfriend?"

"Hm, so I see. He was quite persistent in his asking," she said, her eyes trailing over his neck. "I'm guessing that you said yes then."

He wondered if it was possible to do himself an injury by blushing too much. “Yes.”

“Good. I could tell, the last time I saw you, how much you adored him. I’m happy for you, sweetheart.”

Emerson stared at his mother. *You could?* he thought desperately. Then he found his voice to say, “You’re okay with this?”

She gave him a shaky smile. “Yes, dear. I told you months ago I was okay with you being gay, and I can’t think of anyone better then Jonah to entrust with your heart.” She smiled at him then. “He’s a good boy.”

A soppy smile cross his face. “Yeah, he’s kind of wonderful,” Emerson confessed.

His reverie was broken by his mother’s laughter. “Oh my, but you do have it bad. And I suppose Jonah’s equally as enamored with you. I can’t imagine that boy playing around with your heart.”

Nodding, Emerson tried to ignore the flicker of doubt he felt about that. “He said he….” Embarrassment stole his voice, so he waved his hand around, hoping that would suffice to tell her. “I believe him,” he added in a whisper.

“Good!” his mother said. She clapped a hand on his shoulder and smiled at him. “Now. My next topic of conversation is out. Knowing Jonah, I guess that I don’t have to worry if you were safe. That boy has always been too careful with your well-being to put you in danger.”

Emerson stared at his mother in horror. “What?” His voice pitched a little too high.

“Any other boy and I’d be worried, but not with him.”

He felt his blush return. He hoped she attributed it to general embarrassment at the topic of conversation and not that he was recalling how he and Jonah hadn’t exactly been careful. He knew condoms weren’t needed for hand-jobs, but Jonah hadn’t used one when he sucked him off. “Good, I guess?” Emerson finally managed to choke out.

His mother simply laughed at him. “Though I do feel I should express my concern over your alternative lifestyle choice.”

Emerson stared at her, uncomprehending. She already knew that he was gay, and she had just told him that she wasn’t upset about that.

"Well, you are dating a vampire, or so it would seem." She was smirking at him.

"Oh my God!" Emerson covered his face. "That's it. I'm never letting Jonah near me again. I already had to listen to Zack's comments."

His mother laughed again. "I knew there was a reason I liked him."

§

EMERSON grabbed his wallet and keys and headed out the door. Though he missed seeing Kierstyn and his mom more frequently than once a week, he really liked not having to leave the house an hour before an event in Austin now that he was living with Zack and Greg. Being able to walk to class and Hang Out was pretty satisfying.

When it had come time to pack up and move into the townhouse, Emerson had tried to tell his mother he had changed his mind. After all, since Greg's father was loaded (so much so that Greg was now in his fifth year and getting an additional degree in Geography), the two of them had been able to handle the rent for the three-bedroom just fine, so it wasn't like they needed Emerson's help. His mother had refused to let him stay with her and Kierstyn, though. With only Kierstyn to care for, his mom was more than capable of taking care of the store. Besides, she argued, Dad would never forgive her if she let Emerson put his life on hold once again. Walking to Hang Out, Emerson was very grateful she'd kicked him out.

When Emerson walked into the café, he grinned at the sight of so many familiar faces. He had been so happy to get back to regular meetings and had been surprised at how pleased he was to see Alex the first meeting back. He'd been so happy to hear Alex's delighted, "Emerson!" and to share stories about their summers.

After Emerson grabbed his coffee, he sat down next to Alex, who was talking to a cute Asian girl. "Em, this is Surya, she's a second-year English student."

Emerson smiled welcomingly, pleased to meet her. "I'm Emerson."

"Em's an artist," Alex said.

"Nice to meet you, Emerson. Alex was just telling me about the last club night you guys had."

Emerson grinned. Every few weeks, Hang Out did group nights out to some of the under–twenty-one or eighteen-plus clubs in Austin. Despite being dry, the nights often ended in crazy, outlandish stories.

He was so caught up in the reminiscing that he was caught off guard when Alex smirked and filled a lull by saying, "So, Emerson, Ben told me last week that he was really disappointed you were taken."

Really, he was surprised when he felt himself blushing.

"So it's true? You've got a new boyfriend?"

"We got together over the summer."

"Well…?" Alex waved a hand, signaling for Emerson to tell more.

"It's my friend Jonah."

"The infamous pen pal? Congrats, Em," Alex said with a grin.

Emerson felt his blush deepen as he realized that the nearby members had turned to look.

It wasn't long before they were all listening in and demanding to know everything about the new boyfriend. What was his name? Where did he live? What did he look like? What was he studying? How had he got together with Emerson? And most importantly: when would they get to meet him?

"Since he's not going to be in Austin until Christmas: Christmas," Emerson replied. This was greeted with disappointed moans.

It was about then that Emerson realized how very much he was enjoying bragging about Jonah, his boyfriend.

By the time most of the members of Hang Out had trickled out of the cafe, Emerson and Surya were bonding over *The Princess Bride*.

"Have you read the book?" Surya asked as they stepped from the coffee shop.

"Yeah, I read it when I was eleven and didn't understand half of it, so I had to reread it senior year. Was so glad I did when I realized how much of it I was getting for the first time."

Surya nodded. "Oh yeah, I read it last year and was a good fifty pages in before I realized that the abridgements were ironic."

Emerson grinned. Oh yeah, it was good to be back in Austin.

§

EMERSON picked up on the third ring, and Jonah didn't bother fighting the tingling rush that went through him at the sound of his voice. God, okay, he should have got over his thing about calling Emerson ages ago. "Hello?"

"Hey, gorgeous," he said cheerfully to his ceiling. "Did you miss me?"

"Jonah!" Jonah smiled. Emerson could never fake that kind of enthusiasm. "You have a phone?"

Of course Jonah had a phone, now that he didn't have to worry about falling in love with Emerson every time they spoke. "All I ever needed was the proper motivation," he teased. He was totally planning on talking Emerson into trying phone sex.

Naturally, Emerson missed the innuendo entirely. "Oh," he said, a little shyly but not nearly embarrassedly enough for him to have caught on to Jonah's train of thought. "So how are you?"

Well, never mind. Jonah could postpone that part of his agenda. Right now he was happy just to talk to his boyfriend. "Lonely. Tired," he admitted, realizing as he said it how true it was. "Book signings suck."

That, at least, was only partially true. Though Jonah had perhaps had unreasonably high expectations of what a book signing for a first-time author might be like. Mostly, people hadn't had any idea what his book was about or that he even existed, though a few had stuck around for a reading and some more had browsed around the book store and come around later for a signature and some small talk. Still, it hadn't exactly lived up to what Jonah had built it up to in his mind, despite his best attempts not to get his hopes up.

Emerson wasn't having any of it. "Aw, my poor, successful baby. Just remember, each signature is another person reading your book."

True. And just holding a physical copy of the finished product was kind of its own reward. But Jonah was still disappointed and not above pouting until Emerson made him feel better. "It's not like it was that busy." He paused and seriously thought about it. "Mostly it was really awkward." Trying to talk to a bunch of strangers about a book he'd sweated over for months that they'd never heard of—yeah, Jonah was good with people, but not *that* good.

"Still, you wrote a book and had a book signing. That's… incredible, Jonah."

Okay, that was enough ego stroking for one day. "It's pretty cool," Jonah admitted. Hell, he was only twenty. There was lots of time for fortune and fame yet. "So… you want to celebrate with me?"

Clearly he and Emerson were going to have to have a talk if Emerson couldn't even figure out when *Jonah* was using a line on him. "Sure," he said, sounding confused, "but won't it be kind of difficult when I'm 1700 miles away?"

"Not *that* hard," Jonah said with an audible leer. "You just have to use your imagination."

"Um. What?"

Damn, that must have been too subtle. "Did I mention that I miss you?" Jonah tried.

Emerson's voice softened. Maybe he was finally getting it. "I miss you, too, you know."

"Great!" Jonah exclaimed. He was frankly amazed that it had been that easy, come to think of it. "So you'll do it?"

"Do what?" Damn it! "Jonah…?"

Oh well, might as well just go for it. Jonah let some of the sexual tension he was feeling seep into his voice. "Unzip your fly, Emerson."

"What!?" Emerson yelped. "Jonah! You can't be serious!"

"I am dead serious, Emerson." And also really fucking horny. "Come on. It'll be hot!" Emerson's little outburst had reminded him of the kinds of noises Emerson had made when Jonah had had his dick in his mouth—not that Jonah was likely to forget *that* any time soon.

"I am not going to—do… *that*."

God, he couldn't even *say* it. Things were not looking good for Jonah's phone sex plan. Jonah pouted a little, though if he were honest with himself, he hadn't actually expected Emerson to give in on the first try. He had the not-so-sneaking suspicion that Emerson might not be as experienced as his drunken correspondence might have implied. "Why not?"

"Because… because… I'm not!"

That was illuminating. Jonah quirked his lips. Well, if Emerson wasn't going to give him any new jerk-off material, Jonah would just have to amuse himself another way. "There's nothing to be embarrassed about," he teased, his voice as serious as he could make it given the circumstances. "I have seen you naked, you know."

"Oh, Jesus," Emerson said in a mortified whisper. "Jonah, I'm not—it's different when you're actually there."

Okay, this was getting borderline cruel. Guiltily, Jonah said, "Alright, Em, relax. I shouldn't have sprung that on you. Sorry." Not sorry enough not to do it again at some later date, but at least Emerson would probably see that coming.

"Just… can we talk about something that doesn't have to do with sex?"

That reminded him—they were overdue for some serious conversations. "We're going to have to talk about it eventually, you know. But yeah, we can talk about something else for now. How are things in the townhouse? Settling in okay?"

Emerson had been torn on the issue of moving in with Zack and Greg even before his father had died, Jonah knew, but his mother had insisted that she could do fine without him, that he needed to experience living on his own.

"Good," Emerson answered. "It's nice having my own bed here now, since I pretty much lived here last year. Zack has a tendency to kick in his sleep."

And just like that, Jonah's brain was back to sex again. "Emerson, if you're trying to keep my mind out of the gutter, mentioning your bed is not the way to go." He paused, considering. "Also, if you ever find yourself sharing a bed with Zack again, please feel free not to let me know."

Spluttering, Emerson defended, "Zack has a queen! And it's not as lumpy as the couch!" Jonah could almost see the blushing pout. "Also, you're impossible. I talk about sleeping and you… infer things."

Jonah rolled his eyes. "If I told you I was in bed right now, what would you think about?"

"That you were tired?" Emerson offered stubbornly.

The kicker of it all was that it probably wasn't even a lie. "I can see that I have my work cut out for me," Jonah teased. "But never mind. Anxious for classes to start up again?"

"Yeah, I just got my studio assignment. Eve's pretty excited. We're right next to each other."

Jonah grinned. "I bet you can't wait to critique the inevitable vagina triptych."

Emerson's groan filtered down the line. "I'm more worried about the effect she'll have on my productivity. She's very… distracting."

"I'm sure you'll manage fine."

"I suppose. How about you? Excited?"

"Yeah, and nervous, I guess," Jonah admitted. "I feel like that kid who got held back a couple of times, you know?"

"Why?" Emerson asked. "Because you'll be older? You're not going to be the only older student, you know. Also, bet you most of them don't have a book published."

"Yeah, but that just gives me more to worry about," Jonah said. "What if it sucks?"

"Jonah," Emerson said patiently. "It doesn't suck. In fact, it's the opposite of suck. I read it in two days, and *not* because you wrote it.

Well, that was true, but…. "You threatened not to talk to me for a week when you finished it!"

"Because you made me cry!" Emerson exclaimed. "That's a good thing, Jonah. It means I cared about the characters. That doesn't happen when it sucks."

Jonah blushed, which surprised him. He hated feeling like he was fishing for compliments. On the other hand, well. Sometimes it felt like Emerson's opinion was the only one that mattered. To cover his embarrassment, he improvised, "I dunno, the first couple pages of *Twilight* made me want to cry."

Emerson snorted. "Crying because it's bad and crying because the characters move you are two different things."

"Okay, okay," Jonah conceded hastily. He was having a hard enough time not Googling himself as it was. "Let's talk about you again before my ego explodes."

"Point," Emerson said with a huff of a laugh. "I really should be more cautious about feeding your ego."

"At least until my first B minus."

Emerson laughed again. "Well, I really don't think—"

"Emma?" Jonah heard Zack's voice in the background. "Where the hell are you? It's time to go."

"Damn," Emerson muttered. "Zack is bellowing. They've got a show tonight, and I promised I'd go, and they've got to leave soon…."

It was easy not to be hurt, less so not to be disappointed. "It's alright, Em. It's not like we had an appointment or anything. I just wanted to hear your voice. I'll e-mail you my new number, okay? And you can call me whenever you want."

"Okay," Emerson said reluctantly. "Just… you know I'd rather stay and talk. I really do miss you."

"I miss you too," Jonah said lowly. "Hey, only four more months 'til Christmas, right? Now go have fun. I love you."

"Right. Four months," Emerson echoed. "And I—I know."

Perhaps surprisingly, it was easier not to be disappointed by that response. Emerson had been in love with him for years, if Jonah was any judge, and Jonah had been kind of a horrible person to have a crush on until very recently. If Emerson wanted to make him wait, well, Jonah had nothing but time. "Good!" he said. "Now get going before Zack leaves without you."

§

"EVER wonder what's actually in beef jerky?"

Jonah plucked a stick of beef jerky off the rack on the counter and brandished it at Emerson playfully before giving it a few experimental shakes. Emerson watched the show with amusement.

"Um, no?"

Jonah flipped the package over and started to read out the ingredients. "Beef—okay, that's not surprising. Worchester sauce, salt, again, not very surprising. Soy sauce. You know, this isn't nearly as bad as I thought. I mean, it's not high in food value, but—well, there is a whole lot of salt. Twenty percent of your daily intake? Sheesh."

Emerson stared at his boyfriend. "Why are you worrying about the nutritional value of beef jerky? You never eat the stuff," Emerson pointed out. Jonah hadn't touched beef jerky since he ate four sticks before he got the flu when he was ten.

"I am concerned for the well-being of your patrons!" Jonah said, looking indignant.

Emerson quelled the urge to quirk his lips as he attempted to give Jonah a look that was both serious and dubious. "Right. The well-being of my patrons. And it has nothing to do with you just being bored?"

"Me? Bored?" Jonah arched his eyebrows. "I have no idea what you're talking about." He tossed the beef jerky in the air a few times and then dropped it back into the bucket.

"You know, you might find something more entertaining somewhere else," Emerson pointed out kindly. "You don't have to stay here."

"But what if I want to stay here?" Jonah smiled. He had his elbows on the counter and was leaning across the space. "See, I could go somewhere else, but nowhere else comes with a boyfriend."

"Oh?" Emerson asked, leaning over the counter himself. Jonah's eyes were dancing; Emerson wanted to kiss him.

"Yeah. See, right here comes complete with eye candy." His tone was somber. "Here I get to watch a cute guy serve customers, or even better, get to see his really hot ass every time he goes to find something on a shelf."

Emerson felt his face heat up. "Oh you do, do you?"

"Oh, yeah. My boyfriend is super hot and very sexy."

Suddenly, Emerson realized that their faces were very close. He had slowly been drifting forward as Jonah spoke, responding in kind to the way that Jonah's face had been tilting up. A few more inches, and they'd be able to kiss. "You ever going to tell him that?"

"Hm, maybe. Probably shouldn't, though. His ego is huge, and it would all go to his head."

Emerson tried to play along, attempting a glare, but he was smiling a bit too much. "That's not very nice."

"No?" Jonah murmured. "Maybe I should tell him anyway, then. About how gorgeous he is and how he's been driving me crazy all day."

Their lips were almost touching at this point. And when Jonah finished that last sentence, Emerson tipped his face forward to place a loving kiss on Jonah's mouth. "Lunatic," he muttered against Jonah's lips.

"Lunatic? Is that a nice thing to call your boyfriend?" Jonah demanded, pulling back, his face once again filled with mock outrage.

Emerson didn't even try to stifle the grin. "Only if it's appropriate."

"Are you suggesting that I'm not sane? I'll have you know, I'm so sane that I make sane people jealous of my saneness."

He blinked at that. "Your saneness? You mean 'sanity', Mr. Big Shot Author? And speaking as someone who's sane, I'm not feeling jealous."

"Ha! You're not jealous because you're not sane!"

Emerson forced his lips into a pout. "Am too!"

"Are not!" Jonah let out a delighted cackle. "You are crazy! Crazy about me!"

"Oh my God, that was terrible. Absolutely terrible. I can't believe you made such a terrible pun," Emerson said, his voice filled with uncontrolled laughter.

"Honestly," said Jonah with a huff that belied his somewhat less-than-sane grin, "it's like you don't even know me."

Jonah was once again relaxed against the counter, elbows firmly planted and forearms stretched toward Emerson.

"Sadly, I know you all too well," Emerson said. Jonah grinned widely at that, and Emerson was so captivated that he didn't look up when the door's bell rang.

"Sadly? Again with the insults! If I was a less secure man, I'd start doubting your love and affection for me!"

"It's hard to imagine a world in which Jonah Cherneski isn't a very secure man."

Emerson and Jonah both jumped at the third voice joining in on their conversation. Jonah turned so that he could get a view of the door, while Emerson glanced over his shoulder to see—Justin Grossman. Justin was standing just inside the door, hands stuffed into his pockets and wearing a smile.

"Hey, Emerson." He shot Emerson a smile, then turned to Jonah and gave him a nod. "Jonah."

"Justin." Jonah shifted his weight so that he was standing up straight and tall; his face was tight, his tone wary.

As the shock of seeing Justin wore off, Emerson felt a smile cross his face. Despite the somewhat messy end of their short courtship, Emerson had more good memories about Justin than bad. “Justin. How have you been?”

Welcomed now, Justin walked forward. “I’ve been good. I was back in town for the holidays—needed to visit the folks before they nagged me to death about neglect.”

Emerson offered another smile. He remembered Justin’s parents well. They had been… “overprotective” was not too strong a word. “How are they?”

“Good. Mom and I were in town today, and I thought that I might stop by to say hello.”

It was Jonah who answered next. “Well, here you are, and you’ve said hello.” His voice was as hard and unwelcoming as his body language. Both arms were crossed tightly over his chest, and—did it look bigger than before?

Emerson took a moment to stare at his boyfriend. What was up with Jonah? Usually he was nicer than this.

Justin broke the awkward pause this time. “So. How’s life treating you?”

Emerson grinned wide. “Very good.” His life had been too good these past few weeks for him to answer any other way.

“Going to school?”

“Yeah, design at U of T.”

“Wow, great! You were always so talented. It’s good to hear you followed your dreams of being an artist.”

Emerson felt himself blush. “Thanks.”

Justin gave him a bright smile before he turned to Jonah. He didn’t seem put off by the tense line of Jonah’s shoulders or the way a small frown was creasing the skin between his eyebrows. “And what about you? English at U of T?”

“No. Creative writing.”

“Ah.”

Emerson stared at Jonah. Why had Jonah just lied? Well, sure, he hadn’t exactly *lied*, but why not mention that he wasn’t at U of T? Shaking himself, he tried to regain the thread of conversation. “What about you?"

"I'm studying at Stanford." Justin's pride was obvious.

Emerson smiled. "So you did pick Stanford in the end."

"Well, it wasn't much contest. They offered California weather," Justin said with a wink.

"I can't argue with that—not after being to San Francisco," Emerson agreed.

"You were in San Fran? What'd you see there?"

"Went to visit with Jonah." Emerson tipped his head in his boyfriend's direction.

Justin's eyes flicked back and forth between them. "Jonah was in San Fran?"

"Yes." Jonah's voice was tight. "I'm living there at the moment."

"At the moment." Justin arched one fine eyebrow. "Decide against U of T in the end?"

"No. I did some traveling after high school." Jonah looked unhappy to admit it.

Justin arched an eyebrow. "What happened to all the plans for Jonah and Emerson's Excellent Adventure at U of T?"

There was an awkward pause before Emerson finally managed to say, "Jonah went for the school of life instead. Did the backpacking and crappy job thing."

"Ah…. So, Jonah, creative writing at USF?"

Emerson had to hand it to Justin for his continued attempts to engage a man in conversation when the man was wearing *that* foreboding look.

"Yes," Jonah said shortly, standing tall and looking down his nose at Justin.

Justin nodded. "Home for the holidays, then. They been good so far?"

Jonah nodded. "Very."

There was a long, awkward pause. Again. Emerson looked back and forth between the two men in front of him. Jonah looked so intimidating. Emerson frowned. What was up with Jonah? Why was he acting so…. Oh. Wow. Okay, Emerson was feeling a bit stupid now. He couldn't exactly blame Jonah for being antsy about Justin's presence.

Emerson decided to break the silence. "We haven't seen each other since my trip to San Fran last summer, so yeah, it's been a very good break so far." Emerson offered a smile.

Justin gave a knowing nod. "Must be difficult being so far away from a friend. I know you two were always close."

Emerson felt himself heat at that. Yes, Justin had always known how close they were—and how close Emerson wanted them to be. The subtext hit Emerson hard, though he wasn't quite sure what it was about that comment that made Jonah bristle so much.

"It was," Jonah said. "But it's more difficult to be far away from my boyfriend." There was another pause. Emerson restrained the urge to smack the back of Jonah's head. That was… tactless.

Justin gave a barking laugh of surprise. "Boyfriend? So you two are…?" Jonah nodded once, sharp. Justin's grin grew. "Well, damn. So you finally pulled your head out of your ass, Cherneski? 'Bout damn time you did right by Em!"

Emerson felt heat bloom across the tops of his cheeks. Damn, he had forgotten how forthright Justin could be.

"Um," said Jonah, who was looking thrown and off-balance. Emerson also noticed that his chest seemed smaller again.

Justin gave an easy laugh. "Man, I was *so* jealous of you when we were in high school."

Jonah stared at Justin. "You were?"

"Of course. Emerson was crazy in love with you and wouldn't let me get anywhere. He turned down every date." Justin shot Emerson a grin as if they were sharing a private joke. Emerson felt a little too uneasy about the whole situation. His relationship with Jonah and their honesty about their feelings still felt too new to be poking fun at himself for being secretly in love for so long.

"And it didn't help that you were on record as being straight. You get a little bent on that trip of self-discovery?"

Jonah frowned. "Something like that."

"Well, it's good to see you two together. You always were disgustingly perfect for each other." Justin grinned. Jonah continued to look displeased, and Emerson felt another rush of embarrassment. "How long has this been going on?"

"Since July." Jonah's voice was still tight.

"Last July? You mean it took you two more years to get your ass in gear?"

Jonah went stiff again, his face flushed red. He still looked angry, but there was an uncertainty to him now.

"Jonah was traveling a lot. He lived all over the country for two years. Snail mail kind of slows things down," Emerson was quick to say. Whatever mistakes he and Jonah had made on their road to here were for no one else to judge.

Justin gave Emerson an odd look. "Ri-ight." His gaze flicked over to Jonah.

"So!" Emerson burst out, disliking the tension that kept building in Jonah's body. "How long are you in town for?"

Justin smiled again. "Two more weeks. I leave the day after New Year's."

Emerson offered another smile. "Nice long visit, then."

"Yeah," he nodded. "Look, I was hoping that we could get together for drinks while I was here. We haven't seen each other for almost three years. Time to catch up, yeah?"

Emerson nodded, but before he could reply, Jonah shifted to stand up straight again and said, "Drinks would be good." His voice was a little too loud.

Justin turned to look at Jonah. There was another brief pause, and then he recovered. "Right. Well, whenever is good for me. Em, maybe we could do coffee this week? Vinnie doesn't arrive until the twenty-sixth, so Jonah may rather we wait for drinks until then."

"Vinnie?" Emerson didn't remember ever meeting a Vinnie before.

"Yeah. Vincent—my boyfriend."

Oh! Justin had a boyfriend! *Thank you!* Emerson thought, feeling relieved. Maybe now Jonah would calm down.

"So maybe drinks the twenty-seventh or twenty-eighth?" Justin was saying. "Just think Jonah might like someone to talk to while we lament our bio mark." He gave Emerson a wink and flirty smile at that.

Emerson smiled back. "Okay. Sounds like a plan. I live in Austin these days, and usually I'm only in the Bend for shifts here or to see my mom, so how about I give you my number and we can set a time up for coffee?"

Justin agreed it was a good plan and whipped out his phone to input the number Emerson recited for him. Then he was putting his phone away and making his excuses. "Mom was headed into the natural products shop next door when I decided that here sounded better, but I should get back to her before she forgets I'm with her today and leaves without me. Wouldn't want to have to walk home!"

Emerson gave a laugh before waving Justin off. "See you later!"

Then, with one last, "Later Emerson! Jonah," Justin was gone.

Silence filled he shop in his wake. Jonah was still looking agitated.

Best to get Jonah talking about it now, Emerson thought. Fortunately, it often didn't take much to get Jonah talking when something was bothering him—if you knew what you were doing. And Emerson had had years of teen angst to perfect his technique. "Well, it should be interesting to meet 'Vinnie'," Emerson tried.

Jonah grunted.

"It was good to see Justin again," he tried next.

"I don't like him."

Ah-ha! Success. "I could tell."

"He's a flirt! He has a boyfriend, you have a boyfriend, and he was flirting." Jonah huffed and crossed his arms.

"A total flirt?" Emerson arched an eyebrow at his boyfriend. He had to admit to himself that he was kind of enjoying Jonah's display of jealousy. It wasn't often that Emerson got to see *this* kind of proof of Jonah's love. "Now who does that sound like?"

Jonah frowned at him.

"Did you know that when we go out together, you flirt with every single person who's paid to give us service from bus drivers to waiters?"

Jonah's eyes went wide, and his arms loosened. "What! I do not!"

"Yes, you do. You always have."

"I have no idea what you're talking about!"

Emerson stared at his boyfriend for a moment and realized that Jonah was being fairly honest. "Jonah. At the Starbucks last week, why exactly do you think the cute barista gave you a free cookie?"

Jonah pouted. It wasn't entirely unexpected. "Because I'm obviously a hungry growing boy?"

With a roll of his eyes, Emerson replied, "Because you were flirting, and she was hoping to convince you to come back for more *coffee*. Soon."

"But…! But…!" Jonah stammered before letting out a pathetic whine. "It's not on purpose!"

Oh, geez. Emerson had long ago gotten used to the way that Jonah flirted. He had started about the same time they got to high school. Jonah was just an outgoing and personable guy, and he couldn't help but flirt. Or at least behave in a manner that most people construed as flirting.

There was a time when Emerson had been jealous, had hated the way that Jonah flirted with everyone because he thought it meant less when Jonah was teasing and joking with him. Until he realized that Jonah didn't remember them, didn't let his gaze linger or check for reactions in them after he got what he'd gone to them for. No, Jonah took their attention while they sold him coffee or while they helped him find a book, but he never sought out their attention simply for the sake of it.

"Jonah! I'm not complaining—" and he wasn't "—because I know you don't want the barista—or the bus driver or the waiter. I'm just saying: there's a reason I liked Justin in the first place." Emerson paused then to let that sink in. Then he gave Jonah his best meaningful look. "Also, there's a reason why I turned him down."

"Oh." Jonah stared at him, then blinked. "*Oh*." Emerson knew his boyfriend was brighter than he looked.

Jonah shot a glance at the closed door. "Can I blow you now?"

Then again…. Emerson blushed fiercely. He was sure his face must be beet red. "The store is still open, Jonah. You're going to have to wait. Also—there are a lot of windows in here!"

"I could totally hide behind the counter!"

Emerson glared at his boyfriend. Judging from Jonah's look, he hadn't quite pulled off "menacing."

"Oh, fine, but don't think you're getting out of it. Your dick is mine later."

"Jesus, Jonah," Emerson said, his face still hot. Sometimes

Jonah's horndog tendencies were very embarrassing. Though…. "Like I'm gonna argue with that," he muttered.

Jonah's grin was wide and delighted. "So we're agreed then!" He clapped his hands together in emphasis. Emerson just hid his face in his hands. And wished that it was already time to close the store.

§

EMERSON was happily curled up on the couch, leaning against Jonah's side and lazily watching the film credits roll past. Jonah's arm was tossed over his shoulder, and his fingers were tracing random patterns over Emerson's bicep.

"So, there's a conversation you've been avoiding having with me."

Emerson frowned. "What?" He glanced up in time to see Jonah's eyebrow arch.

"Don't give me that look. You know what I mean. You promised that we'd talk when I got here for Christmas."

"Uh…."

"Emerson, our sexual histories."

Emerson glanced away. He could feel the heat fill his face. Oh, *that* conversation.

Jonah's fingers stopped moving, and soon he was rubbing the palm of his hand up and down Emerson's arm in a soothing touch. "Em, I really should know."

"I don't—there's not much to tell," Emerson admitted, uncomfortable. He was pretty sure that there was a lot to tell when it came to Jonah's sex life. Unlike Emerson, Jonah had dated in high school, and Emerson was pretty sure that most of his girlfriends had let him get to second base. And that didn't even take into account his girlfriends and boyfriends since he'd left Hudson Bend.

"Ri-ight," Jonah drawled. "Says the guy who wrote me a drunken letter about how he lost his virginity at a frat party."

Blushing, Emerson pushed his face into Jonah's chest. "It wasn't—it was just a hand job," Emerson muttered.

"Uh huh. A hand job that was awful? Don't think that I forgot about that."

Emerson covered his face, embarrassed by the memory of the hand job and the letter he'd sent Jonah. "Why can't you just let this drop?"

"Because I—Em, as far as I know, you've kissed three men, one of which while drunk, and you've had one drunken hand job that was bad. So, I'd really like to know if there's more than that. I'm a little… concerned."

"Concerned?"

"About what you're comfortable with doing."

Emerson fidgeted, his hand now dropped from his face and fiddling with the hem of Jonah's shirt. "There isn't much more than that. I kissed some of the guys I dated. I swapped hand jobs with some of them."

There was a moment of silence as Jonah seemingly digested this information. Then he asked, "You ever been blown before?"

Emerson lifted his head so that he could look Jonah in the eye and then arched one eyebrow.

"Besides me," Jonah amended.

Emerson looked away again, uncomfortable with the memories. He didn't want to have to look Jonah in the face as he remembered that night. "Once," he admitted grudgingly.

Jonah nodded. "So, hand jobs, one blow job, and some making out. Anything else?"

Emerson stayed silent. Of course there was something else, but he really didn't want to tell Jonah about it.

"Em."

"Jonah," Emerson parroted back, putting the same serious tone on the name.

"Emerson, what aren't you telling me?" Apparently Jonah would not be swayed from this topic. Emerson wondered if maybe he could just ignore Jonah. Maybe if he said nothing Jonah would give up?

"Emerson, is there something you're embarrassed about?" There was another pause as Jonah waited, and Emerson refused to answer. "Something you wish you hadn't done?" Jonah said, and Emerson could tell by the tone of his voice that he was just working things out. Emerson wished he were somewhere else right now. He straightened up and turned his face away. "Em, you can tell me. I won't judge you, not about this."

Jonah's hand landed on his back, rubbing up and down coaxingly. Emerson was beginning to get that he wasn't going to get away with not saying anything. He bit his lip in consideration and then took a deep, shaky breath. "I was drunk and upset…."

"So you made a mistake?"

Emerson nodded. Then, when he said nothing more, Jonah asked, "Someone wanted a blow job?"

Emerson crossed his arms over his chest. "No." He chewed his lip before admitting, "I went back to his…."

He could sense Jonah shifting behind him. He could sense that Jonah was tensing his muscles. "Em, what happened at his place?"

Emerson swallowed. He could do this. He just needed to start out slow. "Um, he wanted…." He stuttered to a halt.

"Em, okay, you're starting to freak me out a little. He didn't force you into anything, did he?"

Emerson's body jolted in shock. "No," he blurted out. "I—I let him." Emerson rubbed his palms up and down his biceps. "I—he wanted to…." Emerson couldn't get the words out.

There was a long pause, and then Jonah finally said, "Okay. So, he asked to fuck you. Am I right? And you said yes?"

Emerson felt himself go hot. God, to hear Jonah say it like that filled him with mortification. He knew he wouldn't be able to get words out, so he nodded instead.

"When you were drunk and upset?"

Emerson nodded again.

Jonah reached out and gripped Emerson's chin in one hand and turned Emerson's face to look at him. Jonah was frowning when he said, "So he fucked you even though you obviously weren't with it enough to consent?"

Emerson frowned in return. He couldn't let Jonah think that way. "Don't."

"What?"

"Don't make it sound like he forced me. I said yes. I—it was a mistake, obviously, but it was mine to make."

Jonah didn't look appeased. In fact, he looked even angrier.

Emerson swallowed hard and pulled his chin from Jonah's grasp. "Can we just—"

"Forget it? No." Jonah ran both hands through his hair. He took a deep breath and then let it out in a sigh. He sounded calmer when he next spoke. "Okay. Did you enjoy it?"

Emerson felt himself flush once again. He couldn't possibly respond to that.

"Right. I'm guessing then that it was about as good as the other first time you've mentioned." Jonah let out another sigh. "So, is it something you want to ever try again, with me? I mean, not right now or even next week, but eventually? Or we can put it aside to discuss later."

"No," Emerson blurted, then continued before he could stop himself. "I—I do want to. I want you inside me," he told his shoes. "Just not—"

Jonah cut in, though it was kindly done. "Okay. So, that's something that we'll talk about later. Until then, is there anything else I should know? Any no-goes?"

Emerson looked up, surprised. "No."

Jonah gave a decisive nod. "Good. Now, it's my turn. Though you probably figured some things out."

Emerson felt hot and uncomfortable at the thought. "Jonah, I don't—"

Jonah interrupted him again, this time with a strange, upbeat cheeriness. "Yes, you do. Jesus, Em, this is a conversation you should have with all new partners. Now, as I'm sure you've guessed, between Evan, Elijah, and Xie, I've had all the combinations of masturbation, oral, vaginal, and anal sex. Before that there's not much to tell—I went down on a couple girls in high school, got a few hand jobs."

Jesus, and Emerson hadn't thought it was possible for his face to get any hotter.

Jonah ignored his embarrassment. Instead, he continued with that cheery voice, though now a smile was curving the corner of his lips. "And I'm guessing that it makes you uncomfortable to think about or talk about this. But you need to know two things. One, I'm clean. I've been tested recently, and I've not slept with anyone else since Elijah.

Two"—he paused here to grin wide—"I like sex *a lot* in all its shapes and forms, so don't be embarrassed about asking for what you want. I don't want you to ever be too embarrassed to ask me to do something you want to do." Then his grin turned saucy, and he scooted closer to Emerson. His hands came to wrap around Emerson's hips in a gentle caress. "For example, if you asked to, say, give me a blowjob, or if you really wanted me to suck you, I'd be happy to help you fulfill either desire."

"You would, would you?" Emerson said, unable to help the smile from settling on his own mouth. He shifted forward, sensing that Jonah would let the conversation end now. He lifted his face up to be kissed and placed his hands on Jonah's chest to encourage him.

Jonah gave a happy, humming moan of, "Yes." He wrapped both arms around Emerson's waist. "I would."

"Hm, then what about if I wanted you to kiss me? Would you do that?"

Jonah's grin was filthy when he murmured, "Oh, I could be convinced." Then he obliged, and Emerson stopped worrying about it.

§

"DO YOU have to?"

"Yup."

"Are you sure?"

"Yes."

"Couldn't you stay a little longer?"

"Classes start up tomorrow, Em."

Emerson gave the pout that he was quickly learning Jonah found alluring.

"Just think, in four more months I'll be done at USF, and then I'll be home again."

"For good."

"For good," Jonah agreed. "I'm not going to start traveling again. Well… not alone, anyway."

Emerson couldn't help the shy but pleased grin that stole over his face.

"I wish I could kiss you goodbye. Again."

"Jonah, we talked about this."

"I know…."

"Not in public in Texas, you goof."

"I *know*." Jonah let out a dramatic sigh. "Doesn't mean I don't want to. I want to pull you close and kiss you hard, and maybe get some groping in."

"Groping?" Emerson asked, blushing furiously, though still pleased by the attention.

"Yes, groping. Your ass is made for it. Very round, very squeezable." He tilted his head, craning it a little as if to get a look at Emerson's ass while remaining in front of him.

"Jonah!"

"Fine, fine. Besides: mission accomplished. Since I'm not allowed to kiss you, this was the only way to leave you red and flustered."

Emerson knew his face was red, mortified. "Jesus, Jonah. Get on the damn plane, would you?"

"Alright, alright," he said with a smirk, and then his eyes went soft. "Love you."

"I know. Miss you."

Jonah gave a very large grin. "I know." Then he was kissing his fingers and blowing a kiss as he slowly backed away. Emerson stayed put, watching until Jonah finally turned his back and boarded his plane.

CHAPTER 15

NOW

"OH, GOD, there he is," Natalie sighed when they'd cleared the crowd standing in the lobby. "He is such a dreamboat."

Jonah gave her an arch look. "'Dreamboat'?"

"I could talk about how much I want to lick him if you'd rather."

"Ew, no." Jonah made a face. "Gross."

Natalie bristled. "He is not! He is a perfectly gorgeous specimen of masculinity."

Now there was a point Jonah couldn't argue with. Matt Greguol was tall, though not quite as tall as he was, blond-haired and broad-shouldered, with good, strong features and smiling blue eyes. Also— "Totally straight," Jonah said immediately. "No question."

"Seriously?" she asked him, obviously impressed. "How can you tell? Teach me, O Wise One."

For a minute Jonah forgot his misery and almost smiled. Maybe it hadn't been such a terrible idea to allow Natalie to talk him into this. "Well, for one thing, no self-respecting gay man would show up to his own gallery showing in *that* T-shirt, even if he did fill it out that well."

"Jerk!" Natalie laughed, slapping him in the chest. "Circumstantial. Give me more."

"Okay, okay. See those guys over there?" He motioned as discreetly as possible with a nod of his head.

"Sure."

"I know a couple of them through Emerson."

"Gay?" Natalie asked.

"Out and proud," Jonah confirmed. "Anyway, see the expressions on their faces?"

"They look like you that one time Mom took you to the pet store and told you that you couldn't have a puppy."

"Bingo," Jonah said. "Also, he is totally staring at that girl's cleavage. Despite his obvious art student status, definitely a boob man. You're in, Tits McGee."

"Jonah!" She elbowed him sharply in the side. "I'm going to pretend I didn't hear that, but only because I still need your help. What do I do?"

There was no way, Jonah thought, that she could possibly be serious. But one look at her face confirmed it. "Nat, I don't know if you've noticed, but I am sort of the last person on earth who should be giving anyone advice right now."

Then Natalie's earnest gaze slid off his face to a point somewhere behind him, and her pleading pout turned into a small smile. "You're right," she agreed, nudging him to turn around. "I think you've got better things to do."

Jonah said, "Oh," because seeing Emerson again after a week was like a punch in the gut. He barely heard Natalie pat him on the back with a "Go get 'em, tiger" before she made herself scarce, and then Emerson was throwing back a glass of wine and worming his way through the crowd to stand in front of him, looking sad and tired and fucking *beautiful*.

If Jonah weren't still so angry (hurt), he'd have kissed him.

At least Emerson looked as miserable as he felt. Jonah felt a vicious stab of satisfaction at that. "Hey," Emerson said in a rush, like he had to force it out.

Jonah kept his voice soft, because he didn't know what would happen if he didn't. "Hey, Em."

Emerson licked his lips, shifted his feet. Jonah stood statue-still. "I—Jonah, I—I didn't think I'd see you here."

Part of Jonah wished he hadn't. This thing between them was delicate, and there were a lot more ways for it to go wrong than there were to fix it. So while part of him was desperately, fiercely glad to see Emerson again, to *talk* to him, the part of him that was afraid they really couldn't fix their relationship would have been happier not to. He shrugged and gestured across the room, where Natalie was cozying up to Matt. "Natalie brought me along for gay bait."

Emerson followed his line of sight to where Matt was explaining a clay sculpture of a boy with wings strapped on with real leather to Natalie. "Oh," he said. "She could have just asked me. Matt may be pretty, but he's ruler straight."

Well, duh. The sculpture was wearing *pants*. Jonah fought the urge to sigh. This was not the conversation he'd been hoping to have. He let his gaze flicker around the room. If Emerson wasn't going to *talk*, Jonah was not obligated to listen. "Right."

"Right," Emerson echoed. Jonah looked at him despite his resolution not to and found that he was fidgeting, staring at his hands. "So." Eventually he seemed to gather himself up to say something of slightly more import. "Could we—could we maybe go outside and—and talk?"

Jonah was so not ready for this, but life rarely waited until you were ready. He'd learned that lesson well enough. "I… that's probably a good idea, yeah."

Emerson nodded, sucking his lower lip into his mouth and chewing on it the way he always did when he was upset. "Okay. I—follow me, I guess?"

§

THEN

"—EVER since Greg walked in on them *in flagrante,* as you would say, things have been complicated. Which, by the way, what were they thinking? The kitchen of all places? Zack has a bedroom, you know? Anyway, Greg's still mad at Zack for sleeping with Hayley, Zack is still avoiding Greg out of guilt—which has led me to feel like I'm stuck as an extra in *Mission Impossible* more than once—and Hayley wouldn't stop pestering me about how long I've known Greg's in love with her, so I spent a lot of time hiding in my room."

And Emerson's friends accused *him* of being drama-prone. Jonah smiled. "Emerson. Is it possible you're a little stressed out?"

Emerson huffed over the phone. "We can't all be Zen masters of calm, you know."

Oh, what the hell. Jonah wasn't giving up on one of his fondest fantasies just because Emerson kept shooting him down. "I know something that will take the edge off," he said suggestively.

"What?" Emerson obviously hadn't caught the innuendo.

"Emerson," Jonah said patiently.

A beat, and he could practically see Emerson blushing. "Oh," he said. "*That.*"

"You don't have to say anything if you don't want to."

"What, you mean you just want me to sit here and, and…." Emerson's voice got very quiet as he hissed, "And j-jerk off while you…?"

Jesus. Wasn't *that* a wonderful mental image. "Well, I wouldn't mind if you wanted to contribute, but yeah, that is exactly what I'm suggesting."

"But…," Emerson floundered. "What's in it for you?"

You mean aside from the excruciatingly hot noises you actually can't stop yourself from making? "Emerson," said Jonah patiently, "the idea of you getting off to the sound of my voice is kind of its own reward." He waited a second for that to sink in. "It's on my top ten list, okay?"

"Okay," Emerson said quietly.

Jonah opened his mouth. "Wait, was that 'okay' as in—"

Emerson sounded perfectly mortified. "Yes."

Swallowing around a suddenly dry throat, Jonah went to the kitchen to get himself a glass of water. "God. Okay, close your door. Lock it if you can. I don't want any interruptions."

Emerson's shaky exhalation rattled down the line. "Okay. Now what?"

"Are Zack and Greg home?"

"I think Greg is out with Hayley. She's—it's a trial date or something? Honestly, I really don't get it. After spending the last week listening to her angst over Greg, I've never been more glad that I'm gay—"

"Emerson!"

"What?"

"Zack?"

"He's downstairs."

"Turn your radio on, then," Jonah decided. "Not too loud, but nobody gets to hear the sounds you make except for me." He thought about it, about what it would be like to touch Emerson knowing that every time he made a sound, everyone in the house knew it was because of Jonah. "Unless I'm there with you."

Emerson's breath hitched. "Jonah—"

"Do you have lube?" Jonah interrupted. "No, of course you do. Get it and lay down on the bed." He downed his water quickly and went to his own bed, lying down on his back with one arm behind his head.

He waited. "Are you ready?"

"Um."

That was probably as good as he was going to get until Emerson was a little more into it, and that was okay. Jonah had been planning this for ages. He knew how to get Emerson to loosen up. Letting a lazy down-home drawl creep into his voice, he said, "What are you wearing?"

"Jonah!"

"Aw, Em, you know I couldn't help myself. But tell me. I wanna know. I wanna picture you, what you look like spread out on the bed for me. I'll go first if you want."

A long, shaky breath. "That… that would be okay."

"Alright. You know how I told you the thermostat is on the fritz? Well, it's about eighty degrees in here, Em. I had a cool shower when I got home from the gym, and I was still damp when I got dressed, so my clothes are kind of sticking to me. Anyway, like I said, it's hot, so I just put on one of my sleeveless shirts and some jeans." He paused a minute to let Emerson have some time to process before dropping the bombshell. "No boxers."

Emerson swallowed audibly. "Oh."

Jonah prompted, "Your turn."

"Okay. Um. It's Saturday, so. I haven't been out. I'm—it's my old high school gym T-shirt."

Jonah licked his lips. "It's a little too small for you now, isn't it?"

Emerson said, "Um. Maybe?"

He'd worn it to bed once at Christmas time; it was tight across the chest and arms and sometimes rode up in the back. Jonah was a fan. "Nice. What else?"

"Jeans?"

"Which ones?" *Please let it be the ripped ones.* He knew they were Emerson's favorite, though he never wore them out of the house. A good thing, since they'd probably cause a riot.

"The ones with the holes in the knees." Jonah mentally fist-pumped. "Um, socks. Underwear. That's it."

"Are you hard?"

"Jonah!" Emerson squawked.

Smirking to himself, Jonah decided that if he hadn't been before, he was well on his way now. "I am," he said, easing his hand out from behind his head and snaking it down his body to pop open the button on his fly.

"Yes," Emerson whispered.

"Good. That's the point, you know. Get you hard, get you all worked up for me while I tell you all the things I want to do to you. I really do have a list, you know." And while sharing the whole thing would probably only get Emerson to hang up on him, there was no reason not to share bits and pieces. "You wanna know what's on it?"

Breathy, high-pitched whine. "I—yes."

Atta boy, Jonah thought. "Are you touching yourself, Emerson?"

"Not… not yet."

"Are you waiting for me to tell you?" The silence indicated that he was, which was actually unspeakably hot. "That's so—God, Emerson, that's on the list, you know. I want to watch you touch yourself for me, watch you make yourself come. You'd be so embarrassed, wouldn't you? But that would only make it better."

Deep, shuddering breath followed by a strangled little moan.

Well, that answered that question. Jonah pulled down his zip. His jeans were just too damn tight. "Unbutton your fly, but don't touch yourself yet." Now, how to draw out as much pleasure from Emerson as possible…. "Here's how this is going to work. I'll tell you some things on my list, and you tell me if it's something you might want to try. As your reward, I'll tell you what to do, how I want you to touch yourself. Does that sound good?"

Another moan. “Okay.”

“Good. Hmm, well, I already told you one of my favorites: watching you get yourself off for me.” Jonah could just see it: Emerson spread out on his back on the bed, red-faced, eyes screwed shut as he touched himself. “Would you do that for me, Emerson? Let me watch you?”

Emerson groaned. “Yes,” he whispered.

Jonah’s dick jumped, scraping unpleasantly at the teeth of his fly; he winced and pushed the fabric down. “God, Emerson, I wish I could see you right now. Take your jeans off. All the way. Socks too.”

A few rustling sounds made their way over the line, and then finally Emerson’s voice, breathless and raw. “Okay.”

“Hmm, you know what else I want, Em?” Jonah asked, curling a lazy hand around his own erection. He wouldn’t stroke himself, not yet, not until he let Emerson do the same. “I want to see what you look like with my cock in your mouth. Would you do that for me, Emerson? Suck my dick?”

He was pretty sure of the answer, or he wouldn’t have asked, but it still sent a jolt through him when Emerson let out a shocked noise. “Would you, Emerson? Tell me.”

“Yes!”

Jonah shuddered. “You want that, Em? Want my dick in your mouth?”

“God, Jonah.” Emerson sounded totally wrecked.

Jonah took pity on him. “Put your hand on your cock. Just through your underwear. Don’t grip it yet, but you can rub it if you want. Just lightly.”

The moaning was getting louder. Emerson was definitely enjoying himself immensely, if the sounds were anything to go by. “You like that, Emerson? You want me to keep going?”

“God, yes.”

“Then while we’re on the subject, I’m sure you’ve noticed how much I enjoy sucking you.”

“Uhh.”

“I don’t mind telling you, Emerson, I love it. Love making you come apart, making you feel good. I like the way you feel in my mouth.”

"Jonah!"

"Take your shorts off," Jonah said a little breathlessly, scrabbling for the lube. "Right now, Emerson. Get your hand on your cock, I wanna hear you."

That earned him the loudest groan yet, followed by a hot whimper as Emerson started jerking himself off. Jonah was totally going to convince him to do this on speakerphone next time so he could hear *everything*. Jonah himself tried to set a slow pace, knowing that with how vocal Emerson was he wasn't going to last for long. "Tell me what you do when you jerk off, Em."

"Oh, God," Emerson gasped. "Jonah, I—"

"Do you play with your nipples? Your balls?"

Emerson's breath caught on a loud moan.

"You do, don't you? Do it now." Jonah fisted his own cock faster. "And then get the lube, Emerson. Make sure you're nice and slippery for me."

"Jonah," he whimpered. "God—close."

"Me too," Jonah admitted hoarsely. "Tell me what you want, Emerson. Huh? What else do you do to yourself to get off?"

"Jonah—" A deep, choking groan.

"I bet you push your fingers up inside yourself," Jonah said, imagining it. "Get them good and wet and fuck—fuck yourself on them. Do you?"

The sound Emerson made was answer enough, and Jonah squeezed hard around the base of his dick in a desperate bid not to come until he heard Emerson fall apart. "Do it for me now, Emerson. I want to hear you. It's my fingers you've got inside you"—he shuddered hard at the idea and allowed himself a single stroke—"and I've got my mouth on you, Em. I'm fucking you with my fingers and my mouth—"

Emerson cut him off with a gasping wail that went on and on, and Jonah let go of the phone to jerk his cock with both hands until he came all over himself, shuddering.

When he could breathe again, he wiped his hands off on his (probably ruined) shirt and reached for the phone. "Emerson? You still there?"

"Oh my God," Emerson said. Jonah detected equal parts satisfaction and embarrassment. "Um."

"So," Jonah said conversationally, "is it presumptuous of me to say you'd like to do that again?"

"God, you're smug."

Jonah hummed in agreement. "Also extremely satisfied. In case you were wondering."

"I… might do that again," Emerson hazarded.

"And the rest?" he asked, referring to the laundry list of depraved acts he'd recited.

"Um. Those too."

Looking down at his twitching dick, Jonah decided that he really had to stop getting into this kind of post-coital situation with Emerson, or neither of them was ever going to get out of bed again, and they'd die of dehydration. "No pressure," he assured him. "Just, you know, when you're ready."

"Jonah." Emerson sounded almost amused now. "All evidence to the contrary, I am perfectly capable of telling you 'no'."

Laughing, Jonah said, "I know it." Then he let the laughter fade from his voice. "I have to go—big project due Monday. Call you next week?"

"You will if you know what's good for you."

"All right. Love you, Emerson."

He caught the hitch of breath as loudly as if it were one of Emerson's moans. "I—yeah. Goodnight."

§

EMERSON ambled into the room and sprawled out onto the couch. He was feeling loose limbed and content. So much so he was pretty sure nothing could get him down right now.

Zack was already sitting on the couch and watching a football game on the TV. He grunted a greeting that Emerson happily returned with a cheery "hello."

Zack turned his head slowly to regard his friend. "What's with you?"

"What?" Emerson said, though he couldn't stop the silly grin.

"You? You're all… cheerful." Zack somehow made this sound like a bad thing.

Trying to appear cool, Emerson shrugged. "No reason."

Zack grunted again. "If I didn't know better, I'd say you got laid."

Emerson felt himself turn bright red. Sometimes it was not a blessing to have friends who knew you so well.

"Emma? Okay, that blush says you did, but I know you couldn't have because Jonah isn't here, and you would never cheat on that boy."

Improbably, Emerson's face felt warmer.

"Em… why are you blushing? You look like I just found you sleeping with your boyfriend…." Zack slowly trailed off. Then he let out a bark of laughter. "You didn't?"

Emerson sank into his seat.

"Well, shit. You know, I have to give that boy of yours credit. I can't believe he talked you into phone sex."

Letting out a groan and covering his face, Emerson wished he could block out the sound of Zack's knowing laughter.

"Remind me to compliment his skills next time I see him."

Emerson was wrong—something could ruin his mood.

§

DESPITE the major distractions provided by free beer, live music, and not being able to figure out what time zone he was in—a condition exacerbated by the beer—Jonah managed to meet Emerson at the door when he finished his exam.

Then again, "meet" might not have been a strong enough word for what Jonah actually did, which was haul Emerson bodily inside by his wrist and push him very carefully up against the wall so he could kiss him properly. Emerson made a brief noise of surprise in his mouth—Jonah had switched his flight a day earlier—but then he relaxed with a quiet sound of appreciation and let Jonah eat at his mouth until Greg stopped playing the guitar and someone whistled.

Emerson turned his head away then, which was fine since it gave Jonah access to the long, pale column of his neck instead. He applied his mouth to Emerson's pulse point immediately. It was just wrong for

Emerson to go around without Jonah's marks somewhere on his body, and he wanted this first one to be somewhere everyone would see. "Um," Emerson said, and Jonah felt him swallow, felt the vibrations of his vocal cords under his lips. "Zack, did you"—his breath hitched—"what did you give him to drink?"

Zack had handed him a beer the second they'd got in the door, and then after that there had been an arm-wrestling match (Jonah won, but it was close) and a drinking contest (despite the size differential being very firmly in Jonah's favor, Zack had beaten him handily, not that he was going to admit it). He remembered something about tequila, or possibly Jägermeister. Or both.

"Jonah." The tone was encouraging. The hands pulling at his hair, however, were going in the wrong direction. "Jonah, you should probably stop before I die of embarrassment."

With a heroic effort of willpower, Jonah dragged his mouth away from Emerson's neck. His hard work did not go unrewarded: there was a decent-sized bruise already purpling the skin. Satisfied, he kissed Emerson on the mouth again, with somewhat more restraint this time. "I missed you."

"I guessed," Emerson said, flushing prettily and fingering the mark. "Are you always like this when you're drunk?"

Jonah thought about it. The first time he'd been drunk was high school prom. He'd gone down on Deanna Carlisle for the better part of two hours in the back of the limo, making her come over and over again, and she'd jerked him off three times before they finally gave up and he took her home.

They never did make it to the dance.

"Yes," he decided.

"Jesus," Emerson muttered, shoving him away. "I need a drink." He wasn't fooling Jonah, though; he'd felt his erection when he had him up against the wall.

Jonah wasn't so drunk as to be unreasonable. He knew Emerson was never going to put out for him when so many people were hanging around. Besides, it was a good opportunity to get to know Emerson's friends, most of whom he'd only met a handful of times before. It didn't stop him from wanting to grab the back of his T-shirt and drag him upstairs and fuck him stupid, but there would be time for that—or at least the part of it that mattered—later. In the meantime, he vaulted over the back of the couch to sit next to Hayley and make increasingly improbable song requests.

When Emerson walked by on his way back from the washroom, Jonah didn't hesitate to reach out and pull him down into his lap.

"You're disgusting," Hayley informed him seriously, gesturing with her wine cooler as Jonah bit Emerson's shoulder playfully through the fabric of his T-shirt.

Jonah narrowed his eyes. "What kind of fag hag are you, anyway?"

She laughed and leaned into his shoulder. "It wasn't a complaint."

"God, Hayley, don't encourage him." But it wasn't like Emerson made any real effort to escape from Jonah's evil clutches, unless you counted the squirming, and Jonah was sure that was mostly a delightful punishment. Jonah got him back by curving his hand around the flesh at Emerson's waist under the hem of his T-shirt, letting his fingers drift lightly over the sensitive skin.

Zack obviously wasn't pleased by the headway Jonah was making. "Jonah, if you undress him on the couch, I *will* get the ice from the cooler. Don't test me."

"Spoilsport," Hayley griped, eyeing Emerson speculatively. Jonah put a proprietary hand on his thigh, still distracted by Zack's ice idea.

After a few more minutes of good-natured teasing, Greg lured Hayley away—or actually, now Jonah thought about it, vice versa—to "look at the stars," which was code for "have sex outside" if Jonah had ever heard it—and a pretty Asian girl took the seat next to him instead.

"Hi," she said brightly, sticking her hand out for him to shake. "I'm Surya."

Reluctantly, Jonah unpeeled himself from Emerson. "Jonah."

"Yes, we all know who you are," she smiled.

"Oh? Has Emerson been telling stories? Only half of them are true, I promise." Jonah poked him with his left hand. Emerson barely looked away from the conversation he was having with one of his former TAs, just slapped Jonah's hand away from his stomach.

"No, I mean, he does," she rambled, "but that's not—that is—God, this is embarrassing."

Jonah waited patiently for her to get the point.

"The thing is, I'm an English student," Surya finally said. "Um. One of my profs sort of recommended your book this semester."

Jonah said, "Oh."

"And I just—I was wondering. I mean it's sort of a personal question. But. It always seemed to me—I mean this was *after* I met Emerson—"

The poor girl had to be drunker than Jonah. Maybe even drunker than Greg, who from all reports was buck naked on the back porch with Hayley. Jonah did his best to follow her babble.

"But it *is* about him, right? About you?" Surya managed to spit out at last.

Jonah looked up. Emerson was still chatting away at the TA, who was starting to list to one side where he was perched on the armchair. Then he looked back. He didn't need to answer.

Surya sighed. "God, that's so romantic."

"It was a *tragedy*!" Jonah protested.

"Not the story itself. The gesture, you know, the gesture was romantic." She looked a little teary-eyed. "Don't—you never talk about this, do you," she sighed, seeming to deflate and sink into the couch. "I'm the only person ever to fangirl you outrageously and make a fool of myself. God, I should have stayed home. I have another exam tomorrow anyway—"

Wow, where to begin. "Uh, I'm not exactly, you know." Jonah flailed his hand around, meaning "recognizable," though even in his somewhat compromised state he realized that it was probably not obvious. "People don't just come up to me on the street and say, 'Hey, you're that guy who wrote that book named after that Eagles song.' My picture isn't even on the cover."

"But you *live here*," Surya pointed out. "Or you're from here, whatever." For the first time, Jonah noted her accent: definitely northern, maybe New Hampshire? Jersey? He was too drunk to tell. "Didn't it make the papers? 'Local boy makes good' and all that?"

Jonah stared. "I wrote a book about a closeted gay protagonist," he pointed out. Even if the character himself had never come right out and said it, it was pretty much there on the page for everyone to see. "We're in Texas!"

Surya was clearly still waiting for him to get to the point, so he added, "I didn't even know you could *buy* my book in Texas!"

"Well, to be fair, I did buy it on the Internet. It was cheaper!" she defended. "Oh my God, if I bring it over tomorrow, will you sign it for me?"

Jonah considered his plans for the next three days. None of them involved clothes or even getting out of bed for longer than it took to keep hydrated. "Let's aim for next week," he decided.

A sudden draft and a tug on his hand got Jonah's attention, and he looked around to see that everyone was leaving.

"Zack is kicking everyone out," Emerson explained. "Well, not really. They're going a few houses down to play pool in Jim's basement."

Jonah stood. "Are we going too?" He noticed that Emerson hadn't let go of his hand.

"No," said Emerson. Something about the way he said it made Jonah shiver.

Emerson didn't even let Jonah say goodbye to the guests at the door. As soon as they were left alone, he put his palms squarely on Jonah's chest and stood on his toes, brushing a feather-light kiss across Jonah's mouth. Humming in approval, Jonah let him lead, keeping the contact fleeting, teasing, until Emerson made a really hot frustrated noise and dug his hands into Jonah's hair instead.

Then Emerson started backing him toward the stairs, and really, Jonah wasn't so stupid that he would resist *that*. He let himself be pushed along, up the stairs, stumbling, until his knees hit mattress, and he toppled over backward. He sat up in time to see Emerson close and lock the door behind him.

Jonah raised an eyebrow as Emerson crawled up over his body to kiss him again. "Exactly how much have *you* had to drink?"

"Enough," Emerson said with a slight flush. He pushed up the hem of Jonah's T-shirt with both hands and laid a hot, wet kiss just to the right of Jonah's belly button.

Never one to dissuade Emerson from taking the initiative—it happened infrequently enough as it was—Jonah gave a mental shrug. "Am I allowed to participate?"

Emerson looked up at him through slitted eyelashes. "Participation is mandatory," he affirmed, deftly sliding Jonah's belt out of its loops. He'd certainly got better at *that* over the Christmas break—they'd practiced it enough. "Pop quiz at the end."

Something important was going on, but Jonah wasn't quite with it enough to be able to work out exactly what it was, partly due to alcohol consumption and partly because Emerson was rubbing his palm in small circles over the cotton covering the head of his dick. "Was that a really awful double entendre?"

"I'll show you double entendre," Emerson muttered, which made *no sense*, and it made even less sense after he worked Jonah's boxers down to his knees and put his mouth on Jonah's cock, but Jonah was too invested in positively reinforcing this unexpected new behavior to mention it.

Oh, Jonah thought, caught between dazed and incredibly turned on. So *that* was what had Emerson's metaphorical panties in a bunch. Suddenly energized, Jonah propped himself up on his elbows to watch Emerson—face flushed a brilliant red—lick carefully around the head of his erection. *Well, all right then.* And that was really all it took for the sex filter between his brain and his mouth to give way. "Jesus," he breathed. "God, Emerson, do you have any fucking idea what you do to me?"

Emerson breathed a low groan of approval and took the tip of Jonah's erection into his mouth, and Jonah just about did himself an injury trying not to shove his way deeper.

"So hot," Jonah told him, barely trusting himself to let go of Emerson's comforter with one hand so he could cup his cheek. He curled his thumb under Emerson's lower lip, brushing across it gently. "Love your mouth, feels so good. Make me so fuckin' hard, Emerson."

Emerson whimpered around Jonah's cock, and Jonah swore, ran his thumb over Emerson's lip again, pushed the pad just inside as Emerson started to suck him.

It was almost too much to see and feel and hear at the same time: Emerson's flushed skin and the sight of Jonah's dick pushing between sinful lips, the almost unbearable heat and suction and the vibrations of Emerson's constant moans. Jonah lost the plot completely when Emerson wrapped a confident hand around the part of Jonah's erection he couldn't fit in his mouth. He began spewing filth he could barely even hear over the roaring of blood in his ears. "Fuck, Emerson, you should see what you look like right now, kneeling over me like this with my dick in your mouth. It's fucking unreal, you know that? Sucking me so good."

Another moan muffled by Jonah's cock, and then he had to pull his hand away from Emerson's face, or he was going to pull Emerson's mouth down until he had Jonah all the way down his throat, which would be so fucking hot but not—not this time, definitely. Emerson worked him faster, left hand thankfully keeping Jonah from bucking out of control as he felt the orgasm curling tighter and tighter inside him, Emerson's lips and tongue and hand tormenting him. "Fuck, Em, don't stop, you're gonna make me come, gonna—"

Emerson sucked him through it, his eyes burning into Jonah's the whole time as Jonah cursed and came, Emerson's tongue never letting up on the underside of his cock. He gave himself half a second to recover, and then he did what he'd been wanting to do since they made it to the bedroom and fisted both hands in Emerson's hair and tugged until he was close enough to kiss.

They both reached for Emerson's belt at the same time. Still muzzy and uncoordinated, Jonah left him to it and jerked down his fly instead, helping Emerson push the fabric down. Then Emerson pulled away from Jonah's mouth to sit up, color high and pupils dilated as he jerked himself furiously, lips pink and parted and swollen and generally just a picture of debauchery.

Jonah wanted in on it. "Jesus, don't—" Emerson shuddered, and Jonah swallowed past the roughness in his throat and said, "Don't come yet. Fuck—where's your lube?"

Thankfully Emerson didn't ask questions, just gasped out, "Pillow," and fuck, that was so *hot*; either Emerson had been planning something like this, or he jerked off so much he didn't bother putting the lube away. Jonah grabbed the bottle one-handed and flipped open the cap, seizing Emerson's left hand and pouring.

"Show me," Jonah said hoarsely at Emerson's blank look. "Show me what you do when we're on the phone together, Emerson. I wanna see what you looked like all those times I got you off, when I told you all the things I wanted to do to you."

Gasping, Emerson spread the lube over his cock, still working too fast for Jonah's liking. He reached out and covered Emerson's hand with his, fascinated by the sight of it, of both of them working his cock together.

"God." Emerson let his head fall back, displaying the mark Jonah had put on him hours earlier. "Faster, please."

Jonah licked his lips. "Not yet, Em." With his free hand, he poured more slick over Emerson's fingers. "You know what I want."

Emerson shuddered helplessly, and Jonah slowed their hands further. Emerson sobbed out, "Jonah, I can't—"

"Yes, you can," he interrupted. "You can, and you're going to, Emerson. Come on, I want to see it. I want to see you put your fingers inside you. I know you do it to yourself when I'm not here."

"Jonah—"

Sensing he needed a little more encouragement, Jonah took his free hand and guided it to his entrance. "Do it, Em. Fuck yourself on your fingers. Do it for me, and then I'll let you come. It'll be so good, Em, I promise."

Trembling, Emerson pushed a finger inside himself, and Jonah's mouth went dry as he took in every detail: the straining lines of his body, the slack crescent of his mouth, the dribble of come beading at the head of his cock. "Emerson. Fuck. Another one, now."

Emerson let out an inhuman sound but complied.

Jonah got his hand on the bottle of lube again, but Emerson wasn't paying him any attention. "Now move them, Em. Nice and slow. You like that? Like the way it feels having something inside of you? Fucking you?"

Emerson shuddered again, and Jonah took pity on him, moving their hands slowly on his erection. "Asked you a question, Emerson."

"God." Emerson blushed furiously, voice barely audible over his heavy breathing. "Yes."

"What's that, Em? I didn't hear you." Jonah rubbed his thumb in a circle over the head of his dick.

Emerson let out a startled shout. "Yes, fuck, I love it, okay? I—"

In one smooth motion, Jonah added his middle finger to the two pistoning inside Emerson's ass and *pressed.*

Emerson's whole body went taut as he screamed, dick jerking under their hands, covering them in sticky white. Jonah worked the finger inside him until Emerson came back to himself, falling onto all fours over Jonah on the bed and pressing his face into Jonah's shoulder. "Jesus." Jonah could tell how embarrassed he was from the heat of his skin.

Ignoring the mess they'd made, he pulled Emerson to him, pressing a reassuring kiss to his neck. "Em."

Except for the slight tensing of his body under Jonah's hands, Emerson didn't acknowledge him. Okay, Jonah figured, maybe he wasn't up to talking about it yet. That was fine. Jonah was a good enough talker for any two people. "You were amazing, Emerson. Okay?"

Some of the tension seeped away, and Jonah felt him nod. "Okay. Now that that's out of the way, how about some Kleenex? You're sort of limiting my reach, and I stand to lose some key layers of epidermis in a few minutes if we don't clean up."

The exaggeration bought him a tiny laugh, and Emerson rolled over far enough to grab the box of tissues. With that out of the way, Jonah pressed a soft, lingering kiss to Emerson's mouth. "Now get as much sleep as you can," he said with a smile. "You're gonna need it tomorrow."

§

EMERSON sighed happily at the feel of Jonah's strong arm around his shoulders, the smooth chest beneath his head and the steady heartbeat by his ear. They were curled in bed together, neither one of them in any hurry to leave. They had been stretched out lazily all afternoon, not wanting to break the post-coital spell.

Emerson had something to ask, though, and he hoped that it wouldn't spoil the blissed-out mood.

"So," he got out, his voice husky with laziness, and possibly from the fact that Jonah had had him screaming earlier.

"So?" Jonah drawled back.

"I was thinking…."

"Uh oh." Jonah's murmur sounded sleepy and content.

"Har har," Emerson shot back, before moving on from the tired joke. "I was thinking that since Greg's spending the summer back home, his bedroom will be empty."

"Yeah. Thinking about filling it?" Jonah asked. His fingers began making random patterns over the curve of Emerson's shoulder.

"Thought maybe you'd like to." The fingers stopped moving. Emerson rushed on. "I mean, it'd only be for the summer, Greg will be back for more classes in September, but I figured it makes more sense than you renting a place for only four months."

"Em… are you asking me to move in with you?"

Emerson couldn't discern anything from Jonah's tone. He hesitated before he lifted his head to get a look at Jonah's face. Jonah was grinning. "Yes… for the summer. Only if you want to."

The tightening of the muscles in Jonah's arm was the only warning Emerson got before he was suddenly rolled onto his back. "Well, let me think. Do I want to be under the same roof as my very sexy boyfriend? Hm…."

"Jonah," Emerson protested, feeling only a little embarrassed.

"Though you do realize Greg being gone is kind of irrelevant. After all, why use his bed when this one is so comfy?" Jonah gave a lascivious grin and patted the mattress by Emerson's head.

Emerson flushed. "Right. You're keeping your stuff in Greg's room. I'm not telling my mom you're moving into my room! It's bad enough you keep giving me hickeys that she refuses to politely ignore like any sane parent."

Jonah grinned. "So she knows you are well-loved and desired."

"Thanks, Jonah, but really, too much information for her. Or me. She tells me stories about her 'youth', Jonah. Stories!"

Jonah laughed. "Poor baby. How about I make it better?"

"Better?"

"Yeah. I'm thinking a bed for the summer needs repayment." Jonah's hand snaked upward and grabbed the lube.

Emerson licked his lips, uncertain as to where this was going. "Jonah?"

"Don't worry, Em." Jonah must have picked up on the wariness to his tone. "It's for my fingers only."

"Fingers?" The word came out breathy as Jonah was sliding down his body, placing random kisses on Emerson's skin.

"Yeah. Don't you want to know how much better a prostate massage makes a blow job?" The sound of the lube top snapping open seemed really loud to Emerson. He watched, unable to tear his gaze away as Jonah began to pour slick onto his fingers. "Promise you'll love it," he murmured into the jut of a hip bone.

Jonah always kept his promises.

§

"EM, I'M bored," was the first thing that Jonah said when he entered Emerson's room and flopped down on his bed.

Emerson looked up from his computer, where he had been playing around with a picture of Jonah in Photoshop. "Hello, Jonah, it's good to see you too. So happy you decided to come see me."

"Don't pretend you aren't delighted to see my fantastic body," Jonah said without missing a beat. There was a pause before he continued, "Em, come make out with me!"

"Are you whining for sex?" Emerson asked. If he was honest with himself, he wasn't exactly surprised.

"Maybe. Is it working?" Jonah asked hopefully.

"No." Emerson turned back to his computer screen.

"E-em!" Jonah threw a pout in Emerson's direction. "Come on. I'm bored! And horny. Please?"

Emerson steadfastly ignored him, even though he kind of really wanted to give in. After all, he had been sitting here waiting for Jonah to get in from work. And he did still want to implement his plans for the evening. Still, he really didn't want to reward this kind of behavior.

"You know, you could just act like a normal person and try and seduce me when you want sex," Emerson pointed out archly.

"Seduce? But that's the beauty of having a boyfriend; I shouldn't have to always put in so much work when it comes to getting make-out time!"

Emerson stared at his boyfriend. "After that, I'm not sure I'll ever have sex with you again."

"What?!" Jonah squawked, sitting up on the bed. "You can't do that! You're contractually obligated to sleep with me—it's part of the deal."

Emerson continued to ignore Jonah in favor of his computer. "Not if I'm not your boyfriend anymore, I don't."

Jonah made another noise; this one sounded something like a cross between a cat and a chicken. "What?!" He stared at Emerson. "Are you saying you're going to dump me because I won't seduce you?" Jonah asked incredulously.

"Hm," Emerson hummed distractedly. "It does sound like that, doesn't it?"

"Right." Jonah stood up then and walked over to Emerson's chair. He placed one hand on the back of the laptop and firmly pushed it closed. Once Emerson could no longer pretend to be occupied with the computer, Jonah wrapped both hands around his face and proceeded to kiss him.

Oh, jackpot. He knew that Jonah wouldn't be able to hold out forever. Though Emerson had been very impressed with how quickly Jonah had folded.

Jonah used every trick he had ever learned to turn Emerson to jelly. "Come to bed with me," Jonah whispered against Emerson's lips. "I promise to make it up to you."

"Can't you make it up to me right here?"

"I'll break my back," Jonah replied sardonically. "Then how could I properly make things up to you?"

Emerson sighed with mock resignation. "Fine, but only because you're no use to me with a broken back."

Standing, he let Jonah pull him over to the bed and then push him down onto it.

Emerson loved this part. He loved the first tentative touches and long make-out sessions. Loved just lying with Jonah as they let fingers play over each other's skin lazily and their lips dance together in lingering kisses. He loved just taking the time to feel, to get both of them worked up. Sometimes Emerson just wanted to do this without moving toward sex.

Jonah's groin pressed down into his own, rubbing their hard cocks together.

Then again, sometimes getting off was much more appealing than just making out.

Jonah wasted no time in sliding both of his hands underneath Emerson's T-shirt. He smoothed both palms over his ribs, then used his nails to tickle the skin of his belly and reached up to pinch both nipples with his fingertips.

"How about we get this off you, yeah? Then I can make things up to you by paying proper respect to both nipples."

Emerson agreed with that idea. He wrapped both arms around Jonah's shoulders and rolled them over.

"Emerson?"

"My turn to be on top," Emerson said before stripping off his shirt. "Now make it up to me."

Jonah grinned and leaned in to place a kiss to one of Emerson's nipples.

Like with everything else that involved sex, Jonah was very good at this. Emerson curled both hands in their rightful places in Jonah's hair and started to moan.

By the time Jonah moved across Emerson's chest with a series of wet kisses to the other nipple, the first was red and swollen.

Jonah pulled away from torturing the second nub to grin up at Emerson and whisper filthily, "So, baby, now that you've got me where you want me, did you have any other suggestions?"

Emerson looked down at Jonah and tried to smile. Yes, Emerson did have another idea for how they could pass the time. Another idea that he was pretty sure Jonah would go for. However, he was still feeling a little nervous about it.

"I did have one idea," Emerson admitted.

"Oh?" Jonah arched an eyebrow. Emerson blushed; Jonah's look was far too knowing. His brow was arched in a way that suggested that he knew Emerson had some sort of plan.

Emerson leaned forward, ostensibly to start kissing Jonah's neck. Mostly, though, he just wanted to hide the telling blush.

Jonah ran two warm hands over Emerson's back and made encouraging noises as Emerson kissed and licked.

"Em-er-son," Jonah said in a sing-song, if somewhat breathy, voice. "What is it that you want to do?"

"I've been thinking," Emerson said slowly, still hiding his face.

"Yeees," Jonah said. He was smirking now for sure.

"Well," Emerson tried again. He had to remember that this was

Jonah, and Jonah wanted to do anything and everything that involved sex, not to mention that he knew how much Jonah was looking forward to this in particular. Jonah had a tendency to run his mouth about it when they were fooling around.

"I think—I know—" Emerson didn't want Jonah to think he wasn't certain about this. "I'm ready," Emerson whispered softly in Jonah's ear.

Jonah's arms tightened their grip spasmodically, and he went very still. "Ready?" His voice was hoarse.

"Yeah," Emerson breathed. "I want you to be inside me."

Suddenly Emerson was once more on his back with Jonah hovering over him. "Really?" He looked like a kid who had just been offered an entire chocolate cake all to himself. Hell, he looked like Emerson had offered him every chocolate cake *ever*. "Are you saying I can fuck you?"

Emerson nodded decisively. He was still feeling nervous at the prospect—Jonah fully erect wasn't any smaller than he had been before—but Emerson wanted this. "Yeah, fuck me, Jonah. Please?"

Jonah's smile was wide, but soft-edged. "Oh, well, if you insist."

§

TO SAY that Jonah had been planning this moment for years would not have been an overstatement. Oh, the details varied—Jonah had a vivid imagination and a sex drive like a rabbit on Viagra—but the important stuff, that was always the same. And he hadn't kissed Emerson nearly enough yet.

Settling in for the long haul on his side next to Emerson on the bed, Jonah rested his palm flat against Emerson's stomach as they kissed, immersing himself in the rhythm of Emerson's body. Eventually Emerson seemed to realize that Jonah wasn't just going to rush right to the main event, and he relaxed, slipping one hand beneath the hem of Jonah's T-shirt.

"Take your shirt off," Emerson breathed, and Jonah complied, sitting up long enough to pull it over his head before moving over to straddle Emerson's waist. He still hadn't met his kissing quota, but he hadn't ruled that all of those kisses had to be on the mouth.

For example, there was the fading bruise on Emerson's collarbone to address, and the firm curve of his shoulder, the dip of his sternum, the hollow of his navel. And that was all without taking his pants off. Jonah had his work cut out for him.

"Jonah," Emerson gasped when he scraped his teeth up the skin of Emerson's stomach to the left of Emerson's belly button. He knew it tickled and raised his head, smiling a little.

"Yes?"

"You're… quiet." Emerson was blushing worse than he usually did during sex, like he couldn't quite believe he'd actually mentioned it.

That was because the stream-of-consciousness filth he usually subjected Emerson to seemed totally inappropriate for an act Jonah was determined to treat with reverence, but he wasn't going to admit that to Emerson. Jonah kissed his stomach again. "I'm strategizing," he reassured him, tracing his nose over the trail of hair leading down into the waistband of his jeans.

"Strat-strategizing?" Emerson stuttered as Jonah peeled his jeans away from his hips.

"Mhmm." Jonah took in the sight of him, and Emerson squirmed. He was much better at letting Jonah admire him than he once had been due to long hours of practice, but his modesty always seemed to return every time they tried something new. "About how I'm going to make you come first." No—the jeans had to come all the way off now. They would only be in the way later. He sat up and tugged them off gently, caressing Emerson's calves as he did, easing his legs back to the bed with care.

Emerson cleared his throat. "First?"

Jonah smoothed a palm up Emerson's inner thigh, watching as his cock hardened in anticipation. "Think I'll blow you," he decided, situating himself between Emerson's legs. He let the backs of his knuckles graze Emerson's erection before pressing a wet kiss to the skin at the base. "That okay?"

"When have I ever…," Emerson started, but he cut himself off with a groan when Jonah sucked the head of his dick into his mouth. He tried again. "Exactly how many times were you planning—?"

Jonah hummed consideringly, resisting the urge to smirk as Emerson gasped and fell silent. When he pulled off to answer, he kept his hand moving slowly on Emerson's cock. "I don't know *exactly*. How many times can you come in one night? I've been meaning to find out."

"How is this my life?" Emerson wondered aloud.

Jonah ignored him and went back to the task at hand. Mouth. Whatever.

"You're supposed to"—Jonah took him deep, and Emerson gurgled before finding his voice again—"supposed to be fucking me, remember?"

Did Emerson think Jonah was going to forget? Not likely. "I will when I'm ready. More importantly, I will when *you* are ready."

"But—" Emerson started.

Jonah rubbed his thumb in a slow circle around the head of his dick, vaguely amused. "Exactly who is it you think is in charge here?"

After that Emerson just moaned and let Jonah get on with making him come his brains out. At least once to take the edge off, Jonah figured, and, if he were honest, to turn Emerson into putty; he was much less prone to fits of anxiety after Jonah had sucked him into incoherence. To that end, he slid his hands under Emerson's ass, massaging the firm muscle as he licked down the column of flesh. He could have slipped a finger into his mouth, wet it to slide between Emerson's cheeks, but he was saving that until….

Emerson bucked under his mouth, panting and moaning as Jonah flicked over the head of his dick with his tongue. Usually Jonah drew out Emerson's climax until he was literally begging, but he had other plans for tonight. Emerson would have lots of time to beg for what he wanted later. Instead he let Emerson thrust down his throat and swallowed around the head of his dick until he came, panting loudly and cursing, body rigid, and then he was quiet and wordless and pliant.

Emerson was still breathing hard when Jonah tapped him on the hip. "Turn over."

"Jonah…." Emerson was trembling, again or still Jonah couldn't be sure.

"Trust me," he murmured, kissing the top of Emerson's right thigh.

With a little more coaxing, Emerson turned over, and Jonah devoted his attention to caressing the smooth plane of his back, easing away any tension. He pressed his lips to the back of Emerson's neck and mouthed down his spine, hands framing his sides. "I love you like this," he said huskily, dropping a chaste kiss on the dip of his oblique. "The way you go all pliant after you come. It's a pretty good ego boost, Emerson."

Emerson murmured in agreement; from his tone he wasn't turned on again yet, but that would change. Jonah shifted his palms inward and sat up a bit, played with the curve of Emerson's ass with his thumbs, skated a teasing touch across the skin where thighs and buttocks met, pressed his mouth to the top of one cheek.

Emerson's breath hitched, and Jonah smiled into his skin. "I should—stop then," Emerson said a little unsteadily.

Jonah licked sideways across the top of his ass. "Oh?"

Nodding into the pillow, Emerson continued, "Your ego—is already"—Jonah sucked the flesh into his mouth, teething it lightly, and the last word came out as a mostly incoherent sigh—"huge."

There was no way Jonah could be expected to ignore a perfect setup like that. "'S'not the only thing about me that's big, Em."

He felt Emerson laugh a little, but before he could retort, Jonah pushed up and out with his hands, exposing Emerson's hole to his view. Emerson tensed again, but Jonah leaned in before he could mount a protest and flicked his tongue over the pucker of skin.

"Oh," Emerson said, a soft explosion of air. "God, Jonah, what—"

Whatever he was going to say was lost in a broken sob when Jonah repeated the action, pulling Emerson open further and just going for it, tongue swirling and prodding and stabbing at Emerson's opening.

"Fuck," Emerson mewled. "Oh, God, J—fuck!"

Murmuring his agreement, Jonah moved his hands in again. "Hold yourself open for me, Em."

"Jonah—"

Jonah pressed the thumb of his right hand over Emerson's hole, pushed just a little. "Do it, Emerson."

The wet gasp Emerson made at that was mostly eaten by the pillow he had mashed his face into as he shifted on the bed, quaking. Jonah put one big hand on the small of his back to steady him and grabbed his dick with his other hand, stroking gently as he worked his tongue inside.

The sounds Emerson was making were pure vowels now, just meaningless expressions of extreme pleasure. Jonah released his cock to wet a finger in his mouth and slid it deep alongside his tongue, pushing and stretching at the muscle until it was loose. He fumbled one-handed in the drawer beside the bed, and it was a good thing they'd started buying lube in bigger bottles, because he didn't want to spare a second looking for it.

The second finger slid in easily, followed quickly by a third, at which point Jonah had to sit back a bit and just watch as his fingers disappeared, reappeared, over and over again. Then he curled his body low over Emerson's back so he could whisper in his ear. "You're beautiful like this, Emerson. Open and trusting and so turned on." Emerson thrust his hips down against the bed, and Jonah readjusted himself so Emerson couldn't move, could only take what Jonah gave him, bumping purposefully against his prostate every time he pushed inside.

"Please," Emerson sobbed, his eyes closed, cheeks bright red.

Jonah brushed a kiss lightly across the top of one flushed cheekbone. "Soon," he assured him. "Let me take care of you."

"Jonah." Emerson bucked beneath him, and Jonah sucked at a spot on his neck. "Please! Don't—don't make me beg."

Jesus. Jonah had to remind himself to be good; the list of things he liked more than hearing Emerson begging for him was extremely short. "You wanna come, Em?" Emerson whined. Jonah worked his fingers harder, faster, licking a line up Emerson's neck to his ear. "Let go, then, sweetheart. Come for me."

Curling his hands into his sheets, Emerson did, convulsing hard around Jonah's relentless fingers, mouthing a steady litany of, "Jonah, Jonah, oh—"

Jonah needed to kiss him *right now*, but he also—he cursed his lack of foresight—he also needed to take his jeans off before they cut off the circulation somewhere important. He stood just long enough to kick off the rest of his clothes and then rolled Emerson over so he could thank him properly, one long, deep kiss and then a trail of sucking bites down his chest again.

"Jonah. If you b-blow me again I will fucking—"

Jonah never did find out what Emerson would fucking, because when Jonah lapped at the mess covering Emerson's soft cock he stopped threatening and started thrashing. "Oh, God, Jonah, don't," he whimpered. "I can't, I *can't*—"

"Never know 'til you try," Jonah said philosophically, though he was careful to be gentle. He knew how sensitive Emerson would be, so he concentrated his initial efforts on cleaning the come from Emerson's stomach, then his balls, before carefully working his way up his dick.

That was too much, apparently; at the first twitch of his cock, Emerson shuddered all over and sat up, pushing Jonah away so he could reach into the nightstand for a condom, which he thrust into Jonah's hand roughly. "If you don't get inside me in the next thirty seconds, I am changing my mind."

Jonah looked down at the seemingly innocuous packet and swallowed hard as the stark reality of the situation hit him all at once. In a few seconds he would be inside Emerson.

Now is not the time for performance anxiety, he reminded himself firmly, ripping open the package quickly and rolling the condom on.

Thankfully, Emerson saved him from a truly embarrassing crisis by turning around on the bed.

"What are you doing? Come back here." Jonah flipped him over easily, crawling up Emerson's body until their faces were centimeters apart. At least he could be sure that Emerson was at least twice as nervous as he was.

Emerson licked his lips. "I thought—"

"I want to see your face while I make love to you for the first time," Jonah said, a little more honestly than he meant to. He bit the inside of his cheek in an attempt to rein in his emotions.

Emerson said, "Oh." His hands were shaking a little when he passed Jonah the lube, but Jonah wasn't really in a state to comment on it. He slicked his erection and shifted forward another inch.

Then he was pressing inside one micrometer at a time, one hand curled firmly around the base of his cock. With the other hand he reached for Emerson and tangled their fingers together, gripping tightly. True to his word, he never let his eyes slip from Emerson's face, though he desperately wanted to look down and see, watch himself disappear inside Emerson's body.

It was tight—God, of course it was, Emerson was practically a virgin, and Jonah wasn't exactly small—and gut-wrenchingly hot, and maybe Jonah should have thought about the fact that he'd been hard enough to pound nails for an hour before fucking Emerson, but there was no going back in time. "Talk to me, Emerson. You want me to stop?"

He really, *really* didn't want to stop, but Emerson was being *quiet* for once, and that had Jonah worried.

Emerson shook his head, bit his lip, shifted his legs—and all the breath went out of Jonah in a rush as Emerson bent at the knee and pulled him in until their bodies were flush together. "God, Emerson, *Jesus*," Jonah cursed, taking Emerson's other hand as well and leaning down to kiss him slow and deep, pouring out his love and affection until he could practically taste it on Emerson's lips. His dick was throbbing so hard he had to start saying the alphabet backward in his head to get control again. "That talking thing," Jonah reminded him, pulling back gently. "You're supposed to do it with your mouth, Emerson."

"Just… give me a minute."

That wasn't a bad idea. Jonah could use a minute to collect himself too. He kissed him again, just a soft touch of his lips this time, on Emerson's mouth and jaw and ear. He released Emerson's left hand to rub soothingly down the side of his body a few times, then up his thigh and down again until he had Emerson's cock in his hand.

Emerson turned his head away like he was embarrassed.

"Hey," Jonah said softly, kissing his cheek as he started to move his hand. "This isn't exactly a hardship, you know." He kept his face there until Emerson turned his head again and met his eyes. Then he amended, "Not to make a terrible pun or anything," and shifted his balance just a tiny bit to get a better grip.

Emerson opened his mouth, presumably to say something, but what came out was a low, satisfied-sounding moan. There was no mistaking the timbre for anything other than pleasure, and it was all the encouragement Jonah needed to draw his hips back, pulling out almost to the tip. He couldn't help but look down as he did so, seeing

Emerson's hole spread wet and slick and wide to accommodate his length, his hand wrapped around Emerson's cock, hard again under his fingers.

"Aw, Christ," Jonah groaned.

The breath went out of Emerson in a rush when Jonah pushed forward again, and he made another one of those insanely sexy sounds he seemed to have an endless supply of and arched his body up a little. "God, if you could see yourself," Jonah breathed.

Another thrust, then another. Emerson closed his eyes, lips parted and glistening slightly; Jonah licked them, pushed his tongue into his mouth. "Love the way you feel."

Emerson shuddered.

Okay, Jonah thought. *Let's have some more of that*. Shifting both hands to Emerson's hips, he sat back, angling his hips until—

Emerson gasped, his eyes flying open. His hands latched onto Jonah's forearms. "Jonah. God."

Emerson met him evenly on the next thrust, legs wrapping around Jonah's waist, and Jonah felt the pleasure of it all the way through. "You like that?"

Stupid question—Jonah could *see* the answer, had had it in his hand a second ago—but he never could shut up. "So good for me, Emerson, I wanna make it good for you too, but you gotta tell me."

"More," Emerson gasped between moans.

Jonah thrust deeper.

A hot, desperate sound forced its way past Emerson's lips. "Hard-harder."

Christ, Jonah didn't want to hurt him, but it would be so good, and if he was asking for it—

"Yes," Emerson said, half-whine and half in triumph. "God! Jonah, I lo—"

Fuck, fuck, fuck, Jonah wanted to hear him say it more than *anything*, but now was really not the time. He leaned down and kissed the words from Emerson's mouth as he reached between them to put his hand on Emerson's dick again, smearing the small amount of fluid at the head and using it to ease his way down the shaft. It was hardly enough, but it didn't seem to make a difference. After half a dozen strokes, Emerson bit Jonah's lip hard enough to draw blood as his body seized around Jonah's cock, all tight, fluttery heat.

Jonah held on for maybe another three strokes, and then it was too much. He pulled his stinging lips away from Emerson's as his orgasm tore through him, setting fire to every cell in his body and then pouring out of him in a rush as his dick pulsed again and again, leaving him hollowed-out and boneless.

After a few seconds he reluctantly moved over, pulling out of Emerson's body so he could dispose of the condom and catch his breath. Or kiss Emerson again. Kissing Emerson was better than breathing anyway, so he did, gently, until Emerson finally opened his eyes again.

"There you are," Jonah said with a small smile.

Emerson's color was still high, and he was feeling a little vulnerable, if the way he dropped his eyes was any indication, but he reached out and put his hand on Jonah's chest above his heart, so that was something.

Jonah took a deep breath and told himself to be brave. "If you mean it," he said, "now would be a good time."

Emerson took a sharp breath.

"I mean," Jonah continued around the lump that was trying to form in his throat, "I don't know if you've noticed, but I've kind of been head over heels in love with you for years." Maybe he'd been wrong? Maybe Emerson hadn't been about to say—

"Me too," he said before Jonah could get any further. He was blushing furiously now, but he managed to meet Jonah's eyes. "I mean, I—I love you."

And Jonah *knew* that, he did, had known it for almost a year, but hearing it was different. Better. So good that he actually didn't have anything to say—if he could have spoken. Which he wasn't sure he could.

"Are you—" Emerson said cautiously after a minute.

"Shut up, there's something in my eye," Jonah told him, and fuck the mess—he wrangled Emerson around until he was lying on Jonah's chest and held him there until he fell asleep.

§

JONAH paused at the door to Emerson's room for the first time in weeks, feeling twitchy. Emerson was stretched out on his bed, head propped up on his left hand, a pencil dangling from the fingers of his right arm. There was a sketch pad lying on the bed near his hand, but Emerson wasn't paying it any attention. He seemed to be staring aimlessly into space.

Jonah knocked softly on the open door, and Emerson looked up with a smile. "Hey!" He dropped the pencil and flipped the sketch pad shut, leaning up to place them on the dresser.

"Hey." Taking the invitation, Jonah entered and dropped down onto the bed beside his boyfriend, catching a quick kiss as he did so.

Emerson's mouth opened warm and sweet under his, but Jonah kept the touch just this side of serious. He didn't want to get distracted.

"What's up?" Emerson asked a few seconds later when he pulled away, reaching one hand up to brush his fingers over the crease between Jonah's brows. "You look so… pensive."

"Good word," Jonah said with a quick smile, taking Emerson's hand in his own and giving it a squeeze.

"Well, I learned from the best." Emerson turned so that he was on his side, facing Jonah. "Now, talk."

Jonah rolled onto his back and looked up at the ceiling, reaching his right arm so that it wrapped around Emerson's shoulders, pulling him closer to Jonah's chest. "A couple of Natalie's friends are getting a house together in September. I guess one of her friends' dads owns a place he rents out here in Austin or something."

"That'll be nice for her," Emerson said after a hesitant moment. "I mean, Natalie's pretty mature and responsible…."

Smiling slightly, Jonah turned his head and pressed a kiss to the top of Emerson's head. "Yeah, no, of course. It's just, their parents all want to have a man around the house, you know? I think they're worried the girls might get taken advantage of or something. And I guess I'm sort of the prime candidate."

"Well, you're big and intimidating as well as taken and kind of gay," Emerson pointed out, lifting his head to smirk at Jonah a little. "You're pretty ideal for the job of protecting their daughters' virtue."

That was, Jonah had to concede, a fairly valid point. But that didn't mean he had to like the idea. "I guess."

"And trust me," Emerson said, "it's much better to move in with roommates you already know. Greg will be back in a few weeks, and he'll need his room back. School will be starting soon. You need to have this figured out by then, or you're going to be stuck driving back and forth. And that sucks."

Jonah made a face. Emerson was right about that. "I know. I guess I was just thinking…."

"That could be dangerous," Emerson teased. "Go on."

"Well, it's not like I actually sleep in there anyway," Jonah hedged. "And why should I when there's a perfectly good bed across the hall with you in it?"

Emerson's expression took on a guarded quality, and he shifted so that he was lying on his stomach, propped up by both elbows. "Are you hinting at what I think you're hinting at?"

"I don't want to move," Jonah said. "I like it here. It has you, and Zack has stopped glowering at me over breakfast. I never use my room unless you're working anyway. I'll still pay rent, and we can use it to buy groceries or something."

Emerson's cheeks pinkened, and he averted his eyes. "I don't think that's a good idea."

"It's a great idea," Jonah countered. "Think of the time we'll save walking between houses!"

"Jonah, when is the last time you worked on your writing?"

Thrown by the seeming change of subject, Jonah thought about it. "I don't know, Tuesday while you were at work? What does that have to do with anything?"

Emerson persisted. "When was the last time you worked on it when I was home?"

"I have better things to do when you're at home," Jonah said. He ran his eyes and then the tips of his fingers down Emerson's spine appreciatively. "Case in point."

"That's not healthy, Jonah!" Emerson protested. "It was great for a summer, but school starts again soon, and we're both going to have homework to do as well as work. We're going to need our own space. Besides, what if we have a fight?"

"We never fight." Jonah turned onto his side and pressed their noses together. "Come on, Em, don't you want to live together?" When Emerson's eyes slid closed, he brushed his lips across Emerson's in a brief, gentle kiss.

"Of course I want to," Emerson said. "That's the problem. Jonah, you can barely keep your hands to yourself in public. What about when one of us needs to study? Or has an assignment due?"

"Hey! I can control myself," Jonah said, wounded. "If you told me no, I'd back off!"

"Well, I'm not very good at telling you no anymore. And that still leaves you ignoring your own homework. I just don't think it's a good idea, Jonah."

Part of him had to admit that Emerson did have a point, but Jonah wasn't ready to give up so easily. "We could give it a month-long trial period," he proposed. "If it isn't working out by the end of September, I can always move out then."

But Emerson shook his head stubbornly. "It'll be too late to find a place to rent by then. You'll be stuck in Hudson Bend 'til next year."

"That assumes it won't work out. Em, I've spent enough years of my life apart from you."

"We're not going to be apart. We live in the same city. We go to the same school. Considering that for the past three years we've hardly seen each other at all, that should be plenty." Emerson took a deep breath. "We spent the first eight months of our relationship apart, Jonah. Of course we didn't fight. Just because we haven't yet doesn't mean we won't. We're not ready to live together, and you know it."

Bristling, Jonah pulled away. Obviously Emerson wasn't going to see sense right now. "We'll never know unless we try." Emerson wasn't the only one who could be stubborn.

Emerson put his hand on Jonah's arm before he could sit up. "I'm not saying you can't stay over on weekends. You can even keep your key. We'll move in together once we graduate, I promise."

After a long moment, Jonah decided to drop the subject lest he inadvertently prove Emerson's point. With a sigh, he settled back into the bed and curled his body into Emerson's. "I guess I'd better take advantage of you while I still can." He pushed Emerson over on his side and insinuated his left hand into the back pocket of Emerson's jeans.

Emerson gave him a wide-eyed look. "You are incorrigible."

"Nah, just horny," Jonah corrected. "How long 'til you have to leave for work?"

"Uh." Emerson shuddered when Jonah kissed feather-light up his neck to his ear. "Two hours," he said a little hoarsely.

"Mmm." Jonah pulled his hand out of Emerson's pocket and sneaked it under the back of his T-shirt instead. "Plenty of time."

§

EMERSON was still panicking and fretting over the whole situation some three hours later as he was driving back into Austin. By the time he pulled into the driveway at their place, Emerson had decided that the easiest thing to do was to bring the subject up with Jonah. That way Jonah could confirm or deny his suspicions, and Emerson wouldn't have to live in doubt. It was simple.

He found Jonah in his room, laid out on his bed and reading a book. It wasn't that surprising; Emerson took a minute to appreciate the familiarity of the sight.

Emerson cleared his throat and managed to smile back when Jonah gave him a bright grin. "Hey, Em, how'd the day go?" he asked as he put his book aside.

His hands were trembling a little, so he stuffed them in his pockets. "Alright." He licked his lips. "Kind of boring, actually. Until this cute kid came in. You'll never guess who his mom was."

Jonah arched an eyebrow. "Who?"

"Deanna Carlisle."

Jonah sat up. "You're kidding."

Not a very insightful start to the conversation. That comment was terribly ambiguous, though to Emerson the "you're kidding" sounded more like "oh, shit, you caught me" than it did "what a surprise!"

Emerson bit his lip, then forced himself to continue. "Which was surprising, because no one ever told me she had a kid. Not all that shocking, I guess, except the kid looked like he was about three years old already. I mean, she must have got knocked up when we were still in high school."

Jonah snorted and stood, tossing his book to his nightstand. "Christ, no wonder she moved away for a few years."

"So you didn't know?" Emerson really hoped the heat he could feel wasn't a slight blush. "I mean, you took her to prom."

Jonah turned back to face him, his voice sounding careful and deliberate. "Yes… but guess who else moved away after high school? It was just a date. We didn't keep in touch."

"Oh? I would have thought that you…." Emerson wasn't sure how to finish that. Would keep in touch with people you slept with? Would have already known about the kid? Would have at least shared an e-mail with a girl you were friends with and had dated?

Still, the unfinished thought left a frown on Jonah's face. "That I what, Emerson? Whatever you're trying to say, spit it out."

Emerson found he couldn't just spit it out, though. "You went to prom together—well, that's not true, is it?" Suddenly all the bitterness of that one night came rushing back so fast and strong Emerson felt like he was choking on it. "More like you *missed* prom together. I mean, when you tell people you've hired a limo but then don't show up? People tend to notice, Jonah."

Jonah crossed his arms and stood up straight. "Are you actually accusing me of—" His quiet tone sounded dangerous.

Emerson wrapped both arms around himself. "I should tell you more about the kid! He was very adorable. All bright hazel eyes and tan skin and wavy brown hair," Emerson blurted out, feeling desperate and shaken.

Jonah went stone-faced. He stared at Emerson, his eyes hard and his face unyielding. His arms were still crossed, and Emerson couldn't help but notice how very tall Jonah was. "Get out."

Emerson felt himself jerk in surprise. He stared at Jonah. He hadn't seen Jonah looking so angry in years, and certainly not since Jonah had put on muscle mass or since they had started dating. "What?"

"Get out of my room. You know, maybe you were right. Maybe we shouldn't live together."

Emerson winced. Sure, he had been the one to say that them

living together would be a bad idea, but that was because they were too crazy about each other to keep their hands to themselves, not because they weren't good together.

Hurt filled his chest. "What? Because I wanted to know if you knew about Deanna's kid? Which, considering that you were *fucking* her around the same time she got pregnant, isn't unreasonable."

Jonah's nostrils flared. "You know what's not unreasonable? Having a boyfriend who asks you straight up about things instead of coming at you sideways with outrageous accusations. Now get out of my way. If you're not going to leave, I will." Jonah took two steps forward.

Emerson ignored him, filled with rage. How dare *Jonah* get angry? "Alright, fine, then. Do you have a fucking kid?"

Jonah's arms dropped to his side. His hands were balled into fists and clenched next to his hips. "Emerson, so help me God, if you don't get out of the fucking doorway, I don't know what I'll do."

He took another few steps forward, and Emerson stared at him. Jonah had never looked more frightening. Surprised, Emerson took two steps to the left, instinctively getting out of the way.

Jonah stormed past him, his steps hurried and angry, decisive. He had just reached the top of the stairs when Emerson recovered. He spun around and hurried after Jonah's retreating form.

Over the sound of Jonah's boots clattering down the steps, Emerson demanded, "Why won't you answer the question?"

The only response Emerson got was the sound of the front door slamming shut.

Emerson stood frozen at the top of the stairs for long moments, staring at the closed front door. It was hardly the first argument that he and Jonah had had. There was that time in 7th grade when Emerson had ignored Jonah for a week after Jonah crashed his bike while borrowing it. Then there had been the epic battle of 10th grade when Emerson had accidently stolen the affections of Jonah's latest crush, and Jonah had exploded into a ball of jealous and righteous fury. Both arguments had been big and world-ending at the time.

Neither compared to right now.

Fighting with Jonah when he was in love with Jonah, when he knew that Jonah loved him back? Was a million times worse.

He felt like he had been hollowed out. Like something had reached in and pulled out everything that kept Emerson moving, that held him up. Except they had left his heart, which felt like it was being squeezed into a pulp.

Jonah loved him. Emerson knew that. Still, it wasn't very encouraging the way Jonah had run out. And the way he had looked at Emerson, just before he left. Like Emerson was a stranger that he wanted to hurt. Jonah had never looked at him that way before.

And Jonah had—Jonah had threatened him. He had stood there and said he didn't know what he'd do to Emerson if Emerson didn't move. He'd stood there looking so tall and enormous, and Emerson had actually been frightened. Of Jonah!

It was not the first time that Emerson had seen Jonah use his height that way. He had been taller than everyone else for years, and it had been almost as long that he hadn't been ashamed of using it to his advantage. Hell, just last week he had stood beside a freaked-out Hayley in a bar glaring at the guy who wouldn't stop bugging her. The guy had run away just because he was half Jonah's size.

Still, Jonah had never used his height against Emerson. Never. Not even in tenth grade. Even when they were making out or having sex, and Jonah used his size to their advantage, he didn't make Emerson feel afraid. Not like tonight.

Not like tonight when Jonah had stood over him, glaring and threatening, and Emerson had been worried, if just for a moment, genuinely worried that Jonah might throw a punch.

Emerson wasn't sure, but he thought that the idea might be more terrifying now that Jonah had held him down, been inside him, and left bruises on him than it would have been twelve months ago.

Emerson turned from the stairs and stumbled down the hall to his bedroom. Once there he sat down on his bed. Then, still not feeling secure, scooted back until he was pressed into the corner, body curled in close.

Oh God. What if Jonah dumped him?

Something hit his hand. Looking down he noticed the tear rolling down his thumb. Oh, he was crying apparently. Right. Crying because Jonah was maybe breaking his heart again. Only this time it probably was all Emerson's fault.

§

Now

THEY made their way through the crowd of students, professors, and proud parents to a side door Jonah hadn't noticed earlier; it opened on a small, empty smoker's courtyard with a single bench. He didn't sit.

The automatic door closed slowly behind them, and for a long time neither of them spoke. Emerson tucked his hands under his elbows and shifted his feet, looking anywhere but at Jonah.

Jonah was still too angry to be the first to apologize. "Did you want to go first?"

Emerson made a pained face, then said in a rush, "So, I'm kind of insecure and a bit of an idiot when it comes to you."

Jonah frowned. Did Emerson think that was news? They had been stupid over each other for years. Come to think of it, Emerson's insecurity was almost exactly as long-lasting. "Okay… I kinda knew that part."

Emerson wrapped his arms tighter around himself and stared daggers at the ashtray. "Yeah, I guess you would. If anyone knows how crazy I can be, it'd be you."

God damn it, Emerson was missing the point. Jonah made a frustrated sound. "I just—I don't understand how you could think that I'd—"

"What?" Emerson said, meeting Jonah's eyes for the first time in a while and looking like he was going to be sick. "Lie?" He bit his lip again. "I didn't"—a thick, choking laugh. "I'm kind of stupid. I freaked out and convinced myself that you would have found out when we weren't talking. 'Cause I know you wouldn't—I know you wouldn't want to lie to me like that."

"I'm not even *capable* of lying like that!" Jonah burst out. "I could understand, maybe, if you thought I didn't know, but even then—even then you should have known I didn't sleep with Deanna."

"I… what?" Emerson took a step back, his brow furrowing. "You never told me anything about what you did with her."

Of all the asinine things to say—Jonah gritted his teeth. What did Emerson want, an itemized confession of what sexual acts he'd performed with whom, along with dates and approximate times? Should he rate his partners on a scale of one to ten? "In December I gave you my full sexual history." With effort, he reminded himself that Emerson was new to lasting relationships and softened his tone some. "God knows he looks like me, but barring some freaky *X-Files* scenario, Gareth *can't* be mine."

Emerson uncrossed and re-crossed his arms. "So, what, you just skipped prom to go get pizza instead?"

That was enough. "Jesus Christ, Emerson, what the hell does it matter what we did? The bottom line here is you're either going to believe me, or you're not. And if you're not"—if Emerson didn't believe him, didn't *trust* him, even after all this time—"then why am I here?"

Recoiling, Emerson's arms loosened with a spastic jerk, before they changed direction to curl around his torso. "That's not—not what I wanted to… I…." His Adam's apple bobbed as he swallowed hard. "I did something really shitty. I got so upset—Deanna was always everything I wasn't when it came to you, and seeing her threw me so much, I forgot that you—you wouldn't do that to me. I just, I freaked out, and I didn't stop to think until after I'd freaked out at you, and then it was too late."

"Is this an apology? Because usually those start with 'I'm sorry'," Jonah gritted out. He could guess at the reasoning behind it well enough, but he needed to know that Emerson understood what his mistrust had cost Jonah.

Emerson flushed, looking pained. "I—of course it's an apology. I am so sorry, Jonah. I never wanted to hurt you—you're…. I'm sorry I hurt you and made you leave." He licked his lips and curled his hands into fists where they were buried under his upper arms. "'Cause I love you. I do."

The words hit Jonah right at the knees, and only sheer force of will kept him on his feet. There was no way Emerson could fake that kind of sincerity, not when he had so much trouble getting his I-love-yous out in the first place. "Alright, I believe that. But you're not the only one with his heart on the line, here. You can't just go around thinking I'd betray you like that, Em."

"I know! I know," Emerson said miserably. "Did I mention I'm a little insecure? And trying to get better about that?" He took a shuffling half-step forward, expression earnest. "I—I know you love me."

Maybe he was looking for some reassurance that Jonah did still love him—and of course he did—but it could wait a few more minutes. He needed to make sure the issue was well and truly closed, and that meant he owed Emerson an apology of his own. "Alright," he said, bracing himself and trying to resist the urge to hunch. "I guess while we're on the subject, I need to apologize too."

"What?" Emerson shook his head, took another half-step. "I was the one who acted like… like a crazy, jealous person." He gave Jonah a fairly pathetic smile.

"It takes two people to have a fight," Jonah admitted. "As crazy, as angry, as your accusations made me, I could have just told you the truth then. I'd still have been mad, but it wouldn't be like *this*. But I guess I figured if you could really think I'd keep something like that from you, you deserved to keep on believing it."

Emerson swallowed, obviously unhappy but not disagreeing. "Oh. That's"—he cleared his throat, and his gaze drifted away from Jonah's—"that's not unreasonable."

It was, a little, and even if it was *understandable*, Jonah still felt guilty. He could have saved them both a lot of heartache. And besides—"There's something else," he said.

"What?"

Now or never, Jonah told himself firmly. He tried to be matter-of-fact, but his voice came out sounding every bit as tormented as he felt. "When you were standing in the doorway, I think I scared you." He took a deep breath for fortification and plunged ahead. "You actually thought that I'd—and I can't blame you for thinking it. I can't believe I did that to you."

"Oh." Emerson looked down at his feet, to his left, at the tree in the courtyard. "I won't lie—you did scare me a little." He darted a sideways look back at Jonah. "I've never seen you look like that before. I knew you wouldn't hurt me, though."

"I couldn't—I was never going to hit you." Emerson said he knew that, but Jonah had to make sure, had to make absolutely sure, because otherwise—no. He couldn't stand it if Emerson were afraid of him. "You know that, right? I've never hurt *anyone*. But I needed space. I don't get mad a lot, but when I do I need to be alone to think. It's been eating at me ever since." His voice broke, but he was too emotional to bother being embarrassed. "I am so sorry I scared you."

Another step forward and then Emerson was within touching distance, and Jonah couldn't stand it anymore. He reached out, and Emerson finally uncrossed his arms and took Jonah's hands. "I know you wouldn't hurt me, Jonah. I've always known that." He took a shaky breath and smiled a little. "But don't do it again, okay?"

"I swear," Jonah promised.

Emerson let out a long breath of what Jonah assumed was relief. He was near to sagging with it himself. "So… do you think you might want to take your key back now?"

God, if they were okay enough to be joking, they were okay enough to be hugging. Jonah got both arms around Emerson and *squeezed*. "Fuck the key. You're right that we shouldn't live together right now. I'll never get anything done." He smiled a little when Emerson hugged him back. "Well, except for you. What I'd really like is my boyfriend back, if that's on the table."

Emerson pulled away just enough to look him in the eye. "I never wanted to be anyone else's." He flushed a little at the admission. "And you better take that key back, 'cause I am not getting out of bed at nine o'clock on a day off just because you want to come cuddle."

Liar. Jonah leaned their foreheads together. "Yeah, you would."

One of Emerson's arms unwrapped from his back and went digging into his jeans pocket. When it came back out again, it was holding the brass key Jonah had left where Emerson was sure to see it. "It would be easier if you could just let yourself in."

"Hmm, okay," Jonah said, pretending to think about it as he took the key and put it in his own pocket. He could put it back on his keychain later. "On one condition, though." He rubbed their noses together.

Emerson blinked at him, wide-eyed. "What?"

He made it impossible to resist the impulse. Jonah leaned forward just a little further and whispered, "You have to start sleeping naked."

He pulled back just in time to see Emerson blushing and stuttering. "Jonah, I'm not—"

Jonah cut him off with a kiss like a signature on all of their promises. He let it roll on and on, lips and tongue and just a hint of teeth, until his breath was short and Emerson was leaning into him obviously. "What do you say we get out of here?" he said finally.

Emerson pretended to think about it. "Your place or mine?"

EPILOGUE

THREE YEARS LATER

"THANKS for doing this," Jonah said for probably the tenth time, looking over to the driver's seat.

Xie didn't bother looking back, just rolled her eyes as she put the car in park. "Please. Don't think you're not going to make it up to me with free babysitting."

He smiled and turned around in the too-small space to peer into the back, where Tony was slouched adorably in his safety seat. "That's not exactly a hardship," he pointed out before twisting around again and unfolding himself from the dinky car. He loved Xie, but next time she took him house shopping? He was driving. "You know we love having him."

"Well, this *is* my job, you know," she pointed out, slamming the car door shut behind her and somehow managing to wriggle her way far enough into the back to get Tony out of the hopeless tangle that was a baby seat. "So we're kind of even."

She had a point there.

"Can I get anything?"

"The sling," Xie said, pointing with her chin as she hoisted Tony out and away from the grasp of his seventeen thousand seatbelts. I've got his bottle and a toy in my purse just in case."

Once upon a time, Jonah reflected, Xie had refused to carry anything larger than a bare-minimum camera bag. Now, he could fit every book he'd ever be able to write in that "purse." He opened the back door and started sorting out the sling. "Looks a bit big for you," he said apologetically as he held it up.

"It's sized for Bryce right now," she explained, shoving the car door closed with her hip and clicking the remote to lock it. "He took

Tony for his bedtime walk last night." A speculative light came into her eyes, and she looked him up and down. "It'll probably fit you, though."

"You think?" Jonah fiddled with the straps. "Am I doing this right?"

Giggling, Xie managed to help him adjust it one-handed, despite Tony's attempts at sabotage. "It's not rocket science, you know." Then she stepped back, surveyed her handiwork, and declared the harness sound. Tony was summarily stuffed into the sling, and Xie dug her second set of keys out of her purse while Jonah got him settled.

A year ago, when Xie had told him she was pregnant, Jonah had been completely over the moon for her. Then she'd added that she and Bryce were moving back to Texas—to Austin, specifically, as Bryce's father had business interests in Austin—so she could be closer to her parents once the baby was born. Since then, he and Emerson had been spending a lot more time with Bryce and Xie—and, by association, Tony. So when he was finally settled snugly into the sling, he only spent a few seconds fussing about who was holding him. Then he leaned back a little and tilted his head up, waved one fat baby hand in the air until he hit Jonah squarely on his stubbled chin, and quieted again, leaning hard against Jonah's chest like he expected a boob to pop out of nowhere. Smiling, Jonah put his hand on the baby's warm back and rubbed it soothingly. "These people have a microwave?" he asked as he looked around.

"Oh, don't tell me he's hungry already."

"That or he really takes after you," Jonah joked, turning around to show her how Tony was rooting in his chest.

Xie was too short to swat him on the back of the head, so she settled for his ass.

"Nice neighborhood," Jonah finally commented while Xie was unlocking the front door. Neat, cookie-cutter two-and-a-half storey homes lined both sides of the street, their tiny postage stamp yards all immaculately kept and occasionally even trimmed with the proverbial white picket fence. A variety of exterior paint colors and landscape designs kept them from looking too identical. Across the street, in a rare double-wide driveway, were a pair of identical sedans with the license plates "HIS1" and "HIS2."

"Very desirable," Xie agreed absently, slipping into realtor mode. "This stupid lock—"

It finally gave, and she pushed the front door open, immediately toeing off her heels. "Ready for the tour?"

He nodded and stepped inside.

This was not the first time Jonah had gone out house-hunting with Xie. Actually, this was the tenth or so house she'd shown him. Sooner or later he was going to have to confess to Emerson—there were only so many excuses he could make—but before he pitched the idea of buying a house together, he wanted to make sure they could afford a place where they could really be happy. He didn't want Emerson to be disappointed. Xie had shown him some really nice places and some less nice ones, but so far none of them fit. None of them felt like home, though Jonah couldn't quite put his finger on why.

This particular house was obviously home to a few children, if the number of tiny shoes in the built-in cubby in the entryway were any indication. It was painted in cheerful but pale blues and yellows, making the rooms seem bigger than they were, with high ceilings and terra cotta tile floors. Jonah fell in love with it immediately.

"It's a little messy," Xie apologized for the owners. "It just went on the market; apparently the husband is being transferred overseas." She put her purse down in a vacant cubby while Jonah attempted the ballet of removing his shoes without overbalancing with a baby strapped to his chest. "Upstairs or main floor first?"

"Let's start down here." The kitchen would be a make-or-break point, Jonah knew—he and Emerson both liked to cook and entertain, and they were always stepping on each other's toes in their tiny apartment kitchen. Ever since he'd moved in to Emerson's apartment they'd been swearing to themselves that their next place would have a real cook's kitchen, and they didn't have the time or skill set—or the money—to renovate.

But the kitchen was, if not perfect—the counter was water-warped near the sink, and there was a piece of tile missing near the corner by the fridge—certainly more than adequate. There was lots of room. It was open to the dining room on one side and slightly less so to the living room beyond that, bright and airy with lots of headroom below the top cupboards so that Jonah wouldn't be smacking his forehead every five minutes. Tony burped softly into Jonah's shirt—no spit-up, luckily, though Jonah was beyond used to that at this point—and Jonah grinned. "Yeah, I like it too."

Xie rolled her eyes at him like she thought he was crazy, but she couldn't fool him; it was a totally fond eye roll.

A tiny half-bath off the kitchen rounded out the ground floor, and Xie raised her eyebrows as Jonah met her at the bottom of the stairs. "So?"

It was a surprising amount of work to climb the fairly steep steps with a baby strapped to his chest. Luckily, Jonah hadn't quit working out just because he was no longer in school full-time.

"The master bedroom is the first one on the left," Xie informed him from two steps behind. Jonah took the door on his right and pushed it open.

Inside was a child's playroom, sparsely decorated but for kid-sized furniture and the presence of a plethora of multi-colored bins for toys, a great number of which were strewn across the floor. Interlocking foam puzzle pieces covered good-quality hardwood, while paintings of two-dimensional people and animals dominated the wall space—in some instances painted right onto the drywall.

"I think they ran out of easel paper," Jonah said drily.

"Remind me not to let Tony have anything but bath crayons," Xie said with a wince.

Yeah, right, Jonah thought. If Emerson got his way, the kid would have his first set of oil paints by age three.

The next room was obviously the kids' bedroom. It was smallish, but big enough for the bunk beds pushed against the side wall and two child-sized chests of drawers. The ceiling was painted a dark blue, with stick-tacked, glow-in-the-dark stars pasted on to mimic the night sky.

The fourth door turned out to be the bathroom—or rather, another half-bath separated by locking doors on both sides. Through the other door was a prefabricated tub and shower construction, simple and efficient, and then, through yet another set of doors, a master half-bath.

"Well, don't just stand there all day," Xie prompted from behind him, and Jonah started guiltily. He was already thinking of the house as theirs, and what if Emerson didn't like it? What if they couldn't get a loan because his income was mostly royalty-based, and Emerson had only been at his job for a few months?

Tony made a soft, discontented noise, and that was enough of a prompt for Jonah to get moving. One way or another, he had to finish this tour, because sooner or later Tony was going to get fed up with trying to find Jonah's nipple and whine for Xie's.

On second thought, maybe he took after Bryce after all. Jonah pushed open the door.

The master bedroom faced the street, which wasn't ideal, though it wasn't very busy; Jonah could live with it. It was spacious enough for a king-sized bed, two night tables, and two chests of drawers with plenty of room to spare. There was a decent-sized closet set into one wall, and under the big bay window, a cushioned, built-in bench overlooked the street.

Jonah bit his lip. Looking at the bed, he could almost see Emerson in it, sleepy on a Sunday morning, naked with the sheets pushed down to his waist. Stepping out of the bathroom with a towel around his shoulders. Sitting on the window seat with both hands around a mug of steaming, too-sweet coffee.

Jonah was so absorbed in his fantasy that he almost didn't notice Xie standing tip-toe to work Tony out of the sling. "I'm just going to take him downstairs and heat up his bottle," she said with a smile. "But there's one more room you should check out by yourself."

The staircase to the attic folded up into the ceiling, and Jonah stepped back as he pulled the cord to make it descend. It did so with a loud creak, and Jonah coughed at the cloud of dust the action kicked up. Obviously the house's current owners didn't venture up here often.

One sleeve over his mouth to block out the worst of the dust, he climbed the ladder into the attic.

Upstairs was a long, narrow, lofty room stacked high with boxes, each labeled with a precise hand: Christmas decorations, summer clothes (David). The ceiling sloped on both sides; it was just high enough that Jonah could stand comfortably for about three feet on either side of the center line. He judged that Emerson would be just short enough to squeak by without injury.

At first Jonah wasn't sure why exactly Xie had sent him up there. It seemed to be simple, stuffy storage space. Then he realized that it wasn't dim because of a lack of windows—a myriad of boxes and dust conspired to block out the natural light from the two large windows, one north and one south facing, at each gable end.

Emerson's studio, Jonah realized. This was what the other houses had been missing.

Quietly, he descended the ladder again, pushing it back up into the ceiling after he was done. He found Xie feeding Tony at the kitchen table, a knowing expression on her face. "So?"

Jonah rubbed his jaw. Then he smiled. Hell, it still might not work out, but…. "When can we move in?"

§

"WHY are we here again?" Jonah was dragging his feet, a hangdog expression on his face.

"I told you, Mom is thinking about getting a cat," Emerson repeated. His mother had made the announcement a few days ago. His father had been allergic to cats, and so his mother hadn't had one since before they were married. The hurt that Emerson felt at the idea that his father's absence would be so marked was outweighed by his pride for his mother at recovering somewhat from her grief. So here Emerson was on his way to the local shelter to see if he could spot any likely candidates and to show his support for her decision.

Emerson poked Jonah in the chest. "And you should look into being a dog walker. Besides, don't you want to go look at all the puppies?"

Jonah pouted. "Yes… but I'll also fall in love! I will, Emerson! I'll fall in love and want to take it home, and then I'll mope for weeks knowing someone else adopted them! I can't handle this. I can't be a dog walker, Em!" Jonah wailed. "What were you thinking?!"

"That you are an idiot, but one who loves dogs and would want the opportunity to play with some? Also: cat."

Jonah sighed dramatically. "Fine. But there will be moping. And no complaining about it!" Jonah waved a threatening finger in his face.

Emerson just shook his head at Jonah's antics. He ignored his boyfriend's melodramatic moment, pulled the door open and walked in the building and up to the front desk.

"Hi. I'm Emerson, and this is Jonah. We were hoping to take a look at the cats and the dogs."

"Are you thinking about adopting?" asked the girl sitting behind the counter. She was young and pretty with a blond ponytail and bright smile. She was dressed in Hello Kitty scrubs and wearing a name tag that read "Samantha: Admin. Assistant."

"I'm scoping out the place for my mom—she's thinking about getting a cat. And the dogs...." Emerson shrugged. "I'm trying to convince this oaf to be a walker."

"Ah. He looks thrilled at the prospect," Samantha said with a flirty smile.

"He's convinced he will find his first child in with the dogs and that I won't let him keep it."

She laughed. "Well then, cats first?"

She led them into a room filled with cat cages and stood back to let them look.

Emerson began taking a circuit around the room, looking at all the cats, hoping to find one that might suit Linda.

"What about him?" Jonah asked, pointing to the first cat.

"The card says he's twelve."

"So?"

"I'd like to get one that lasts longer than three years."

"Whatever. Her?"

"'Shy and timid. Prefers small families and is frightened by tall or large men.'" Emerson turned to look at Jonah. "So, not planning on ever visiting my mom again?"

Jonah looked back, his face mopey. "Him, then?" he pointed to the next one in the line.

"Jonah... you know, normally you like cats. What's with you?"

Jonah pouted.

"Calm down. You're acting crazy. This day is not going to suck, I promise." Emerson placed a quick kiss to the corner of Jonah's mouth.

Jonah's eyes went soft at the touch. "Okay. Him."

"What?"

"Him," Jonah repeated as he moved to stand in front of a cage with a beautiful black and white cat. It was very friendly, judging by the way it moved closer to Jonah and began talking to him.

"Hm. I think you might be right. I'll bring Mom and Kierstyn by to see him." Emerson turned to Samantha and gave her a nod.

"Sounds good. Should I take you to see the dogs now?" she asked politely.

"Sure." Emerson grabbed Jonah's wrist and dragged him down the hallway. They followed the girl into a room filled with cages and the noise of excited dogs.

"So, here are our strays. Have a look around, say hello to our boys and girls," she said before excusing herself to return to the front desk.

"Aw! Em, this one's missing an ear!"

Emerson stepped up to Jonah's side to see the dog. It was adorable with a white-and-brown coat, large brown eyes, and one torn ear. It cocked its head to look at them. Emerson watched Jonah talk to the dog before eventually saying goodbye and moving on to the next.

He followed Jonah around the room as Jonah inspected each dog, watching as he greeted each mutt, telling them they were adorable and listing all their qualities to Emerson. Emerson grinned, pleased by Jonah's obvious enjoyment. Emerson was pretty sure that his surprise would go over well.

Emerson didn't often try to surprise Jonah; he wasn't a man prone to launching them, unlike Jonah, who had a tendency to come home with surprises of various sizes and nature daily. Jonah had a tendency to walk through the front door and open conversations by saying things like: "I bought you a present today. Don't you arch your eyebrow at me, Em; I can buy you presents if I want to. Okay, so it's not so much a present for you, as it is a present for us. But I did buy it with you in mind—all you. See, I was in Forbidden Fruit buying flavored lube when I suddenly thought to myself that we've never tried any of the other varied products that they sell at their fine establishment."

Emerson blushed just at the memory of Jonah saying this to him. Jonah had said it all like he had decided to pick up gummy worms while he was buying milk and eggs at the grocery store. Emerson had choked on his tea.

"Anyway," Jonah had continued after cheerfully pounding Emerson on the back a few times. "So there I was staring at their selection when it occurred to me that now that you're used to having me inside you, we really should try something new and exciting. Long story short, I bought you a vibrator." Jonah had looked overwhelmingly pleased with himself. Emerson had had little to say to that in response. He had been pretty sure that saying either of his first two thoughts (*But vibrators are for girls!* or *You want to stick something that* vibrates *up my ass?*) was out of the question. Besides, he didn't want to hear a mocking Jonah rant about feminism and equality. He settled for the third option of: "Um, why?"

Jonah had stared at him for a moment. "Because vibrators are awesome?"

No, Emerson had wanted more of an explanation than that. He arched his eyebrows and waited.

Jonah sighed. "Because you want to know what it feels like to have one against your prostate?"

Emerson still hadn't been convinced.

Then Jonah had stepped up toward him and wrapped both arms around his body. "Okay, how about it's something that I really want to do with you because I'm pretty sure it will be amazingly hot, and I can't wait to see how much it turns you on and gets you off."

Emerson wasn't sure what had swayed him: the argument or the feeling of Jonah's arms wrapped around his body, which was so distracting that he forgot to argue and just leaned into Jonah's touch. Really, it was neither here nor there, because an hour later Emerson had found himself lying naked in bed with an equally naked Jonah lying on top of him and a new sex toy pressing into his body. Really, Emerson's life could have been worse.

"Ooh, Em, this one lost its tail!" Emerson jerked as he was brought back to the present. He blushed when he realized just what he was recalling and *where*. Jesus, that had been about two years ago now. Emerson supposed the high degree of surprise and embarrassment coupled with the fantastic sex afterward kept the memory fresh. Still…. Emerson shook the memories off and refocused on the here and now. This was not the time to be thinking about sex. Besides, he was likely to have plenty of opportunity for such considerations later tonight.

When they reached the last cage, Jonah let out a soft "oh" of discovery. Behind the bars was a large, gray-faced dog. He looked somewhat like a Great Dane, though he was covered in curly hair. His nose was pressed to the gate, his eyes wide and imploring, and his tail gave tiny, cautious wags.

"Hello there." Jonah held his hand out so that the dog could sniff him. The mutt quickly sniffed Jonah's hand, and his tail picked up speed.

"Ah, so I see you've met Ringo," said Samantha, returning to the room.

"Ringo?" Emerson asked her, barely glancing at her, too captivated by Jonah.

"Ringo?" Jonah was still looking at the dog, who, upon hearing his name, wagged his tail even harder. "Hi, Ringo. Aren't you a pretty puppy! Yes you are—so gorgeous." The puppy wagged his tail so hard that his whole back end began to shake.

Emerson turned to look at Samantha once again. She smiled at him before rattling off the dog's history.

"Ringo's a new addition. He's a thirteen-month-old Poodle–Great Dane mix. His family brought him in when they realized how big he'd get. They already couldn't keep up with his energy or his exercise needs."

"So they just gave him away?" Jonah looked aghast. "But he's a sweetheart! And you know he just wants to be a good boy, you can just tell. Yes, you can. You are such a good boy, aren't you Ringo? Yes you are!"

Emerson rolled his eyes as Jonah resumed talking baby talk to the dog.

"Can we get a closer look?" Emerson asked under his breath to Samantha. She grinned at him.

She walked to the cage door and unlocked the gate. "How would you like to say hello to Jonah, huh, Ringo?"

Ringo came bounding out of the cage and went straight for Jonah. "Oh, aren't you wonderful." Jonah went down to his knees and ran both hands over Ringo's head and then down his body. Emerson didn't try to fight the grin as he watched Jonah coo at the dog.

"Em, he's a sweetheart!" Jonah said, looking up.

"Yeah, so I see." Emerson walked over and crouched down next to them. The dog turned to him and sniffed Emerson's hands and then face. Emerson scratched his ears and was delighted by the way the dog leaned into it. "He is a sweetie," Emerson confirmed.

"He's not just a sweetie—he's wonderful, aren't you, Ringo?" Ringo turned to Jonah and licked his face.

Emerson had been right—Jonah was definitely falling in love with this one.

"I think this is the one," Emerson said to the girl.

"The one what?" Jonah asked absently as he continued to pet Ringo. Both man and dog were still happily occupied with cuddles.

"The one that we're taking home."

Jonah's head snapped up. "What?"

"I think he'd do well in our family, don't you?"

"Are you serious?"

Emerson nodded. "Well we do have that new house with a yard. It would be a shame to let that go to waste."

Jonah grinned. "A puppy? Really? You're getting me a puppy?"

Emerson nodded again. This time Jonah let out a whoop of delight and launched himself to his feet. Suddenly he was on Emerson, his hands holding Emerson's head steady as Jonah plundered his mouth. Emerson happily submitted, vaguely aware of the girl saying, "I'll just go start the paperwork."

"You got me a puppy," Jonah mumbled against his mouth.

"Hm?" Emerson hummed dazedly. "Well, technically I didn't get it yet," he pointed out.

"Don't care. A puppy." Jonah jumped suddenly, and then looked down. Emerson followed his gaze to see that Ringo's head was resting on Jonah's hip as he stared up at them imploringly.

"Did you just poke me with your nose?" Jonah asked him. Ringo didn't answer. "He poked me in the hip with his nose," Jonah said.

Emerson looked down at Ringo and laughed. "He poked you?"

"Yes," Jonah nodded. "Are you sad about being ignored, sweetie?" Jonah moved one large hand to stroke it over Ringo's head. "Look at those sad puppy eyes."

"They look strangely familiar," Emerson said with a smirk. "Good match for you."

Jonah smiled. "Yeah, I think he's a good match for us. He'll fit right in at our house."

"I have no doubt. I think he'll be happy to join you every morning on your runs." Emerson pressed himself closer. "There is also evening walks, just the three of us."

Jonah grinned, delighted at the thought. "Emerson. You bought me a puppy." Jonah turned to the dog once again. "You're my puppy now, aren't you, Ringo?" Emerson couldn't help but smile as Jonah unwound his arms from him and took a step toward the dog.

Oh yeah, Ringo was going to fit in just fine with their family. Emerson was sure that he wasn't going to regret this surprise. Taking a step closer, he knelt down to say hello to their new puppy once again.

§

JONAH brushed the dust off the tops of the parcels and put the box back in the closet. He'd had them wrapped for weeks, but they'd been lost in the move, victims of poorly labeled boxes. Jonah wasn't used to moving with so much *stuff*, and he'd been looking for them for weeks. Five minutes ago, with the backyard full of well-wishers at Emerson's—now very belated, due to the insanity of the move—birthday party, inspiration had struck, and Jonah had finally located the correct box in the back of an upstairs closet.

Closing the door to the office behind him, Jonah trudged back down the stairs and into the kitchen, where he stuck his head out the back door.

"Emma, your mutt is trying to molest Hayley."

"He is not a mutt," Jonah protested. Between Eve, Zack, Greg, Hayley, and Ringo, the small yard was pretty full. Sure enough, Ringo was doing his best to bury his nose in Hayley's crotch. "Anyway, that puts him firmly in the majority."

Hayley didn't seem to mind too much anyway, the way she was laughing and running her fingers through his fur. "Nice, Jonah."

He grinned. "Any time. Em, can I talk to you inside for a sec?"

"Sure." Emerson handed his barbecue tongs off to Greg and kicked off his sandals at the back step before closing the door behind him. "What's up?"

"Got something for you," Jonah said a little sheepishly.

Emerson took them both, running a finger along the dust-smudged wrapping paper. "But you already gave me my birthday present."

"These are sort of just-because presents," he explained. Though that wasn't precisely true either. It wasn't like he'd gone out and bought them. "Not even real presents, really."

"Stop trying to take them back," Emerson scolded with laughter in his eyes. "Which one should I open first?"

"Big one first."

"Predictable." Smiling, Emerson ran his thumb under the tape and began peeling the edges open. "Should I guess what it is?"

"You should open it faster," Jonah groused good-naturedly. He wanted to see Emerson's face when he realized what it was.

Emerson glanced up at him from under his lashes, coy. "I could put it off 'til later, if you like," he offered innocently, holding out the present for Jonah to take back.

Some of Jonah's anguish must have shown on his face, because Emerson took pity on him then and finished with the wrapping paper. He ran his hand reverently over the smooth cover of the book, tracing the names at the bottom before carefully opening it, caressing first the rendering of the canine Jonah and then each individual page with something bordering on worship. Then he closed it up and hugged it to his chest for a brief moment before setting it on the paper on the kitchen counter and flinging himself at Jonah.

I am getting laid so hard tonight, Jonah thought smugly as Emerson's mouth crashed against his own.

Eventually Emerson seemed to realize that they still had guests and, thus, could be interrupted at any moment, so he pulled away, the apples of his cheeks stained bright pink. "When did this come? I can't believe you didn't tell me!"

"Before we moved," Jonah admitted.

"Jonah!"

"I was going to give it to you on your birthday!" he defended. "But then I lost the box."

"I don't know how you managed on your own for three years," Emerson said with a smile and a shake of his head. Then he looked back at the book Jonah had written, the one Emerson had spent intermittent months of his life illustrating. Somehow they'd forgotten about it for more than a year, and after that they discovered just how difficult it was to find a publisher for a children's book that already had illustrations. "Only three more weeks." Then it would be on bookshelves around the country. Jonah himself could hardly believe it, and he already had three titles in print.

"I know." Having Emerson's name beside his on the cover was so much more satisfying.

"I don't know how you're going to top that," Emerson commented, fidgeting with the smaller package before peeling away the first piece of tape.

Jonah was going to comment that he had his ways, but then Emerson finished unwrapping the tattered red Moleskine, so well-used now that it barely closed, glued-in keepsakes sticking out where they'd come unfolded. Emerson looked up, obviously intrigued. "Jonah, is this—"

"The notebook you mailed me from San Antonio. Yeah."

"You kept it?"

Jonah huffed. That was a stupid question. "Emerson. Obviously I kept it. It was from you."

"No, but I mean—" Emerson opened the cover, his eyes taking in the first page, where Jonah had glued the card he'd mailed with it. "You were supposed to write in it."

A smile tugged at the corner of Jonah's lips. "I did."

And he had—short notes, rambling epics, the occasional doodle or pasted-in memory—for close to five years. Then, just after the deal on the house went through, he ran out of room. But that was okay. By then Jonah had said pretty much everything he'd ever need to say.

Emerson,

This is probably not what you envisioned when you bought me this, but I can't help but hope that you don't mind, because if I don't find some way to tell you this I'm going to lose my mind.

I'm tired of editing the letters I send you, of scouring my own words and trying so hard to make sure I don't accidentally spill my heart all over the page. I should be able to tell you anything, but even though sometimes I think—hope—that you might feel the same, I can't make myself take the risk, and it's killing me.

Emerson turned the page.

Leaving you was a mistake.

Skipping ahead a few pages, he came across a page torn from a magazine, Jonah's short story entry and the accompanying photograph Emerson had taken. A postcard from Grand Teton National park that just said, "Wish you were here." One of Natalie's blackmail pictures of

Emerson passed out at his desk. A childish drawing of a turkey labeled "Harper." Then: *The problem with Elijah is that he isn't you.*

It went on and on. A crumpled plane ticket. A washed-out Sno Cone wrapper from the ballpark they'd played on as kids. A snapshot of Emerson at a museum in San Francisco, half out of focus, and one of the view from the roof of Jonah's apartment building. Every one of Emerson's letters, with what Jonah had wanted to say scrawled in the margins.

The picture of them from the photo booth at Xie's wedding, drunk and flushing and in love.

Jonah's heart beat a little faster. Tucked in at the end of the book was the listing from the sale of the house, Xie's sales pitch highlighted in blue at the bottom:

Warm, well-kept, two-and-a-half storey in a friendly neighborhood. A modern kitchen and open concept main floor make this house perfect for entertaining. Character and built-ins abound. Upstairs features three bedrooms with en suite master bath.

Jonah had been there when she'd written it up—a formality, since they'd already told her they were going to make an offer—and she'd looked up at him with a wicked smile before she penned the last line.

Perfect for growing families.

Emerson closed the book again before he could get to that, and Jonah let out a long breath. There would be plenty of time for that later.

Emerson swallowed, brushing his thumb over the stained cover. "Jonah, I…." Then he looked up, eyes bright, and Jonah had half a second to brace himself before he was caught up in a fierce hug and a sweet, lingering kiss. "Thank you," Emerson breathed, knocking their foreheads together just slightly. Then he laughed a little, choked-off and almost annoyed. "Though, seriously, next time you want to give me something like this?"

"Hmm?" Jonah asked.

Emerson drew back far enough to poke him in the chest playfully. "Don't wait until we have company!"

Jonah peeked over the top of Emerson's head just in time to see Zack mouth, "Get a room!" through the patio door. He grinned sheepishly. "I'll try to keep that in mind." Then he looked back down at Emerson.

"So. How about we get back outside? Your friends are waiting for you to celebrate your birthday."

"Yeah." Emerson rubbed both hands over his face. "Right. I'm going to bring my new book outside."

Jonah smirked. "Showing off?"

"More like I have to show them something, or they will all think you dragged me in here for a quickie."

Emerson turned to make for the door, but Jonah caught him around the waist before he could take a step. "What makes you think I haven't?"

Emerson's eyes crinkled at the corners. "I didn't say you hadn't." Then he tapped Jonah in the chest with the Moleskine. Jonah's hands came up to catch it automatically as Emerson leaned in with a conspiratorial look and a slight flush. "But if you can wait 'til we're alone, I'll make it worth your while." With a quick peck to Jonah's lips, he picked up the children's book and turned to go back outside, a pronounced bounce in his step.

Well, hell. Who was Jonah to turn down an offer like that? Grinning, he followed his boyfriend out into the yard. Life was good.

Like many romance authors in her genre, in real life ASHLYN KANE is an overeducated, overworked, underpaid twenty-something. Writing provides a welcome distraction from her disgust with the job market, as well as a means to help buy shiny new windows for the house she just purchased with her shiny new husband.

When she's not getting up at stupid hours of the day to go to her so-called "real jobs," she can usually be found either at the gym or parked in front of her MacBook, chatting with her various co-authors and trying to create the kinds of dynamic characters she always ends up falling in love with.

MORGAN JAMES started writing fiction before she could spell it. It was in high school that she started writing her first novel about a gay character, and she thanks the Internet for helping her realize that didn't make her crazy. Coincidentally, she also thanks the Internet for the role it plays in her long distance friendship with Ashlyn Kane. Geek, artist, archer, and fangirl, Morgan tends to while away free hours with imaginary worlds and people on pages and screens—it's an addiction. She lives in Ontario with her family and is the personal slave of three cats and a poodle (who isn't named Ringo, but who does like to poke).

Also by ASHLYN KANE

http://www.dreamspinnerpress.com

More by ASHLYN KANE

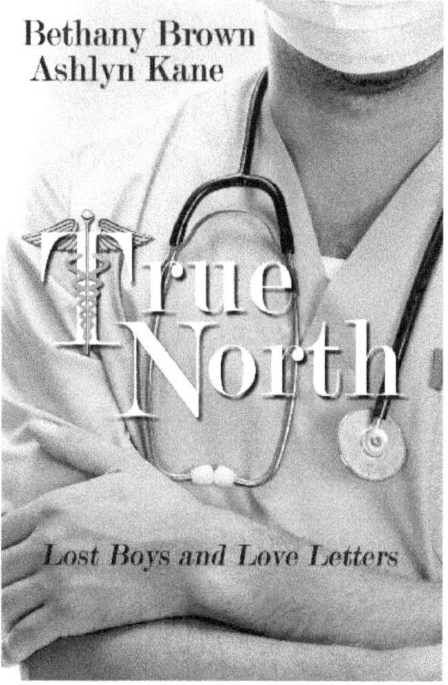

http://www.dreamspinnerpress.com

Dreamspinner Press
For more of the best M/M romance, visit
Dreamspinner Press
www.dreamspinnerpress.com

www.ingramcontent.com/pod-product-compliance
Lightning Source LLC
Chambersburg PA
CBHW050032030726
47506CB00001B/229
9781615818143